MIDSUMMER MOON

LAURA KINSALE

AVON BOOKS ◆ NEW YORK

MIDSUMMER MOON is an original publication of Avon Books. This work has never before appeared in book form. This work is a novel. Any similarity to actual persons or events is purely coincidental.

AVON BOOKS
A division of
The Hearst Corporation
105 Madison Avenue
New York, New York 10016

Copyright © 1987 by Laura Kinsale
Published by arrangement with the author
Library of Congress Catalog Card Number: 87-91599
ISBN: 0-380-75398-7

First Avon Printing: November 1987

AVON TRADEMARK REG. U.S. PAT. OFF. AND IN OTHER COUNTRIES, MARCA REGISTRADA, HECHO EN U.S.A.

Printed in the U.S.A.

K-R 10 9 8 7 6 5 4 3 2

THE AVON ROMANCE

Four years old and better than ever!

We're celebrating our fourth anniversary...and thanks to you, our loyal readers, "The Avon Romance" is stronger and more exciting than ever! You've been telling us what you're looking for in top-quality historical romance—and we've been delivering it, month after wonderful month.

Since 1982, Avon has been launching new writers of exceptional promise—writers to follow in the matchless tradition of such Avon superstars as Kathleen E. Woodiwiss, Johanna Lindsey, Shirlee Busbee and Laurie McBain. Distinguished by a ribbon motif on the front cover, these books were quickly discovered by romance readers everywhere and dubbed "the ribbon books."

Every month "The Avon Romance" has continued to deliver the best in historical romance. Sensual, fast-paced stories by new writers (and some favorite repeats like Linda Ladd!) guarantee reading *without* the predictable characters and plots of formula romances.

"The Avon Romance"—our promise of superior, unforgettable historical romance. Thanks for making us such a dazzling success!

Other Avon Books by
Laura Kinsale

THE PRINCE OF MIDNIGHT
SEIZE THE FIRE
UNCERTAIN MAGIC

Chapter 1

For the fourth time, His Grace the Duke of Damerell lifted the knocker with his free hand and brought the tarnished brass crashing down on its mottled-green base. For the fourth time, the sound echoed on the other side of the oaken door, unanswered. Ransom Falconer's mouth drew back in the faintest hint of a grimace.

He and his horse appeared to be the only civilized creatures within five square miles. Had he thought otherwise, he would never have allowed himself such a show of emotion. The overgrown Tudor walls rose above him, gray stone and neglect, an affront to the values of ten generations of Falconers. Admittedly, from where he stood on the threshold Ransom could see the romantic possibilities of the place: shaped gables and tall oriel windows and dark spreading trees, but at the very thought of such sentimentality those Falconer ghosts seemed to stare in haughty disapproval at his back. Without conscious intention, his own aristocratic features hardened into that hereditary expression of disdain.

Princes had been known to quail before such a look. There had been a few kings, too, and innumerable queens and duchesses and courtly ladies, all struck dumb and uneasy beneath the Falconer stare. Four centuries of power and politics had evolved and improved the expression, until by Ransom's time it was a weapon of chilling efficiency. He himself had learned it early—at his grandfather's elegant knee.

1

As it was, when at last the rusty lock creaked and crashed and the door opened on a complaining groan, the figure peering out from the gloom received the full force of His Grace's pitiless mien. The young maid would have been forgiven by a host of knowledgeable Whigs if she'd turned tail and run in the instant before Ransom recalled himself and softened his expression. But she did not. She merely wiped her hands on a grimy white apron and lifted a pair of vaguely frowning gray eyes. "Yes?" she asked, in a voice which might have been testy had it not been so preoccupied. "What is it?"

Ransom held out his card in one immaculately gloved hand.

She took the card. Without even glancing at it, she stuck the engraved identification into one bulging pocket of her apron.

Ransom watched his calling card disappear, shocked to the core of his pedigreed soul at such poorly trained service. "Mr. Lambourne is at home?" he prompted, keeping his voice quietly modulated. She might be a country mouse of a maid, a shade too softly rounded to be in vogue, but she was a pretty chit with those misty-gray eyes and elegant cheekbones, made more striking by the stark simplicity of her coiled chestnut hair. Not that His Grace the Duke of Damerell was in the habit of dallying with housemaids—she was not at all in his usual style in any case—but he found no advantage in needlessly frightening her. Ransom even allowed himself a moment's human pleasure, his glance resting briefly on her full lower lip before he looked up and lifted one eyebrow in expectant question.

She blinked at him. He found himself experiencing a peculiar sensation. Her eyes held his, but it was as if she did not even see him standing there, but looked past him at some distant horizon. Her mouth puckered. She lifted her hand, resting one delicate forefinger on that sweetly shaped lower lip.

"Square the coefficient of the diameter of the number three strut," she murmured.

"I beg your pardon?"

She blinked again and dropped her hand. Her eyes came into soft focus. "Can you remember that?"

"I'm afraid I don't . . ."

His voice trailed off as she rummaged in her huge pocket and drew out his calling card. After another moment's search, she located a pencil lead and scribbled something on the back of his card. "There," she said, with husky satisfaction. She dropped the card into her pocket and looked up at him with an absent smile. "Who are you?"

His earlier affront at her excruciatingly bad training returned, cooling his momentary startlement back to full reason. "I believe I delivered my card," he said pointedly.

"Oh." A becoming blush spread up from her modest collar, but he forced himself to ignore it. Well, not to concentrate on it, at any event. She had skin like an August peach, soft and golden and touched with pink.

She was rummaging again in her apron. The Pocket, as he termed it to himself, seemed to be burgeoning with peculiar paraphernalia. A jay's feather, a tiny telescope, a tangled length of wire, and a flat-toothed metal disk with a hole in the center—all appeared from the depths into which his card had vanished. She looked down, poking out the tip of her tongue in a child's gesture of concentration.

It was not The Pocket so much as the sleepy hedgehog she produced that left him nonplussed. She held the creature out to him, still fussing in her pocket with the other hand. He accepted the animal in dumbfounded silence. She located the card at last and glanced at the engraving, frowning. Then she flipped the creamy rectangle over.

"Oh, yes." She heaved a sigh of relief. "Square the coefficient of the diameter of the—what does that say? Three? Yes, the number three strut." She looked up at him with a small, accusing frown. "I thought you were to remember that."

"Forgive me," he said icily, "but I wish to see Mr. Lambourne, if it won't tax you too much to announce me."

She looked completely blank. He was beginning to think that she was unbalanced in her mind when she repeated, "Who did you say you were?"

He fixed his Falconer gaze with ferocious intent upon the card in her hand. After a moment she said, "Oh," in a satisfactorily flustered way, which assured him that his Doomsday look had not completely lost effect after all. It also had the result of producing another pleasing blush.

She bit her tongue and glanced quickly at the engraving, then back at him. "Um—Mr. Duke, I think you are mistaken in your direction."

He felt himself going pale, all those generations of Falconers gasping in absolute and utter stupefaction. "Falconer." His voice came out with strained gentleness. "My name is Falconer. The other is—my title."

"Oh." She frowned at the card. "Oh, yes. I see that. But—"

"I wish to speak to Mr. Lambourne," he interrupted, still with that disciplined softness that was compounded of exasperation and restrained impatience. The hedgehog rolled up and presented its spines to his palm. Her full breasts rose and fell lightly beneath the plain blouse. He could just see the aureoles, faint smudges against the stiff fabric.

Abruptly, he added, "Am I mistaken in believing that this is the home of Mr. Merlin Lambourne?"

"Well," she said with round-eyed apology. "Yes."

His sources were not so ill-informed as to allow him to fall for that sad little attempt at dissembling. Ransom treated her to the full extent of the Falconer stare. She seemed to have the way of it now, for her breasts rose and fell a little faster in agitation, and she ran her tongue over her upper lip.

"There is no Mr. Merlin Lambourne," she said quickly.

"Indeed." He held her with the stare, while she shifted and looked frightened, and he had the unhappy thought that it was rather like pinning a butterfly to a board. But he was on his country's business, and unpleasantries were common enough in that line of work. He could not afford to leave here without speaking to Merlin Lambourne if the man was still alive.

It dawned on Ransom that perhaps that was what she meant. Perhaps the old man had died. It had been a week since that last ill-fated report, and the report itself had been confusing, with word that Lambourne had appeared on some days in the garden hale and healthy, and on others looking like a walk to the back gate would finish him.

Damn the man, to die before England could make proper use of him. Ransom swallowed a stronger oath and allowed his mouth to soften slightly. "Forgive me. If there's been a recent bereavement . . ."

He let his words trail off suggestively, but she only looked at him without comprehension. And there was no sign of mourning in her dress. So—the old man was still alive, certainly, and she was only trying to fuddle Ransom with this nonsense. He found it ridiculously transparent and wondered that such amateur efforts had managed to prevent one of his best agents from making contact weeks ago with the reclusive Mr. Lambourne.

"Miss." He did not hide his impatience any longer. "Mr. Lambourne has specifically requested that I call on him. I must ask you to conduct me without delay, or I fear I shall be forced to report your recalcitrant behavior to him myself."

This was sheer bluff, but of the type at which His Grace of Damerell excelled. It seemed to work. Her eyebrows lifted, creating a little anxious furrow above her nose, and she put her finger to her lower lip in that absent gesture that managed to set his blood running in a particularly embarrassing manner. "Requested you call? Oh, dear—is that possible? But I—" She gave the card a puzzled look. "Damerell. Damerell. This is most— I'm so mortified, but I'm afraid I don't recall . . ." She took a deep breath and met his eyes with the air of finally seeing him for the first time. "Damerell," she repeated, as if trying to convince herself of the name. "Do come in, Mr. Damerell."

"Falconer," he corrected dryly. "Damerell as in 'the Duke of—' " He lifted his hands, one full of hedgehog and the other full of his horse's reins. "I'm afraid you'll have to relieve me of my burdens."

"Oh!" She blushed again, worse than a schoolroom miss, though he judged her to be well on the shelf if she weren't married. The middle range of twenty, certainly, for though she still retained that pleasing trace of babyish roundness, she'd gained some tiny laugh-lines about her eyes. Ransom's London ladies would have despaired over laugh-lines.

Ransom, perversely, found them enchanting.

She reached for the hedgehog, drew back quickly without finding a break in the spiny ball, and moved closer. She held The Pocket wide with both hands. "Just drop him in."

Ransom looked down for a moment on the top of her head, where the shining hair was drawn into an uneven part. He had an instant's notion of correcting that zig-zag line—a notion which brought a vision of her with the chestnut mass tumbling about her shoulders . . .

For God's sake, he admonished himself. He shook off that line of thought with alacrity.

He cleared his throat and sent the hedgehog tumbling into her offered pocket with a tilt of his palm. The animal squirmed and settled, apparently content with such cavalier treatment.

"You'd best leave your horse," she said, as if he had been about to lead the beast into the hall. "Thaddeus must have gone off. I signaled and signaled, and he never answered."

Ransom draped the reins over the doorpost obligingly, not caring if the hired animal wandered off. It was worth the price of a job horse if he could interview Merlin Lambourne. The misty-eyed maid stood back, holding open the door.

Ransom stepped inside. It was a dark, wide passage, full of odd shapes and unidentifiable masses crowded along the walls and piled in the shadowy corners. She backed up to give Ransom room, knocking over something that fell with a metallic clang.

With little flustered mutters, she righted the object, holding it up and frowning a moment at the webbed network of wire and round weights that hung from a wooden frame. "Whatever is that, do you suppose?"

The distressed puzzlement in her voice made him want to smile. He suppressed the notion ruthlessly. "Perhaps, as its inventor, Mr. Lambourne could enlighten you."

She looked up, squinting at him in the dim light. "Oh, dear. I thought you understood. There is no *Mr.* Lambourne. I'm Merlin."

"Pardon me?"

"I *said*," she enunciated, with the patient expression of a person speaking to an elderly deaf-mute, "that *I'm Merlin.*"

"You're Merlin."

"Yes. You'll have heard of John Joseph Merlin. The Ingenious Mechanick. I'm named for him. I daresay my papa would not have liked it at all, but he was killed, and so Uncle Dorian said it was no business of his. Not that I'm the equal of Mr. Merlin, of course, but I think I've made some progress in my own way. Would you like to see my wing design?"

With a menace that would have made Parliament tremble, Ransom repeated slowly, "*You* are Merlin Lambourne?"

"Have you heard of me?" She looked enormously pleased. "I expect you read my monograph on the Aeronautical Implications of the Perichondral Tissue of *Garrulus glandarius.*"

"No," he said stiffly. "I did not."

"Oh. Well, I can give you a copy. I had five hundred printed." She bit her lip, and then added, "There are four hundred and ninety-seven left, so you may have as many as you like."

He drew a breath, looked at the hopeful expression in those soft gray eyes, and for a silent moment wavered between fury and reason, cursing his fool agents and the nonexistent *Mr.* Lambourne and everyone else from Bonaparte on down. In the lingering pause, her eager lips began to droop.

He watched her fade like a wilting flower and suddenly heard himself say, "Thank you. I shall take twelve dozen."

"Twelve dozen!" She looked astonished, and then doubtful. He prepared to issue a gallant insistence, but she only protested, "If you've only the one horse, you can't carry them all."

"I'll send for my man."

"Ah." She nodded wisely. "Will you give them to your scientific friends? You must have a vast acquaintance, to need twelve dozen."

"Vast. And I shall donate a copy to each of the various lending libraries, of course, as well as the universities."

"Shall you? Indeed! Why— Oh, that is a— Oh, my, I don't know what to say!"

He looked down at her. Really, it was too pathetically easy. The joy on her face made him want to ask for another twelve or thirteen dozen. She took an excited little hop backward and knocked the unidentified object over again. The hall rang to a discordant clatter. She bent hastily, picking up the mysterious framework.

"Sorry." She colored a little, clutching the contraption and peering at him from under her eyelashes with a tentative smile. "Perhaps when I see it in better light I can recall what it is."

And His Grace the Duke of Damerell, the scourge of Whigs, the advisor of princes, the ambassador, minister, man-of-the world, looked down at her and found himself smiling back.

Merlin's problem, Theodore and Thaddeus had always told her, was that she thought too hard.

Uncle Dorian had violently disagreed, of course. Concentration was her best quality, he'd always said. Uncle Dorian had been sure she could accomplish anything. His last words to her had been, "Keep thinking, Merlin. You can fly. The answer is . . ."

The answer is . . . *what?*

How like Uncle Dorian to forget what he was going to say.

For five years that unfinished sentence had haunted her. It seemed she didn't know *any* answers, though she tried and tried to build a machine that could fly. Uncle Dorian's dream seemed so close, sometimes, so near her grasp, and then a test wing collapsed or a propellant gave a vicious pop and her model was left in tatters on the ground. The corridor was lined with pieces of her failures.

She tripped on a discarded orrery, making the wheelworks that moved the miniature solar system ring. A white blur moved quickly near her ear as the duke caught a tottering axle-rod in his gloved hand before it descended on her head.

"Careful," he said sharply.

Merlin ducked and apologized.

The Duke of Damerell, she repeated to herself. Or was it the Duke of Falconer? He seemed excessively sensitive over the difference. But she couldn't seem to focus on anything about him, except his face and his height. Her cursed concentration again, which caught hold of a thought or an image and would not let go. Just now, she could picture him in exquisite detail as she had just seen him, when first she had opened the door. She could see his thick brown hair beneath his hat, ruthlessly trained into neatness, and the dark eyebrows just as fiercely tamed. His eyes had looked yellow-green in the dappled shade outside, and his nose and mouth as elegant and wild as a gyrfalcon's fine-drawn markings. Perhaps that was why they had picked him as the Duke of Falconer. He looked uncannily like a smiling hawk.

She stumbled on something that fell with a dull thump and heard him utter a muffled oath behind her as his hands steadied her shoulders. "Sorry," she said miserably. He kept his hand beneath her elbow as she negotiated the last of the dim-lit passage and turned aside into the central hall.

One look at the jumble that filled the large room made her realize it was no place to entertain a visitor. Merlin knew she was no housekeeper, but when had she let things come to this? A rusted steam boiler, the fraying basket of a hot-air balloon, a discarded vacuum pump, and a damaged paddle—in the pale sunlight through grimy windows the place looked like a battlefield. She picked her way through the silent confusion, bending to slip beneath the massive sweep of a broken wing that cast a shadow across the narrow path like a great, weary bat.

The duke came behind her. He made no comment on the chaos, but she sensed his opinion in the way he inspected the caked grease that had smeared across his glove from the falling axle-rod.

The short flight of stairs to the solar was clear, at least, if only because it provided the single passage from her laboratory to this . . . storage. "Put it in storage," she'd said a thousand times to Theodore or Thaddeus, and never looked to see where the item had gone. Well, now she knew. It had gone to the great-hall and been dumped, and if she'd always been too preoccupied before to notice the accumulating mass, she certainly saw it now.

The solar was a slight improvement. Only half the size of the great-hall, it contained crowded laboratory tables and smaller pieces of equipment, rolls of wire and cases of glass beakers, and hundreds of leather-bound books strewn about in a mild degree of organization. At least she knew where a chair was. Under two feet of journals, which required several moments of exertion to remove.

She stood back from her labors, panting slightly, and offered him a seat.

"Thank you," he said. "I prefer to stand."

Merlin blinked at him. "Oh. Forgive me. I suppose you must have rheumatism?"

A fine curve appeared at the corner of his mouth and quivered there as he said solemnly, "I enjoy the best of health, thank you. But I was taught by a formidable nanny that a gentleman does not sit in the presence of a lady."

Merlin, lost in rapt contemplation of that intriguing masculine dimple, took a moment to realize that by "a lady," he meant her. "Oh," she said, and sat down.

He tilted his head, surveying the cluttered room. His gaze lingered on a large wooden crate from which a tangle of wires led to a set of wheels and pulleys. He stared at the object a moment and then looked down at her with that odd half-smile. In the sidelight from the window his hair danced with gold and red. "It is *Miss* Lambourne, then, whom I have the pleasure of addressing?"

Merlin nodded and hoped he wouldn't begin calling her "*Miss* Lambourne" in that soft and dignified way. She had a feeling that in one of her frequent reveries she would not answer to anything but a sharply enunciated "Miss Merlin, hey!," which was what Theodore and Thaddeus had found to be moderately successful.

"You seem to be quite an inventress," the duke said. "What is that object, if I may inquire?"

Merlin frowned at the wooden crate and wires. "It was to help me string the framework for my full-sized aviation machine. It didn't work."

"I see." He looked around again, as if seeking something, and then at Merlin. His light eyes were alert and piercing. "And what have you made that *does* work?"

Her shoulders drew down. Of all the questions he might have asked, that one was the least welcome. She looked at his shiny boots amidst the dustballs on the floor. "Nothing, I'm afraid. It's very discouraging. I believe the whole problem is weight and propulsion. And stability, of course. The models are so difficult to upscale. The wooden struts are too heavy, you see, and that makes the wing proportions far too—"

"Quite," he interrupted, just as she was gaining momentum in her explanation. "And you've had no progress in anything besides aviation?"

Merlin raised her eyes in surprise. "Oh, no. I've devoted all my thought to the flying machine. And truly, I have had *some* little success with my models—"

"Yes, of course." He was frowning at various objects in turn around the room. "But nothing else? What is that, for instance?"

Merlin looked at the carved mahogany piece that had caught his attention. He was scrutinizing it with an intensity that suggested he hoped it might hold the secrets of the universe.

"Uncle Dorian's old wardrobe," she said timidly. "I keep an extra cloak in it."

His mouth flattened into annoyance, and she added in hasty self-defense, "It gets quite cold in here in the winter."

"No doubt." The duke lowered his brows, glowering at her in a way that made her feel quite giddy. "Miss Lambourne, I must be truthful with you. I've come here in the utmost secrecy on behalf of His Majesty and the Lords of the Admiralty. It has come to our attention that you are in possession of a device which could be invaluable in the defense of your country."

"I am?" Merlin asked in a small voice.

His half-smile returned, this time with a much more unpleasant hardness to it. "I had hoped that you would not be so foolish as to deny it. I can provide you with every necessary evidence of my identity and my position with the government, so you need not fear that you are dealing with the other side."

"Oh, no!" she said. "Of course not." She put her forefinger to her lower lip, just remembering in time not to bite her nail. "What other side is that?"

His gaze lingered a moment on her hand. She quickly lowered it and folded her fingers in her lap.

"The French, Miss Lambourne. You are aware that we are at war?"

"Well, yes, I—" She met the cold disapproval in his eyes and added humbly, "I'm afraid I don't go out much."

"So I apprehend. Let me assure you that we are, indeed, at war and in need of every patriotic effort which our citizens can provide."

A heavy silence filled the room as Merlin tried very hard not to drop her gaze like a chastened child. She had a notion that the duke would not like such craven behavior. She wished that he would smile at her again as he had in the passageway below—an honest smile and not this ironic curl of his lips.

"Miss Lambourne," he said, "will you not help us?"

She swallowed and nodded. He looked at her expectantly. Another long pause followed while the waiting lift of his brows gradually drew down into another frown.

"Miss Lambourne, I beg you not to play games with me. Where is the invention?"

"The invention," she repeated, her eyes widening in comprehension and distress. "*My* invention? Oh, dear, but it wouldn't be of any use to you at all. It's far from ready—the wings aren't at all satisfactory, and the body from the model won't work in full size. I have to put all the stabilizing and maneuvering equipment at the aeronaut's feet, and there's very little space. I haven't even tried it myself yet."

He gave a huff of impatience. "I don't mean your damned flying machine!" He swept the room again with a frustrated glare. "There must be something else—haven't you anything else?"

"No, no, I told you—I haven't wasted a minute! I've worked on the aviation machine since Uncle Dorian died. And I'm very close. Truly I am. I'd like to help you, but it's much too soon to experiment with a human being. Perhaps if you could wait another few months—"

He leaned over her suddenly with one hand on the back of her chair and the other covering her fingers in a hard grip. "Miss Lambourne—my dear Miss Lambourne—please try to understand. This is no trifling matter. A week ago a man was found dead. His throat cut. He was trying to reach my office with messages of the greatest importance. They were in cipher, Miss Lambourne, but one of them mentioned you and this—invention. It is very possible—probable—that the code was broken."

He looked at her with an intensity that made her feel hopelessly stupid. "Is that very bad?"

With a harsh laugh he let go of her. "Only if you value your life and your country. I intend to remove you and this invention of yours to a safe place, Miss Lambourne. Immediately."

"Remove me! Oh, I'm afraid that is impossible, Mr.— um—"

"Duke," he suggested. "Please don't tax your mind with trivialities. Just gather your things and let us be on our way to a safer place."

She stared at him. "You cannot be serious. I can't leave now, just on the verge of perfecting my wing!"

"For God's sake, we'll take your wing with us. In fact, we'll take everything with us. I don't know what my agent meant by a revolutionary despatch apparatus, but he was no fool. I'll swear it wasn't a bloody fantastical flying machine."

Merlin rose instantly in defense of her dream. "I'm sure that was exactly what he meant, sir! What better way to deliver despatches than by air? Why, if it is military despatches you have in mind, just think! You could have orders across the Channel in a matter of hours."

"Nonsense," he said. "More likely I could have a broken head in a matter of seconds."

Merlin stood up, deeply affronted. Finding herself nose-to-chest with his muscular form was somewhat daunting, so instead of tossing him on his ear as she had desired to do, she said coolly, "Shall I see you out?"

"I'm not going anywhere, Miss Lambourne. Not without you."

"But that's— But you—" She spread her hands. "Oh, this is quite stupid. There is only the aviation machine. Why should you insist on my going with you if you think it's worthless?"

He leaned against the cluttered laboratory table and crossed his arms with a casualness that aggravated her temper. "Disabuse yourself of the notion that it was your flying machine which so impressed my late colleague. I don't employ agents who are prone to hyperbole. If man had been meant to fly—"

"Thank you very much, Mr. Duke, but you needn't repeat that old adage. I'm familiar with the sentiment."

"Falconer," he said.

"Pardon me?"

"Ransom Falconer. Fourth Duke of Damerell. Most people call me Your Grace, but really, I believe I could come to like Mr. Duke just as well. Shall you ring for tea while I take a look round?"

Merlin drew in a dignified breath. He appeared to have every intention of standing there against her laboratory table forever. With what she considered to be freezing politeness, she said, "Please look all you like, but you will have to move aside a step if you would like tea."

"Certainly." He straightened, with a brief flash of that smile that had pleased her in the hallway below. It softened Merlin's annoyance and made her feel suddenly shy again.

She ducked her head and reached for a large box on the table, taking hold of the crank and sending it whirling. After a moment, she leaned over as she was cranking and carefully closed a small metal flap between two wires. A blue arc of light crackled inside a glass jar. Merlin stopped turning the crank and put her mouth close to the cone-shaped depression in the box. "Thaddeus!" she called. "Thaddeus, do you hear me?"

From the box came a faint, steady hiss as she waited. She tapped nervously on the table, aware of her guest's eyes upon her back. The duke would be wanting his tea, she thought, and hoped that Thaddeus would answer.

The silence stretched, filled only with the hum of the box. Merlin doubled up her fist and rubbed it on the tabletop. A duke. She had an idea he would be accustomed to better service than this. For the first time in her memory, she looked around her laboratory and thought that it seemed a hopeless, shabby mess. The hedgehog squirmed in her pocket, and she absently reached for a sunflower seed and dropped it inside.

The sound of the alarm bell made her jump. Thank goodness, Thaddeus had heard her signal. His voice came out of the box, faint and hissing and none too pleased. "Aye, Miss Merlin? What's it now?"

"Tea, Thaddeus," she said, trying to sound very certain of herself. "I have a guest."

There was a fuzzy pause and a crackle and then Thaddeus's voice again. "—tea, you say? And do—" The voice was lost in noise and then returned. "—middle of—back garden and up to me knees in mud, Miss Merlin?"

Merlin pressed her lips together. The duke was staring a hole in her back, she was sure. "Thaddeus," she said forcefully, "bring us tea immediately."

"Poo—Mi—lin—now. Ye ain't—self!"

"Thaddeus. Stand still. You know I can't understand you if you carry the box about like that. Stand still, Thaddeus. Do you hear me? Stand still!"

The voice answered, suddenly much louder. "Aye, I hear ye, Miss Merlin. You be making your own tea. I'm goin' out to the dairy barn now. I'll be takin' your pesty speaking box wi' me, but don't you go ringin' me little bell for no silly tea. Ye know I got the works o' two to be doin', what with Theo down."

"Thaddeus—" She said his name twice, but he was gone. She had only the hiss of electricity through the ether for response.

With a sigh of defeat, she opened the metal switch. The blue arc sparked and died, along with the hum. Merlin turned, biting her lip in apology. "About your tea—can you wait a minute while I go to the kitchen?"

The duke was staring at the little box and its single wire. "God in Heaven," he said in a strangled voice. "Great God—"

He raised his eyes. To Merlin's astonishment he let out a whoop that rang jubilation off the old stone walls. She found herself grabbed and squashed and pounded in a bruising embrace. As she flung her chin up and gasped for breath, she had only an instant to register the softness of fine cloth on her cheek before he kissed her, full on the mouth—a rough, undignified, and consuming kiss that was all mixed up with the thumping on her back and the ache in her lungs and the really painful way he was standing on the toe of her left shoe—not that she cared, but the hedgehog might be squeezed, and, oh . . . oh, my, well . . .

It was over before Merlin had time to realize it had started—or at least before she had time to realize that she was enjoying being mauled. He let her go and stood back with a grin that made her throat feel peculiar and trembly. "Merlin Lam—" He was as breathless, if not as bruised, as she. "Merlin Lambourne," he declared, between pants. "By God, you are a *genius!*"

Chapter 2

It had been thirty-odd years ago, at the age of five, that Ransom could last recall having such difficulty with his table manners. Trying gamely to swallow the overcooked mutton without choking, he postponed sawing at another bite and put his full concentration on chewing. The toughness of the meat would have made scintillating dinner repartee difficult, but any hopes of mere polite conversation had been quickly put to rest by his hostess.

Miss Lambourne sat across the ancient, scarred table from him. Reading. In the fading light from the low windows, her full lips moved softly, and that little worried furrow came and went in the smooth skin of her brow. She had finished her mutton in a quarter of the time he was taking—for which he could only admire the strength of her teeth—and now between pages she tore off chunks of glutinous bread, alternating bites between herself and the hedgehog. The creature had been deposited in a convenient bowl and placed in the center of the table—in the absence of a suitably imposing silver epergne, Ransom supposed.

"Does it make a nice pet?" he asked, tired of battling with the mutton.

She turned a page.

"Yes," he continued after a moment. "I daresay it has all kind of uses. And quite decorative, too."

The pucker formed between her brows, and she marked her place with a finger. "Pardon me?"

"Does it make a nice pet, I was wondering."

18

"Pet?" Her thick lashes swept down and up. Ransom had the sudden and painful urge to kiss her within an inch of her life again, on the theory that she would surely have to take notice of him then. "What pet?"

"The epergne," he said, with a little flick of his finger toward the spiny centerpiece.

She looked at him blankly for a moment, and then, in a tone he imagined she reserved for agreeing with raving lunatics, said, "Why yes, I'm sure you must be right."

Ransom smiled and wished she wouldn't stare at his mouth while she teased at her lower lip in that damned provocative way.

"Would you pass the salt, if you please?" he asked, to break the moment.

She looked from his mouth to his plate. He could see the slow change, the dawning of common awareness. It was a fascinating process, this transition from deep dreaming to daylight—rather like the passing of a morning's mist into full sun. But no, he thought as he watched her, not so harsh a change as that. More like the lazy rise of a full moon to light the summer midnight.

"Oh," she said, frowning at his laden plate. "Do you dislike mutton?"

"With a strong jaw and the addition of a little salt, I expect I'll manage to hack my way through."

She pursed her lips and looked about the table. After a moment her gaze alighted on the hedgehog. "Oh, dear."

Ransom lifted his eyebrows.

"The salt cellar," she said. "I'm afraid . . ."

He looked at the hedgehog. It stared back at him with beady innocence. *Yes*, it seemed to say between twitches of its sharp little nose, *I'm in the salt cellar, and I'm bloody pleased about it*.

The creature's air of simpleminded spite reminded Ransom of a few Whigs he knew.

"I'll find some." Miss Lambourne rose quickly, getting tangled for a moment in her skirts as she scanned the laden shelves and counters that lined the dining room walls. Ransom watched her begin to push jars and crockery about, opening lids and peering inside and adding to the general disorder in the room as she set each container hastily aside.

When Ransom had invited himself to high tea, he'd imagined that the service would be rustic. He'd not been completely prepared for an inedible meal served by a grouchy old man with a head as bald as a baby's, who seemed to think it the height of effrontery that he should be asked to clear off the dining table so that his mistress and her guest could eat in such unwonted elegance.

On the other hand, Thaddeus Flowerdew seemed to have no qualms about the propriety of the situation. He left Miss Lambourne in the room with Ransom as if it were an everyday occurrence for an unchaperoned lady of the finest breeding to dine alone with a strange man. A few probing questions and Miss Lambourne's usual vague answers had assured Ransom that her situation was shamefully irregular. The fact that it made his own mission much easier to have no proper guardian present did not obscure the fact that Miss Lambourne deserved far better than this.

From the moment when she had mentioned her Uncle Dorian, Ransom had placed her in the social hierarchy. His original assumption that Merlin Lambourne was some obscure country squire had been instantly dismissed when Ransom had realized that he was dealing with *the* Lambournes, allied to crazy old Sir Dorian Latimer by marriage to a niece. The intricate web of connections formed in Ransom's mind in utter clarity. As easily as if he'd had a map before him on the table, he could trace the lines of descent and alliance and place each player in proper perspective.

Miss Lambourne's father would have been the Colonel Winward Lambourne killed under Cornwallis at Yorktown, and her paternal uncle the late Lord Edward of Cotterstock, which meant the present Lord Edward—handsome, stupid poet that he was—was her first cousin and legal guardian.

And her mother—her mother must have been the tragically famous Lady Claresta, the beauty of her age. Ransom had seen her once, when she'd visited his grandfather at Mount Falcon. Ransom had been no more than thirteen at the time, but he remembered. Ethereal and lovely, the bluest of blood and the richest of dowries—and deaf. Stone deaf and completely mute. To this day Ransom recalled her smile. He could see it in her daughter: wistful, kind and dreamy, a smile that had made a thirteen-year-old boy groomed to power and position forget his pride and spend an entire week at her service. On his knees. He had loved her—that sad, silent lady—as only an adolescent could.

He looked at Miss Lambourne, on a stool now, reaching toward the highest shelf with her pretty ankles plainly visible beneath her skirt. He felt a rush of disgust for the relatives who had buried her here. She'd already been born when her mother had visited Mount Falcon, Ransom calculated. And no one had mentioned a daughter. He would have remembered. He never forgot that sort of thing.

"Miss Lambourne," he said abruptly. "Has your family done nothing to provide you with a proper female companion since your mother died?"

There was a clatter of metal as a rusted spoon slid off the top shelf and bounced on the floor. "Botheration," she said, and left it there. In a voice muffled by her upraised arm she asked, "What did you say?"

"A companion," he repeated patiently. "You should certainly have a respectable lady living here with you."

She dropped her arm and looked around at him. "Whatever for?"

"To uphold the proprieties, of course. No young lady of your age and connections lives alone."

"Oh, I don't live alone! Thaddeus and Theo—"

"—are of no consequence whatsoever in this instance. You should have a proper chaperon, a lady of decent breeding. For your own protection, if nothing else."

Her gray eyes were wide and soft in the dimness. "Protection from what?"

He could guess what Miss Lambourne's life had been. Shuttered up with her eccentric great-uncle, who probably had been the only one of the family who would take Claresta and her little girl after her husband had died. Locked up and abandoned, her considerable fortune "administered" by a guardian who had undoubtedly forgotten her existence—it made Ransom's jaw tighten in a way that those who knew him would have considered ominous.

"From all sorts of things," he said harshly. "Any rogue could barge in here and take whatever advantage of you that he liked. Look at the freedom you've allowed me, and never demanded the least evidence of my credentials."

She turned around on the stool, leaning with her hands braced behind her against the shelves. "Yes, we did have a fellow who stole some of Thaddeus's garden tools once. But that was years ago, and Thaddeus and Theo beat him to an inch when they found him. No one's bothered us since."

"I didn't necessarily mean thieves. There are worse dangers which threaten an unprotected lady, if you take my meaning."

Her forehead furrowed. After a moment she said, "I don't believe that I do."

"Miss Lambourne, I know you've lived a sheltered life, but you must be aware that there are men in this world who would not hesitate to . . . to . . ."

She watched as he stumbled, her gaze as innocent and interested as a wild sparrow's.

"Who would not hesitate to take liberties with your person," he finished brusquely, deciding that the case required strong language.

With an expression of utterly naive curiosity, she asked, "What kind of liberties?"

Ransom closed his eyes and released an explosive sigh. "Really, Miss Lambourne, it would not be at all proper for me to discuss such a thing with you. But you may take me at my word. You need a chaperon."

She stood frowning at him a moment longer, and he knew he had not made the least progress in impressing the dangers of her situation upon her. He lifted his goblet and took a swallow of the bitter wine as she turned back and scanned the shelves. She tilted her head back and mumbled, "What was I looking for?"

"Salt."

"Oh. Yes." She stood on tiptoe and reached once more for the top shelf. In the midst of a thumping and shuffling of jars, she asked, "Are you going to take liberties with my person, Mr. Duke?"

Ransom choked on his wine, having been caught observing the trim turn of her ankles again. "Most certainly not!" He set down the glass and added in a more controlled voice, "As a gentleman, I do not go about ravishing unprotected females, I assure you."

"Oh," she said, without much interest. She stuck her nose in an open jar and sniffed loudly.

Ransom watched her, amused in spite of himself. She clearly had no notion of what he was talking about. He found her attitude rather pleasing after years of experience with hard-eyed courtesans and simpering young misses who contrived to swoon at the mere mention of a stolen kiss.

He sipped at the wine again and then set it down with a grimace. He was determined to find a way to rectify the shameful neglect of her station here. He could be certain, at least, that her cousin's irresponsibility was not deliberate. Lord Edward Lambourne had fortune enough of his own, and a brain too small to leave room for more than folly and fashion. No, it was pure self-centered preoccupation that had resulted in this travesty of common familial duty. And as much as Ransom abhorred it, he could see possibilities in the situation which could work to his own advantage.

Miss Lambourne was proving distinctly difficult to dislodge. He'd spent the afternoon attempting to reason with her, but had succeeded only in gaining permission to take the speaking box and use it for whatever patriotic purposes he might be able to imagine. He could imagine quite a few. Indeed, he wanted to shout in triumph every time he thought of the speaking box and the infinite possibilities of communication through thin air.

But he needed Miss Lambourne, too. Not only to begin work to improve the instrument, to adapt it to use at sea or on a battlefield. And not only to prevent the secret from falling into French hands. No, it was more than that which made him want to remove her from this place as soon as possible.

He was afraid for her life. He had not exaggerated the way his agent had come to a violent end. She was in danger, he was certain, and that was why Ransom was sitting here chewing tough mutton and making himself a nuisance to an elderly grump and his muddled mistress. And why he had no intention of leaving without her.

She gave a crow of success from her stool and hopped down with a dusty jar balanced precariously in one hand. As she set it before Ransom, he could read the large initials N.A.—C.L. on the label, but the quantity of spidery writing underneath was illegible. Miss Lambourne handed him a spoon and sat down, pink and a little breathless from her exertions.

"N.A.—C.L." He frowned at the white crystals. "Are you certain this is salt?"

"Oh, yes. That would be the chemical formula, you see. Sodium chloride. Uncle Dorian often labeled things that way. He was a great chemist, you know." She seemed to realize that her reassurance might not be quite the thing to make Ransom completely easy in his mind, and added, "But of course, he would never have kept anything poisonous in the dining room."

"Of course." Ransom peered dubiously at the label, where among the faded script the words "Salt" and "Co. Lvs." were legible, along with an abbreviation. "Dare I ask what this 'Aphro.' signifies?"

She squinted at the lettering and waved a vague hand. "I expect that means that it's African salt."

He sprinkled a little on his forefinger and touched his tongue to it. The familiar rich and bitter flavor filled his mouth, unmistakeable. He nodded, satisfied, and spread a generous amount over his mutton, hoping to disguise the meat's blandness if not its texture.

"I believe we'll reach Mount Falcon by mid-afternoon tomorrow." He attacked the mutton once more, taking advantage of her momentary attention by employing the old "assumption-of-success" tactic to advance his ends. "We'll carry the speaking box with us, and I can arrange to have several trustworthy fellows pack up everything here and follow directly. You won't be separated from your work for more than a day or two."

She took a deep breath—a bad sign, Ransom knew. "Mr. Duke, I've been trying to tell you that I can't leave."

"Yes," he said, taking another diplomatic tack along with a salty bite of mutton. "But you haven't told me why."

"Indeed, but I have. There's my wing—"

"—which you can test at Mount Falcon. As I said, all of my resources will be at your service. The west ballroom will be entirely yours, and we have no end of open lawn and steady wind. Much better than what little cleared ground you've got here."

She bit her lip. A faint sign of progress, to Ransom's keen eye. He waited, ready for the next objection.

It came as predicted. "But to move everything," she said. "It will take months to reorganize."

Ransom refrained from commenting on her concept of organization. "I'll assign you my personal secretary." He took another bite of mutton. "The man's a genius at making order out of chaos, I assure you. Everything will be at your fingertips."

She looked tempted, and then sulky. "But the speaking box. You'll be wanting me to work on that instead."

"Indeed not—not unless you insist. I would like you to explain its functioning to my secretary, and I'm sure"— here Ransom stretched the truth considerably—"I'm quite certain that he can adapt it to our needs with very little further help from you."

"And then there's Theo," she said, as Ransom continued stubbornly with the mutton. The salt had somehow made it surprisingly flavorful. "He's been ill for the last three months. Thaddeus would never leave without him."

"Yes, of course." Ransom put a tone of deepest empathy in his voice. "Identical twins. They won't want to be separated, naturally. That's why Thaddeus will have a room right next to Theo's, where he can be available to carry out the doctor's smallest instruction without the burden of all this other work the poor fellow's been carrying." Ransom shook his head dolefully as he finished off another bite of mutton. He was beginning to enjoy himself. Yes, he was beginning to enjoy himself indeed. He felt exceptionally—astonishingly—well. "Thaddeus has been doing the work of two. I don't see how he's managed. And now if you stay, he'll have to be keeping a strong guard over you in addition to everything else."

"A strong guard?"

"Why, yes, of course, Miss Lambourne." Ransom smiled at her, finding that in the lingering light from the window she looked lovelier than ever. His pulse began to quicken, watching the mobile curve of her lips, and the fine, soft line of her throat. "French agents," he said, but somehow the perilous urgency of that thought was fading. She was so ripe and perfect, so adorably kissable. "If they've cracked our code—" He lost the thread of that particular sentence and kept smiling at her, fascinated and elated by the shy dip of her head as she glanced at him. "How lovely you are," he murmured. "So soft . . ."

He saw her chin come up and her misty eyes widen. "I beg your—"

"Ah—I suppose I shouldn't say so." He had no idea why he *had* said so, except that a feeling of vast happiness was expanding inside him. He took another delicious bite of mutton, and another, and looked down to find that he had finished it off. "Blast," he said. "Is there more of that?"

She was staring at him, her lips slightly parted. At his question, she looked startled and began to rise. "I'll ask Thaddeus."

"No." Ransom stood up, too, and caught her arm as she turned toward the door. "No, don't bother with that. I want . . ." He paused, looking down into her beautiful eyes. He slid his arms around her and drew her against him. Happy; he was so happy, reveling in her soft shape, her body in his arms. "I want you," he whispered, bending to her ear. "Come with me."

"Mr. Duke," she said in a breathless voice.

He laughed. "Call me Ransom." He rocked her gently, drawing her closer. "Little Merlin. Lovely Merlin. Wherever did you get such a name?"

"My—my uncle—" She struggled, but he held her easily, like a tiny bird in his hands.

"I'll call you Wiz," he said, kissing the corner of her mouth. "My own wizard. God, you make me feel so good."

"I don't mean to," she said in a small, muffled voice. She was wriggling, trying to get her hands against his chest. "Oh, dear—are you going to take liberties with my person?"

"Yes. Oh, yes. I'm going to be wickedly improper. But I don't care." Elation and desire sang through him. He caught one of her hands and kissed her palm. "I've been proper all my life. I want to make love to you."

"Oh," she said. "Dear me."

He smiled into her palm. "Beautiful, silly Wiz. Come with me. Let me love you."

"This won't change my mind," she mumbled, and then drew in her breath as he kissed the soft skin of her inner wrist. "I won't leave."

"You don't have to leave. I can love you right here."

She made a small sound, which might have been "Oh" but came out more like a sigh. Ransom recognized that feminine music from a thousand amorous encounters, but this time it filled his soul with special joy. He squeezed her in a burst of adoration and then bent down to lift her. She seemed less substantial than a feather, easy to kiss and cuddle as he strode through the door and turned toward the spiral stairs.

He had a moment's thought of Thaddeus, but it only made Ransom chuckle to think of confronting the ancient retainer with Miss Lambourne in his arms. He felt confident, daring; he felt positively heroic. He kissed her and pressed her head against his shoulder, subduing her faint wriggling protests and ducking to miss the stone ceiling as he mounted the stairs.

His mind seemed to be exceptionally quick and clear. He impressed himself with his quick identification of the bedrooms, based on some long-ago lesson in late medieval architecture. The room he chose held a four-poster bed hung about with thick curtains of an awful, heavy green. He kicked the strap-hinged door closed behind them and leaned his shoulders against it, letting her struggle and slip down to her feet.

She tried to pull away, but he held her close, burying his face in the curve of her shoulder, sliding his hands up and down her arms. She smelled like dusty sunlight, warm and human, not perfumed and pomaded like other women he had known. Lord, oh, Lord, he wanted her . . . He said so, his voice a low groan against her skin, and then hugged her to him in sheer delight. He wanted to laugh. He wanted to hear her laugh. He lifted his head and tilted her chin up, kissing her nose and her eyelashes, smiling down at her.

"Mr. Duke," she stammered. "R-Ransom, I don't at all think you should be doing this."

"Ah." He nuzzled her temple, breathing her special scent. "There's nothing else I'd rather be doing."

She caught her lower lip in her teeth, and a surge of heat went from his chest to his feet in response. He bent and ran his tongue across her mouth, teasing her lip free and nibbling at it himself. Her breath came faster, warming his cheek. She squirmed in his hold.

"Don't you like it?" he murmured. "Oh, Merlin, sweet wizard, let me show you some magic. You'll think it's wonderful. Have you ever felt like this before?"

"No, I—" She gave a little gasp as he circled her nipple with his thumb. Her gray eyes widened, and then she ducked her head against his shoulder.

He chuckled and held her close. "Don't be shy, pretty Merlin. I want to see your face when I touch you."

"Oh, my," she said to the depths of his coat. "I do believe there was something in the salt."

"Something in the salt—" He nipped at her neck with a playful growl. "Something in the salt, hmm? A love potion, Wiz?" He caught her face in his hands and tilted it up to him. "You don't need potions. I wanted you from the moment I saw you."

He kissed the shocked "O" of her lips, slid his fingers into her hair, and held her hard against his mouth: a deep kiss, a man's kiss, to brand her his by force. He felt her resistance and then, slowly, her softening.

It was enough, that small compliance, to make him sweep her up again and carry her to the bed. He yanked off his coat and bent over her among the pillows, grinning. He kissed her nose. "Do you know," he murmured, "in London they say I'm not romantic. All those china-doll debutantes. I think I'm romantic. Don't you, Wiz?" He sat beside her, caressing her cheek with the back of his fingers, letting them slide down to the buttons at her throat. "Has anyone ever been so romantic?"

"I'm sure I can't say." She wet her full lips. "I really don't go out much."

He stroked her skin where he'd loosed the buttons. She wore no wealth of undergarments. Only a light camisole separated his palm from the soft offering of her breast. As he touched her, her body tightened. She stared into his eyes with dawning wonder, as if he were some magical beast that had just appeared for her perusal.

"How do you feel?" he asked playfully as he traced an erotic pattern on the warm curve of her skin. "Do you like this?"

"What?" Her intent gaze had gone unfocused as she gazed at the base of his throat. "Oh . . . yes, I—oh, my. What are you doing?"

"I'm going to love you, Wiz. I want you to feel"—he bent over her, just barely brushing her skin with his lips—"delicious."

In fact, Merlin felt as if she were chocolate melting under a hot sun. She drew in a deep, shuddering breath, wondering why, if this was what he meant by taking liberties with her person, anyone would ever object to such heady pleasure.

He tugged her blouse free and spread warm fingers around her torso, sliding his hands upward, carrying the camisole along. His thumbs brushed the underside of her breasts, then circled her nipples again. Merlin jumped and bit her lip, torn between shyness and delight. But there wasn't room for both in her mind—there wasn't room for anything but the stunning bloom of stimulation as his tongue washed across the tip of her breast.

Small puppyish sounds came from her throat as he leaned over, pressing her into the goosedown with his weight. "Merlin," he whispered. "Little bird, sweet sorceress . . . Ouch!" He rolled suddenly to the middle of the bed, boots and all, clutching his ribs. "What the devil—" For a moment he frowned at her waist and then grabbed at the pocket of her apron, flipping it away from him so that the contents went spilling out onto the floor with a metallic ring. He grinned, leaning on his elbow and looking down at her. "Booby-trapped, are you?"

Merlin just stared at him, lost in this new pleasure, fascinated by his nearness: the beguiling unfamiliar scent of him; the solid, warm feel of his body pressed against hers. She followed the line of his jaw and the laughing curve of his mouth with her eyes.

"Ah, God," he said. "When you look at me like that . . ." He made a low, velvety noise in his throat and bent over her again, his tongue a warm invasion in her mouth, his boot and thigh a hard pressure against her leg. With one hand he drew her skirt up around her waist, exposing the full length of her legs. Before she could tear her lips free to voice a belated spurt of modesty, he captured her wrist and brought it against him, sliding her open palm downward from his chest to his abdomen. He pressed her hand to the hard shape beneath his breeches, groaning against her mouth as she touched him. Suddenly his hand left hers and tore at his buttons, and then she felt his naked flesh against her palm, smooth and hot and insistent.

Merlin whimpered, confusion and excitement surging through her. Never had she felt like this, never been this close to another person in her memory. It felt wonderful, a tingling through her limbs, a weakness like water, shyness and exhilaration and a sweet, soaring need. She wanted something, and he knew what it was. He had to, for he gave it to her when she couldn't name it herself.

He covered her with his body, holding her down, spreading kisses across her face and throat. His heat nestled between her legs, seeking, sliding against her sensitive skin until she moaned in answer. She arched her back up to capture more and found him waiting, felt the heavy intrusion, a response that was so perfect and unexpected that the pain of it was lost in the pleasure.

His hands cupped her face as he pushed gently into her. He felt like sun and soft grass and summer wind, and then rougher, like gathering weather, like hard rain and howling gusts. She gave herself up to him, soaring, a wing-free hawk in the wild arms of the storm. His power rocked her and carried her to blue-lit heights, so high she could barely breathe, and then higher yet again, panting and straining, upward and upward until his lightning exploded around her and she cried out in mingled pain and joy.

She clutched at him, as if she were falling, reeling down through the sun-shafted clouds. He gathered her close, murmuring comfort and love, warming her cheek with his heavy breath. He nuzzled her throat, burying his face against her skin. "Merlin." It was a groan. "I've never felt like this. I think I—" He swallowed and made another wordless sound. "You'll say this is impossible, and my God, it is impossible, but I think I love you." He stroked her torso and then her face, tracing her eyebrows and her lashes. "I love you. Merlin, Merlin, I love you. Do you believe me?"

He sounded so desperate, so suddenly human. She opened her eyes, trying to focus on the question he'd asked. "Of course," she mumbled in confusion, taking refuge from his intensity in quick agreement. She pushed ineffectually at her skirt, but he caught her hand.

"No," he said. "You're beautiful. Don't be shy of me." He ran his fingers along the smooth, damp line of her inner thigh. "Did you like it, Merlin? Did I please you at all?"

Her mind felt like jelly. She could only nod again, not even understanding the question.

He caught her hand and carried it to the joining of his legs. "You pleased me," he said. His voice was strange and thick. "Lord, that's the understatement of the century. Do you feel that? For God's sake, I already want you again. Merlin, sweet Merlin—I want you. All of you. I want you to think of me and nothing else."

"But my wing design," she protested. Her voice sounded weak and breathless as he shifted his weight across her. "I have to think of that."

"The devil take your wing design. Must you be so bloody literal?" Stiff cotton rustled as he pulled her blouse halfway down her shoulder. He kissed the soft skin of her underarm. "Sweet Jesus, you are lovely. I can't bear it. I have to love you again."

"Shouldn't you take off your boots?" Merlin asked timidly. "Thaddeus will be furious if you get mud on the counterpane."

He looked up, offense and laughter chasing one another across his handsome features. "I didn't change for dinner, by God. Why should I change for dessert?" He leaned over her. "Besides, His Grace of Damerell never has mud on his boots."

"Oh." The syllable came out a gasp as Merlin felt the hard length of him penetrate her again in one smooth thrust. His hands slid beneath her buttocks, lifting her into him.

Merlin's body answered with a surge of excitement. She knew what to expect now, knew where the deepening rhythm led. It was as wondrous as any discovery she had ever made. In her intensity she abandoned shyness, the wing design forgotten along with the rest of the world. When he kissed her she kissed him back. His tongue swept into her mouth, and his arms tightened around her, drawing her with him as he rolled onto his back.

He took longer this time. Much longer. He pulled the blouse and camisole off her and caressed her shoulders and neck and breasts. Over and over, Merlin trembled on the verge of that lightning explosion. She worked clumsily at his shirt buttons and tugged at his cravat, baring the smooth, hard muscle of his chest and throat. A faint sheen of perspiration turned his skin to shadowed marble in the deep twilight.

He pulled her down until she could taste the salt of excitement on him. "Merlin." His voice was breathless at the base of her throat, his hands sending sparks from her breasts to her belly. Suddenly he clasped her to him hard and rolled atop her again. She heard her name in broken, whispered repetition, and then it was lost in a low moan, in his fingers gripping her arms and his face buried in her hair.

She thought for a wild moment that they might die of this, that the breath would never return to her lungs and the exquisite agony would burn her to ashes. But she lived through the climax, through the burst of lightning and the long fall, and a moment later felt his thrust, prolonged and shuddering, and a sound from deep in his throat that had no meaning beyond ecstasy.

The daylight faded, and with the last of it, Ransom's illusions. He lay with his arms around her, staring at the deep shadow of her hair against the pillow. He felt, for a few moments, suspended: hung between the brittle heights of elation and the strangling, sickening swamp of horror.

It was a peculiar experience, as if he saw himself—a man, with a woman, lying sated on a bed in the gathering dark. He knew himself content. He knew happiness; that much was left of the wild tide of emotion that had swept him to this moment. He knew that the quiet rise and fall of her breasts beneath his hand gave him pleasure. Simple pleasure, heart-deep. A satisfaction he had never in his life felt so completely.

But that was the man on the bed. The man who had taken a woman as if he owned her, when he did not. Who had just violated every sense of decency and honor Ransom had upheld for a lifetime. The man lay there, in possession of an innocence still lovely in destruction—able to feel the smooth curve of her arm, to smell the warm scent of dust and love on her skin.

Ransom hated that man. Betrayal burned through his veins, turned to raw anguish as the last moment of unreality passed and he *became* that man.

"No," he groaned in helpless fury. The crime was committed; he had done it. *He* had—the man who should have protected her. His duty, his morality, his honor as a gentleman . . .

She turned toward him, and in the deep dusk he could see just enough to know that she smiled. Remorse gutted him. He wanted to howl with it. He laid his head back and covered his face, pressing his fingers into his skull until he ached with the strain of holding back his cry of rage.

"Mr. Duke," she whispered, and touched his arm.

He grunted, unable to command his tongue.

"Mr. Duke," she said, a little louder. "I know I don't get out much, but really . . ." There was a tone of wonder in her voice. "I don't believe I've ever met anyone quite like you."

Ransom began to laugh. He laughed until the bed shook with it, until she sat up and began to make ineffectual attempts to relieve him—little fluttering pats on his back and singsong "There nows," as if he were weeping instead.

And he wanted to weep. He could not believe it. Never in his lifetime, not raging or drunk or sober, had he discarded all control and let his passions have free rein. To act without thought was the greatest sin he could imagine. Ransom had been trained to discipline from his first rational moment, had been drilled in the consequences of power, in his duty to wield it with precision and care.

He was human; he had his desires and his weaknesses, but to act on them to the ruination of someone else, to the injury of an innocent girl who had every right to expect all the strength of his protection . . .

"Oh, God," he said, his voice a rasp of stupefied rage. He turned his face downward into the pillow. "Oh, God," he moaned, and curled his hands over his face. "Oh, God . . ." he hissed into his palms. *"There was something in the salt."*

Chapter 3

"Never thought to see the day," Thaddeus grumbled, thumping a plate of burned bacon and tomato down in front of Ransom. "Never thought to see a bastard eatin' at me own table."

Ransom swallowed the urge to take out a few more of Thaddeus's already scarce teeth. "Mind your own affairs," he said stiffly. "I'll make it right."

"'Tis me affair, ye bleedin' sod." A cup of cloudy, lukewarm tea hit the table with a clatter. "I took care of her, I did; it's what me an' Theo's done for years, all right and tight, and then you come along in your gentleman clothes and smooth talk and what's she know about it? Ain't never seen a blighter the likes o' you, she ain't. Don't know a randy sonofabitch from a mare's hind end—"

"*Enough.*" Ransom's command would have frozen King George in his royal tracks. "I said I'd take care of it."

Cold toast rattled ominously in its rack as Thaddeus dropped it in the general vicinity of Ransom's plate. "Spilt milk," the old man said darkly. "I'd like to know how you'll be cleaning it up."

"I'll marry her."

Thaddeus stopped on his way to the pantry door. "Will ye now?"

Ransom made no answer. He bit into his charred breakfast and glared.

"When?" Thaddeus persisted.

35

"When I obtain a license."

"Bishop Ragley's to home, over at Barnstaple. Half an hour an' ye can be there."

To his utter disgust, Ransom felt himself flushing. Ragley, for God's sake. One of his grandfather's oldest cronies. Ransom could imagine it, confessing the sordid story to the stiff-necked cleric, asking—begging—for a special license. His gorge rose just contemplating the humiliation.

"I'll ride into London and bring the license back," he said, and then felt double disgust at the notion of explaining his intentions to a meddling servant.

Thaddeus turned and shuffled back. "That won't do, sir. Won't do at all."

"Get on with you," Ransom snapped. "Cursed impudence."

"Cursed blackguard," Thaddeus muttered.

Ransom thrust his chair back and roared, "I'll marry her, damn your eyes! What more do you want?"

"Today."

Ransom stared at the old man, his jaw quivering with suppressed rage. Thaddeus stood his ground, holding out a jam-pot as if it were a knight's shining sword. In a concerted effort to gain control of his temper, Ransom narrowed his eyes and looked down. He selected the least-crumbled piece of toast and put it on his plate. After a moment Thaddeus moved forward and spooned a blob of marmalade onto the bread.

"She's sleepin' like a lamb up there," the old man said. "Like an innocent babe."

"I'll speak to her when she wakes."

Thaddeus plopped another spoonful of jam onto the toast. "Never knowed a mother, not as she could remember. Ain't had no proper life at all."

"I can see that," Ransom said sourly.

"Sure ye can." A third scoop of marmalade hit the mound with a liquid plunk. "Fine gentleman like yourself, knows just how to take advantage of a trustin' lady."

Ransom clamped down on a retort. Another spoonful of preserves quivered where Thaddeus dropped it and then slithered over onto the blackened bacon.

"Her poor mother, that fine, gentle lady, she must be turnin' over in her grave," Thaddeus went on, spooning a further heap of marmalade onto the growing mound on Ransom's plate. "And we promised her—lying there on her deathbed, she was—me and Theo promised her we'd take care of that little girl. And we done fine, too, until here comes Mr. Fancy-Dancy"—preserves splattered across the bacon and dripped from the wrinkled tomato—"without a by-your-leave, all set to turn our Lady Claresta's little girl into a wh—"

"Don't you say it." Ransom came to his feet, shoving his chair aside. In the sudden silence his words filled the air with soft menace. "If you value what's left of your life, old man, you won't finish that sentence."

Thaddeus drew himself up, his bald head coming no higher than two inches below Ransom's shoulder. The manservant glared at Ransom for a long moment and then began vigorously scraping the last of the marmalade out of the pot and spooning it all over Ransom's food. "Bullyin' meself for your own sins," he muttered. "Hit me, hit me, see if it makes ye feel a right one. Go on, now, while I ain't lookin'. While me back's turned, that's the way. Me old neck'll snap like a twig, I warrant. I won't feel a thing. Won't have to worry for me poor mistress no more, won't have to work on me hands and knees in the garden, won't have to—"

"Oh, for the love of God." Ransom flung his tattered napkin down onto the table. "Go saddle up my horse." He kicked the chair out of his way. "On second thought, don't touch my horse. If your cooking skills are any example, the beast would be lame before it reached the front gate."

"Where're ye goin'?" Thaddeus asked, hope and belligerence mingled in his querulous old man's voice.

"I'm going to Barnstaple. I'll be back with the bishop this afternoon."

* * *

From the window of her laboratory, Merlin watched him ride out of the dooryard.

So.

He was gone.

It left a funny feeling inside her, that departure. Funny and quivery and sad, a lot like the way she had felt when Uncle Dorian had died, but worse, for this time she felt it was somehow a failure of her own, that this man who had arrived in her life like a burst of electricity had wanted to befriend her but had found her lacking. Last night he had held her in his arms, after his strange, angry laughter faded, and then when she'd awakened, he'd been gone.

She'd bathed in cold water as usual, except this time it wasn't usual, for she'd washed away all the traces of the astonishing experience of the evening before. She'd tiptoed to the door and heard him, downstairs with Thaddeus. An odd panic drove her away when what she'd really wanted was to see him again—to touch him, to hear the laughter in his voice.

Merlin, Merlin, I love you. Do you believe me?

She looked down at the leather-bound stack of papers she'd assembled. Twelve dozen, she'd counted out, and then in a burst of hope added a few extra, just in case he had more scientific friends than he had first imagined.

But he was gone now. Merlin bit her lip and rubbed at the binding with her fingertip.

Well, she thought. *Perhaps I'll donate them to the universities myself.*

The bell on the speaking box shrilled. Merlin swallowed the stupid lump in her throat. He hadn't even taken the speaking box, in the end—the invention he had come for.

The bell rang again. Thaddeus, Merlin knew. There was no one else to call her. She sat waiting, knowing that he would give up soon. He always did. And the stairs to the solar were too much for his ancient legs.

She was safe here. She was alone with her work, as she'd always been. After the bell went silent, she slid off her stool and began to dig amidst the confusion on the table, looking for the last equations that she'd balanced before Mr. Ransom Duke had exploded into her quiet life and then faded out again.

Her dogged concentration faltered at noon, when she saw Thaddeus carry a tray for his brother across the yard to the cottage. Certain that he would be occupied for an hour with Theo, she slipped downstairs for a solitary lunch. Somehow she didn't want to talk to Thaddeus. Not today. Not when he would ask questions. Questions like who her visitor was and why they had left the table in the middle of dinner and why the bed in Uncle Dorian's room was mussed and why her own was not.

She frowned at the marmalade-covered breakfast plate that lay abandoned on the dining room table. There was a trail of jam across the wood that ended at a tented napkin. The napkin emitted a faint crunching sound. Merlin lifted the material. Beneath it, the hedgehog rolled up, clutching the last of a jam-covered slice of bacon.

"I'm not going to take it," she assured the little animal softly. "You can open your eyes, silly."

The hedgehog ignored her. She replaced the napkin. After a moment the modest crunching resumed.

Merlin sliced herself bread and cheese and sat down. All morning she'd been occupied, lost in struts and stabilizers. It had come as a profound relief to put her mind to familiar puzzles, to slide easily into the elegant world of numbers, of theories, where questions had answers, if one only thought hard enough.

Now, emerging from that comforting trance, she was aware of the silence of the empty house. Her own breathing was the loudest sound she heard. It seemed to Merlin to ache, that silence. It made her throat fill up with pointless tears.

She stared blindly at the jumble of discarded junk that filled the corners of the dining room. Leaning against the wall beneath the window was a kite she had begun months ago. The framework was there, the short tail and the smooth, silken body, carefully modeled after a hawk's wings curved in the downbeat of flight. She knew the kite would fly. Beautifully. What she didn't know was why.

Her gaze drifted lazily past the kite to the half-finished anemometer she'd copied from a diagram by Sir Francis Beaufort. The little twirling cups would measure wind speed. There were a pair of them—why she'd made two, she couldn't remember, but a thought hung like a tickle at the back of her mind.

She rose. For a few minutes she stood frowning down at the kite and the anemometers. Then abruptly she grabbed them up and spread the kite across the table. After a frenzied search for tools, she bent over the kite and began to work, her mind empty of everything but her sudden purpose.

A half hour later, she was ready. The kite's pure curve sprouted new decoration: the two anemometers, one each mounted above and below the wings, and a tall pole, salvaged from the great-hall and attached at the apex. A string was centered lower, near where a bird's legs would have been. Half an hour of concentration had produced a pulley that would control the angle of the kite relative to the pole to Merlin's satisfaction.

She maneuvered the unwieldy apparatus out the door and down the passage, stopping only to stuff a notebook and pencil into her apron pocket. As she stepped into the yard, a stray breeze caught the kite. The anemometers spun.

Merlin watched them, one above the other, and gave a little squeal of excitement. The wind in the dooryard gusted and died, but she knew where it would be blowing more steadily. She tucked the kite under her arm and trotted out the garden gate, headed for higher, open ground.

It was almost dark when she found her way home, dragging the pole and the kite behind her. She was utterly happy and exhausted. Her notebook was filled with observations, with every variation of wing and wind speed. She'd scribbled down equations, crossed them out and scratched in more. She'd watched the birds and with her new knowledge seen things she'd never really seen before—the arc of a soaring wing and the changing angle of a feathered curve as a buzzard came to rest in a tree. The exhilaration of discovery carried her into the dooryard and past the carriage before she even noticed it was there.

It was Ransom's voice that broke through her reverie. She looked up and saw him striding toward her. The delight of the afternoon welled up into a cry of pure joy.

"Mr. Duke," she called. "Oh, Mr. Duke, I've *done* it! You won't believe how simple it is! It's the curve of the wing, you see. I have it all down. I measured everything. The wind speed varies with the curve, and the angle against the—"

"Merlin!" His furious shout cut her off, far louder than necessary from a yard away. He grabbed the kite and tore it out of her hands. Silk ripped under his fingers as he tossed the delicate framework aside. It landed and snapped, settling in a shapeless mass.

His hands closed tight on Merlin's arms, but she was looking beyond him. "You broke it," she said stupidly.

"Are you all right?" he demanded. "Are you hurt?"

Merlin dragged her eyes away from the heap of silk and stared up at him. "You broke it."

"Where have you been?" he cried. "Not flying some damned kite? I've been out of my wits, curse you." He began to pull her toward the house. "I come back and find your chaos of a laboratory in shambles—if the mind can conceive of such a thing—your precious Thaddeus knocked over the head, and no sign of you. I've got my agents out searching over half the shire." He shook her as he walked. "You might have had your throat slit. Or worse, by God. Far worse."

Merlin stumbled along beside him, unable to focus on anything but her broken kite and his last words. "I don't see what could be worse than that."

His grip tightened. "Don't you? Well, let me tell you, my innocent babe, being raped—" He broke off suddenly, and even in the twilight she could see the dark rise of blood in his face. He looked sideways at her, his mouth set in a terrifying curve. "Never mind that. The bishop's here."

"The bishop," Merlin repeated in a small voice. "What bishop?"

"What difference does it make? Ragley."

"But—is he here for dinner? I don't think there's mutton enough for—"

"Lord, we won't have him sit down to one of your elegant dinners," the duke snapped. "He can do his business and be gone."

She pursed her lips in desperate confusion. "What business?" Then she sucked in her breath and lunged against his hand, trying to break into a run. "Not Theo! Oh, no—you can't mean you've sent for a clergyman for Theo!"

He stopped, so abruptly that Merlin tangled in her skirts and would have fallen if he hadn't kept the punishing hold on her arm. "Theo is in exactly the same health as you left him. Ragley's here to marry us, of course."

"Marry us." She shook her head. "Marry us to who?"

"*To each other*," he shouted.

Merlin scrunched away from him. "M-marry? But—"

"It's a little late for buts." He pushed her through the door, and then halted in the dim-lit passage. Merlin exhaled as he let her go and stood rubbing her arms, afraid to look up at him while he was in this temper. The change from pleasure to persecution left her numb, disoriented. What had she done to make him so angry?

As if to further confuse her, he cupped her face and tilted it upward, bending to press his forehead against hers. "Don't ever do that," he said in a voice that shook, a voice far different from his earlier tone. "Merlin, don't ever scare me like that again."

"You broke my kite," she said tremulously.

He tucked a trailing strand of dark hair behind her ear. She waited for an answer to her accusation, for a reason, but he seemed not to have heard her. His gaze had wandered downward to linger at her lips, and his fingers brushed across her cheek with a feather touch. Merlin drew in a shaky breath just an instant before his mouth closed softly on hers.

Warmth seemed to slide down over her like satin, leaving her knees feeling too tenuous to hold. She leaned on him. He supported her, held her easily against his solid shape. She could feel the muscles in his thighs grow taut. For an instant the lightning of the night before flared between them, silver-hot, and then he broke away. "I don't think," he whispered ruefully against her temple, "that I'll regret this so much. I think that it might suit me very well."

Merlin dragged her heavy eyelids open. "What?" she said in a hazy voice.

He gave her a gentle push forward. "Come. The bishop's been waiting four hours."

Their entrance to the dining room was heralded with a thump and a clang as Ransom knocked over an abandoned bellows which collapsed in a heap at his feet.

A tall, elderly man in white stockings and a black frock unfolded from his chair, but Merlin had eyes only for Thaddeus's bald head, gleaming above a blood-stained bandage. "Thaddeus! Whatever on earth happened?" She pulled out of the duke's grasp and rushed to the manservant. "Oh, no, did that wretched scaffolding of mine in the barn fall on you? I'm so sorry, Thaddeus, I know I promised to pull it down, and I was going to, I truly was, but you see I had a splendid notion this afternoon, and I was afraid that I'd lose what it was, you know, if I didn't put something together just then, and—well, you see . . . I suppose I . . . just forgot."

"Aye, that you did," Thaddeus said, pushing her away as she tried to pat his shoulder. "Forgot it the last six months, you have, but that ain't what crowned me! Some bleedin' Frenchie, the duke here says"—he waved a hand toward Ransom—" snuck up on me like the creepy little snake he was. And I'm sorry, Miss Merlin, that I am, but he did make a wee mess of your room."

"It isn't important now," Ransom said sharply. "Bishop, may I present Miss Merlin Lambourne?"

Merlin blinked at the thin cleric. He was observing her with a sad, faintly accusing gravity, as if she had just died and been refused admission to Heaven. She managed a curtsy—one that must have squeaked from all the rust on it, she feared.

The bishop inclined his head. "It is most gratifying to perform the Lord's service and be of comfort to you in this moment of darkness, Miss Lambourne. I trust you will find strength in knowing that I bring His holy blessing to bestow upon your union."

Merlin made no sense of that. She glanced quickly at the duke. His mouth curved into a thin line of annoyance, but he said nothing.

"High time." Thaddeus thumped the table and stood up, tottering only a little. "Me an' the parson agree on that. Let's hie on over to Theo's room and tie the knot."

Merlin felt Ransom's hand beneath her elbow, turning her toward the door. She set her feet frantically. "Tie the knot! Thaddeus, are you mad? You don't really suppose I'm going to marry anyone!"

"Well, o' course ye are, Miss Merlin. Why not?"

She struggled for an answer. "Because I can't. I've never known anyone who was married!"

"Well, I 'spect the duke here can tell ye all about it." Thaddeus arched his brows. "What he ain't managed to get across already."

Ransom's fingers tightened on her elbow. "Keep a civil tongue in your head," he said coldly, "or you may find you don't care for your new master."

"Hmmpf. Ye can just lay them hackles, Mr. Big Dog. 'Tweren't my doin' she's got to be married, no sir. And she don't understand a word of it no how, that's plain as a pitchfork."

The bishop cleared his throat. "Perhaps I should speak privately with Miss Lambourne. I feel that, indeed, she may not recognize the gravity of her spiritual position."

The grip on Merlin's arm tightened until it hurt. "I hope I made myself clear, Bishop. No blame whatsoever can be attached to Miss Lambourne. Her 'spiritual position' is perfect innocence."

"Well put, my lord duke." The bishop fixed Ransom with a disapproving gaze. "You must certainly bear the entire weight of this incident on your own conscience.

Still, as a friend of your family, and of your late grand-sire, I hope you will permit me to say that Miss Lam-bourne might benefit from guidance—other than your own—in such a delicate situation as this."

Merlin could feel the duke's fingers tremble and bit her lip in apprehension. For a moment she feared he would begin shouting again—there was that much rage and more in the bruising pressure of his hand. But instead he let go of her. She heard him take a deep breath and exhale it slowly. He touched her shoulder, turning her toward him, and brushed her cheek with a brief caress. "All right. I'll be waiting, Wiz. Outside with Thaddeus."

Little good such gentle endearments had done him, Ransom thought bitterly, staring upward at the midnight shadows of the canopy. She might have been with him now, in this same bed where he'd loved her before, if Ragley hadn't made such a cock-up of the whole thing.

He must have botched it royally, the pontificating old bumbler. Ransom could think of no other reason why he was sleeping here alone while Merlin had retired to her own bedroom, with Thaddeus to guard the door and the bishop in the next room down the hall to preserve what was left of propriety.

And worse, for the ancient cleric to have called Ran-som on the carpet—Ransom himself, by God, as if he were some common parishioner—and demand to know if he had a proper affection for this female he proposed to marry. If he *loved* her, for pity's sake! The old warhorse of Westminster Abbey was lapsing into senility. Love her! How the bleeding Hell could Ransom possibly love her? He'd only laid eyes on her the day before.

Oh, he was willing to do his duty, all right. More than willing, in all honesty. He was growing tired of the in-conveniences of courtesans and mistresses, of the jeal-ousies and expenses and petty tantrums that had to be endured in order to meet his physical needs. He'd been less and less inclined to tolerate them lately, choosing to spend his time in London at Whitehall instead of at Madame's—undoubtedly why he'd been so disgustingly susceptible to that thrice-damned aphrodisiac.

The worst of it was, Ransom was as hungry for her as he'd been under the influence of her cursed potion. He was having a devil of a time getting control of himself. In fact, he was failing utterly. He lay there burning and ready for her, and thanked God that Thaddeus and the bishop were such a pair of old maids as to insist on chaperoning her themselves. Otherwise, Ransom had a clear and humiliating knowledge of just how long he would have held out against his own desire.

He threw the bedclothes back and got up. He wanted to pace, but the hard contact of his bare toe with a carved chest effectively banished that notion. He sucked in a sharp breath and fumed at Thaddeus, who had left Ransom barely enough candle to get undressed and into bed—probably on the theory that he'd stay there more readily without a light to guide him elsewhere.

A thin shaft of moonlight poured between the curtains drawn across the bay window. Ransom pulled the musty damask aside slightly and took an exploratory look out the open casement. Ground fog filled the yard, creating a billowy floor just a foot or two below the window. It was an illusion, he knew—the distance to the pavement was undoubtedly greater than he'd like to know about—but the appearance satisfied his private discomfort. His secret fear of heights was something that he lived with—if not exactly comfortably, at least without undue agony. He had contrived to arrange his life so that the problem had faded to the status of a minor nuisance. It had been months since he'd even thought of it, and he dismissed it now, feeling only a brief twinge of uneasiness thicken in the back of his throat.

He stood with his arms spread above him, leaning on the curtain rod. A light breeze caressed his unclothed body. To his chagrin, the night air did nothing to cool the heat in his veins.

She was, he thought, the most baffling and entrancing creature he'd ever had the misfortune to meet. None of his seasoned strategies worked with her, not reason or temptation or force. Not mild force, in any event. He had no doubt he could break her if he cared to do so, but his mind passed over the possibility with distaste. Unsentimental he had to be, but only the extremity of life or death would bring him to apply that kind of pressure.

He glanced back into the dim room, unwilling to return to the suggestive depths of the great bed. With a soft grunt, he swung himself into the padded window seat, settling his back against the stone wall. The curtain fell into place, enclosing him in a cool space between the fabric and the glass.

He tilted his head back, contemplating the irony of the situation. The most eligible widower in His Majesty's domain: rich, titled, powerful, and more than passably attractive, if his female admirers were to be believed—flatly refused, on account of a broken kite.

It should have been amusing. Ransom tried to summon a laugh, but it came out more of a snarl. The bishop had regaled her with the wages of sin and social stigma, Thaddeus had called her a bird-witted fool, and Ransom had used every appeal from sweet whispered compliments to one highly salacious kiss, which made him groan and shift restlessly just to remember. And she had taken it all with that bewildered slow blink of hers, and that fingertip resting on her full lower lip until he thought he would burn to cinders if he could not take advantage of the soft invitation.

All for naught. She'd listened, and then turned to Ransom and asked why he'd broken her kite.

He'd made the fatal mistake, then, and still he did not know what it was. He'd apologized for the kite: he was sorry, he'd been afraid for her, it had just been a moment of clumsiness, and it was only a kite, after all, was it not? He would give her a hundred better ones.

"It was an experiment," she'd said gravely.

"A kite?" Perhaps he'd allowed just a hint of skepticism to creep into his voice.

"Yes," she said. "Now I know how to fly."

Humoring her, he'd judged it best to say nothing to that. And after a moment, giving him a long, deep look from those mist-colored eyes, which seemed unexpectedly to penetrate to the very heart of him, she'd said, "I cannot marry you."

Ransom clenched his jaw and leaned forward, burying his face in his arm. It was the failure that galled him. He did not like to fail, and the state of his physical passions made this debacle a particular torture. He'd not felt so hurt, so angry and ill-used, since he'd been falsely accused of stealing Latin noun declensions from his younger brother's phrasebook.

He leaned back and closed his eyes. Lord, but he was tired and frustrated, to become as sensitive as a schoolboy over the befuddled Miss Merlin Lambourne. He tried to relax, to clear his mind, but the moment he drifted toward sleep he began to dream of Latin grammar, and of kites that tangled on the ground and would not fly.

He wrenched his eyes open on a low moan. The room was quiet. Outside, the moon had set. The fog had risen, blotting out the night sky. He nodded off again, this time to a nightmare of flying, on a kite that took him ever higher, horrifyingly high, so high that he could not even imagine the ground, until suddenly the kite dissolved and he began to fall—his worst fear, his personal terror—and he had no breath to scream, no hope—

He came awake in a shivering sweat. The diamond-shaped windowpanes were cool and hard against his face. He lay against the glass and metal network, holding his breath while his heart thudded in his ears. At first the other noise seemed part of that, only a distant echo of the sound of his own night fear. He exhaled slowly.

As he took his first conscious breath, his mind and body snapped to full awareness. He froze. The pounding of his blood rang in his head, but it could not conceal the sound he heard.

Footsteps.

There was someone else in the room, and the still air was laden with the smell of ether.

Chapter 4

It was the sickening-sweet smell that penetrated Merlin's consciousness first. In some dreaming, deep corner of her mind, she recognized it from long ago days in her great-uncle's laboratory. She turned over with a groan and lifted her head, mumbling, "Uncle Dorian?"

Darkness and silence answered her. Awareness prickled, pulling her from the edge of sleep. She struggled up with her hands braced in the depths of the down mattress. "Uncle . . ."

It came to her suddenly that Uncle Dorian was long passed away. The chemical odor burned in her nose, nauseatingly strong. She fumbled for the counterpane in the pitch blackness and threw the bedclothes back.

The rude impact against her face caught her completely by surprise. Her scream choked into a gagging whimper under the saturated cloth and strong hands that forced her mouth and nose into the strangling muzzle. She kicked out, once and hard. Her foot connected with yielding flesh. The answering grunt of pain seemed distant as thickness smothered her thoughts and dragged her down, until she was lost in emptiness and the stench of ether.

When she came to awareness, she was afraid to open her eyes. Sickness pressed in her throat, aggravated by the rolling motion that rocked her body from side to side in a warm cradle. She lay as still as possible, glad of the firm support that at least held and protected her from the worst of the motion. As the nausea receded, her mind struggled to shake off the lingering effects of the ether. She pieced together the movement and the sound of horse's hooves and the rhythmic squeak of wheels and decided that she was in a carriage.

With a sense of detachment, she concluded that she had been kidnapped. For a while, it seemed unimportant. It was enough to overcome the last waves of sickness and meditate vaguely on the notion that her abductors were rather thoughtful to press a cool, sweet-smelling cloth to her forehead.

Eventually, though, she began to come to her full senses. Detachment tightened into a knot of dismay. It had happened, just as the duke had warned her—the enemies of her country were dragging her off against her will, to be forced to work on their nefarious projects, or to be tortured, or to have her throat cut, or . . . or . . . What had Ransom said would be worse than that? She couldn't remember, but she was sure it must be horrible. She stifled a moan and peeked beneath her lashes at her surroundings.

It was daylight, the gray and watery sun barely illuminating the elegant red satin interior of the carriage. She was being supported in a surprisingly comfortable position across one seat. The opposite seat was occupied by another victim, a man laid out bound and gagged, still unconscious, his bruised and bleeding head lolling helplessly with the motion of the coach. The sight of his injury made Merlin cravenly glad that she had not had the chance to put up serious resistance to her captors.

The bound man was no one Merlin knew. She hoped that Thaddeus and the duke and Bishop Ragley had escaped safely. The fear that they had not made her go weak and trembling and awful inside. She lay thinking warm, miserable thoughts of how they had only wanted to take care of her, especially Ransom, how his shouting at her had only been concern, and she had been too stupid and obstinate to listen.

Oh, but she should have listened to him! He would be beside himself when he found out she'd really been abducted. The thought of how furious and frantic he might be made a hopeful lump rise in her throat. Perhaps he would rescue her. She would forgive him for shouting at her if he did. She would even forgive him for breaking her kite.

She began rehearsing suitably grateful and contrite phrases under her breath, such as, "Mr. Duke, I can't thank you enough for saving my life, and I know you didn't mean to ruin my experiment." Or, "It really doesn't matter that you made fun of my flying machine, Mr. Duke, not since you risked your life to rescue me." Or, in response to his abject apology for destroying her kite, "It's nothing, Ransom. Really it doesn't matter. I can make another one, I think. Yes, yes, I can, I'm sure of it. Almost sure of it. Oh, Ransom—" She sniffed, suddenly overcome by the realization that most probably she would never see Ransom or Thaddeus or Theo or her flying machine again. "Oh, Ransom," she whispered. "I'm so sorry I didn't listen to you."

"Are you indeed?" he said. "I'm bloody glad to hear it."

Merlin jumped, so abruptly that she nearly slid off the seat with a deep sway of the carriage. She scrambled upright, catching the lavender-scented compress as it fell from her forehead. "Ransom!" she gasped. "Whatever— I was afraid you— But what are you doing here? Oh, no," she wailed, "they've captured you, too!"

He had been grinning at her, resting casually back against the seat with his beaver hat cocked, but at that he looked indignant. "They most certainly have not. That fellow in the other seat turned out to be a poor hand at fisticuffs in the dark. Dropped him with one good right."

He looked pleased with himself. Merlin sat holding her forehead and trying to puzzle out the sequence. "So you have rescued me already," she said.

"In a manner of speaking."

"My," she said wonderingly, "I must have been carried a long way for you to have to bring a coach to fetch me home."

His self-satisfied smile turned grim. "You aren't going home. Not just yet."

"I'm not?" She pursed her lips. "Well, I suppose I might wait a day or so, if you think it necessary. But I hope I can remember how I made the kite that long."

"I'm afraid a day or two won't suffice, my girl. I'm taking you to Mount Falcon for an indefinite visit."

She sat up straight. "You can't do that. I don't want to go."

"Consider yourself abducted, then."

"I will not! You've rescued me."

He smiled. "Actually, I fear I'm the one who kidnapped you. You didn't recognize my shriek when you nearly unmanned me with that gallant kick last night?"

Merlin blinked. She frowned at him, and at the unconscious man on the opposite seat, and pressed her aching temples. Finally she said in a glum voice, "I don't believe I understand."

"Poor Wiz." He slid his arm around her shoulders and drew her close. "You don't have to understand. Just let me take care of you."

She resisted him for a moment and then gave in to the steady, comforting pressure of his embrace. She drew in a shuddery sniff and blew her nose on the lavender cloth. "That seems altogether too s-simple."

"Does it?" His breath ruffled her hair. "It's begun to seem quite perfect to me, Wiz."

She said tremulously, "I suppose you still want me to marry you."

He rubbed the back of her hand, a gentle touch that made the knot in her chest go queer and melting. "I think it's the right thing to do. It's a hard world, Wiz. I wouldn't want you to suffer for my sins."

"I liked what you did," she said in a small voice. "I think Bishop Ragley is stupid to call that a sin."

He was silent for a long moment. His finger traced the bones in back of her hand. He took a deep breath and let it out harshly. "Some times and some places, it is most definitely a sin. It was unforgivable, what I did. I'll live with it all my life."

Merlin bit her lip. "Will it make you very miserable?"

"Ashamed," he said softly. "Unspeakably ashamed, to have hurt you."

"But you didn't hurt me."

"In the eyes of the world, Wiz, I've ruined you. I know you don't understand that. I hope you never do. I hope you let me make the only reparation I can and allow me to marry you."

"But my flying machine . . ." Merlin hesitated. "You don't like it."

His fingers paused in their gentle rubbing. "I never said I didn't like it."

"My 'damned flying machine,' you called it. 'A bloody fantastical flying machine.' You said I would most likely break my head." She swallowed. "That's what you said. I remember."

"Well, most likely you *would* break your head," he said in a reasoning tone. "I wouldn't stand by for that any more than I'll let you be condemned for what I've done to you. I'll do my best to keep you from hurt, Wiz. I swear it."

"But you don't understand." She shifted in restless frustration. "I'm building a *flying* machine. It's going to *fly,* not fall."

She felt the deep breath he took and held. "Merlin," he said gently, "people don't fly. Birds fly. If people launch themselves off a cliff with a pair of wings attached, they fall. They're killed." His arm tightened around her shoulders with a faint shudder. "I don't imagine it's a very pleasant way to go, either."

"You don't understand," she said despairingly. "You don't understand. Wouldn't you like it, to be able to fly? To go as high as you could and see everything; to go as far as the wind goes, as fast . . ." She sat up away from him. "I can do it. I know I can. It's more than just attaching a pair of wings. Oh, it's much more than that. It will work. Someday. I'm certain of it."

He had a very odd expression on his face, dismay mixed with amusement and something else, something warmer and more affectionate. "Then at present I fear that we shall have to agree to disagree."

Merlin looked at her lap, disappointed in his lack of response to her dream. "I suppose so."

She felt his gaze on her, alert and probing. The carriage rocked along in silence. At length, he said, "But you wish not to marry, I take it."

She did not answer.

"Merlin," he said softly, "your flying machine isn't *you*. Don't let it overwhelm what's really important."

"But it is important!" she burst out. "It *is* me. I mean . . ." She paused, struggling for words. "There's nothing else to me but that. It's what I *am*. I'm going to invent a flying machine that works. Uncle Dorian always said so."

He scowled, leaning his elbow on the windowsill and pinching the bridge of his nose. Merlin watched him from beneath her loosened hair, noting the way the vague sunlight picked out his strong cheekbones and the clean, commanding line of his jaw. Though he frowned, there was still that touch of warmth about his mouth, amusement mixed with impatience that softened the unyielding angles and planes of his face.

He was like no one she had ever seen before—completely composed on the outside, perfect, immaculate in his dress and manner and yet radiating energy, a focused power that would sweep every obstacle from his path. It dawned on her that he really *had* kidnapped her, that he was carrying her away against her will, and she had not made the least move to stop him after that first instinctive kick. Which hadn't, she thought gloomily, appeared to have hindered him in the slightest.

He toyed with her fingers, lifting each one separately and letting it fall with the sway of the carriage. "I think," he said finally, "that it might be best if you left off with your work on the flying machine for a space."

Merlin stiffened, pulling her hand away. She stared down at her balled fist. "That's impossible, Mr. Duke." She heard a very faint breath of amusement from him and corrected herself quickly. "Mr.—um—Ransom, I mean."

He lifted her chin. "That's very nice," he said. "To have you use my Christian name. I don't hear it very often."

"It's easier to remember." She tucked her chin in, trying to evade his touch. It was hard enough to keep her mind clear without having him look at her in that disturbing way. "And I'm very sorry, but I cannot stop working on my aviation machine in favor of the speaking box."

"Well, then," he said easily, "don't work on either. Think of your stay at Mount Falcon as a holiday."

She bit her lip, frowning stubbornly.

"Merlin." His voice was very soft. "It grieves me to hear you say that there's nothing else to you but your great-uncle's fanciful dreams. It's not true."

"It is. What else have I invented? Oh, once I made a kettle that would boil water with electricity, and there's the speaking box, but who would care about something like that?"

"I suppose there might be some harebrained fellow who'd take an interest in a speaking box, but I wasn't talking about inventions. There's more to life than mechanics and chemistry."

"I like mechanics," she said. Then, in a burst of honesty, she added, "I'm not very partial to chemistry, though."

"There are children, for instance. Have you never wished for a family?"

Merlin opened her mouth. She closed it. She thought of the house where she had been brought up—quiet when her great-uncle had been there and quieter still after he had died. Her chest felt hollow, and her lips went quivery and out of her control. "No!" she said defiantly. "Uncle Dorian said children were quite a nuisance. Noisy. And always wanting a sweet when one is trying to concentrate."

He studied her. "I see."

"No," she said more firmly, "I don't care for children in the least."

"Have you ever actually met one?"

"Perhaps not, but Uncle Dorian told me all about them. He preferred to keep hedgehogs."

Ransom glanced at the bound stranger on the opposite seat, making sure the man's injured head still lolled without conscious volition. He took Merlin's hand and leaned near her. "Wiz," he said, making his voice as gentle as he could, "do you understand that because of what happened between us, there is a possibility that you might bear a child?"

Her eyes widened. "But I don't want one."

He found, to his chagrin, that her answer cut him far more deeply than was reasonable. He swallowed the angry retort that rose to his lips. "I'm afraid," he said carefully, "that it is no longer a matter of what either of us wants. If I— If you carry my child, then—" He broke off, overwhelmed suddenly by a vivid image of the chapel and crypt at Mount Falcon—two small marble memorials and a larger one above them.

His throat closed on old and familiar emotions: guilt and frustration and grief for things that had never been. He had not married for love. He had never expected to do so. Yet somehow his gay young wife of ten months— his grandfather's choice—had left a space in him that had remained empty for twelve years. He had not really known her. He had not known the twin daughters who lived three hours longer than their mother. And abruptly the thought that Merlin Lambourne did not care to have his child brought a wave of profound and unexpected desolation.

He glanced away and let the hurt roll over him, waiting for common sense to reassert itself. Outside, a sheepdog in a nearby pasture bunched its woolly herd and worried them through a gap in the hedgerow. Ransom watched until the little scene dropped out of sight and then said with his best diplomatic neutrality, "I suppose we need not address the problem unless it arises."

Merlin did not appear to share his complacence. She was frowning at him with her full lower lip set in a pout. He supposed she could have no idea how seductive she looked, sitting there wrapped in a wildly rumpled dressing gown over the night rail she'd had on when he'd stolen her out of her bed.

That *had* been rather dashing of him, he thought with a revival of humor. He wished he were carrying Merlin Lambourne off to a desert island where he could spend the next decade or so ravishing her.

His intense physical attraction to her still surprised him. He had thought that after two days the effect of the aphrodisiac could not possibly still linger. But there it was. Since that triple funeral twelve years before, there had been no pressure for him to remarry. No more important family alliances to be made, no lack of male heirs in the direct line, with his younger brother Shelby and Shelby's son. There had been no reason for Ransom to even contemplate burdening his active and ordered life with marriage—until his baser instincts had entrapped him and he had found to his chagrin that he was not so very sorry to be caught.

"Just where *is* my hedgehog?" Merlin demanded suddenly. She bent double, stretching her neck to see under the seat. Her thick hair fell loose and tangled over one shoulder as she made little huffs of exertion trying to reach into the back corners.

Ransom bit his lip, wanting to close his fingers around that tender nape, torn between kissing and strangling it. "Left behind as a hostage," he said. "It was a difficult choice, but I could only save one of you."

She came upright, flushed and so distressed that he was ashamed of himself.

"Merlin, Merlin—" He shook his head and touched her cheek. "What an ogre I must be, to have you look at me so! Your hedgehog is perfectly safe. So are Thaddeus and Theo. I'll have them all transported to Mount Falcon as soon as may be."

Merlin tripped on her nightgown as she descended from the carriage. Ransom caught her by one arm, and a strange man in a wig and a frilly coat caught her by the other. She stood favoring her stubbed toe, gaping up at the structure before her.

"Where are we?" she asked in a voice that seemed tiny in the enormous courtyard, standing at the foot of the colossal stone steps that led upward to the huge columns that held up a gigantic portico which overshadowed the monumental door.

"Mount Falcon," Ransom said.

"But I thought—I thought we were going to your home."

"This is my home."

"Oh," Merlin said, and stared. "Oh, my."

Ransom chuckled. "I've heard stronger opinions, I assure you." He glanced at the man in the wig. "I've had to bring along a criminal, I'm afraid. Remove him from the carriage and lock him in one of the empty strong rooms." His mouth quirked a little at the servant's impassive expression. "No need to treat the rascal kindly, I assure you. If you care for your position, you'll keep a constant guard. I will deal with him later."

There was a crash of metal on metal, loud from as far away as where they stood at the foot of the steps. The great front door swung silently inward. Another lace-cuffed servant bowed and stood back to make way for the upright, slender lady who glided through the opening and came to stand at the edge of the portico.

"Damerell," she said. "What is the meaning of this?"

Her voice sounded small and thin, sharp as steel, but dwarfed by the massive columns and the ponderous architecture that spread away from the portico and curved back in stately wings around the forecourt. As the bewigged footman passed her and descended the steps, Merlin saw that neither he nor the woman were as tiny as they had first appeared against the monumental scale of the building. The servant stood shoulder height with Ransom himself, and the lady only a hairsbreadth shorter.

"The meaning of this," Ransom repeated in a bemused tone. "I must say, Blythe, that a simple answer to that question escapes me at the moment. Would you care to meet our new guest?"

"Damerell," the lady said, never taking her eyes from Merlin as Ransom began to lead her up the steps, "are you inebriated?"

"Merely because I've taken to bringing home pretty girls in their night rails? Come, Blythe, you don't doubt this is government business! May I present to you Miss Merlin Lambourne?"

Blythe's blond eyebrows lifted. Merlin tried a curtsy, her second in two decades, and left off when the footman grabbed at her as if he thought she were swooning.

"I was under the impression that the person you intended to bring back was a man," Blythe said.

"As you see, she is not. Merlin, I give you my sister, Lady Blythe. She keeps us all on the straight and narrow path to Heaven. Never an easy task, I fear."

"Hullo," Merlin said shyly. "I'm sorry I'm not dressed, but I was in bed when Ransom came and got me."

Blythe's blue eyes widened. Her eyebrows climbed higher. "This is some joke, I assume. In poor taste, at that. Damerell, Duchess May would like to see you in the Godolphin Saloon. Miss . . . *Lambourne* may come with me."

"That's very kind of you, Blythe, but I would like Miss Lambourne to be introduced to our mother immediately."

For a moment Lady Blythe pursed her lips, her fine, pale skin suffusing with bright spots of color. "I find this offensive, Ransom," she said in a low voice. "Pray remember there are servants present."

"Exactly," Ransom said. "I wish for everyone to understand fully Miss Lambourne's position as an honored guest at Mount Falcon."

Blythe looked Merlin up and down, her mouth curled and her nostrils flaring as if she scented some unpleasant odor. "At least make her decent before you take her in to Duchess May."

"Tactics, my dear sister. I quite know what I'm doing. Come along, Wiz. They'll have raised the ducal standard at the gate as soon as we came through. My mother keeps a sharp eye out for that. She'll be waiting.''

Happy to escape the withering stare of Lady Blythe, Merlin tagged at Ransom's side through the door and into the Great Hall. She stopped, craning her neck to follow the tiered arches upward three stories to the ceiling, where frescoed angels battled red-eyed demons for possession of a golden coronet held out by a man in a Roman toga.

''Painted by Antonio Verrio,'' Ransom said. ''A nice comment on my illustrious forebear's politics, I think.''

''Oh.'' Merlin wondered if his forebears had been Italian orators. Before she could ask, he was guiding her up the steps through the largest arch and down a long vaulted-stone corridor where the echo of his boots mixed with the scuff of her slippers. She looked back and forth at the pairs of marble busts that stared at one another across the corridor in endless procession. More forebears, she guessed, all draped in their togas.

A footman stepped forward and bowed, holding open a tall door. Sunlight poured through into the chilly hall, and Ransom urged her ahead of him into the pool of light.

''Mamá,'' Ransom said, and strode to take the hand of the lady who rose from her chair. As he leaned to greet her, both of them became silhouettes against the sun streaming through the great windows. Merlin lingered near the door, not at all anxious to face another freezing perusal.

''Good afternoon, Damerell.'' The lady's voice was firm and pleasant, very like Ransom's own. ''You've brought us a guest.''

The silhouetted duchess held out her hand toward Merlin. Miserably aware of her frayed dressing gown and tumbled hair, Merlin clenched her fists and bobbed in place, wishing she could duck behind the huge door and hide.

The dowager duchess moved forward out of the sunlight. Merlin squinted against the contrast. She stood helplessly and tried to smile while Ransom's mother looked her up and down.

As her eyes adjusted, Merlin saw the duchess's serene face change—not to a frown, but to delight. "I have it!" she exclaimed, reaching for Merlin's hands. "Claresta's daughter. My very dear! Oh, my very dear. You are the image of her when you smile."

Merlin found herself smothered in a sweet-smelling embrace—as smothered as she could be by a lady so much smaller than herself. The duchess gripped Merlin's hand and drew her imperiously back to Ransom.

"Wherever have you found her, Damerell?"

He smiled. "You've guessed who she is. Shall I take all the pleasure out of your life by telling you the rest?"

"Of course not." The duchess's voice rang with indignation. "It was a rhetorical question. I shall put my mind first to determining why she has arrived in her dressing gown and slippers, and then to why you have brought her. You look the veriest waif, my dear. Come, will you sit here?"

She guided Merlin to a gilded chair upholstered in flowery needlepoint. Merlin sat perched in the middle of it, afraid she might smudge the creamy armrests with the leftover laboratory grime on her fingers. She could see the rest of the saloon now that she wasn't looking into the light. The scale of it daunted her. The sitting room was larger than the great-hall at home, dominated by a life-sized painting of an Arab horse and faded tapestries of hunts and battles. A crystal chandelier sent red and blue and yellow rainbows spinning across the rich carpet.

The duchess startled Merlin out of her openmouthed study of the grandeur. "Oh, Damerell—tell me the poor child doesn't suffer as her mother did!"

"Not at all," Ransom said cheerfully. "I'm sure she'll speak quite lucidly, now that she's decided not to catch flies on her tongue."

Merlin shifted and blinked under their combined looks. There was a lengthy silence. "I believe frogs are quite good for controlling flies," she offered, since they seemed to expect some comment from her on the subject.

Ransom got a peculiar pucker around his mouth. The dowager duchess looked from Merlin to him and back again.

"What is your name, my dear?" the duchess asked.

"Merlin Lambourne, ma'am. I'm named after John Joseph Merlin."

"The Ingenious Mechanick," Ransom supplied, when his mother looked blank. "I believe we have one of his ingenious clocks hereabouts someplace."

"Do you, indeed?" Merlin sat up eagerly. "May I see it?"

"Of course you may. Not just now," he added, as Merlin leaped to her feet. "You're taking a holiday from mechanics, remember?"

Merlin's protest was lost in the duchess's exclamation. "I have it! I have guessed it. You are engaged to be married."

Merlin turned in astonishment. Ransom inclined his head toward his mother, but did not look so pleased as he had at her earlier successful conjecture. "A very near miss, Mamá," he said quietly. "I have asked her."

The duchess frowned, her eyelashes fluttering in concentration. She looked back and forth between Ransom and Merlin. Her son started to speak, but the duchess waved him into silence. "No, don't tell me anything. I shall consult my cards." She stood and took Merlin by the elbows, brushing her dry, smooth cheek against Merlin's. "Welcome, my dear. Do go and settle in. I'm sure your baggage will be following you shortly. Damerell never forgets that sort of thing." She smiled mischievously. "Not even in the midst of capturing French spies and rescuing young ladies out of their beds in the wee hours of the night."

Merlin found herself ushered out the door, along with Ransom.

"How does she know about that?" she asked. "How does she know my mother's name?"

He shrugged. "She claims it's feminine intuition." There was a tinge of annoyance in his voice. "It's rather her hobby. She loves to prove that while we benighted men must muddle along on nothing but our own reason, she can guess anything on the slightest of evidence.'' He stopped at the foot of a spiraled staircase where a maid waited to escort Merlin up. ''She's a bit too bloody good at it sometimes, too.''

Chapter 5

Ransom took secret pleasure in the timeless rhythm of being dressed by his valet. It was not something he mentioned, to his valet or anyone else, any more than he would have explained publicly why he used the state apartments of his huge ancestral home as his living quarters. When everyone else had removed to the fashionably, and luxuriously, redecorated bedrooms upstairs, Ransom had stayed in the drafty state chambers below. Not because he particularly reveled in the chill grandeur, or because he had shared the ducal quarters with his grandfather from the age of eight, or even because he was now, in fact, the duke himself.

No, he preferred the state bedchamber because it was on the ground floor. Not something which could be admitted. Ever. To anyone. Better to be ridiculed in the papers and teased for having a pompous mind than to reveal his fear of heights. It was his one unconquerable weakness, the hidden source of every mysterious eccentricity that had made the rounds of gleeful gossips. No one had guessed, and no one would. Weaknesses were not a thing the Duke of Damerell allowed himself. Besides, after meeting Merlin Lambourne, Ransom was beginning to suspect that perhaps he *did* have a pompous mind.

An hour after he had sent her upstairs, he sat back looking up at the gilded plasterwork on the ceiling, relaxing under the even stroke of his valet's razor. It was Ransom's only real leisure, this half-hour period that occurred three times a day. Riding, breakfast, luncheon, dinner—top boots, trousers, frock coat, silks; they followed one another with comforting regularity. In town or in the country, the nature of his business might change, but the procession of clothing stayed the same.

Ransom allowed his eyes to ease closed. Miss Lambourne had caused a rift in the daily routine. It felt good to settle back into it, taking this chance to go blessedly blank. A man needed such times to relax without thinking, to have a moment without responsibility, a moment of self-indulgence, without the weight of politics and decision pressed on him—

"'Pon my honor, big brother, here you are snoring away while the country goes to rack and ruin!"

Ransom tilted his chin so his valet could reach beneath his jaw. Footsteps and a laugh drifted closer to his chair.

"The French have landed! The King's made Fox his prime minister. Wake up, Damerell. I've been elected MP for Cork-in-the-Cowbyre."

Ransom opened one eye. "Good God," he murmured. "We're in it now."

"'Tis a respectably rotten borough." His brother Shelby cast himself into a chair. "Only myself and a herd of prize Jerseys to please."

Ransom sat up, glancing in the mirror and indicating a fleck of foam beneath his ear that the valet had missed. "I suppose now you'll forever be urging the dairy cause."

"Jerseys are dun cows." Shelby looked struck. "Begad, a seat for *dun* territory!" His shout of laughter over his own pun rang in the huge room.

Ransom ran his thumb across his jaw and stood up, nodding to the valet, who whisked away the towels and basin. "How deep in debt are you this time?"

"No worse than usual." Shelby began a restless prowl of the room. "Where've you been, you scurvy fellow? I've been hearing dark tales from Blythe."

Ransom shrugged into his shirt and began buttoning it.

"Hah!" Shelby said. "I know that black-hearted smile. Who is she, brother? Is she pretty?"

"Very."

"Unmarried?"

"Presently."

"Rich?"

Ransom sat down to pull on his boots. "Is this interrogation leading somewhere?"

"Certainly it is. You know what excellent use of a pretty, unmarried heiress I might make."

"Only too well. Miss Lambourne is strictly out-of-bounds."

"Too good for me, eh?" Shelby lounged against the window frame with the afternoon sun turning his hair to molten gold. "Well, I don't doubt that. I'm a damned paltry fellow."

"You're a damned wastrel," Ransom said, accepting his cravat from the valet. "Beyond that, you're sharp-witted and pluck to the backbone and the handsomest devil on two legs, and it's my heart's wish that you'll quit the gaming tables and make a man of yourself."

Shelby drew in a breath. His ready grin faded to a bitter, lopsided smile. "As I said, a damned paltry fellow."

Ransom paused in the motion of folding. He looked toward his brother. "Shelby—"

"No, don't!" Shelby exclaimed. He shoved his hands in his pockets. "One of these days you'll tempt me too far, and I'll take your infernal gift money and make you promises I never mean to keep."

For a long moment, Ransom frowned at his younger brother. Daily, he asked himself what demon it was that inhabited Shelby, that forced him to spend all that brilliance and wit on deep play, instead of using the limitless prospects with which he'd been born. He might have made an extraordinary military man—a master of tactics— or a shrewd and charming diplomat. He could have been a dazzling speaker in the House of Commons or at the bar. He might have managed Mount Falcon—a responsibility Ransom would have been only too glad to share— and brought it to a peak of production, instead of gambling away four of the five estates that had comprised his generous inheritance. That he had an income at all was because their grandfather had seen the handwriting on the wall and left the fifth and richest property wrapped up in a neatly entailed trust with Ransom as the trustee. Ransom doled out a small allowance to Shelby and then did his damnedest to hold what was left in prime condition for the benefit of Shelby's three children.

But the waste, Ransom thought. The things that might have been. It drove him to distraction, the bloody waste of a life . . .

"Stop looking as if you don't know where to bury me," Shelby said. "Do I stink so much?"

Ransom set his jaw against the rush of love and frustration. "Foully," he said, resuming the task of folding his cravat.

Shelby's mouth tightened. "Must everyone march to your lockstep, big brother? Be satisfied I let you bully poor Woodrow into trying to match your stride."

"I'd rather have you. To better it."

"Well." Shelby tilted his head back against the wall, stretching with elaborate casualness. "Well, well. Haven't given up on the black sheep yet? Will you never learn, Ransom?"

Ransom turned a level gaze on his brother. "Never," he said softly. "Shelby. Not ever."

Something came into Shelby's face, blunting the sharp edge of insolence. His lips quirked as he stared at the toe of his polished boot. "Damn you, Ransom. I said don't."

Ransom kept his look steady. Sometimes he came so close, it seemed, so near to the key. Thirty-four years old, Shelby was, with his son Woodrow and two daughters and a future. There was still a future there. Ransom would not allow it to be otherwise.

Shelby frowned at the floor for half a minute before his handsome face slipped into a lazy sneer. He looked up into Ransom's waiting gaze. "Watch yourself, my lord. You'll drive me back to London's card tables tonight."

"Touché." Ransom turned back to the mirror. "Consider the topic closed."

Shelby made an inelegant sound and turned to the window. Ransom continued dressing in silence. Just as the valet gave his midnight-blue frock coat a final brush, his brother straightened up and said, "What the devil . . ."

Shelby leaned toward the window, staring outside. Ransom moved forward, looking through the transparent ripples of the window glass into the formal garden. Among the roses and lavender a knot of houseguests and servants was gathering. He could hear the nervous laughter and shouts of warning, could see that the pointing fingers were focused on a spot somewhere on the roof above his head.

He swore. Ignoring the watch fob that the valet held ready, he strode for the door. The servant lunged after him, just reaching the knob in time to throw the portal open. Ransom burst through at a violent pace with Shelby on his heels.

It was really quite easy to reach the wind vane. After being sent to her room—until her clothes arrived, Ransom had said—Merlin had quickly grown tired of examining the elegant furniture. She negotiated the scaffolding outside the window and carved balustrade, and only paused a few moments to puzzle over the identity of the row of sculpted figures which looked down in majestic stone silence over the courtyard. More forebears, she decided. Ransom seemed to have a quantity of them.

The ten feet from the balustrade to the attic story was no difficulty—she stood on an enormous stone thistle topped by a gilded crown to climb that—but the steep slope of the pediment roof required some ingenuity. She finally dragged herself up the slippery leaded surface by hanging on to the ankle of the posturing Atlas who held up a golden globe.

The dragon-shaped wind vane that had attracted her attention stood a few feet away. Merlin straddled the peak of the roof and slid along, eager to investigate the mechanism that registered not only wind direction, but the temperature as well, on a compass and thermometer in the wall of the Great Hall so far below. She reached for her pocket, intending to locate pliers, but her hand met only the bare skin of her leg.

She looked down, remembering for the first time that she was still in her nightgown. "Oooh . . . botheration," she said. And then, because she had climbed so far for nothing, and because it sounded like something Ransom would say, she added, "*Curses.*"

As if the word had conjured him, she heard his voice, faint and strained on the light wind. She looked around.

Far below, like figures in the wrong end of a telescope, a group of people huddled together among the garden walkways. Two ran to join the group, turning tiny faces up to the heights of the house. Merlin smiled, thinking she recognized Ransom. She grabbed the wind vane and hauled herself to her feet, tottering on the peak of the roof as she waved and hullooed back.

The Ransom figure stopped stock-still. He raised an arm. Merlin answered with another vigorous wave, but the distant man only pressed his forearm over his face and did not move again. The other latecomer gestured wildly, seeming to shout at him. Merlin dropped her hand, puzzled to see the second man tear off his coat and come running back toward the house. She caught a flash of his golden hair just as he disappeared from her view beneath the edge of the balustrade.

Standing there with everyone looking up at her, Merlin began to feel a flush of shyness. They certainly did seem to think she was something extraordinary. More and more people gathered, and as each one arrived, several others would point and they would all stare, clustering in smaller groups and breaking up again. Only the one she thought to be Ransom stood still, his head bent and his hand still covering his eyes.

Merlin sank onto the roof, dangling both legs over one side of the peak. She did not want to climb down now, not with everyone watching her. It was better to sit and feel the breeze and think of how fine and high she was. Perhaps they would grow bored and forget about her. The view was quite remarkable, out over the flat-roofed wings of the house, studded with ornamental parapets and towers, across the elegant gardens to the fields and the village and the high Sussex downs in the distance. In a far break between the hills, she fancied that a gleam of silver was the Channel. If she had a flying machine, she mused, she could be there in moments, sailing high above the waves.

"Miss," someone said. "Miss—"

Merlin scrambled to her feet, startled by a voice so close.

"Don't jump!" he cried, just as Merlin spotted his blond head peering up from behind the gilded crown that topped the giant stone thistle.

She stared at the golden-haired stranger. "Jump! Why ever would I do that?"

He closed his eyes, panting audibly. "Thank God. Just a . . . just a moment; let me catch my breath. I'll have you down in an . . . instant."

"I'm sorry," she said, "but I don't want to come down just yet."

His eyes popped open. They were very blue eyes. He was a very handsome man, with a face rather like some of the beautiful statues she had passed on her way to the roof. "You don't want to come down yet," he repeated blankly.

"Not really. I hope you haven't gone to any trouble."

"Trouble? Oh, no. Not at all. Nice view, ain't it?"

Merlin smiled. "Oh, yes. I'd like to stay up here forever."

He had caught his breath. He looked down at the waiting crowd. The breeze ruffled his blazing hair and lifted his lawn shirt from the dark marks of perspiration across his shoulders. Leaning with his arm around the thistle, he grinned back up at Merlin. "You know, I think I could fancy that myself."

"If you grab his ankle"—she pointed at Atlas—"you can get up here. I can see all the way to the water."

"Yes, I imagine you can." He followed her instructions, hauling himself up to her level. "What's your name?" he asked as he settled beside her.

"Merlin. After the Ingenious Mechanick, you see."

"Do I?" He grinned again. "What a clever chap I must be. I'll wager excellent odds that you are the pretty, unmarried female my brother brought home today."

"Oh, are you Mr. Duke's brother? You're not very like. Except when you laugh at me," she added as his face creased.

"I'm Shelby," he informed her. "Look down there. Poor Damerell, he's not laughing now."

Merlin bit her lip. "Do you think he's angry at me?"

"Oh, well," he said airily, "not especially. I'd only advise you to stay up here for a week or so."

"I suppose I've done something very wrong," she said in despair.

"Unusual, Merlin dear. Unusual."

"I wanted to see the wind vane."

"Yes, well, I realize that's one of our top attractions, but perhaps you might have asked for assistance before you tackled the summit. But there," he added, as she squeezed her lips together to control their quivering, "it's not such a disaster as that. Don't cry, love . . ."

"Oh," she said on a sudden, deep sob. "I want to go home!"

"Then you shall." He circled her shoulders and drew her against him. "We shan't keep you prisoner here if you don't like it."

"Oh, yes, you will," she mumbled, wiping at her eyes with her sleeve. "Ransom will. He kidnapped me."

The comforting weight on her shoulders lightened. "Did he now? I didn't think he was such a villain as that."

She hiccoughed. "Well, he is. He kidnapped me and broke my kite and now I have to give up my flying machine to w-work on his stupid s-speaking box. And look at them." She pointed. "They're all *laughing* at me. I hate him! I want to go home."

Shelby was frowning. "Speaking box. What's that?"

"Oh, it's just a stupid thing I made so that I could stay in my laboratory and talk to Thaddeus when he was in the garden." Merlin sniffed. "I wish I'd never thought of it. Ransom wants it for his war."

"Like a telegraph, do you mean?"

She licked a stray tear from the corner of her lips and sat up a little straighter. "No. I read about that—Mon-

sieur Chappe's semaphore towers with the signaling arms?
I thought that was very clever, but Thaddeus wouldn't
learn the signals. So I made the speaking box, and I just
talk to him.''

"Just talk to him. Not shouting or anything?''

"No. The electricity carries my voice through the ether,
you see. Sometimes it buzzes a lot, especially if Thaddeus won't stand still when I'm talking to him. But since
I worked out how many turns to take on the coiled wire,
it's not so bad.''

"Hmm,'' he said. "Hmm.''

"Ransom says the French have found out about it, so
he kidnapped me.''

"Yes. I begin to see the light.'' Shelby's voice sounded
odd. "It may be that he's right, Merlin. You might be
safer here.''

Merlin gave him a hurt look.

He smiled at her. "Come, what is it that you don't care
for about the place? Look around—it's really rather nice.
Pretty gardens, good food, lots of room to ride . . .''

"I don't know how to ride.''

"Walk, then. Look at all those fields.''

"Well,'' she said doubtfully, "Ransom did say there
was lots of open lawn for me to test my aviation machine.''

"There, you see? And if I know my brother, he'll chop
you down another couple of woods if you don't have
enough space now. Where is your aviation machine? Have
you brought it with you?''

"No. Ransom said he would have it transported. But
he doesn't like it, so I'm afraid he won't.''

Shelby shook his head. "Don't worry about that. If
Damerell promises he will do a thing, he'll move Heaven
and Earth to do it.''

Merlin looked down at the waiting group below. Ransom stood a little away from the others. He seemed to be
staring at the ground with passionate interest, his hands
pressed over his temples like the blinkers on a carriage
horse, as if he did not want to see beyond. She put her
finger to her lower lip and worried at it, sniffing again.

"Merlin," Shelby said softly, "don't go home. I'd like to be your friend."

She let out a shaky breath. "I suppose I could stay. For a little while. If my flying machine really comes, that is."

"It will." He squeezed her hand. "Come down with me now, and I'll undertake to protect you from that ogre waiting for us below."

"He'll shout at me."

"Undoubtedly. But you must be brave, dear. He's been shouting at me all my life, and I'm still quite intact." He shrugged and grinned. "Physically, at any event."

Merlin sighed. She gathered her nightgown around her legs and launched herself down the slope of the roof. Behind her, Shelby's cry of dismay broke off as she caught the Atlas's ankle and swung neatly around to land on the stone thistle.

Looking back, she saw him close his mouth with a snap. He hesitated and then waved jauntily down at the crowd below just before he matched her move with a slide and a catlike leap. He landed, slipped, and saved himself with one hand on the gilded crown. Cheers and shrieks drifted up from the ground below.

"Heigh-ho!" he cried. "I think I hear a bit of feminine concern for my well-being."

Merlin scrambled down the side of the thistle and walked to the balustrade. "Yes," she said. "Two of the ladies have covered their eyes."

"Hah." He jumped wide of the thistle, landing in perfect balance and eliciting another set of cries from below. "I appreciate this, my dear. It should raise my value immensely in certain quarters. I venture to say I'll be rescuing ladies morning and night from up here."

Before she climbed over the balustrade, she looked to see if he was following. He beckoned her back, and she let go of the stone railing and returned to where he stood in the shadow of the thistle.

"Merlin," he said with soft, sudden emphasis. He took her hand and turned it over, palm up. "Do you keep your promises?"

"Yes," she said. "Of course I do."

"Promise me one thing then, love. Promise me you won't tell anyone else—*anyone*—about the speaking box."

"Well—Thaddeus already knows. And Ransom."

"Thaddeus is your gardener?"

Merlin gave him a sheepish smile. "Thaddeus does everything I don't want to do."

"A fine fellow to have around. But you won't tell anyone else?"

"I suppose you mean because the French want to kidnap me?"

He squeezed her hand. "Promise?"

She hesitated and then nodded.

"Good." He lifted her palm and placed a kiss in the middle of it, then rubbed it flat against his own. "Honor of a gentleman. And a lady. And Merlin"—he looked directly into her eyes—"believe me, I'll find out if you don't keep it. If you think you're in trouble now . . ."

Merlin bit her lip, a little unnerved by the sudden hardening of his friendly expression. He looked every bit as intimidating at that moment as Ransom had ever done. "All right. I promise."

He smiled, and his face changed like the sky on a windy day—from clouds to sunlight. He gave her a pat and light push toward the balustrade.

The climb down the scaffolding went faster than Merlin had anticipated. Long before she was ready, she found herself on the ground, surrounded by strangers: neatly uniformed servants and men and women in elegant dress. They all stared at her. There was a great deal of tittering and chuckling and speaking behind hands, and Merlin was glad when Shelby took her arm and brushed past them.

She was not so glad when she saw where he was taking her. A few yards apart, Ransom stood unmoving. He looked like one of his statues, marble-white and inhuman. Merlin set her feet and tried to pull away, but Shelby held her fast.

"Pay your accounts, love," he murmured. "Believe me, I know what comes of putting them off."

She looked up into Ransom's eyes. There was not one trace of reason or understanding there. He made no greeting, spoke no word of reassurance, only grasped her arms and tore her out of Shelby's grasp. "Ransom—" Shelby said in a warning voice, but his brother gave no sign of hearing. When Ransom spoke, his voice was like the whisper of steel in a sheath, so low she could barely hear it.

"Come with me," was all he said. The pain of his fingers made her arms go prickling and numb. He released her as suddenly as he'd taken hold and began walking away.

Merlin looked after him, dumb with terror. Her feet took her forward, puppetlike, because she could not conceive of what might happen if she did not obey.

They left the staring crowd behind. Ransom did not once turn back to see if she was following, not until they were inside the great house and through the arched passages and beyond the spiraling staircase. Not until he had jerked his head at a liveried footman and huge double doors had shut with a resonant thunder, closing them alone in a splendid room.

She was aware of glitter around her, of rich blues and golds and a bed whose canopy rose up like some giant beast from a fantasy tale. But it was Ransom she watched with unnerved fascination. He turned on her, and for an instant fear bound her as he reached for her hands.

Afterward, Merlin was not sure what she had expected. Violence of some kind, a punishing rage. His face promised that in its brutal intensity. She had scrunched herself smaller in anticipation of the noise and pain. But all that came was silence, except for the sound of his breathing, and the warm whisper of it on her skin as he clasped her hands between his and carried them to his mouth.

He stood for a long time with his eyes closed, rocking slightly, pressing her hands to his lips.

She looked up at him. Harsh lines edged his closed eyes. The skin across his cheekbones was white and taut. He just stood there, not speaking, clinging to her hands until her fingers throbbed with the pressure of his grip.

If he had done as she expected, raged and shouted and bullied her, she would have pulled away from him. She would have knotted herself up in a ball and withdrawn, and when her chance had come, she would have run away. But to see him like this, reduced to this terrible silence . . .

"I'm sorry," she said in a trembling voice. "Ransom, I didn't mean to . . ."

Her words trailed off into confusion. She was sorry—for what, she did not understand. Obviously she should not have climbed the roof. Obviously everyone thought it was quite criminal and peculiar. They had laughed, all those elegant strangers. They had laughed at her, and therefore in a way at Ransom, because he had brought her here. Within an hour of arriving, she had disgraced him. And Ransom was not a man who would easily tolerate disgrace.

"I want to go home," she said miserably. "Would you let me go home?"

He took a deep breath. Like someone waking up, he opened his eyes and closed them briefly. His hold on her hands loosened.

Merlin tried to straighten her numbed fingers. He lowered them, but kept them between his palms. His hands shook a little as he laced them with hers.

"Merlin, I can't send you home." His voice sounded hoarse and unlike himself. "It's too dangerous."

"But—" She wanted to argue, only she had no arguments that could possibly match his. There was a lump the size of an egg on Thaddeus's head to prove his words. She looked up into Ransom's eyes and said, *"Please."*

"I can't." He rubbed his thumbs across her hands in a jerky motion. His mouth had a distraught twist to it that gave his face a queer look, like hard stone crumbling. "Merlin, don't. Don't ask me anymore."

It sounded more a plea than a command. Merlin hung her head, defeated by that. His arrogance could be resisted. But when he spoke to her with such a tone in his voice, there was nothing to do . . . nothing but move into his arms and remain there, with her heart feeling weak and foolish and her body wanting his closer.

She felt him go tense as she pressed herself nearer. He let go of her hands, and then seemed not to know what to do with his own. "Merlin," he whispered. "Ah, Merlin. Have a little mercy. Do you think I'm made of iron?"

She shook her head.

"No." He made the word a bitter sound. "I suppose you know better than anyone that I'm not."

Beneath her cheek she could feel his heart, a strong and excited beat that belied his stiff resistance. "I think I've forgotten what you're made of," she said. "Perhaps I'd better examine you again."

He exhaled in a hollow whoosh. "Damnation," he said in a different tone, a kind of plaintive resignation.

Merlin snuggled closer. His embrace enfolded her, drawing her hard against him. His cheek rested on her hair. He stroked her back in a rhythm that was at first simple comfort and then, with a slow drift downward, something more.

It started as only the heat of his palm through her dressing gown. He spread his hand across her spine and began to outline tantalizing circles on the small of her back.

She tilted her head up, recognizing this for what it was. His cheek slid against hers, very smooth, smelling faintly of soap and mint. His arms tightened, just slightly. Sweet and subtle, the touch of his breath on her neck became a light kiss.

Merlin sighed, curving her neck with all the pleasure of a cat stretching beneath a stroking hand. Her lips parted. She held her breath. It was like the brush of rose petals on her skin, like the beat of a captive bird's wing, but more than that. Warmer. Stronger. She made a small sound of aching pleasure.

"What a shameless hussy you are," he whispered, and she could hear the smile in his voice. "What am I going to do with you?"

She bit her lip, pulling back in mild surprise. "Oh, dear. *You* haven't forgotten?"

"Don't look so dismayed." He looked down at her with a sleepy, sensual grin. His hands moved down her back, rocking her against him. "I haven't forgotten, Wiz. I remember all too well."

She smiled. "Well . . . actually . . . so do I."

He covered her mouth with a hard, sudden kiss. "You'd drive a saint to distraction," he growled against the corner of her lips. "And I am not a saint."

"Oh, no," Merlin agreed. "You're a politician."

He stopped the delightful play of his tongue at the edge of her mouth and looked down at her. Humor made boyish crinkles at the corners of his eyes. "At least you know what kind of low company you've fallen in with."

"Low company indeed!" A new voice brought ice ringing in the soft air. Merlin jumped, half-turning in Ransom's arms. His sister Blythe stood in the doorway, her hand still on the handle of the silent, well-oiled door. She looked shocked and shaken, but her lips trembled with dawning rage.

"Blythe," Ransom began, but his sister interrupted him, stepping into the room and closing the door with an echoing bang. Just before it shut, Merlin caught a glimpse of hovering figures outside.

"I had thought to offer my presence to avoid a scandal, since you had so obviously forgotten the proprieties after that incident outside," Blythe said. "But, Ransom, I never expected—" Her voice broke on a shaky squeak. "Oh, Ransom, how *could* you? It was bad enough that you marched her to your *bedroom,* but I managed to smooth over that. You were beside yourself, everyone could see that. But *t-this—*"

Merlin had begun to try to wriggle out of his arms, but his hold on her tightened.

"I'm sorry," he said in a calm voice. "You're right, of course, Blythe. I shouldn't have left you with awkward explanations to make."

"Awkward! Ransom, do you realize you could lose your privy appointment over this?" Blythe paced into the room, chafing her thin hands. "The King has already made it clear that he disapproves of your association with Mr. Fox—''

"*Friendship* with Mr. Fox," Ransom said deliberately. "Of long standing."

"Nevertheless, it would be far too easy for you to be tarred with his brush. Everyone knows he's just lately married that woman who's been his . . ." She hesitated. Merlin saw a frown begin descending on Ransom's face. ". . . his concubine," Blythe rushed on. "For decades. And now for you to be involved in a scandal like this— for God's sake, Ransom, only think of what it will do to your prospects! Everything we've worked for will be ruined."

"I really don't think my career has been a joint project, Blythe, as much as you wish it were so." He let go of Merlin, only to take her hand and hold it firmly when she tried to move away. "And I don't believe this 'incident,' as you put it, need be blown into a scandal."

Blythe tossed her blond head. She narrowed her eyes and looked with distaste at Merlin. "We've seventeen houseguests here presently, and at least fifteen of them saw you drag Miss . . . *Lambourne* into your bedroom. I didn't count how many were standing behind me when I opened the bedroom door."

"Without knocking."

"I didn't expect there would be a need to knock," she said icily. "I was trying to make that very point to my observers."

"Well, Blythe, I would advise you to turn about and inform your 'observers' that a man in love must be allowed a little room for eccentricity." Ransom's hand closed very hard on Merlin's. "Miss Lambourne and I are engaged to be married."

Chapter 6

"We certainly are not!" Merlin cried. "I told you I couldn't marry you."

"Engaged," Blythe exclaimed, as if Merlin hadn't spoken. "Ransom, you cannot— You wouldn't— Not to this . . . *person?*"

Merlin waved her arms as if she could blow the very notion away. "Of course not! I'm going to work on my flying machine."

Blythe didn't even look at her. "Why—we don't know who she is! It's insane. Lady Edith Massingill I could countenance, or even that Jennings girl that the Spencers have been pushing on you, but *this*—"

"I'm not a *this,* if you please," Merlin interrupted. "And I want to go home immediately."

Blythe gave Merlin a look of disgust. "By all means, Miss Lambourne. Take yourself off at once."

Ransom stood silent, one eyebrow raised. His grip tightened on Merlin's hand as she tried again to pull away.

"I want to go home," Merlin insisted. "I hate it here."

"Well, you may rest assured that you certainly aren't wanted—"

"Blythe." Ransom's warning tone cut his sister short. "Stop your tongue, before you find you've said something yet more stupid."

Blythe turned. Her mouth went to a sharp, quivering line. "Stupid," she said, in a thin voice. "Is it stupid for me to want to help my brother?"

"Certainly, when you're in this emotional state. God knows what you're thinking with, but assuredly it isn't your head."

Merlin frowned, struck by the concept that a person could think with something besides his head. Her own skin was flushed with anger and her tongue wanted to say things that admittedly didn't seem to be arising from a rational consideration in her brain. She decided, after a moment, that she was probably thinking with her spleen.

Following that logic, she glanced at Ransom. It was clear that he was thinking with his head right now, but a few moments earlier . . .

Merlin tilted her head. She liked it when things began to make sense. Ransom's actions fitted nicely into a pattern. She suspected that she might have a much easier time understanding his reasonings and rages if she guessed which part of his body he was thinking with at the time.

And understanding that, Merlin saw that Ransom had left himself wide open to a counter-accusation by his sister on just what part of *him* had been in control of his wits when he took Merlin into his bedroom and into his arms and kissed her.

But Ransom apparently knew his sister better than Merlin did. Blythe simply stood as if he had delivered a devastating blow. Her shoulders drew inward, and she clenched her hands. In a low voice, she said, "I'm sorry, then."

Ransom's hand relaxed its grip on Merlin's. "Blythe," he said gently, "I've been stupid, too. Very stupid. But if you want to help me out of this pinch, then you'll have to use that brain of yours."

Ah, Merlin thought. Clever. She could see the effect Ransom's sudden softening had on Blythe. She still wasn't thinking with her head. It was her solar plexus now, Merlin guessed, that little spot above one's stomach where pride and hopefulness curled. Blythe looked up at Ransom like a dog would look up at its master, chastised and eager to correct its mistake.

"You're right," he went on. "I've made a serious blunder, for myself and for Merlin, too, by bringing her in here. I've risked my own reputation, and I've no doubt ruined hers. So . . ." He paused. He didn't sound upset. Instead, his voice had taken on a familiar quality, a certain rhythm and emphasis. "What is the situation?" he asked in a rhetorical tone that Merlin recognized as the same one Uncle Dorian had used when he'd wanted her to follow him in an intricate line of reason. "We have to live with the mistake that's already been made. We can't pretend that no one else knows of it. We can't hope that our witnesses, left to themselves, will interpret it kindly, or simply forget about it, or refrain from spreading the story. Some of them might, but numbers are against us. Among seventeen houseguests, there are bound to be at least a dozen confirmed gossips, any one of them with connections that might lead back to the King or Mr. Pitt."

"Yes." His sister looked bleak. "Lord Parrymore and Mr. Littlejohn are dining at St. James's two nights hence."

Ransom seemed unperturbed, though his words belied it. "Worse and worse. Parrymore's after my hide for siding with Mr. Fox over the slavery issue."

"Oh, Ransom," Blythe wailed. "I just can't understand why you allowed this to happen."

"But that's no longer the point," he said patiently. "You waste your thought and energy over what's too late to change. Think forward, Blythe. What now?"

Blythe pursed her lips. "If we can't change it," she said as if reciting an old formula, "we must turn it inside out."

Ransom was silent, not answering the quick glance that asked for approbation.

"Well," Blythe went on after that slight, hopeful hesitation, "that must mean making people approve instead of disapprove."

Ransom waited.

"Yes . . . of course," she said thoughtfully. "Turn a scandal into a romance."

Ransom lifted Merlin's hand and bent over it with a sweeping bow.

"But it must not be announced immediately," Blythe said. "That would look too much like a forced affair."

Ransom inclined his head to this wisdom.

"I'll manage it," Blythe said crisply. "Just a hint in the proper ears, I think, for now. Perhaps it need never go farther than that."

"Perhaps not. I might be quietly jilted at some later date."

Blythe smiled. "Yes. Yes, I see that you might."

"I'm sure you'll know just what to say."

Blythe started for the door. Merlin managed to get a small sound past the lump of fury in her throat. Both Blythe and Ransom turned in her direction.

"I am *not* engaged," Merlin said very clearly and evenly.

Blythe stiffened into a militant pose. "Miss Lambourne. My brother's political career is at stake here. I'm sure he would thank you to cooperate."

"He certainly would," Ransom said mildly.

Merlin took a deep breath. "My spleen," she warned, "is trying very hard not to think."

"Indeed?" Blythe said. "Does it trouble you often?"

Merlin ignored her and looked at Ransom. "This isn't fair."

His jaw tightened just perceptibly, and his eyelashes swept down and up. An instant later the expression was gone, uninterpretable, vanished into a slight, practiced smile. "Love and war, my dear. I'm afraid we haven't a sufficiently comfortable margin for fairness just now."

She pressed her lips together. Ransom's simple lesson in politics for Blythe had not been wasted on Merlin. Blythe was going to spread word of the engagement. There would be no stopping her, clearly, as long as she thought it was in her brother's interest. And Merlin didn't believe for an instant that he would allow himself to be jilted. She began to suspect he had planned the whole scene to bend matters to his will. Perhaps, just perhaps, he had been thinking with his head all along . . .

"Come with me, Miss Lambourne," Blythe said, dragging Merlin with her in a commanding sweep toward the door. "You must be made presentable. I want to brush over this incident and begin introducing you as soon as possible."

Merlin allowed herself to be pulled along. She'd already forgotten Blythe in concentration on this new suspicion of Ransom, this new understanding that what he appeared to feel might not be what he felt at all. As she passed through the door she looked back at him. He smiled at her, another smooth and reassuring smile. And suddenly, for the first time in her life, she questioned the value of the evidence before her eyes.

It was a lie, that smile. It was not the truth.

Merlin touched her lower lip. She did not smile in answer as Blythe led her away.

Ransom closed the door behind them and turned back to the tall windows. He held out his hands, examining them. They seemed reasonably steady—a complete contrast to the shaking mass of nerves inside him.

The image of Merlin's silhouette against the sky still burned behind his eyes. Every time he pictured the moment, it got hard to breathe and harder to think. His mind had gone to jelly; he had no clear recollection of how she had gotten down or how they had ended up in his bedroom. He had a better idea of how she had wound up in his arms—that was obvious enough. He thanked God that Blythe had interrupted when she had, or he'd be in that bed with Merlin right now, seventeen houseguests and Mr. Pitt be damned.

He shifted, uncomfortable in his visions, in his blood that ran hot and cold, thinking one moment of Merlin soft beneath him and the next so high—so appallingly high— above. He pulled his open palms down his face and shuddered.

At least something had been salvaged from the wreckage. He'd hemmed in Merlin a bit closer on his determination to make her an honest woman. And she knew it. She'd given him that look, those beautiful gray eyes all solemn and accusing, as if his effort had been a crime instead of an honor-bound duty and an opportunity no other woman in the kingdom would resist. And for the love of

God, he'd wanted to go down on his knees and say he was sorry for it. Sorry for his scheming and his machinations that came to him as naturally as his heartbeat. He looked for advantage and struck, on instinct, because that was what he had been taught to do all his life.

But he'd never before met someone who saw through him and said nothing. Who only looked at him in that misty-eyed vague way, like a fawn would look at the wolf who had orphaned it.

"A pox on her," he muttered as he stalked toward the door. "You'd think I was offering her a *carte blanche*, instead of honest vows."

"Your Grace," said the voice, without a trace of impatience, a day later in Ransom's study. "Forgive me, Your Grace."

Ransom drew a breath, admitting the intrusion to his conscious mind on the fifth quietly spoken "Your Grace." He looked up from the papers in his hand. "Yes, Collett?"

His secretary laid an envelope on the soft leather surface of the desk. "For your immediate attention, Your Grace."

Ransom scowled as he sat up and reached over, recognizing the seal of office that marked the message. "Yes, of course. You did quite right." With a nod of dismissal, Ransom sent his man off. Collett was obviously relieved that this monstrous breaking of the rules had been justified.

Every living soul at Mount Falcon knew that during his five afternoon hours at government business—reading and writing bills, studying strategy, practicing arguments and counter-arguments—Ransom was not to be disturbed on pain of unknown but undoubtedly horrific tortures. He had been particularly jealous of his privacy this day, when the last three had been spent rescuing Miss Lambourne from French spies and watching her climb unnervingly high roofs.

If he was truthful with himself, which he generally tried to be, he had to admit that his usual intensity of concentration had been cut up considerably this afternoon. His political propositions had frequently dissolved into annoying speculations on the length of Miss Lambourne's eyelashes and the way that one little curl of hers kept escaping her silly spinster's bun to lie in tempting silkiness against the soft skin beneath her left ear. He was descending rapidly into a state of dangerous irritation.

He broke the seal and flipped open the folded parchment. The message, as he'd expected, was innocuous. "My dearest lord duke," it said. "I beg you to stay in the country and continue your own work, as there is nothing to occupy you here during the Recess. Though your offer is kind, you cannot rescue me from the exigencies of new office. It pleases me more to think of you in that great ridiculous palace of yours, desperately plotting ways to communicate from one end of it to the other in less than a sennight. Your servant, Castlereagh." At the bottom of the page, in a different ink, the writer had added, "*Postscriptum.* A very good *bon mot* makes the rounds these days, told on the Duke of York, that when an Irish officer was introduced at the levee, as Major O'Sullivan O'Toole O'Shaughnessy, the duke exclaimed, turning up the whites of his eyes, 'O J—s!' ''

Ransom rubbed his chin. The new secretary of war's oblique approval of his encoded message concerning the development of Merlin Lambourne's speaking box was satisfactory, but the significance of the *bon mot* was not immediately clear. His Royal Highness the Duke of York was not known for his wit, but Ransom doubted the Irish-bred Castlereagh took such an exceptional delight in this particular manifestation as the postscript implied.

He refolded the note and tapped it against his palm. After a few moments, he lit a candle and held the paper over the fireplace grate, turning the note until it was well alight before he dropped it, making sure it had gone completely to ashes before he went back to his desk.

He settled into his familiar chair. Silence descended on the study again, except for the comforting tick of the mantel clock. He had finally succeeded in composing a paragraph that had eluded him for half an hour and was preparing to put pen to paper when the discreet "Your Grace" whispered again through the quiet room.

Ransom threw down his pen. *"Yes?"*

Collett turned white around the lips. "Forgive me, Your Grace. But the Lady Jaqueline . . . Your Grace, I've tried . . . but you must know—that is . . ." He spread his hands and clenched them. "She rather insists upon seeing you, Your Grace."

Ransom pressed his steepled fingers against the bridge of his nose. He searched for the words of that elusive paragraph. They were lost. He let out his breath in an explosive sigh. "See her in," he snapped, not in the mood to let Collett off the hook by moderating his tone.

"Yes, Your Grace." Collett disappeared. A moment later a vision of feminine height and beauty burst into the study, flashing eyes of gemstone violet.

"I want my children," Lady Jaqueline announced in her gorgeous voice, that voice that still throbbed with the French vowels of her childhood. She stopped in front of Ransom's desk, poised in a theatrical posture that would have been ludicrous on any other woman. But not on Jaqueline. Magnificent as a goddess, she stared at him like Diana on the hunt.

"I believe your daughters are in the nursery at this time of day." Ransom rose with a studied degree of politeness. "Woodrow might be there also, as he has no lessons this afternoon."

"You know what I mean. I want them *with* me!"

"Of course. I hope you will spend as much time with them as you wish."

She tossed her head. An amethyst that matched her eyes sparked in the russet depths of her hair. "Your *Grace*. You are as cold as the fishes in the sea. You steal my children from me just as you wrenched away all my other rights."

"I'm not withholding the children from you. I've made it clear, more than once, that you are welcome to live here with them."

"Live *here?*" Without moving, she managed to drench her lovely figure in revulsion. "Impossible."

"It's not impossible. You could avoid Shelby if you wished."

She drew in a hiss of breath at that name—the name that had hung in the room unspoken since the moment she had entered.

Ransom shrugged, deliberately casual. "God knows, the place is large enough. You could miss one another for weeks at a time. And he's only here at the end of each quarter"—his lips twisted in brief ruefulness—"when his allowance runs out."

"You are *cold,*" she said again. "I want my children. I will take them out of this place to somewhere that the light can reach their poor hearts."

"No," he said calmly. "You will not."

"I must." She raised a tragic hand to her breast. "It is my mother's duty."

"As it was your mother's duty to abandon them in an opera house in Florence seven years ago?"

"That," she said, and swung her pale hand in dismissal, "that would not happen again." Then she clasped her fingers and raised them toward him. "I swear it."

He shook his head, drawn against his will into a faint smile at her theatrics. "Jaqueline, you know I cannot trust you."

"But I swear it!" she cried in her throbbing goddess voice. "How can you doubt I would walk through Hell for them, my little ones, that I would never let their sweet faces from my sight?"

"Do forgive me. But I doubt it."

One perfect tear appeared, glistening on her pale cheek. "Oh! I said you were cold. Now I say you are ice. You have no life in you. No love. Have you never known passion once in all your frozen days?"

He let out a slow, careful breath, holding back the rise of anger. "Perhaps I simply prefer to keep my passions in check."

"True passion cannot be held in check." Her chin came up in a scathing tilt. "True passion burns here"—she pressed her heart—"where you have *nothing.*"

"*Brava.* May we bring the curtain down now, if you please? I have a considerable amount of work before me."

"So. You will deny a mother her children?"

Ransom sat down and picked up his pen. "Jaqueline, I give you every child in this house. As long as you don't take them past the outer gates."

Still she hovered like a breaking storm, the sound of her deep, offended breaths blending with the scratch of his pen. After a moment, he added without a pause in his writing, "And you know, of course, that the place is far too heavily guarded for you to have a chance of spiriting them away. Not to mention the legal consequences should you attempt to do so."

True silence descended then. Ransom finished a page, writing nonsense, anything, just to maintain the fiction that he did not fear she might try to do exactly what he warned against. Jaqueline was passionate—no question of that. It was only a question of which passion gripped her at a given moment.

He took his time, sanding the paper, brushing it clean, just as if there were real meaning in the words. When at last he looked up, he saw which way the wind had turned.

She was not crying. The crocodile tears which came to her so easily never showed when she was truly moved. In real sorrow or pain, Ransom had never seen that magnificent face disfigured by common sobs. Instead, her perfect lips had softened, and her eyes had grown clear and dark with bottled misery.

"I could not," she whispered. "You know I could not. It would hurt them, to take them away like that. And they have been hurt so much already. I only wish . . ." Her fine voice faltered, impossibly pure even in breaking. "It's only that I am so lonely sometimes. Ransom . . . can you understand that? That I'm in the midst of a crowd always, and yet I sleep alone and wake alone and think of . . ." She hesitated. "I think of . . ." But she did not say it. She made a sound, a little aching sound of pain, and turned away.

Ransom rubbed his forehead. He shaded his mouth with his hand and leaned on his elbow. "Jaqueline," he said, "what can I do to help?"

She looked over her shoulder. "Ah, yes. Help. The Dukes of Damerell. Always wanting to *do* something. To meddle. It was your meddling that dissolved our marriage."

"It was no work of mine."

"You, your grandfather—what do I care? You're all the same. *Dukes*." She made the title an epithet. "What chance have I against men who bend Parliament itself to their will with the flick of a finger?"

"Would it were so easy," Ransom said with a grim half-smile. "And if recollection serves, you brought the divorce and"—he paused, and then said them bluntly, the words that had branded his brother an adulterer—"the accusation of criminal conversation yourself."

She whirled, and light glanced off the jewels in her hair. "At your grandfather's urging! It would bring Shelby back to me, he said. It would make him see his duty. It was never, never to go so far—" She stopped suddenly, twisting her hands together. "It was a trick. Your father hated me. You know he did," she said as Ransom opened his mouth to protest. "I am an *opera* singer. One might as well say I am a whore."

Ransom sighed. "I suspect that, to my father, opera singer said quite enough."

Her regal head went up. "He did hate me, then."

"He only thought you should have loved your husband and children more than you loved the stage."

"I tried that! Do you think I did not try? Where was Shelby those years when I stayed home and played the wife? Gaming. Every night. Gaming and flirting and worse. God knows, I found out there was worse at the court proceedings. And for that . . . for *him* . . . I gave up my career. I gave up everything I loved. I bore his children. I lived in poverty. I watched him gamble away my own money—*my* money, and my shares in my father's theater! And then I must needs hear chambermaids testify as to who he had spent it on."

Ransom met her accusations with silence. He had no answer to them.

"Well," she said finally, "I shall go. I don't wish to see the children now. I cannot laugh with them as I should."

He stood up and went to her as she fumbled with her reticule. Her perfectly shaped lower lip was full and trembling. He took her hand and squeezed it. "Don't run away, Jaqueline. Not as Shelby does. Please. That's your gift, is it not? To make us all laugh when we would much rather cry?"

She raised her eyes, dark and magnificent with those real tears she never shed. "Do you feel like crying sometimes?"

He gave a small shrug. "I'm too old for that, don't you think?"

She bit her lip. He saw her swallow convulsively, as if a silent sob had almost escaped.

"We both know our parts very well, don't we?" He gave her cheek a gentle pinch. "You and I. We're not the ones who weep. So go and make those young ones of yours laugh. Sing them a happy song."

It was a challenge impossible for her Thespian soul to resist. She was a trouper to her toes; it was bred in her blood to answer her cue—no excuses, no sentiment, no time for the silly weakness of defeated dreams. For an instant she composed herself, and then her lips curved in that legendary smile, the one that had brought a hundred men crawling to her feet for favor. It was no task to understand why Shelby had worshipped her. It was harder to know why she'd accepted him. More money, greater titles and positions had been offered her in plenty. But it was Shelby she had chosen—penurious, volatile younger son—and Ransom could only account for that one way.

If she loved his brother yet, he forgave her all her passionate mistakes. Even the children, even her attempt to use them, that false abandonment in Florence made in hopes that Shelby would come to their rescue. Ransom knew the truth, though he would never let her realize it. He had been the rescuer in place of his brother. He knew how well she'd seen to their care before her "disappearance." But he'd brought Shelby's children home for good from that adventure, unwilling to risk more. It was war between them now, Shelby and his Jaqueline, and Ransom would not leave innocent lives in the breach.

But she was here. It always happened like this. She stayed away as long as she could stand, and then she had to see her children.

"*Bravissima, cara mia,*" he murmured, with a nod for her manufactured smile and a vast, unspoken respect for her gallantry. "You are without equal."

"Yes. I am a performer *nonpareil,* am I not?" She turned without waiting for an answer, her voice trailing behind her like a velvet cape.

After the door had closed, Ransom sat down. He lifted his pen and toyed with it, staring at nothing in particular for a long, long time. Then he squeezed his eyes shut and pressed his eyelids with unsteady fingers. "Yes, you are," he said to the empty room. "And so am I, Jaqueline. So am I."

Chapter 7

Merlin was concentrating. She was sitting on the huge stone steps of Mount Falcon, hugging her knees and thinking about Ransom and the possibility that he was lying. Not only with his words, which wasn't such a strange thing—Merlin had been known to tell a fib or two herself in her life—but with his smile.

And worse . . . with his kisses.

She tried to make it into a problem of logic, as if it were some equation she could master, some whim of natural law that had eluded her. But she knew she was failing, that the deep ache in her throat was muddling her reason and making her conclusions nonsense.

She wished she could fly.

It seemed more important than ever now. More beautiful and simple to be able to soar away from these new emotions that plagued her. To be able to ride the air on the strength of logic and mathematics, instead of struggling on the ground with thoughts which made her blood grow warm and her eyes go blurry. She had been happy enough in her solitude, until Ransom had come and shaken her out of it like a windstorm would shake a baby bird from the nest. It had happened too soon for her, this being flung from her refuge into the greater world. She'd been left on the ground without wings.

She could not imagine why he wished to marry her. She had heard all his reasons, his talk of her reputation and his duty, but after the past few days at Mount Falcon it was blindingly clear that she could never be anything but an embarrassment to him. The rules of his world were impossibly alien. She could not speak or look or move without breaking one of them—without glancing up from her investigation of a cleverly hidden mousetrap behind the sideboard to meet the shocked gaze of some guest whose name she could not remember, or scrambling out from examining the axle design under a carriage in the courtyard to find the coachman looking at her as if she had just sprouted a beard and pointed ears.

Then there was the fountain in the center of the east garden whose intriguing rotating mechanism she dearly wanted to investigate. Fortunately, she had managed to stop herself while still teetering on the marble edge of the pool, with only one bare foot in the water, before the elegant couple strolling among the roses had turned too very pale. Now she just sat, with a damp hem, not daring to do anything at all.

She looked up at the echoing sound of horseshoes on cobblestone, and saw Shelby trotting under the arch and across the great courtyard toward her. His bay mount danced to a stop as the smooth, silent wheels of Mount Falcon went into motion and a groom appeared from nowhere to take the horse as Shelby dismounted. He came up the steps two at a time and sat down next to Merlin, ignoring the footman who stood waiting above to open the huge front door.

"Hullo," he said, bending a little to look into her face. "What's to do?"

"Nothing," Merlin said glumly.

"Ah." He leaned back with his elbows propped on the next step. "Bored?"

She nodded and rested her chin on her hands, staring out across the countryside beyond the open end of the courtyard, where the grassy lawns fell away from a steep stone wall down to an elegantly designed lake and a stream. "I don't think my equipment is ever going to come."

"Oh"—he swished his riding crop idly back and forth across the steps—"I imagine it will."

She could hear the smile in his voice. She looked sideways at him, her lower lip set contentiously. "Why? Because Mr. Ransom Duke promised?"

The smile became a grin. "My brother keeps his promises."

"I've been here three days."

"Well, give him a little time to work. He's not God Almighty. Much as he'd like to think so."

Merlin turned back, crossing her arms under her chin and hunching in a smaller ball. "I don't think it's going to come. I don't think he wants me to work on my flying machine."

"He gave you his word."

"Hmmpf. He also kissed me."

There was a sudden shift in the relaxed body sprawled beside her. "Did he indeed?"

"Yes," she said. "And I've figured it out. It's his way to lie, you see. He doesn't want to lie with words, because he wants everyone to say what you do—that he's so honest and noble and everything—so he smiles at me and kisses me to make me think something that isn't true."

Shelby sat up very straight. "To make you think what, for instance?"

"Oh . . . that I'm going to marry him. That he kisses me because I'm . . . nice, or something. When he really just does it so I'll do what he wants."

"And just what is it," Shelby said in a voice that had suddenly gone low and vicious, "that he wants?"

Merlin blinked, startled by the tone. "Why, to make me work on the speaking box, I suppose. I can't think what else it might be."

"Can't you?" His blue eyes glittered with that cold threat she'd seen in them once before. He swung the riding crop in a savage sideways cut at the air. "I'm afraid I can."

Merlin wet her lips. "Oh?"

He looked uncomfortable suddenly. The riding crop flicked from side to side. "Merlin, this isn't the kind of thing a fellow usually speaks about to a lady, but you're rather—unprotected, just now. I mean, there's no one else who's going to tell you."

"Tell me what?"

"Listen, Ransom is . . ." Shelby shook his head, and the grim frown faded to something not quite so angry. "I mean, my brother does his damnedest to be some kind of bloody hero—and don't think I don't appreciate it sometimes, even if I hate his guts for it more often—but the fact is, he's a male. He has . . . desires, just like the rest of us. At least, I suppose he does. Hellfire, I know he does. He frequents a stable of high-flyers in London that would give a lesser man altitude sickness."

Merlin's mouth dropped open at this news. "Then why won't he let *me* fly?" she cried.

Shelby looked around at her, shock in his gilded blue eyes. Then abruptly he began to laugh. He threw back his head and covered his face, howling with it. Merlin sat waiting, offended but resigned. She was growing used to this reaction.

"Merlin, Merlin—" he gasped finally. "What am I going to do with you?"

She lowered her chin onto her crossed arms again. "That's what Ransom says."

Shelby sobered. After a pause, he said in a different, tighter voice, "Damn. I never thought I'd be so disappointed to find out he was a bounder like the rest of us human beings."

"What's a bounder?"

Shelby's eyes narrowed. "It's a low-down, underhanded, slimy *snake*, that's what it is. Curse him, with all that self-righteous cant about 'bettering his stride,' and you being 'out-of-bounds.' Out-of-bounds to poor old black-sheep Shelby, of course, while he plots and connives at bringing you to ruin!"

"Oh, well." Merlin moved her hand in dismissal. "He's already done that."

Once again, Shelby turned to her with his blue eyes widened by shock. "You're joking."

"If you mean when he carried me upstairs and stayed with me all night—" Merlin found herself blushing at the way he was staring at her. "And he—and we . . . Oh, dear." Shelby was growing bright red, except for the white spots over his cheeks and at the corners of his mouth. "Was it really such a bad thing?"

"Oh, my God," Shelby groaned. He ran his hands through his hair. "Oh, my God, Ransom—you blackguard—you dirty, filthy, rutting *beast,* you didn't . . ."

Merlin pressed her lips together. She buried her face in her arms and said in a muffled voice. "I can't see why everyone thinks it was so terrible."

"I don't believe it," Shelby said, his voice rising. "My brother. *Ransom.* I always thought it was *me* who was the villain, because the damned gaming has me by the throat. But I never did anything like this. I never hurt anyone. All those lies they told about me at the trial, and Ransom sat there beside Grandpapa looking so bloody . . . empty. As if it were killing him inside and he couldn't show it. As if he cared. God, what an actor. What a genius! Making me feel like the lowest wretch alive for things I hadn't even done, while he was probably out ravishing innocent girls right and left without ever a crack in that poker face of his!"

Merlin could not quite follow every point in this discourse, so she said nothing. She only pressed her face deeper into her arms.

"Hero," Shelby snarled. "He's a damned despicable dog. What a show he's put on all these years, the lying bastard. I ought to kill him. I ought to call him out. But he wouldn't come. He'd drip brotherly love and honor. Faugh, it makes me want to retch, he's so good at it. Making us all so desperate to dance to his tune while he has his own sweet lying way!"

"I know," Merlin said sadly. "He thinks with his head, while all the rest of us are thinking with our solar plexii."

"Our what?"

"Right here." She tapped herself. "Where there isn't any logic. Where you're thinking now."

He frowned at her. "What do you mean, where I'm . . ." He paused. His lips relaxed a little from their trembling stiffness. A moment later he blew out a huge sigh. "Merlin, you have the damnedest way of putting things."

"I just learned about it myself. That you can think in different places besides your head. For instance—"

But she left off as the cold look descended again on his face. "I've a mind to get out the pistols right now," he hissed beneath his breath, "and inform that blighter the wedding will take place before dark."

"It wouldn't do any good."

"Hah. If he values his worthless life, it would."

"You don't understand. I don't want to marry him."

"That's extremely high-minded of you, Merlin, but it won't wash." Shelby stood up. "He's not going to leave you in the lurch. Not after I'm finished with him."

"Wait! Shelby. You don't understand!"

He paused, looking down at her, his perfect form very tall and imposing against the background of the sky. "Believe me, Merlin, I understand more about this than you do."

"But I'm *not* going to marry him. That's just what he wants, for me to marry him—so I'll have to do everything he says and never be allowed to work on my aviation machine again! I couldn't bear that, Shelby. I couldn't bear it!"

"You mean he's asked you to marry him?"

"Yes! A million times. He's been plaguing me with it ever since . . ." She trailed off, seeing Shelby grow red again.

"Well," he said, and then seemed at a loss.

"You know how he is," Merlin added, hunching on the stairs. "He always gets his own way."

Shelby sank back down onto the steps. "Yes," he said savagely. "I know all too well. And he'd smother you. You don't know how to contend with him."

"I'm trying to learn. Usually I can decipher things faster. But he isn't like mathematics. He never does what I expect. If I think he's going to laugh, he shouts; and when I think he's going to shout, he kisses me. And he'll never bring my equipment here for me to work on like he promised.''

Shelby shook his head. He cut at the steps with his whip in a disgusted move. ''No, he's done that much, anyway. Trust Ransom to keep his precious word. When I was out riding a few minutes ago, I spotted four wagonloads of it being hauled through the outer gate.''

Merlin jumped to her feet. ''It's come?'' she cried. ''Why didn't you tell me?'' She picked up her skirt and flew down the stairs, breaking into a run at the bottom. When she reached the arch that lead into the stableyard, she saw the four ox-drawn wagons, swarming with servants who were preparing to unload.

''Not here!'' She rushed up to the best-dressed one with the wig who seemed to be directing things. ''Don't unload here. Come to the front—it's much closer to the ballroom. And we must call Ransom's secretary; he's going to organize everything. Leave it there, leave it there—'' She waved her arms at a groom who had grasped the first thing that came to hand, a refracting telescope made of brass.

The man in the wig looked at her in astonishment, but when Shelby came up behind with a quiet command to ''Do as she says. Take it to the front and fetch Mr. Collett,'' the servant nodded and snapped out orders. The drivers flicked their long whips, and the oxen lumbered forward through the echoing archway into the main courtyard.

Collett was waiting on the steps holding a portable writing box by the time the four wagons had creaked to a stop. Merlin ran to him. ''Here it is,'' she cried, spreading her arms in a happy sweep.

The ruddy-cheeked secretary scanned the jumble of items piled five feet above the side panels of each wagon. ''Yes, miss. I see that.''

''Can you organize it? Ransom said you could.''

''I shall do my poor best.''

Merlin frowned. ''Oh. I'd hoped you'd do your best best.''

"As indeed he will," Ransom said, coming forward down the steps. "You must speak straight to Miss Lambourne, Collett. The finer nuances are lost on her."

"Yes, sir," Collett said. He descended the last two stairs and joined the head footman in looking things over. After a few moments of conference, they set up the portable desk on a stone balustrade of convenient height, and began unloading, with Collett taking careful notes as each item came free of the pile.

Merlin watched, lost in satisfaction. She did not notice Shelby walk quietly up to his brother.

"Your Grace," Shelby murmured. "I wish to speak to you."

Ransom raised his eyebrows, that pointedly spoken "Your Grace" all the warning he needed to know that Shelby was not in a trifling mood. "Certainly," he said. "At your convenience."

"My convenience is right now."

Ransom inclined his head. He followed Shelby to a spot a little distance from the commotion of the unloading. "I understand that wedding bells are in the air," Shelby said, with an ironic twist to his finely sculpted mouth that made him appear suddenly much older.

Ransom hesitated. Blythe's hints had spread rapidly, it seemed, for he knew she'd never have gone to Shelby in person with news of that sort. He watched his brother, noting the high color in Shelby's cheeks and the way the tip of his riding crop vibrated in a tiny, jerky motion, like the tip of a cat's tail as it prepared to leap upon a mouse.

"I most sincerely hope so," he said carefully. "Do you have some objection?"

Shelby's smile was more like a sneer. He looked toward the wagons where Merlin hopped about, dusty and bedraggled, getting herself in everyone's way as she anxiously examined each item as it was unloaded. "Do you really think she's duchess material, Ransom?"

Again Ransom had to search for words, unsure of his brother's motivation. At length, he decided on lightness. " 'Love is blind,' I believe the saying goes."

Shelby turned on him with a curling lip. "Oh, Ransom, do you speak of love? How quaint. How charming. How very, very *like* you to be so sentimental."

The sarcasm hung heavily in the air between them. Ransom took a deep breath. "I've grown quite fond of her," he said.

"Have you? What a fortunate development. And did you discover this affection before or after you slept with her, my oh-so-honorable brother?"

Ransom could feel the blood drain from his face and then return in a hot flush. He hated himself for that betrayal, and for the way he looked abruptly away, unable to meet Shelby's eyes. A hundred explanations rose to his lips, and he discarded them all as what they were. Excuses. Self-justification that Shelby had every right to scorn. And in the end Ransom could say nothing, only stand there and endure his brother's contempt. It was not so easy to swallow as he might have hoped.

Shelby said softly, "I could have forgiven you almost anything. I used to wait for it—" His hand clenched on the riding crop. "God, you don't know how I've longed to see it. Some slip. Some little weakness, to show you're my brother and not some God damned walking saint. You could have cheated at cards or made a shady business deal. I wouldn't even have cared if you'd seduced one of those scheming little debutantes who're always throwing themselves at you. Serve her right, I would have said, for parading her charms and dragging a man off to dark corners in the garden. But somehow, brother dear, I don't think Miss Lambourne did any parading. I don't think she wanted you at all. I think you took advantage of her in the lowest, ugliest way imaginable."

Ransom closed his eyes. *It wasn't like that*, he wanted to shout, but his tongue wouldn't move. He stood frozen for one long breath and then shook his head, still unable to look at Shelby.

"I wish I could say this does me good," Shelby whispered. "I wish I could say I was glad to see you with that look on your face. But I can't. It makes me sick."

Ransom suddenly found the capacity to speak. He slanted a vicious look toward his brother. "I'm going to marry her," he said in a hiss.

"She doesn't want to marry you."

"For God's sake, what difference do you think that makes?"

Shelby narrowed his eyes. In a mockingly light tone, he said, "Why, I suppose if it were my life, I'd rather jump off the cliff at Beachy Head than be bound to you for the rest of my days."

Ransom stood very still, trying to contain the pain of that thrust, to keep it locked up in a hard ball like the one his fist made. "I meant," he said quietly, "that there is no other choice. For her own protection."

"Oh, yes. I understand completely. You must do your noble duty, no matter who is hurt."

"I'm not going to hurt her."

"She doesn't belong here, Ransom. She's miserable."

He scowled. "It's only that it's new. Look at her now that her things have come."

"Yes. And how long will you let her have them? As long as it suits your convenience. As long as Your Grace cares to play this little game of the speaking box."

With a sharp look, Ransom said, "She told you of it?" Shelby nodded.

Ransom pursed his lips. "Do you suppose she's told anyone else?" he asked.

"No. I had her promise not to."

Ransom managed a humorless chuckle. "She's probably forgotten all about that. With any luck, she's forgotten about the speaking box, too."

"What do you want the thing for, anyway?"

Ransom squinted at the play of sunlight on the stones of the courtyard without answering.

Shelby laughed, a sound tinged with bitter self-mockery. "Never mind. I can guess. Didn't suppose you'd want to confide the whole patriotic story to your ne'er-do-well brother."

"Shelby—"

"Oh, no, Your Grace." Shelby took a step back, pointedly avoiding Ransom's offered hand. "That game is over now. We've come to an end, you and I. Enough of this striving to overcome my character flaws. Enough of lectures and honor and disappointment when I fail. I shall wallow in my small sins, Your Grace. Gambling, indebtedness, the occasional willing female—I shall glory in them, knowing that someday, perhaps, they may grow great enough to match the fine example of my older brother, whom I have always so admired."

With a cold, economical move, Shelby turned away. Ransom watched him descend the steps and stroll up to Merlin. He put his hand on her shoulder and bent to her ear. Merlin listened to him, then looked up into his face with a smile. There was complete and unquestioning pleasure in that expression. Trust. She and Shelby knelt together to examine the latest item off the wagon, and Merlin's dreamy laughter floated up to Ransom where he stood above them on the stairs.

He held himself very still, fighting back the alternating waves of fury and chagrin. Shelby rose and held out a hand to help Merlin to her feet. He tucked her arm in his and leaned close as he guided her toward Collett. They made a striking couple. Shelby would make any pair look striking. Ransom could feel his brother's fatal charm even from this distance.

It filled him with outrage, with that sense of foul ill-usage which had possessed him the first night Merlin had turned him down. He'd forgotten that moment of self-doubt, sure in his strategies and his success once he'd brought Merlin to his home ground.

He had not counted on this. He didn't know Shelby. Not anymore. A tiny, unfamiliar thread of fear curled in Ransom's chest. As expert as he was at judging his peers, at manipulating and second-guessing his political opponents, his own brother was an enigma to him. He could not guess what lay behind the sneer and the cold derision, whether it was disillusionment or a twisted relief that Ransom was no better than his brother in the end. But he sensed that for Shelby, some bridge had been crossed and burned.

Ransom had failed him. As he had failed Merlin, and honor, and himself.

It was a bitter, bitter cup from which to drink.

"Damerell." A feminine voice broke into his bleak musings. Blythe touched his arm. "Whatever is going on here now?"

He tore his eyes away from Merlin and Shelby. "Surely you can puzzle that out for yourself, Blythe. Miss Lambourne's equipment has arrived."

She let go of him. "Yes, that's quite apparent. I meant why are you allowing Shelby to hang all over her when we're trying to encourage another story entirely? This commotion has succeeded in attracting half the house party. 'Tis you who should be playing the lover in such a scene."

He drew in a sharp breath. "But it isn't me, is it? I'm afraid there are some elements here which have escaped my control."

"Nonsense. Shelby is just being his usual impossible self. And now—" She smiled, tilting her head toward four new arrivals on the scene. "You see? This will drive him off soon enough. I'm so glad I thought to mention to the nursemaid that the children would not want to miss all the fun."

"Uncle Demmie!" The shrill voice of one of Shelby's twin daughters drifted down from the open door. A bundle of pink skirts and blue eyes and awkward arms and legs tumbled toward him, followed by another, identical set. In a moment they had him, one by each hand, and stood behind him peering out at the wonderful sight in the courtyard below.

He let them hang on him, smoothing their silky hair that was as bright as Shelby's own. Above, twelve-year-old Woodrow hovered in the doorway, auburn-haired like his mother, but with Shelby's chin and eyes. Jaqueline herself stood behind him, showing not a hint of the emotion that would be boiling behind her cheerful smile.

Shelby had not seen her yet. He was looking toward Ransom and the girls. Ransom could never fathom how Shelby felt about his children. He was affectionate and easy enough when around them, which wasn't often, but he almost never mentioned them at other times. Ransom thought they were rather like puppies to his brother: fun to pet and cuddle and easy to forget.

Blythe moved away, greeting some of the guests who were gathering. Ransom clasped his nieces' damp, small hands in his. "Come—it looks rather like Christmas, does it not? Let's go and see."

The two girls hung back, but a slight pressure was enough to carry them along with him as he descended the steps. It was a wonder that two such parents as Jaqueline and Shelby could have produced three such timid children. Or perhaps, Ransom thought cynically, it was not a wonder at all.

Down in the courtyard, Merlin looked up at Shelby's firm tap on her shoulder. "Look here," he said. "Have you met my daughters?"

Merlin straightened from the electrostatic generator she'd been carefully unwrapping from its cover of musty linen. "Daughters?" she repeated, and then saw the two little girls peeping out from behind Ransom's legs. "Oh. Oh, dear."

"Augusta and Aurelia," Shelby said.

For such large names as those, they seemed to be very small girls. Merlin stood nervously as each one came out from behind Ransom and performed a little curtsy. After they had returned to their refuge, Merlin dipped in a curtsy, too. "I'm sorry," she said with a trace of defiance, "but I don't have any sweets."

They giggled.

"They probably don't deserve any," Shelby said. But he reached in his pocket and produced two sweetmeats wrapped in colored paper. Augusta and Aurelia came out one by one and accepted the treats with another pair of solemn curtsies.

"My," Shelby said, "but you have trained them well for me, Damerell. Do they sit up and beg?"

Ransom merely looked at him, careful to keep his face impassive.

"Perhaps I'd better think of placing them elsewhere, the poor innocents," Shelby added casually. "Where I'm certain their *virtue* is safe."

It was hard—it was a physical pain in Ransom's chest—to hold back and not react, to keep his hands loosely clasped around the twins' and not doubled into fists to smash in his brother's face. He looked at Merlin, who was eyeing the children warily.

"What's that?" Aurelia pointed to a tripod supporting a large gold orb in the center and seven arms with various sized balls at the ends.

"A pa-pa-pa . . . a pa-planetarium."

They all looked up at the new voice. The slender boy who'd come silently closer flushed wildly under the inspection and glanced with wide eyes at Ransom.

"I believe you're right, Woodrow," he said. "It is a planetarium—is it not, Miss Lambourne?"

Merlin frowned at it. "Possibly."

"Oh, yes," Woodrow said. "It is. See, this is . . . Ma-Ma-Mercury, and Ve . . . nus, and there is the Earth and the . . . ma-ma-ma-*moon* . . . to ga-ga . . . go around it. Ma-Ma-Mars and Ju . . . pa-pa-piter and . . . Saturn and Uranus."

"Why, of course," Merlin agreed, taking a closer look. "There are the rings on Saturn and the twelve moons of Jupiter."

Woodrow reached out a tentative hand, glancing frequently out of the corner of his eye at Ransom as if he expected to be stopped at any moment. But when no prohibition came, he took hold of the little crank. The whole apparatus began to turn, spinning the moons around the planets and the planets around the sun.

The twins erupted in cries of awe. Merlin peered at them suspiciously.

"What's that?" Aurelia pointed again.

This time Merlin knew. "An electrostatic generator," she said smugly. "Don't touch it."

Woodrow snatched his hand back and held it behind him, glancing fearfully again at Ransom.

"What have you been doing, Damerell—beating the boy?" Shelby exclaimed. "I can't bear all these hangdog looks."

"I'm . . . sorry . . . sa-sa-sa-sir," Woodrow said, staring straight ahead. Ransom only looked at his brother, his mouth tightened in a terrifying line.

Merlin decided that she liked Woodrow. He didn't screech like his sisters, and he didn't seem to expect any sweets. "Ransom scares me, too," she whispered, leaning close to the boy. "He's a duke, you know."

Woodrow rolled his eyes toward her.

"And he's trying to make Woodrow into one," Shelby added in a louder whisper. "Myself having failed to pass muster."

"Oh, no!" Merlin looked at Woodrow with deep sympathy. "How awful."

Woodrow's clear young skin flushed red. "I'm . . . sorry, ma'am," he said.

"Oh—" She waved her hand. "I'm sure it isn't your fault. Have you been kidnapped, too?"

This question seemed to leave Woodrow at a complete stand. His mouth opened and shut again, and he looked miserable.

"I'm afraid Woodrow made the mistake of being born into this position," Shelby said. "He also is my—"

He stopped so abruptly in mid-sentence that Merlin glanced up at him in surprise.

"—my son," Shelby resumed after a moment, in a voice that had gone suddenly stiff. "Mine and that lovely female's standing at the top of the stairs. How do you do, my dear Jaqueline? It has been such a very long time."

Jaqueline, framed in the doorway, inclined her head with a smile. Merlin thought she was breathtaking—as riotously beautiful as Shelby was handsome. She seemed friendly, too, her eyes lingering on Merlin with that engaging smile.

Merlin smiled back. She expected the lady to come down to join them all. Instead, Shelby leaned over and took Merlin's hand with a warm squeeze. He put his lips close to her ear and murmured, "Come here, Merlin. I have something to show you."

He put his arm through hers, turning away from the others. Merlin had little choice but to allow him to lead her out of earshot of the sudden murmurs, though not out of sight of the curious glances the guests and servants sent after the two of them. Shelby stopped next to an ornamental urn full of trailing flowers.

"What is it?" Merlin asked.

"Only this, my love." He picked a flower and kissed it lightly, before he reached up and tucked it into her hair. "Only this."

Merlin looked up at him, mystified. But he made no further explanations. He only took both her hands and smiled down into her eyes, the look in his blue ones much too enigmatic to define.

Chapter 8

"Well, I never," Blythe exclaimed. Her slippers clicked as she hustled to Ransom's side. "You're not going to allow him to proceed with that nonsense, are you?"

He gave her a sour look. "What do you suggest, Blythe? Pistols at dawn?"

"I suggest you do something instantly, before he—" Her slim body went stiff as a blade. "My stars, he's not going to . . . *Oh*, he wouldn't *dare*—"

But Shelby did dare. Under at least twenty-two pairs of staring eyes, he pulled Merlin closer and pressed a gentle kiss to her temple. No one spoke, not even a murmur— the guests too well-bred and the servants too well-trained—but the silence screamed with unholy glee. Ransom felt himself flushing, which was an embarrassment almost as acute as watching his brother make love to a woman who was widely rumored to be Ransom's fiancée.

Merlin turned away from Shelby, apparently in shyness, but Ransom saw the way her eyes sought the wagons. She pulled her hands from Shelby's in a move that might have been coy or might, knowing Merlin, just have been vaguely impatient. Whatever she meant by it, the withdrawal saved her from instant and irreparable ruin. She was the picture of demure confusion as she looked helplessly back toward the others.

Ransom grasped the opportunity without delay. He strode down the steps, calculating furiously for the best way to bend this scene to account. If only Merlin would turn to him for protection, would take *his* hand and look up at him . . .

It did not happen. As he reached her, his arm outstretched in offered protection, she only paused long enough to take the flower from behind her ear and set it in his open palm.

"That tickles," she said. And left him with it.

She made her way back to Mr. Collett and began poring over his inventory. When she looked up and asked the secretary a question with just exactly the same expression of intensity and pleasure on her face that Ransom had hoped she'd turn on *him,* he felt the flower stem snap between his fingers. He grasped Shelby's wrist and slapped the broken remains of the flower into his brother's upturned hand. "Keep it," he hissed under his breath. "As a memento of my profound appreciation and respect."

Shelby inclined his golden head in a little mocking bow. From beneath those gilded eyelashes, he seemed to be studying the base of the steps with profound concentration. Five stairs above, Jaqueline stood with a twin clinging to each side of her skirt, calmly pointing out items that might be of interest to small, wide-eyed girls. Her voice was smooth; her smile remained radiantly cheerful. For her, it would be humiliation indeed to allow the facade to slip now. Just as painful as it was for Ransom to know that he'd not managed to keep the flush from his face and the anger from his gestures.

His undisciplined reaction fit his plans well enough, thank God—it highlighted him as a jealous suitor—but he despised the spectacle he must have made. People had always talked about him: why should they not? He had enemies who held him in hate and admirers who held him in awe, and he'd endured all the rumors those feelings implied, but he had yet to become a common buffoon for the gossip mills. It was a new experience, to see the sly smiles and faintly lifted eyebrows. He did not like it.

He did not like it at all.

Blythe slipped purposefully among the guests, answering God-knew-what in response to the polite murmurs of interest. Ransom was just moving to control his sister, whose aid was likely to be about as helpful as that of a loose cannon on a rolling ship, when a simple dogcart drawn by an elegant black pony emerged from the arched entry to the courtyard.

Ransom paused between relief and dismay. In the driver's seat perched a tall figure, as immaculately black as the pony except for the starched white punctuation of an ecclesiastical collar. The Right Reverend Edwin Peale brought his trap to a halt and waited for a groom to take his horse and a footman to help him from his vehicle before he spoke.

"Your Grace," he addressed Ransom without even a curious look toward the chaos of equipment in the courtyard. "How do you do today? But you needn't have bestirred yourself to meet me at the door like this. I assure you I quite expected to wait if need be. I know what a busy schedule you keep."

"My pleasure," Ransom said, just as if he hadn't completely forgotten the long-standing appointment. And as if it weren't the last thing he would normally do to come to the door in person for the likes of the Reverend Mr. Peale. However, Ransom had his hopes for the clergyman, none of which would be served by doing what he was in the mood for—giving the man the cut direct.

Not that it would make much difference. Mr. Peale had his own hopes, and they made him devilishly difficult to offend.

He was already in the process of advancing those hopes. After greeting Ransom, Mr. Peale sought out Blythe, taking her hand and bending over it with a bow that Ransom suspected had been rehearsed for a minimum of two hours to find just the right blend of pressing warmth and reserved dignity. Not an easy combination, but necessary for a man with dreams of both a bishop's office and a brilliant match.

Blythe exhibited an equally contradictory response. She turned quite scarlet, a weakness Ransom was not presently in a position to fault, and managed to put flattered pleasure on her face and annoyance in her voice, so that the overall effect was one of blushing flusterment. Merlin had done it more attractively, Ransom thought, but on the whole he was not displeased. Matrimony was imminent, he hoped, with one well-meaning and meddlesome sister soon to be removed to a happy home some distance away. India would do nicely, he felt.

For the moment, though, he was stuck with all of them: Mr. Peale fluttering around Blythe like a mating moorhen; Shelby and Jaqueline exchanging gay comments that did not quite mask their venom; and Merlin, who was dragging up the steps an enormous winglike contraption that resembled nothing so much as the left half of a huge, dead bird. She brushed off the protests of Collett and his numerous underlings, insisting on handling the item herself. It stuck in the doorway, but after a few minutes of tugging and twisting and anxious maneuver, the thing tilted up like the single wing of a dying swan and passed through. The last Ransom saw of it was the white tip, sliding along in little jerks across the marble until it disappeared into the Great Hall's gloom.

Ransom did not have to endure Mr. Peale in close quarters until the next day. The clergyman had an invitation to stay for the month, and he'd timed his appointment with Ransom to be excruciatingly seemly—not too soon to appear overly anxious, but with plenty of time left to woo Blythe into accepting.

Ransom met his aspiring brother-in-law at the breakfast table, in a mood mellowed by a brisk morning ride and the sloppy greetings of his two nieces, who had waited for him in the Great Hall with news of the wondrous transformation of the west ballroom. Ransom postponed viewing this marvel in person, pleading a prior appointment, and invited Mr. Peale to accompany him to his study.

A footman held open the door. Inside, Ransom's desk was immaculate, and the rest of the furnishings glowed with evidence of meticulous care. The ornate fire grate was spotless, the damask curtains drawn, and the tall windows polished. Perfect order reigned, the result of decades of demand by Mount Falcon's masters. Ransom gestured toward a chair, and then widened the scope of the move in order to sweep a curled hedgehog off the seat and deposit it on his desk.

He sat down in another chair and looked expectantly at his guest. "Now, Mr. Peale. How may I serve you?"

The clergyman glanced at the hedgehog. Ransom met Peale's eyes with an absolutely neutral expression. Mr. Peale cleared his throat.

"Your Grace, allow me first to express my deep gratitude for your condescension in giving me leave to speak to you."

Ransom moved his hand just slightly in denial. "Come, Mr. Peale. Let us have no talk of condescension. No doubt our forebears fought side by side at Runnymede. And there have been many connections between our families since."

Not very subtle, that. But then, Ransom had no desire to sit in his study all morning while Peale worked his way around to a declaration without prompting.

The young reverend swallowed. A vein worked in the side of his throat, and his long hands clenched. He was a good-looking man, light and lithe in build, with neat black hair and a frame that Ransom suspected could wield more power than was immediately evident. "If I may be so presumptuous, Your Grace," he said, "I would like to say that I have dared to dream of another connection between our families."

Ransom waited. He found this careful reverence cloying. It was not as if Peale were some low-bred social climber. If the man hadn't been of noble descent, Ransom would never have been wasting his time in the hope that his high-stickler of a sister would consider Peale's suit. The clergyman was quite Blythe's equal in background, with three earls, a marquess, and a cousin with royal ties to match her ducal connections. It was the misfortune of the blue-blooded Peales, however, to be poverty-stricken, while Blythe had fortune enough to support all three of the earls and leave a generous allowance for the marquess if Mr. Peale could land it.

"It would be an honor to be associated with your family in any manner," Ransom said. Out of the corner of his eye, he saw the hedgehog unroll on his desk. "Pray continue, Mr. Peale."

"Thank you, Your Grace. In view of my circumstances, I had feared this interview might be difficult, but you allow me to dare hope my aspirations are not beyond the realm of reality."

"I presume they are not," Ransom said, "though I should be better able to judge if you would tell me what they are."

But this was going too fast for Mr. Peale. He took a deep breath and looked at the floor. "Might I ask your leave to present to you my prospects?"

Ransom gave a silent sigh. "Of course, Mr. Peale."

In the discourse that followed, Ransom had ample time to allow his mind to drift. He knew all about the reverend's prospects, what little there was to know. Among all those earls there was not a man who could offer Mr. Peale a living—at least not in the style to which he was accustomed. But Blythe's portion would take care of that, and Ransom was not really so heartless as to pack them off to India. He had a position in mind at Yorkminster, where Blythe could put her energy into the advancement of a young cleric in powerful church circles. Circles which seldom intersected with Ransom's own.

He steepled his hands while Peale talked on, watching covertly as the hedgehog made its slow way across the polished surface of his desk. The small creature stopped to investigate an inkwell, its shiny nose twitching around a stick of sealing wax, then headed for the edge.

". . . and of course," Mr. Peale was saying, "I have my mother's property, which is not large, but very well kept, and I hope would bring—"

"There is no need to think of selling your maternal legacy," Ransom interrupted, standing up. "I'm sure that something can be arranged in the way of a position for you, Mr. Peale. I shall begin some inquiries this afternoon. I fancy that a friend of mine in York may be of some assistance in that regard."

"Your Grace, I— How can I possibly express my gratitude?"

"Don't think of it." Ransom caught the hedgehog, careful of its flattened bristles, and drew the animal back toward the center of the desk. Its front paws made small scrabbling noises on the shining wood. "You have a fine future before you, Mr. Peale. I don't doubt that."

Peale clasped his hands. His knuckles turned white. "Your Grace. That brings me then to . . . to my purpose in asking to speak with you."

Praise the lord, Ransom thought. *Out with it.*

"Your Grace," Peale said, and stopped. The hedgehog began another determined trek toward oblivion. "Your Grace . . ."

Ransom closed his eyes and opened them. "I shall be the most graceful fellow in the county," he murmured.

"Forgive me." Peale made a little apologetic cough. "I seem to have become quite tongue-tied."

"Really, Mr. Peale, there is no need to feel ill-at-ease, I assure you. Do go on."

"Your Grace . . ." The reverend bent his head, staring at the rug. Ransom reached out to catch the hedgehog before it toppled over the edge. "Your Grace, I should like to beg your permission to pay my addresses to your sister Blythe."

"Damn!" Ransom jerked back, sucking his middle finger.

Mr. Peale looked up with a stricken expression.

"Ah—" Ransom clutched his bleeding finger in his other hand. "Pardon me. You were saying?"

"Your Grace," Peale repeated. "I beg you to allow me to ask for your sister's hand in marriage."

"Yes. My sister." The hedgehog scrabbled again toward the edge. Ransom grabbed for it. His forefinger caught the creature under its belly.

Instantly, it curled itself into a ball with his finger trapped inside. A hundred spines drove into his skin. "My *God,*" he ejaculated, before the trap tightened even more and a strangled howl closed his throat. He yanked his hand back, but the hedgehog had a death grip on his finger. A guttural sound of agony escaped him. He reached to try to tear the animal off and got a palm full of pinholes for the effort. "Get Merlin," he ordered through clenched teeth. "Bring Merlin, quickly."

Mr. Peale stood staring.

"Now!" Ransom roared.

"Your Grace. Pardon me, Your Grace, but—"

"Bring Miss Lambourne."

"Instantly, Your Grace!" Mr. Peale made a rapid exit from the room. Ransom sat down at the desk and pressed his forehead into his free arm. His finger throbbed and ached, and if he made the slightest move the spines drove deeper, creating a sensation closely akin to holding his finger over a searing flame.

He waited. Seconds passed. He made a hissing sound of anguish into the crook of his elbow. Minutes went by. He groaned and panted and cursed dumb animals. The hedgehog showed no inclination to relax its curl. Ransom gave a soft keening moan, and then with his face still hidden in his sleeve he began a muffled pleading with the hedgehog.

"There's nothing to be afraid of," he promised the animal. "There's not a wolf in sight. I'll give you a nice bowl of cream. How do you feel about worms? Do you like worms? We'll have tea together. Where the bloody hell is Merlin? For God's sake, oh, no—please. Don't squeeze any harder. Please don't. Listen to me. Worms and cream. We'll have worms and cream. Nice, juicy worms. The gardeners are standing by. I'll give orders on the instant. But I can't pull the bell unless you let go of my finger—"

"An' would you be likin' me to pull it for you, sur?"

Ransom's head came up. He winced, having caused the hedgehog to clench harder with the abrupt move. In front of his desk stood a stranger with a freckled grin and eyes of devil's green to match his Irish brogue.

"Major Quinton O'Sullivan O'Toole O'Shaughnessy." The officer introduced himself with a flourishing bow. "I was just now proceeding down the hall to a visit with His Lordship Shelby Falconer, by way of inquiring about a small matter of pecuniary interest. The door was open, you understand, and the Lord above preserve me, but I couldn't help but hear you speaking in so distressed a manner. And, sur, me blessed mother would not want her only son to miss an opportunity to be of service."

Ransom had opened his mouth to snarl a dismissal when recollection of the war secretary's message and that ridiculous *bon mot* hit him. "What did you say you're called?" he demanded.

"Ah, forgive a poor son of the Ould Sod, but me name is O'Sullivan O'Toole O'Shaughnessy. 'Tis a burden the Good Lord and me superior officer have asked me to bear."

Ransom glanced at the hedgehog clamped on his finger. "We all have our trials, don't we? Who's your superior?"

The Irishman looked very directly into Ransom's eyes. In a soft voice without a trace of the brogue, he said, "I believe you've had a note from my commander quite recently."

"Have I? I receive a large amount of correspondence. Tell me, Major, have you been introduced at court?"

The officer grinned. " 'Oh, Jasus,' His Grace of York said when he heard the name. It was embarrassin', sur, an' me commander standin' right there to hear it."

"I don't doubt that." Ransom managed a thin smile. "Welcome to Mount Falcon. Will you make us call you by that mouthful?"

"Indeed, sur, an' you may call me O'Shaughnessy. Or Quin. Bein' a friend, like."

Ransom winced as the hedgehog loosened an instant and tightened again. "How long can you stay?"

Quin shrugged. He tilted his head so that the morning light from the windows emphasized the handsome deep red in his hair. "Well, sur, among other things, such as lookin' after those particular ladies as might need lookin' after, I wouldn't like to be leavin' before this little matter of His Lordship's bill is clear."

Ransom frowned, not pleased that Shelby had been used in such a way—luring him into debt to one of the

War Department's agents. Ransom would have put a rapid halt to such a ploy if he'd known about it. He filed the matter away for investigation, intending to make mincemeat of whoever was responsible when he found them out. But he had to admit that the debt made a most convenient cover. And it was comforting to know that Castlereagh had taken Ransom's project seriously enough to send extra protection.

As satisfied as he could contrive to be while a hedgehog was using his finger as a pincushion, Ransom nodded shortly. He shifted in his chair. "That should be an adequate reason to stay a while, then," he said in a testy voice. "I don't intend to advance any money on my brother's allowance in the foreseeable future."

"Well, now, that is a shame, Your Excellency's Highness. But only what I was expectin'. I had heard you was a great farthing-pinch."

"Yes, I am. And I'm not at all fond of levity when my finger is being lacerated by a hedgehog. I don't suppose you have any notions on how to make the damned thing uncurl, do you?"

Quin's green eyes crinkled merrily. "Why, no, sur. By my soul, I can't say that I do. But I was after calling in the gardener, wasn't I? To be bringing tea, was it? Some beautiful juicy worms, plump as gooseberries, for Your Honor's Noble Grace."

"Go away." Ransom glowered. "I'll deal with you later."

Quin laid his hand on his breast. "By the rod of St. Patrick—I never thought Quinton O'Sullivan O'Toole O'Shaughnessy's own father's son would be treated so uncivilly." He looked up past Ransom toward the door. "But here now—perhaps this is a lady who needs my attention."

With a rush of relief, Ransom exclaimed, "Merlin, thank God—" He stopped as Blythe glided in. There was no sign of Merlin. He dropped his forehead into his free hand and groaned.

"Damerell," Blythe said.

He looked up wearily. His finger had passed into a throbbing numbness. "Yes, Blythe?"

His sister glanced toward Quin. Her hands had been balled into small white fists, but as the green-eyed Irishman grinned and bowed, her fingers relaxed slightly. "Oh—are you occupied?" she asked with sudden and unusual diffidence. "I shall come back."

Quin reached out and caught her arm lightly as she began to turn away. "Dear lovely ma'am," he said. "Pray don't take the sunlight from me poor empty life so soon."

Blythe's eyes widened at this familiarity. Ransom braced himself for an icy retort. Instead, he had the astonishing experience of seeing his stiff-necked sister allow a stranger, and an ill-bred one at that, slide his hand suggestively down her arm and lift her hand for a lingering kiss. Blythe stood very still. Frozen by shock, Ransom supposed. After Quin straightened, she remained for a full half minute staring up at him before jerking her hand from his and marching out of the room.

"That was well done," Ransom said dryly.

Quin winked. "Every duty has its rewards, me wise old mother was fond of saying."

"I can assure you that my sister's favor will not be one of them."

"Your Dukeship's Highness may say that same. But I'm thinkin' "—Quin swept a bow—"that a man might be wont to study long before acceptin' Your Grace's reckoning. 'Tis not meself with the hedgepig stuck on me hand."

"Perhaps you'd prefer a hedgepig stuck on your ar—"

"Hold your loose tongue, sur, if you please! Yet another lady graces our humble selves with her fair presence."

Ransom twisted—carefully, this time—to look toward the door. Merlin stood outside, peering in, dressed in her familiar apron with the bulging pocket.

He tilted his head back against the high back of his chair and closed his eyes with a harsh sigh of relief. "Get it off me," he ordered. "This instant."

"Oh, my," Merlin cried. "Oh—are you hurt?" He heard her rush toward him. "Here, let me—"

His bellow of pain drowned the rest of her words. The hedgehog reacted to her hasty attempt to pry it open by clenching with a force that thrust spines deep into his flesh—all the way to the bone, he was certain. He jerked his arm and the hedgehog out of reach. After an infinite moment of purest agony, he wrenched his eyes open to see Merlin wringing her hands.

"Oh, no. Oh, no—I'm so sorry!" she moaned. "Oh, your poor hand! What shall we do?"

"I believe I shall retire, dear ma'am"— Quin began moving toward the door—"before His Dukeship becomes cantankerous."

"Oh, Ransom." Merlin paid Quin no attention at all, but grabbed Ransom's free hand as the Irishman closed the door behind him. She clutched Ransom's palm between hers in a gesture that at any other time he would have found highly gratifying. As it was, he just managed to prevent himself from cursing her to bleeding Hades and back. "Oh, Ransom," she repeated, and slid to her knees beside his chair, holding his hand against her cheek.

He took ten deep, even breaths. Trust fate, he thought, to put Merlin in a devoted mood when he was paralyzed by pain. He spread shaky fingers against her soft skin and muttered, "Damn the luck."

"What?" She raised wide, gray, miserable eyes.

"Never mind," he said. "Never mind."

She turned her head and pressed her lips into the curve of his palm. Instantly, his whole body began to sing a willing song, an ardent humming in his veins that clashed with the anguish in his arm, creating a peculiar desperation, a need to draw her close and crush her against him as if that might wipe out the pain.

He swore again, feeling foolish and furious. He cupped the nape of her neck, drawing her up to him as he bent in spite of the searing pain in his finger. It was stupid and farcical and it hurt like the devil, but her lips were warm, impossibly soft, impossibly generous in opening to his sudden demand.

"Curse it," he muttered, pulling away and burying his face in his arm on the desk. "I really don't think I deserve this."

"What can I do?" Merlin asked in a wretched voice. "What can I do?"

Ransom bared his teeth in the imitation of a smile. "Very little, it would appear."

"But it's hurting you. I don't want you to be hurt. And it's my fault. I probably left the hedgehog in here. I'm sure I did. I often do things like that." She bit her lip. "Oh, Ransom. Can you forgive me?"

He took a deep breath. Her gray eyes were lovely, the lashes like soft smoke against her skin. "Merlin . . ." He sighed. "At some time before I die, I will probably forgive you."

Her dusky eyebrows drew together. With pained amusement, he watched the irony go right past her, leaving that luscious, misty puzzlement on her face. She lifted her hand and touched her lower lip. Ransom moaned. He rested his head on his trapped arm and reached out to catch her hand. "Don't do that, please." He clasped her fingers, keeping hold of her hand. "You make me feel quite uncivilized."

"I don't mean to."

"I know. You never mean to, do you?" He squeezed her hand. "Just sit here with me, Wiz."

She looked at the hedgehog sadly. "I know exactly how it feels."

"Oh, really? Have you had several score of hatpins driven into your flesh lately?"

"No. I mean I know just how the hedgehog feels."

Ransom sighed. "And I thought I was the sympathetic figure here."

"I'd like to curl up in a ball myself right now."

"Why don't you try it? And then ask yourself what would make you uncurl."

Merlin looked up at him. He gave her a faint smile, meaning to reassure, but she did not respond. The familiar, distant look of concentration was in her eyes, that way she had of looking at his nose and at a point a hundred miles away at the same time. It made her seem infinitely vulnerable and precious, that look—like a child smiling in its sleep. A fierce sense of his responsibility for her gripped him. He had torn her out of the safe existence she had known, forced himself on her body and her life. The price of that was a commitment, and Ransom was not a man to evade his duty. He propped their clasped hands on his knee and waited intently for her to come back to him.

"I have it!"

"*Ah,*" Ransom croaked, as the sharp sound of her voice made the hedgehog flinch.

Merlin scrambled to her feet and began searching frantically in her pocket. She pulled out a handful of metal springs and tossed them on the polished surface of the desk. Two broken pencils followed, a small mirror, and a snuffbox. She made a sound of vexation, holding The Pocket open and peering inside. Another diving search produced what appeared to be an extensive collection of clock innards. Ransom refrained from inquiring where they had come from, but he determined to look into the state of the Mount Falcon timepieces immediately.

"Here," she said. "Here, I can feel it . . ." She pressed her fingers into the very bottom of The Pocket, scrabbling for purchase on whatever item was escaping her. After a breathless struggle, she held it up triumphantly.

"A sunflower seed," Ransom said.

"It loves them!" She rushed around the desk and leaned over, scooting the single seed toward the bristling ball on Ransom's hand. "There. There. Watch."

A minute passed.

"I'm watching," Ransom said.

She waved him into silence. He tilted his head, observing the way the sun caught her hair as she bent, staring at the bristling ball in profound concentration. Her hands were braced on the surface of the desk, her fingers spread in unconscious grace, unadorned by anything except a grease smudge on one slender thumb. The plain cotton blouse gaped slightly, giving him a tantalizing glimpse of a shadowed curve beneath.

"Come here and kiss me," he said. "A watched hedgehog never uncurls."

She looked up, brushing back an escaped lock of hair. "It doesn't?" Her expression was dubious. "I've never watched one very long."

"Merlin, I'm in pain. Severe pain. I need distraction."

She frowned at him. Then a little gleam of a smile curved her lips. She examined her fingers. "I suppose . . . if you aren't trying to make me do something I don't want to."

"Of course not. It's in the nature of a strategy. A diversion. I think this hedgehog is modest. It doesn't like people staring at it. We have to make it think we've forgotten it entirely."

She moved around the desk again to his side. The little smile was gone. Her face was solemn, her magnificent gray eyes as clear and soft as moonlight. "Would that really help, do you think?"

Her expression, her tone, the faint tension in her brows—all told him the question was utterly serious. His mouth went dry. "No," he whispered honestly. "I just want to kiss you."

She lifted her hand. With her forefinger, she traced the outline of his mouth. Ransom closed his eyes. Desire was there, hot and instant and hard to control. The first fluttering touch of her lips on his made his fingers grip the arm of his chair. The fact that his injured hand was suddenly free to participate in this reaction hardly registered in his conscious mind. He lost himself in the awkward kiss, in the shy tender warmth, lifting his chin to cajole for more . . .

"It worked!"

Her abrupt withdrawal left him feeling provoked, and not a little silly.

"Look," Merlin said, ignoring his mumbled profanity. "I told you."

Ransom didn't need to look. He was examining his freed finger, hoping that it wouldn't have to be amputated. The punctures did not appear to be quite as deep as he'd feared, though they stung viciously and bled all over the ink blotter. He wrapped his handkerchief around them and glared at the hedgehog, which had made short work of its single seed and was waving its button-black nose in the air, looking for another.

"I find you *de trop*," he informed the animal. "Kindly proceed to your original destination, and I hope you break your spiny little neck on the way."

"Here." Merlin had located another sunflower seed. "Come here."

She held open The Pocket and waved the seed over the hedgehog's nose. It trundled eagerly after the lure, leaning off the edge of the desk and stretching its forepaws until gravity took over and the animal tumbled into Merlin's apron. She dropped the seed in after, and then swept the rest of her springs and clockworks in on top. There was a faint tinkling as the hedgehog shifted about until it was satisfied with its position.

"I hope," Ransom said dryly, "that you'll dispense with carrying a miniature bodyguard after we're married."

The moment the words left his mouth, he wanted them back. A major tactical error—to speak as if the resolution of their controversy was a foregone conclusion. And the instant tightening of her eyebrows told him that the slip had not passed unnoticed.

To retrieve a blunder, his grandfather had always taught him, seize the offensive.

"Why won't you?" he asked, before she could voice the inevitable denial.

Her lashes swept downward. "I like my hedgehog. And perhaps I think I need a bodyguard."

"You know what I mean, Merlin. You were about to say you won't marry me."

"You always put words in my mouth."

"Was I wrong?"

"That's not the point—"

"It is to me. I want to know *why,* Merlin." He stood up and walked around the desk to confront her, spreading his arms. "Am I too old? Not rich enough? Ugly?"

She frowned, tucking her chin in a little as he moved closer.

"Merlin." He caught her arm, gently, but enough to block her escape route past him. "Don't you like me at all?"

Her lips worked. He took note of that and pressed his advantage, running his palm up her sleeve and caressing her cheek. "I like you, Merlin. Very much."

She frowned harder. Her lower lip set mulishly. "I don't believe you," she said under her breath.

"Do you think I'm lying? Haven't I kept my promises to you? Haven't I transported your equipment here and given you a place to work and brought in the best doctor in the county to see to Theo? Haven't I taken care of you? How can you say you don't believe me—Merlin, for God's sake, do you think I kiss every female who walks in the house the way I kiss you?"

"I don't know."

His hand closed a little tighter on her arm. He was beginning to lose his temper. "Allow me to assure you that I don't!"

Her eyes flashed up. "I'm sure you would, if you wanted them all to abandon their flying machines!"

"Merlin, I have never said—"

"Of course you've never said. Not out loud. You just kiss me."

"And you take that to mean I want you to abandon your flying machine."

"Yes!"

Between clenched teeth, he said, "Would you be so kind as to explain to me the reasoning behind that?"

She opened her mouth and shut it again. He felt her wriggle and tense beneath his fingers. "Because," she said in a burst of feeling, "you think with your head!"

He stared at her a moment. Then he let go of her arm and rubbed his eyes. His injured finger throbbed dully.

"You are beyond my comprehension, Merlin. You really are. I'm offering my house, my protection, my name . . . I don't know what else I can give you."

"Wings," she whispered.

His patience shattered under the weight of frustration and hurt. "I am not going to let you kill yourself in a damned-fool attempt to fly!" He grabbed her shoulders in spite of his injured hand. "Do you hear me? I am not."

She endured the sharp shake without a word. He wanted to kiss her; he wanted to crush her against him and keep her safe from every possible harm. But a strategically placed hedgehog and the knowledge that she saw his lovemaking as some kind of coercion deterred him. He thrust away from her and walked to the window.

"You live in a fantasy world," he said in a low voice. "It's a lovely world, Merlin, and I—I've felt rather privileged to share a little of it. But the real world is still here. It's still as cruel and unforgiving as it's ever been." He raised his eyes and gazed out at the trimmed sweep of green lawn. "Sometimes it seems like I've spent my whole life trying to protect the people I care about from it."

"Perhaps they don't need so much protection."

He glanced back at her. "Ah. A gem of wisdom from the lady who wishes to attach wings to herself and leap off a cliff."

"It's not so simple as that."

"Is it not? You jump. You fall. You break your neck. It seems fairly straightforward to me."

She bent her head. But he could see the way that little pucker formed between her brows.

"Merlin," he said, "I'm sorry. I seem to lose all my diplomacy around you. But, my dear, I already have your innocence on my conscience. I don't want your demise there, too."

"I don't think my demise is any of your concern," she said to the floor. "I'll do what you like on the speaking box, and then I'll go home. I am not your responsibility, Ransom." She turned away from him, toward the door, and then stopped and looked back. There was an expression of clear determination on her face which he had never seen before. "I suppose if my 'innocence' is on your conscience, it will just have to stay there. Perhaps I do live in a fantasy world, but I'm not going to marry you and give up my aviation machine so that you can keep your good opinion of yourself."

Chapter 9

It was Woodrow who brought the awful news to Merlin. He dropped it innocently a week later, in the west ballroom, staring up at the wing framework she was stringing.

"Mr. Pa-Pemminey uses aluminium," he said matter-of-factly.

Merlin turned around. "Uses aluminium for what?"

"For wings. He said that one needs the strength of . . . sh-sh . . ." As always, Woodrow lowered his eyes, and his stutter worsened whenever she looked straight at him. "Sta-sta . . . s-stretched aluminium wire."

"Strength! The strength is in the canvas skin. Stiff wire is a poor trade for the elasticity to be found in catgut. And who is Mr. Pemmican?"

"Pa-Pa-Pa-Pemminey." He took a breath. "He lives in a . . . tower on the ca-ca-ca . . . *cliff* at Ba . . . Beachy Head. I ride there sometimes. He's ba . . . building a flying ma-ma-ma . . . machine . . . too."

She gasped. "He's building—" Her mouth worked like a gaping fish. "And he's using aluminium wire!" She grabbed Woodrow's thin shoulders. "He's not tested it yet?"

"I don't think so. Pa-please, Ma-Ma-Miss Lambourne, don't ba-ba . . . be angry! I'm sure he hasn't . . . ca-ca-ca . . . *completed* it. He ca-came to Uncle Damerell last fall and asked if the . . . ga-ga-ga-*government* wanted to . . . ga-give him funds to finish. Ba-but my uncle said he was . . . ca-ca-ca . . . crazy."

"Last fall!" Merlin moaned. "Last fall! Why, he will have flown it across the Channel and back by now."

"Oh, Ma-Ma-Miss Lambourne, pa-please don't . . . ba-be upset. I'm . . . sure he hasn't. I ga-go to . . . see him almost every fortnight. It isn't far. And he was very angry with Uncle Damerell. He . . . said it was a ca-ca-ca . . . *crime,* that the ga-government would allow Ba . . . British genius to . . . starve. I don't think he has very ma-much . . . ma-ma-ma-money, you sa-sa-sa-sa . . . you understand. And aluminium wire is expensive."

"But *last fall!* He must have found another sponsor by now. Not everyone is such a cod's head as your uncle, Woodrow!"

Woodrow cast down his eyes again. He shuffled his feet. "I'm . . . sorry. I don't know. Mr. Pa-Pa-Pemminey did . . . say, last . . . time I went, that he'd been . . . ta-ta-talking to-*to* . . . some interested pa-pa-pa . . . *parties.*"

"Interested parties." She made a sound of dismay. "Oh—were they *very* interested?"

"I don't know. I'm really . . . sorry. That's all he . . . ca-ca-called them. 'Interested . . . pa-parties.' "

Merlin chewed her knuckle. And then she squared her shoulders and turned around and went back to work with a vengeance.

Very early each morning before anyone else was awake, she reserved two hours, because she'd promised, and worked on making the improvements Ransom had requested for the speaking box. The secretary Mr. Collett was always at her service during those times, ready to fetch anything she needed on the instant, to transcribe her notes himself and lock them into a box he carried in and out of Ransom's study.

It was communication over greater distance that Ransom had asked for. Distance and power. She built a battery with more cups and plates, and refined the coiled wires. In some of the cool summer dawns Collett carried the portable portion of the box off to a far corner of the estate, and they learned together that the voice came clearer through the ether when one partner was high—speaking from the third floor of the house or listening on a distant hill. Merlin began to contemplate ways to catch the effect without the help of hills and houses.

She dutifully thought about the speaking box all through her solitary breakfasts, planning ahead to the next day's work, and then turned her mind to her real goal. By the time she reached the west ballroom she was focused entirely on the flying machine, tense and frowning in anticipation of the enormous job ahead. The only thing that interrupted her concentration was her daily meeting with Ransom, whom she passed in the Great Hall every morning as she left the breakfast room.

He had not spoken to Merlin for three weeks. She wasn't sure how she felt about that. Most of the time it was very convenient, since it meant she had no distractions, no one pestering her over stupid notions like Duty and Reputation and The Honorable Thing To Do.

He was always in riding clothes, just coming in the door from outside. He would stop when he saw her, and every day her insides would give an odd little squeeze at the sight of him, so fiercely elegant in his polished top boots and immaculate coat while she still had jelly on her fingers and mud clinging to her hem from a dawn excursion with the speaking box. She was learning to notice things like that. To notice the way his breeches were never smudged or torn, but fit his thighs as his coat fit his shoulders—without a wrinkle, completing the tall, masculine silhouette.

He'd bid her good morning the first few times they'd met there in the hall, but Merlin found any encounter with him, even a simple greeting, too much a threat to her concentration, so she only nodded and thought harder about the flying machine and hurried on.

Now he only nodded, too.

She worked all day and into the nights, with the image of the mysterious Mr. Pemminey always hovering over her. Woodrow had ridden his pony to visit her competitor again, and his report was alarming. Mr. Pemminey had indeed found a new sponsor, and he was hard at work on his project—not simply an aviation machine, but one that would carry an aviator and a *passenger,* too! Merlin was appalled. She threw herself into frantic work.

At the morning stroke of three from the clock in the Great Hall she would finally give in to the ache in her shoulders and the scratchy droop behind her eyelids. In the deep-night silence, she trudged alone up the huge staircase and lay down in her clean, freshly aired bed that smelled of violets. For just a few moments she would stare up at the elegant canopy and allow herself to forget the speaking box and the flying machine.

In those moments she always thought of Ransom. And a strange, lonely melancholy would creep through her, before weariness overtook it and sent her into heavy sleep.

"I suggest we use George Reade to speak in the House on that point," Ransom said, and then smiled. "As it will require more than ordinary gravity to ensure belief.

His companion chuckled. "Quite." After jotting in his notebook, the under-secretary of the Exchequer rose. "A most productive conversation, Damerell. And I do thank you for your hospitality these several days. I shall not stop here another."

"No? You won't stay until week's end?"

"My deepest regrets. I mean to set out for London to-morrow morning. But before I go, Damerell, I must see this marvelous winged machine I've been hearing about from your other guests."

"That." Ransom's smile flattened. He waved his hand dismissively. "An overlarge toy."

The secretary smiled. "And yet you've given over your ballroom to it, I understand."

"It entertains the children. Of all ages."

"Sly fellow! You know you can trust me. Are you certain that it isn't a military triumph in the making? By God, Damerell, what an achievement it would be, to make the thing work."

"I'm not holding my breath," Ransom said.

The secretary clapped Ransom's shoulder. "Take me to this folly, dear boy, and let me judge for myself."

"Certainly." Ransom inclined his head in a slight, dry bow and gestured toward the door. He'd determined on a strategy of nonconfrontation to deal with Merlin, deliberately avoiding her, trying to give her time to adjust and—more to the point—to miss his attentions. It was quite clear from their last encounter that he had pushed her too hard, too soon.

So he had thrown himself into his work, isolating himself from the rest of the household. In a place the size of Mount Falcon, that was a simple task. He had only to take his meals in private with whichever guest he preferred to honor and spend the rest of his time closeted in his own spacious wing of the house.

Now he stood back and followed the secretary from the room. "I've yet to see it myself, actually." Their footsteps echoed in the long, arched corridor.

"You haven't? For shame, Damerell. Have you lost all pretense to youth and dreams? Upon my soul, when I think of the boyhood days I sat swinging my legs from the highest elm branch I could find and wishing I were a bird on the wind!"

"What a delightful picture."

"You villain, I see you storing that confession away to use someday when you wish to plague me in the House. But it won't wash. I ain't ashamed of boy's dreams, and nor should you be. Come down off your high horse and admit it, Damerell—you'd love to see this thing fly as much as I would."

Ransom shook his head. "I would prefer to have it dismantled and removed from my premises. But I am in love, you see."

"Hah. The only thing you've ever been in love with is that seat in Westminster Hall. Past time you remarried, Damerell. You're becoming damned stiff-assed in your old age."

"Thank you for the observation. I shall endeavor to improve myself."

The secretary laughed and made a face at him. "Yes, I can see that you take the criticism very well. Come, come, dear friend—you'll forgive me. I know you have the dignity of your position to uphold. And a nice little well-bred wife with no town tarnish on her will be just the ticket.''

''Do you think so?'' Ransom grinned, abandoning his solemn face. He gestured toward the door to the west ballroom. ''Then allow me to introduce you to Miss Lambourne.''

At his signal, a footman bowed and swung open the double doors.

Ransom thought he had prepared himself. He'd been hearing for weeks about the wonderful ballroom from his nieces. It was one thing to hear, however, and quite another to see the great, graceful sweep of canvas that hung by a thousand streamers where his German-crystal chandeliers should have been.

It filled the room, this flying machine. One wing tip touched the painted ceiling three stories above, where Leander swam the Hellespont to reach his Hero, and the other brushed the carved mantel of a Sicilian marble fireplace. A coarse wooden platform covered the intricate inlaid pattern of colored stone on the ballroom floor. Tools and wires glinted in the afternoon sun and ropes drifted everywhere, hung from pulleys and casting long, intersecting shadows through the air and across the floor.

To Ransom's surprise, the huge object had an unlikely beauty of its own. A living presence, as if it were some mythological beast conjured out of legend and hung as a silent trophy in his hall. Amidst the spindly forest of ropes, dwarfed figures moved in and out of the giant's shadow.

''Ransom!'' It was Shelby's voice, suspiciously friendly, beckoning from a far corner of the room. One tall silhouette with two smaller ones attached to it moved out of the shadow and came toward them.

The secretary greeted Ransom's brother with clear pleasure. He had a smile and a pat for the twins, who were too excited by Ransom's visit to remember to be shy. They squealed and grabbed his coattails and began pulling him into the room.

"Marvelous," he heard the secretary say to Shelby as they followed after.

"Yes, it is rather wonderful, isn't it?" Shelby exclaimed. "I've become quite fascinated by the whole thing myself. Spend every afternoon here helping out."

As Ransom's eyes adjusted to the deep contrasts of light and dark, he saw Merlin hunched over a writing stand in the corner, frowning tensely as she scribbled in a large notebook. She didn't look up as the twins propelled him forward. Nearby, Major Quinton O'Sullivan O'Toole O'Shaughnessy was propped against the fireplace mantel, his arms raised, wrapping wire with careful moves around the lowered wing tip. Jaqueline stood by, holding the wing in position for him, craning her neck to watch.

Mr. Peale was there, too, standing next to Merlin and reading numerical equations from a dusty text to her in a solemn, Sunday-morning chant. Woodrow and Blythe—Blythe, of all people!—completed the unlikely group, cutting strands of catgut and sorting them by length in precise rows across the floor. Woodrow was sorting, at least. Blythe was hovering nearby and pointing out his mistakes.

Ransom swallowed his shock at the odd collection of his relatives and guests, determined by habit not to show his surprise. It appeared that half the household had adopted the flying machine as a regular entertainment. He looked around, trying to see what it was that had precipitated such unexpected devotion. Nothing he saw enlightened him.

"What can Uncle Demmie do?" Augusta cried. "Miss Merlin! Can Uncle Demmie take us on the cat's seat?"

Merlin looked up into his eyes. The deep pucker was etched between her brows, and shadows beneath her cheekbones gave her an unfamiliar, hollow look. Ransom had the distinct impression that she didn't even see him. "Yes. Yes, of course," she said in a distant voice. She went back to her writing. "Go to Shelby for sweets. What was that last number, Mr. Peale? One hundred seventy over the square of what?"

Aurelia and Augusta crowed and tried to pull Ransom away, but he detached himself. "Merlin," he said.

"Not now." She shook her head. "Not now, if you please!"

He stared at her tight shoulders, at the taut, slim fingers that gripped the pen so zealously. She ordered Mr. Peale to stop a moment and grabbed another notebook, brushing through the pages furiously. Holding her place with an awkward elbow, she scowled up at the aircraft. She lifted her hand to her lower lip in that characteristic gesture that had so often made his blood run warm. This time, though, there was such an anxious tension in the way she chewed her finger that he had another reaction to it entirely.

"Merlin," he said again. "May I speak to you a moment?"

He received not a blink of response.

"Shall I write your message down in a note, Your Dukeship?" an amused Irish brogue inquired. "And deliver it when she returns to this earthly plane of ours?"

Ransom glanced at Quin. The major was lounging against the mantel, his coat loosened and his deep coppery hair falling in his eyes. Jaqueline coiled the last of the wire between her fingers.

"No, thank you." Ransom made an effort to hold on to his good temper. He smiled at Jaqueline. "Good afternoon. I didn't expect to see you here, I must confess."

"Oh, I come with the children and spend all day." She laughed and leaned just slightly toward Quin, so that her fingers brushed his sleeve. "We find this room most alluring, the children and I."

"I see," Ransom said in a perfectly neutral voice. He doused his quick surge of resentment on Shelby's behalf and resisted the urge to turn and see if his brother was watching.

"Ah, Jackie," Quin said, smiling down at her. "Don't give old Quinton a bad name with His Grace. Pull those lovely claws of yours out of me heart, dearest."

Jaqueline released her light hold. She blew him a kiss. "Vile boy. You take all the joy out of being a fast woman."

Quin's lips curved in a leering smile. "Oh, are you a fast woman, my sweet? Perhaps I spurned you too hastily."

"Too late." Jaqueline neatly avoided his move to catch her. "I am a mother again." She knelt, holding out her arms to envelop her daughters as they pressed wriggling bodies close for a kiss.

From behind Ransom came a high and chilly voice. "Jaqueline, you don't actually suppose such an exhibition will mislead either of my brothers? Ransom is hardly foolish enough to believe that you care so very much for your children when you have ignored them for—"

"Blythe," Ransom said sharply.

Jaqueline glanced up, her violet eyes unreadable. She gave Augusta an extra hug before she rose.

"It is perfectly true," Blythe went on heedlessly. Her face was pale as she frowned at Ransom. "She comes in here every day pretending it's the children, when all the time she only wants to flirt with—"

"Leave her be, Blythe." Shelby's soft voice made them all turn. He stood with the secretary, looking as cold and finely drawn as one of the Grecian statues outside. In the ensuing silence, Merlin's pen scratched and Mr. Peale went on intoning mathematical equations.

"My lord secretary!" Blythe reddened. "I'm so sorry—I did not know you had come in! How do you do? Where would you like to sit? Oh, dear, I'm afraid there isn't much place in here just now."

"Quite all right, my lady." The secretary's voice held only a hint of forced joviality. "I'll only stay a moment. I wished to see the flying machine with my own eyes."

"But do let me ring for tea."

"Please don't trouble yourself—"

"It will only be a moment. Pull that crate up closer, Shelby."

"Really, Lady Blythe," the secretary protested, "I don't wish for a thing—"

"Please sit down there, if you like. Ransom, perhaps you could clear this workbench of that . . . paraphernalia. How is your dear wife, my lord secretary? Has she recovered from her little bout of congestion?''

"Yes, she's quite well." The secretary sat down and then sprang up again. He turned around and carefully removed a screwdriver and a littering of screws from the crate where he'd begun to sit.

"I'll take that," Ransom said. He laid the handful of metal on the workbench. The twins rushed over and scooted up on the bench, scattering screws.

"This is the cat's seat," Aurelia announced. "You can take us on it, Uncle Demmie. Miss Merlin said."

Augusta nodded vigorously. "Yes. Take us!"

"In a moment." Ransom kept his attention on Blythe and the secretary, wary of further blunders from his sister. She seemed to have decided that the situation called for a more formal grouping. She snipped at Shelby until he sat down with a sigh on a heap of canvas cloth, and then went after Mr. Peale. The reverend responded instantly to the object of his passion by politely accepting her invitation to join her upon an old carriage seat that appeared to have been exhumed from some stableyard attic.

Mr. Peale's desertion left Merlin with an open mouth and a frown. She went back to work, and for a few moments continued scratching away with her pen. The writing began to slow. She looked up. Ransom watched. It came as it always did, that reluctant transition, as her eyes left the soft cloudy vistas of thought and focused on the world at hand. For the first time, she noticed him.

She smiled. And it seemed suddenly to Ransom that the three weeks since he'd kissed her had been three lifetimes.

He held out his hand and spoke gently, because she seemed fragile: pale and tense and worn thin as an overstrung wire. "Merlin," he said. "Come here. We're having tea and a bit to eat. I'd like you to meet a good friend of mine."

"I'm sorry," she said. "I have to work."

"You can rest a few moments, don't you think? We'd enjoy your company. The secretary wishes to hear about your flying machine."

"Oh." She laid down her pen. "Of course."

She came out from behind the writing podium, dragging a stray coil of wire that had caught in her skirt. While approaching them, she passed in and out of rope-thin shadows. Sunlight kindled a gleam in her chestnut hair. Blythe leaped up and performed the introduction while Ransom was still frowning at Merlin, disturbed by the new, slender delicacy of her, the impression that she would snap and then crumble under a careless touch.

Blythe poured tea when it arrived, as indifferent as the well-trained maid to the odd surroundings. Ransom took three extra scones onto his plate, returning a casual smile for his sister's raised brows. He moved next to Merlin, who was already expounding on aviation to the secretary, and offered the scones.

She glanced at him, shook her head, and went on talking. Ransom continued holding up the plate, and the secretary took one scone, eating it handily between eager questions.

Ransom waited a few moments. He sipped his tea and watched Merlin. Behind him, Quin had engaged Blythe and Shelby in some sort of Irish blarney—which they seemed to be enjoying, if Shelby's chuckles and Blythe's huffing was any indication. The Reverend Mr. Peale had collared Jaqueline. To Ransom's amazement, the two of them appeared to be content to argue the relative merits of aluminium wire and catgut at length.

Ransom offered the scones to Merlin again. She paused in her dialogue and shook her head. "No, thank you."

The secretary took another one. "And the landing," he said between bites. "How do you propose to accomplish that?"

"Well, I've heard that Mr. Pemminey is using wheels." Merlin frowned. "But I do believe that my skis provide more flexibility. There is the matter of wind resistance, though—"

"I wish you would eat something," Ransom said evenly.

Merlin shook her head as he held up the plate again. "I'm not at all hungry. As for the wind resistance, I'm trying to calculate for that by—"

"You look as if you haven't had a meal for days."

She waved her hand. "Mr. Pemminey is preparing to test his model next week," she said, as if that should be explanation enough.

"Have you thought of a grapple?" the secretary asked. He took the last scone from Ransom's offered plate. "Something like a ship's anchor, if you see what I mean. You could throw it out and release the line as you descended."

"But there is the weight, you see." She worried her lower lip. "Mr. Pemminey seems to have mastered that, since he plans to carry a passenger. But I'm afraid my design could not cope. I'm moving up my test to Monday next. I cannot imagine how Mr. Pemminey has managed to advance so far so fast—"

"Mr. Pemminey be damned," Ransom said under his breath. He set the empty plate down on a convenient intersection of strung wires. "I have a question, Miss Lambourne," he announced.

His determined tone overrode Merlin in the midst of her discussion. Everyone looked toward him.

"I was just wondering," he said casually, "exactly how you're planning to get this apparatus out the door."

Merlin turned toward him. She opened her mouth. She closed it. She twisted to gaze up at the huge sweep of canvas with a look of pure horror transforming her expression.

"Oooh," she breathed. "Oh, *nooo!*"

There was a moment of dead silence.

"There's a poser," Shelby said. "Merlin, do you mean to tell you never thought of it?"

Her throat worked. No sound came out.

"Really," Blythe exclaimed. "Then we did all this for *nothing?*"

"Exactly what have you done, Blythe?" Shelby demanded. "Nothing Woodrow couldn't have accomplished twice as fast on his own."

"Woodrow is a child. I was asked to monitor the accuracy of his work," Blythe said stiffly. "And I certainly wouldn't have wasted my time if I'd known Miss Lambourne hadn't accounted for so simple a thing as transporting her apparatus outside the room!''

"It is a terrible oversight, my dear," said Mr. Peale. "I apologize sincerely if I've encouraged you to spend your precious time unwisely."

"But sure, it's no problem at all." Quin gestured toward the row of huge windows that overlooked the formal garden. "'Tis only a wee bit o' wall blockin' the way.''

Ransom gave the Irishman a sardonic smile. "Don't even think it."

Merlin covered her face. She sank down onto an overturned whiskey keg. "Oh, no," she moaned. "Oh no, oh no, oh no."

The twins rushed to her side. "Don't cry, Miss Merlin! Uncle Demmie will know what to do!" Aurelia patted Merlin's cheek. "Uncle Demmie always knows what to do."

"Of course." Merlin's head came up. Her drawn face shone with relief and hope as she looked toward him.

In the expectant silence, he cleared his throat. "I can't help you this time, I'm afraid."

The clamor of protest made him scowl. He looked away from Merlin's stricken countenance.

"Uncle Damerell?" a timid young voice asked. "Excuse ma-ma-ma . . . me, ba-ba-ba—I have an idea."

Ransom turned to Woodrow and struggled to lighten his expression when the boy gripped his hands together and cast down his eyes. "Yes?"

"The wings," Woodrow said. He took a deep breath. "The wings. We ca-ca-ca . . . could change them, ca-ca-couldn't we? Here." He pointed. "And over there. Ma-ma-ma-make those joints ma-ma-*metal*. Hinges and . . . *screws* . . . sa-so they would fold up and . . . down. Then if you only . . . took out one window . . .''

"*Yes!*" Merlin cried. "I can do that!" She leaped up and smothered Woodrow in a hug. "Oh, thank you. Thank you so much! You're the smartest person I ever, ever met!"

Ransom was preparing to declare that a window would be removed at Mount Falcon over his dead body when Woodrow emerged from Merlin's embrace. The boy was scarlet with confusion and pride.

"My pleasure, Miss Lambourne," Woodrow said, without a single trip over a "p" or an "m."

He didn't even seem to notice the lack of stutter. But Ransom did. With a sigh, the master of Mount Falcon consigned one of its century-old Vanbrugh windows to an ignoble fate.

Merlin rushed back to her writing table, grabbing up the pen and dragging out diagrams and notes from the piles of vellum scattered across the floor. She muttered to herself, making little moans and occasional lamentations, such as: "This will throw me back a month," or "Blast, blast, I can't cut the skeleton there . . . but wait! Could I possibly . . . no—it won't work. It would never stand the strain. It will have to be in the third quarter . . . Mr. Peale! Mr. Peale, where is that Johnson book on integral calculus? Page two hundred and twenty, I believe it was . . . Oh, do hurry—we have no time, no time at all!"

Mr. Peale, with profuse apologies to Blythe, promptly went back to work. Ransom's sister stood looking after her admirer, holding the teacup he had handed her, the corners of her mouth turned down in little white pinches.

"Does he desert you so easily, darlin'?" Quin sauntered up and took the teacup from her hand. He lifted her fingers to his lips. "I find his priorities baffling."

The pinches at Blythe's mouth grew deeper and whiter as a pink flush suffused her face. When Quin lingered with his lips brushing her skin, she snatched her hand away. "I shall not stand for your continued impudence."

"Forgive me, Your Ladyship." Quin bowed contritely. "I can't seem to help meself."

"Nonsense," Blythe said. She turned away.

"Let's go on the cat's seat now, Uncle Demmie!" Augusta clutched Ransom's hand and pulled. Aurelia abandoned her impromptu game of skittles with Jaqueline and added her pleas. Ransom allowed himself to be drawn back toward the workbench, but his attention was divided between Merlin and the secretary, who had decided to take his leave and was already speaking to Blythe.

Augusta dropped Ransom's hand. She skipped to the end of the bench and bent over. The secretary was moving toward them when the floor lurched beneath Ransom's feet. He grabbed at the nearest thing, a dangling rope, and felt it go taut beneath his fingers. At the same time, an unfamiliar creaking clank began a rapid rhythm.

He looked down. His jaw clenched in alarm. The six square feet of planking on which he and the twins and the bench rested had begun to rise from the rest of the floor.

Chapter 10

It was pride and the secretary's amused gaze that prevented Ransom from stepping off when stepping was still possible. He gripped the rope, expecting the contraption to grind to a halt. It did not. His feet passed the level of the secretary's generous paunch. *Now,* Ransom thought, watching the other man's feet appear to grow closer together as his perspective changed. *Step down now.*

His body tensed. It did not obey him.

He only held the rope harder. A sweep of canvas and catgut entered the top of his peripheral vision and began to pass smoothly downward, growing larger as the tools and papers and scraps of canvas on the floor grew smaller. *Now,* he thought again, and again his feet did not move.

His boots topped the secretary's head.

"Jolly clever device, eh?" the politician cried. "I believe I'll stay long enough for a ride myself, Damerell."

Ransom wanted to swallow, but not even his throat would obey him. The twins sat still on the far end of the bench, making little whimpers of pleasure and excitement. He noticed with growing panic that their weight was not enough to counterbalance his, and the square platform tilted alarmingly toward his corner. Everyone in the room was looking up, resembling a group of foreshortened mushrooms with faces oddly white in the gloom beneath the flying machine.

A festoon of rope and wing glided down the side of Ransom's field of vision. He saw his reflection passing in the huge mirror above the mantel, a stranger in a dark coat and neat cravat, looking utterly poised and nonchalant as he leaned against the tautened rope. In the mirror, the tilt of the platform looked to be a few inches, no more. To Ransom it felt like a sickening incline.

"Isn't it fun, Uncle?" one of the twins asked, her voice dim through the pounding of blood in his ears.

Ransom could not look toward them. He tried to move his head and found his muscles paralyzed. The edge of the wing passed him. The upper surface of the canvas spread out to view in a downward, dizzying pitch.

His hand slipped a fraction, slick with sweat. A jolt of terror went from his stomach to his brain. He could no longer look down. His body seemed to have passed from his control. He stared at the far wall as the frescoed murals on it slipped downward. His lips were stiff, but behind them his thoughts clamored a silent prayer. *Oh God dearest God deliver me I'm going to fall I'm going to fall I don't want to fall oh God oh God let me down let me down let me down.*

Something large and shapeless swam into view, descending more rapidly than the rest of the surroundings. For an instant it seemed to Ransom the thing would smash into their fragile perch, and then it passed smoothly in front of his eyes, looking like a giant moth wrapped in a spider's silk and dangling by a dark thread. Belatedly, his mind recognized the limbless torso of a statue that had toppled off its garden perch in the last hard frost of winter. The thing was bound in a net of hemp and hung from a rack of pulleys: the counterweight to his treacherous elevator.

He could see the ceiling now, looming down like a huge umbrella, its mythic figures in grotesquely strained perspective.

"Is this high enough, Uncle Demmie?" a twin asked. "Should we stop?"

He could not even make his tongue move to answer that, though his mind screamed, *Yes yes yes!*

"No, no!" cried the other twin. "Let's go higher! Miss Merlin never let us go this far."

"All right. We're not even to the tip of the wing yet."

One of the little girls stood up. The platform trembled and began to swing. A low sound came out of Ransom's throat, a violent, wordless, animal sound.

"Hullo, Miss Merlin!" one of the girls called. Her voice made a thin echo above the creaking mechanism. "Hullo, Woodrow—do you see how high we are?"

On top of Ransom's own dread was the added terror that the twins might slip off. When the one who had stood up—he could not turn to see which—moved again, Ransom managed a frantic snarl. "Sit down! Sit down and don't get up!"

"Yes, sir."

From the corner of his eye, he saw the movement of pastel skirts. There was a thump, and the platform dipped and swayed like a living thing.

Oh God oh God oh God let me down.

He kept his eyes on the painted wall, moving slowly past in a pendulous swing. The ceiling began to curve down to meet the vertical. He looked at the paint, at the colors, at the brushwork and cracks in the plaster that he had never seen and never wanted to see.

Get me down please God please get me down.

The mechanism creaked to a slow halt. Silence filled the hall. The platform began a sluggish spin.

Damn damn damn damn God damn I can't take this I can't stand it I can't I can't I can't oh God.

He heard voices below. There was a thump and a loud crash, and the boards beneath his feet jumped. He clung to the rope. Blackness threatened around the edges of his vision.

The creaking began again. The platform dropped from under him . . . caught . . . and dropped again.

Ransom lost himself then. His heart simply stopped, along with his mind. The blackness turned to nothing, the soft moaning sounds in his ears went dumb. There was only one thing: there was the rope, and he held on to it. He held on to it for his life and his soul and all the saints in Heaven and the demons in Hell. He held on to it until his fingers went numb and then began to burn. He held on to it while he died, seventy-seven separate deaths, each time the platform jerked and dropped, and jerked and dropped, until a voice somewhere just below his right ear was saying, "So how did you like it, Damerell? Quite a sight from up there, eh?"

It felt as if Ransom were opening his eyes, except that they already seemed to be open. The veil of terror slowly dissolved, leaving him able to see again. He found himself a foot away from Shelby, who was wiping perspiration from his forehead with a handkerchief, his other hand still resting on the wheel and crank where an equally-winded Quin was lashing a rope securely.

Blythe and Jaqueline and Woodrow and the secretary were all looking at Ransom with expectant smiles. A little further away, Merlin and Mr. Peale still bent together over work on their equations.

"Isn't it wonderful, Uncle Demmie? The cat's seat?" Augusta demanded. "Miss Merlin built it, all by herself! She said we should take you up on it. She said we should be sneaky, and if we ever could get you to try it, you would see why she wants to fly."

Ransom amazed himself. He was not trembling. He was not weak in the knees as he shouldered Quin aside and strode toward Merlin. His hands didn't shake. His anger seemed to have wiped out the fear, but in the end his body betrayed him. He opened his mouth to speak, and the only sound that came out was, "D—"

He stopped. His throat worked. To his horror, he could tell that the curse was not going to emerge as a single word, but as a maimed caricature of a word, a stammering collection of nonsense sound like the rising babble of hysteria inside him.

For an instant he was not himself but someone else. Someone who stuttered.

Another instant and that long-forgotten boy was gone, shoved down the deep well of history by adult pride and adult ruthlessness. Ransom drew his lips back in a grimace as he looked at Merlin's pale cheeks and the weariness etched around her long lashes and gray eyes.

"Enough," he said, the word as clear as winter ice. "No more of this folly. You're driving yourself to exhaustion. I won't permit it. I won't stand by and watch you make yourself ill over nonsense. It's time you abandoned your absurd ideas and grew up. You are going to learn how to go on in the world, Miss Lambourne." He turned, sweeping the room with a freezing gaze. "The ballroom is locked and barred from this instant. To everyone."

Without waiting for a response he strode out the door and down the long series of corridors and into his own room. He threw the door closed behind him and went into the dressing room, grabbing a porcelain basin from the wash stand.

He put one hand out to the wall. His legs gave way. He sank to his knees and bent over the basin and was very, very sick.

Merlin did not take Ransom's ultimatum seriously. No one came to banish them all from the ballroom after Ransom left. He had been angry with her, that was all, his temper aroused and then dissipated in intimidation and threats, as it always was.

She worked until three that morning, and rose again at six, but after breakfast there was no sign of Ransom in the Great Hall. Merlin paused until she realized she was looking out the window for him. Then she frowned and hurried down the corridors to the ballroom.

She found it locked.

The footman standing outside the door bowed to her, his wig a light-colored blob in the early morning gloom. "His Grace wishes to see you, Miss Lambourne."

"It's locked," she said.

He looked at her impassively.

"Do open it."

"Forgive me, Miss Lambourne. I am under a specific injunction from His Grace not to do so."

Merlin stared at him while her heart slid slowly to her toes.

"In his study, Miss Lambourne," the footman prompted. "Immediately."

She had a moment of wild rebellious courage, in which the scientific merits of the various possibilities of storming, burning, blasting, or beating down the door passed through her mind. As she paused, the broad-shouldered footman looked down at her with his eyebrows lifted in a faint but unyielding smile.

She saw where she stood in the order of things.

With a deep, shaky breath, she turned away. She went down the corridor a distance, then stopped, turned, and went back. "Excuse me," she said to the footman in a small voice. "But could you point out the way?"

He escorted her, walking ahead down the long archways and around the many turns. At Ransom's study the servant did not pause for permission to enter, but simply opened the door and announced her.

Ransom stood up from his desk. He glanced at a chair, which was enough to make the footman draw it forward for Merlin. The servant seated her, and then—apparently under the order of another ducal blink—disappeared silently from the room. Ransom rested against the desk, his arms crossed, looking down at her.

Merlin hunched her shoulders. She felt like one of the twins called down for disorder.

"Good morning," he said in a voice that strained a little too hard for pleasantry.

She looked up at him. He was very tall. She had a sudden urge to press herself against his immaculate shirtfront and cry.

Instead, she said, "It isn't a good morning at all."

His thick brows lowered slightly. Merlin felt as if she had not seen him for years. He looked different. Not quite so typically self-assured and overbearing, but edgy and somehow more dangerous—like a hawk threatened into challenge. The line of his jaw was taut, his yellow-green eyes dark and dilated.

"I'm sorry you feel that way," he said.

Merlin thrust out her lower lip.

"I understand you've nearly finished with work on the speaking box."

"Yes, Mr. Duke," she said, with what she hoped was killing formality. "I shall be able to go home soon."

"How long?"

"Soon. Another week, perhaps."

"You might have been done a week past, if you had concentrated on that alone."

She said nothing, surprised and a little hurt by this unfamiliar abruptness.

Even more harshly, he said, "My mother and her crystal ball claim you're not increasing."

Merlin blinked. "Increasing what?"

"The number of my offspring."

"Offspring!"

"Yes." He looked away from her, out the window. His fingers tapped a hard rhythm on the edge of the desk. "Children, you know. I believe we discussed this."

"We did?"

He closed his eyes briefly and opened them again. "Since you've been here at Mount Falcon . . . have you been quite on schedule?"

"I've tried." She was astonished and pleased at this unexpected show of interest. "But no matter how hard I work, Mr. Pemminey seems to stay ahead."

He looked at her dryly. "Will the wonders of nature never cease? I meant, you mooncalf, have you had your monthly cycle?"

Merlin searched her brain for what he could be talking about. "Oh," she said at last. "Do you mean my menses?"

"If you wish to put it in good blunt Latin . . . yes. Will you answer my question?"

She nodded. "Just after I arrived."

There was a change in his face, far too subtle to be interpreted. He nodded. "That's some solace, I suppose."

Merlin could not imagine why. She started to tell him that the event occurred with monotonous regularity and was really nothing to be especially pleased about, but he had turned away and was rifling among some papers on the desk.

He held up a sheet. "Here's another schedule," he said. "Your new one."

Merlin took the offered paper. As she read through the list of lessons in riding, deportment, and conversation, her jaw grew slack and her eyebrows drew down. "I can't possibly do all this!" she cried. "I don't have time!"

"I can't agree with that objection. As you see, the times have been carefully calculated by Mr. Collett. You should have ample periods of rest and digestion. It's rather an improvement on your present agenda, I think."

"But my flying machine! That isn't provided for anywhere!"

He toyed with a pen. "You see how many hours there are in a day when one dispenses with frivolities. There is no need for you to work yourself into a decline, you know."

"Ransom!" she wailed.

He lifted his eyelashes, giving her a look as chilly and green-gold as a hunting falcon's. "The ballroom is locked."

"It's not fair! It's not fair! You promised I could work on my flying machine, as long as I built the new speaking box, too."

"I never made any such bargain."

"You did."

"No—"

"Oh, that is a foul lie, Mr. Duke! You said I could test my wing design here. You said there was no end of open lawn and steady winds."

He pursed his lips. "I did not understand all the ramifications at the time."

"A promise is a promise."

He made a sudden move, catching her arm and pulling her up out of the chair. "And a life is a life. I'm not so jealous of my honor that I'll jeopardize your silly neck on account of it. I made you a promise, you say? Well, I'm breaking it."

She stared up at him. Her arm hurt where his fingers dug into her sleeve. One of the buttons on his coat pressed into her skin. "Just like that? I thought that was all you cared about—your *honor.*"

"Think again, my girl. Expedience is my maxim. I've spent my life in politics, remember?"

She tried to wriggle away from him. "And that gives you leave to go back on your word?"

"A time-honored tradition among politicians." His mouth angled in a caustic smile. He held her without effort, in spite of her struggle. "The means be damned; it's the ends I care for. If a lie will save some stupid commander from wasting half his troops in a harebrained tilt at *honor,* you may be sure I'll tell it, and tell it well. I need your speaking box because I think it will save British lives, and I want you here so I can protect yours." His grip on her tightened. "If I made a promise in order to effect those goals, it wouldn't be very bright of me to stick with the promise and throw away the goals, would it? I want the speaking box, Merlin, and I want you safe."

"I'm safe! I'm here, aren't I?"

"Yes. And much good you'll be when you fall off that damned cat's seat of yours and kill yourself!"

She glared up into his eyes. "Is that what you're angry about?"

His fingers shifted on her arm. "What?"

She saw the way his look faltered, just for an instant. "The cat's seat!" She tore herself out of his grasp. "You're angry because of the cat's seat! Why? Are you too dignified to have any fun at all?"

"Don't be ridiculous."

"I only wanted you to have a chance to understand! To see what it's like."

His face grew still and peculiar. The look he gave her was ferociously cold. "Oh," he said, "I saw what it was like. Never fear."

She bit her lip. Merlin was no match for that intensity; she knew she wasn't. It was one thing to battle an equation on a piece of paper and another entirely to face down a living, breathing duke who'd been born and bred to command the awe of lesser beings like herself.

He made no move to catch her back, but her arm still throbbed where his fingers had bruised her. His instant of weakness had vanished; impossible even to imagine now as he regarded her with that golden chilly gaze. Merlin felt her resolve begin to wither under it.

"It's not fair," she mumbled yet again, unable to think of anything more persuasive when he was staring her down like that.

"The devil take fairness," he said.

Merlin plopped down in her chair. She brushed back a strand of hair that had fallen in her eyes. Once again tears threatened. She struggled with them a moment, unwilling to surrender her pride, but then recollected that tears could be quite effective with Theo and Thaddeus when she wished to bend them to her will. She lifted her face, feeling one warm drop slide down her cheek.

For a moment Ransom's expression seemed to change, just the faintest relaxing of his mouth, the slightest clouding of his eyes. Merlin added a loud sniff for effect.

His brows lowered instantly. He straightened up from his position against the desk and produced a handkerchief with a brisk move. "Save yourself the trouble. I can get a much more professional performance from Jaqueline."

Merlin slumped back in the chair. She rubbed her eyes with the crisp linen and then balled it in her fist. Clearly, there was no coaxing Ransom out of his sudden decision. None that she could manage, anyway. But the tears had given her another notion. Perhaps she could not fool Ransom in front of his eyes, but he could not be everywhere all the time. This schedule he'd had made up for her—it only included him for a few hours a day. The rest of the time . . .

"Well," she said abruptly. "I suppose I have no choice."

"None whatsoever."

Merlin stood up. She squared her shoulders and glared up at him. "If *I* ever get to be a duke, I won't be as big a bully as you are, I can tell you that!"

"Since you are exceedingly unlikely ever to get to be a duke, I don't think we need concern ourselves with the prospect."

"One just never knows, does one?" She held out her skirt and turned from him with a flounce. When she reached the door, she stopped and looked over her shoulder. "And if I should, I shall expect you to address me properly. It will be 'Miss Duke' to you, you may be sure!"

A half hour later, in the sharp, slanted light of an early sun through the saloon windows, Merlin faced her troops. They were a sleepy and out-of-sorts collection, but she had no time for patience. At half-past seven, Woodrow and Mr. Peale looked reasonably alert, but if she'd waited until Shelby, Quin, and Jaqueline would normally have arisen, she'd have been halfway through her riding lesson and a day behind, lost to Ransom's crazy whims.

"We must take emergency measures," she announced. "Ransom has locked the ballroom."

Shelby yawned, lounging in one of the needlepoint chairs with his leg thrown over the gilded arm. "Well, so he said he would. Can't you talk him out of it?"

"I tried. He gave me *this*."

Shelby took the sheet of paper that she waved under his nose. As he scanned it, his fine eyebrows lifted. "He must be serious indeed." Then he scowled. "I suppose this is some plot to whip you into proper shape to be his duchess."

"Duchess!" Merlin echoed. "Is that like being a duke?"

Quin stretched deeply and lowered himself onto the foot of the chaise where Jaqueline reclined. "Female duke, as it were."

"How do I get to be one?"

"By marrying my brother." Shelby appeared to be engrossed in some scene outside the saloon windows as he spoke, but his mouth tightened when Quin moved his hand so that it brushed against Jaqueline's ankle. With a twist of his lips, Shelby added, "Not a state I would recommend entering into with anyone. Least of all a Falconer.''

"With respect, my lord,'' Mr. Peale intoned, "the holy state of matrimony is twice blessed.''

"Hah,'' Shelby said.

"Twice blessed?'' Merlin cocked an interested look at the reverend.

"Yes, Miss Lambourne. And not to be entered into without the most rigorous thought and prayer concerning the object of one's hopes. I myself have spent many hours examining the character of my beloved, whose pure spirit and gentle character are not to be improved upon—''

"Yes, but—could I order everyone about then, like Ransom does?''

"Everyone except Ransom,'' Jaqueline said languidly, "who would then have the legal right to order *you* about, and do whatever he pleased with all your earthly possessions.''

Shelby slanted a look toward her, his blue eyes narrowed, but he said nothing.

"He already orders me about,'' Merlin said.

"Does he now? I'd call in the constable, darlin','' Quin said.

"What for?''

"Why, to have him arrested! There's men enough in Parliament to see that the rogue went to the scaffold for his crimes, I'll wager.''

"Aye,'' Shelby said darkly. "I know a few myself.''

"Arrested for what?'' Merlin cried.

"Ah, you're too modest, me love. For kidnapping your sweet self, dear. For stealing your flying machine and various other instruments of great scientific value. I don't doubt all those fellows in Parliament who'd like to see the last of him could come up with a few more hanging offenses.''

Merlin gasped. "Hanging! Are you saying they would hang him for kidnapping me?''

"Naturally.'' Quin was watching Shelby as he spoke. "They're not likely to be showing mercy to such a villain as Damerell. All you have to do is call in the law.''

"Hang him," she moaned. "I won't allow it!"

Shelby threw back his golden head and laughed. "What a capital farce. The Duke of Damerell, arrested and finally brought to book for running other people's lives!" He glanced toward Jaqueline, and the laugh distorted into something less pleasant. "Time and past. Hanging's too good for 'im, I say."

Quin stood up. "I'll ride into the village to send for the authorities right now."

"No!" Merlin cried. "You can't do that! I'll lie! I'll never admit Ransom kidnapped me! I'll say I gave him the flying machine, and everything else!"

Quin paused. He looked toward Shelby with a questioning lift of his brows.

Shelby waved his hand. "For God's sake, you can't think we're serious. Do sit down." His tone was pleasant, but he gave Quin a very queer look, a quick, penetrating glance that reminded Merlin very much of Ransom for a moment.

"Major O'Shaughnessy," Mr. Peale said, "may well be too much given to odd fits and starts."

"Among other things," Shelby said sourly. When Quin winked at Merlin and sat down again near Jaqueline, Shelby's face became a handsome mask. He tapped the chair arm, his fingers picking out a careless, complex rhythm. "Perhaps there's some less drastic way to allow Merlin access to her flying machine."

"Yes," Merlin said. "That's why I wanted to talk to everyone." She whisked Ransom's schedule off the floor where Shelby had dropped it. "It says here that I'm free between the hours of eleven at night and nine in the morning. If I can find a way into the ballroom, and someone can keep Ransom well occupied for that time, then I can keep working without his ever knowing."

"Well occupied between the hours of eleven and nine," Quin mused. He grinned lazily at Jaqueline. "Now—I wonder who in heaven could manage that?"

"You Irish bastard!" Shelby came up out of his chair with one swift shove. "Just what do you mean to imply by that comment?"

Quin looked startled. "Nothing whatsoever, my lord. It was just an idle speculation."

"Then I'll thank you to keep your eyes off my—off of Lady Jaqueline when you're making insinuations."

"Really, Shelby," Jaqueline said. "You do not have to defend my honor, my dear. You never did so when we were married."

Shelby turned away sharply, resuming his stare out the window. "Of course," he snapped. "I forget myself. Do forgive me. Call her a sailors' doxy if you damn well please, Major. I'm sure it's no business of mine."

Merlin looked from one to another with knitted eyebrows. She blinked at Jaqueline. "Is there really something you could do to engage Ransom all night?"

Jaqueline laughed softly. She took Merlin's hand and gave it a motherly pat. "Nothing another woman could not do."

"Oh," Merlin said. "Oh, you mean . . . *that*."

"Quite."

Merlin touched her lower lip. "I don't think I care for that idea." She chewed her nail, trying to imagine Ransom lying in bed with someone else, touching some other as he had touched and caressed and loved her. She twisted the schedule in her hand. "I don't think I care for that idea at all."

"Guileless child!" Jaqueline said. "But about me, dearest Merlin, you must not concern yourself. The duke and I are not at all likely to become lovers. He's far too toplofty and I'm far too spoiled for that."

For once, Merlin found herself rather glad of Ransom's toploftiness. She said diffidently, "Do you have any other ideas, then?"

Quin stood up and sauntered over to the door. He bent and examined the engraved brass lockbox and shining knob. "As for breakin' into the ballroom—by my sainted mother's blood, you may consider that problem as good as solved."

"I might have guessed you'd be a lock-pick!" Shelby exclaimed, swinging around to face them. "Why the devil is a rogue like you hanging about the Mount, anyway?"

"You owe me money, my dear fellow. If you will re-call."

"Oh, I do, do I?" Shelby retorted sharply. "The world's full of my duns, but they don't all haunt my house and call me their 'dear fellow,' by God!"

Merlin blinked, taken aback by the sudden transfor-mation of Shelby from his usual amicable self into a man who looked rather dangerously aware of the consequence due to him. Quin inclined his head in instant submission.

"Allow me to apologize if I've been overly familiar, my lord."

"Too damned familiar by half. I suggest you take your insolence elsewhere!"

Quin kept his eyes focused on the floor near Shelby's boots. "Forgive me, my lord, but I'm not here at your invitation."

Shelby snorted. "What, am I supposed to swallow the notion that my brother wants you here? I find that un-likely in the extreme, but if he should do, I'm quite will-ing to convince him otherwise."

"My lord." Quin lifted his eyes. His usual cocky grin had vanished, and he looked more serious than Merlin had ever seen him. "Accept my humblest apology. I've over-stepped my place."

Shelby grimaced and swung his arm in an impatient gesture. "Oh, for the love of God, you'll gag us all on this sudden syrup. You won't do yourself any good hang-ing about here, for I haven't a feather to fly with now and well you know it. Just take yourself off."

"My lord—" Quin took an unsteady breath. He pressed his lips together. His green eyes left Shelby and rested an instant on Jaqueline.

Shelby stiffened visibly. He looked at Jaqueline. She was stroking one slim finger across the back of another with every evidence of intense interest in the operation.

"Oh, of course!" Shelby threw his hands wide in a mock bow. "Why ever didn't I guess? He's here at *your* invitation, is he, my lady Jaqueline? My apologies again. My profound regrets for thinking to spoil your *af-faire*—"

"Shelby," Jaqueline said. She made the barest sketch of a warning movement with her hand in the direction where Woodrow stood silently near Merlin, drinking in every word with his grave and wide-eyed attention.

Shelby drew in a savage breath. He shut his mouth.

"Miss Merlin," Woodrow said after a moment. "It will have to be me who helps you. All they are going to do is argue, I think."

Merlin nodded. "Yes. I can see that!"

Shelby, Jaqueline, and Quin all began to find something singularly interesting about the walls, the ceiling, and the floor. "Now, darling," Jaqueline said at last, "you know we only nip—"

A gasp from Mr. Peale interrupted her. "He didn't stutter!" the reverend exclaimed. "The boy didn't stutter!"

Woodrow turned scarlet. "I da-da-da . . . I . . . yes, I'm sa-sa . . . *sure* I da-da-did, sir."

"You blockhead," Shelby said to Mr. Peale.

The reverend's mouth fell open. "I beg your pardon, my lord, but I'm certain—"

"No one gives a fig for what you're certain of," Shelby snapped. "I can't fathom what my brother is thinking, to have the bunch of you in residence! A bigger collection of gudgeons and loose screws I've never—"

"But that is the answer, of course!" Jaqueline sat up, smoothing her skirt. "If we wish to distract the duke, we have nothing to do but convene without dear Merlin's flying machine to occupy us. The shouting alone must be enough to drown out her construction noise."

Chapter 11

"Have another blueberry muffin, Miss Lambourne?"

Merlin started awake, to find the muffin already on her breakfast plate. Ransom offered the butter dish, watching her from beneath lazy eyelids.

Merlin cleared her throat, blinking rapidly. "Yes, please," she said, unable to muster a refusal on short notice.

"Did you have a restless night?" he asked mildly.

It was not one sleepless night, but weeks of them that made her eyelids so impossibly heavy. She broke the muffin and buttered a bite of the steaming bread without answering.

"Excuse me, Miss Lambourne," the duke said. "Perhaps you didn't hear my question? I asked if you had not slept well."

Merlin and Woodrow exchanged looks over the delicate green and yellow porcelain flowers that adorned the lid of the Meissen chocolate pot. She should have known Ransom would not allow it to pass. A "social solecism," he would call it, taking her to task in that abominably pleasant way of his for not responding to a civil inquiry. After ten days of her new regime, she recognized the signs.

"Forgive me," she said with a trace of belligerence. "It must have been that the full moon kept me awake."

"Ah. You didn't think to draw the bedcurtains?"

She shifted uncomfortably in her chair. "No. I didn't." She set her lower lip, staring mulishly at the crystal that sparkled in the morning sun. She might have liked these leisurely breakfasts, sitting at a small table in the pretty cornflower-blue room and listening to the pleasant, unruffled tones of Ransom's conversation about everything from the weather to Bonaparte's military strategies to the duke's plans for refurbishing some abandoned lodge on the far edge of the estate. Instead, working on three hours' sleep, stuffed with His Grace's idea of a proper breakfast and feeling the cool morning breeze drifting through the open windows, she always found herself unbearably drowsy in the long minutes while awaiting dismissal.

He did it on purpose, she was sure, pouring himself more coffee and sipping it with maddening slowness. He asked Woodrow about his lessons in that agreeable, interested way—as if it were only idle chatter, when both she and Woodrow knew that the boy was being grilled and his progress measured with merciless accuracy. It always made poor Woodrow stutter so that he could hardly finish a phrase, but Ransom seemed to have infinite patience to wait while his nephew stammered out an answer in complete and coherent sentences.

Merlin thought she would have found some way to escape this torture, except that Woodrow was so pathetically glad to have her there. Not that she ever protected him—not that Ransom ever scolded the boy or even said a cross word—but she well knew that a third person was a welcome buffer to the potent focus of Ransom's interest.

"Yes," the duke was saying in response to some description of Woodrow's Latin lesson. "And that is the root of the word *astral,* of course."

"And as-*tronomy*," Woodrow said, wrapping his tongue around the word with painful effort.

Ransom nodded. "A subject Miss Lambourne undoubtedly finds fascinating."

Merlin sat up straighter, catching this signal that she was expected to participate. Woodrow, well-drilled in his lessons on polite conversation, addressed his next comment to her. "Do you know our family's ma-ma-ma-motto, Ma-Ma-Ma . . . *Miss* Lambourne?"

"No," Merlin said, obediently taking her turn. "I don't believe that I do."

"*Ad as-ta-ta-ta.* . . . *as-tra pa-pa-per aspera,*" Woodrow said.

Merlin hesitated a moment, searching out the words from the stammer. Then she broke into a surprised smile. "*Ad astra per aspera.* 'To the stars by hard ways'! Oh, I like that. I like that very much. Perhaps I'll make that my motto, too."

"No, you ca-ca-ca-can't, I don't think. It ba-ba . . . *belongs* to us, don't it, Uncle?"

" 'Does it not,' " Ransom corrected.

"Does it not," Woodrow repeated. "I'm sa-sa-sa . . . sorry."

"I think I should be able to adopt it as a motto if I like," Merlin challenged before Ransom could have a chance to get back to the subject.

He slanted a look toward her. "As you please."

"No," Woodrow protested. "It's on our ca-ca-coat of arms and everything. How ca-ca-can it be our ma-ma-ma-motto, then, if sa-sa . . . *some*one from another family ca-ca-can have it?"

"I see your point." Ransom took a sip of coffee, using both hands to lift the old-fashioned doubled-handled cup. "I'm sorry, Miss Lambourne. It seems you'll have to be content with the Lambourne motto."

"I don't even know the Lambourne motto!"

"I don't believe I recall it, either. But I saw a coat of arms above your front door, did I not?"

"I don't know. I never looked."

His mouth curled a little. "I suppose if you don't remember it is there, we can't expect you to remember what is on it, can we?"

"No," she said, with equal dignity. "I don't suppose you can. I think it's something silly, though. Like *Semper fidelis.*"

"A proud motto. What could be wrong with that?"

"It doesn't mean anything. 'Always faithful' to what?"

"The country, the crown . . . your family. Any number of worthy causes."

"Hmmpf," Merlin said. "*Your* motto, now—that is quite inspiring. One wishes to fly to the stars, of course, and one knows it won't be easy."

"Say instead—impossible."

"Hmmpf," Merlin said again.

"You are in a pugnacious mood this morning, Miss Lambourne." The little curl at the corner of Ransom's mouth grew more pronounced. "Are you certain you're sleeping well? Everything in your bedchamber is quite satisfactory?"

The only thing wrong with Merlin's bedchamber was that she hadn't been in it enough. But much progress had been made in her secret nocturnal employments: the new joints had been set in the flying machine and the frame restrung with aluminium wire. The wings folded down now and tucked in just like a sleeping bird's. She was almost ready for a test, if she could contrive to have a window removed from the ballroom front—not exactly something she could hope Ransom would fail to notice.

Woodrow, seeing that the conversation was taking a dangerous turn toward Merlin's nighttime activities, waited just long enough for her to answer with a flustered, "Oh, yes! Quite satisfactory!" before he sought to distract Ransom from further questions on that subject.

"Uncle Damerell," he said. "Ca-ca-ca . . . *could* Ma-Ma-Miss Lambourne ma-ma-make up a change to her own ma-ma-ma-motto? Then pa-pa . . . *perhaps* she would like it ba-ba-ba . . . more."

"I have another proposal." Over his double-handled cup, Ransom lifted one eyebrow in Merlin's direction. "Marry me, Miss Lambourne, and my home, my title, and even my family motto are all yours."

Woodrow's eyes grew round. "Oh, yes!" he exclaimed. "Oh, yes, Uncle. What a ca-ca-capital notion! Then she ca-ca-ca . . . *could* live here all the—" He caught Merlin's appalled look and stammered, "Oh! Um—I meant . . . that is . . . I sup-pa-pose it isn't such a ga-ga-ga-good idea."

Merlin glanced apprehensively at Ransom, afraid he would see something suspicious in the boy's sudden reversal of opinion. Instead, Ransom's swift look toward Woodrow held another emotion entirely. "Woodrow—" His voice was sharp with emphatic concern. He set down his cup and reached over to grip the boy's hand. "You musn't think, because your parents have had such difficulties, that every marriage must necessarily be so."

Blood rushed to Woodrow's face under his uncle's penetrating frown. He opened his mouth, but all that came out was a collection of meaningless syllables. Before either Merlin or Ransom could say anything, the boy tore his hand away and pushed his chair back. It fell over with a wooden thump. Scrambling up from the floor with a new rush of "Ohs!" and "I-I-I-" and a sadly tattered "Sa-sa-sa-so sa-sa-sa-sorry!," Woodrow clutched his hands together and pulled them apart and fled the room.

The door slammed shut behind him, leaving Ransom and Merlin in silence.

Softly, Ransom said, "Damn."

Merlin had no answer for that. She blinked at the door, and then looked at the man next to her.

He put his hand over his eyes, massaging the bridge of his nose. His broad shoulders sank a little. "What did I do?" he asked.

Merlin had an idea, but it did not seem possible to tell him that the full intensity of his undivided attention, focused on such a tender subject as Woodrow's parents, was enough to send the timid boy into rout. She just shook her head.

Ransom tapped slowly at the handle of his cup, his long, steady fingers a contrast to the delicate porcelain. "I am doing my best, you know." He stared at his hand. "I'm doing my damnedest to bring him up."

Merlin kept her gaze on an innocuous bowl full of vivid pink and purple sweetpea blossoms. A wisp of breeze played with the petals.

"Why, for instance," he asked pensively, "isn't he afraid of you?"

She shrugged self-consciously. "I'm no one to be afraid of."

He frowned, his hard features growing even more intimidating. Merlin tucked in her chin. She fiddled with the corner of her napkin, watching a dull-coated little songbird that hopped along the windowsill.

"Then why the devil am *I*?"

His demand burst in the quiet room. Merlin started. She looked at him out of the corner of her eye. "Because," she said logically, "you're scary!"

A look of affronted disbelief came over his face. "I am not!"

"Oh, yes, you are."

He tossed his napkin on the table. "Nonsense. Do I eat children? Do I have horns and a tail?"

She met the ruthless golden-green eyes glowering at her from beneath a frowning slash of brows. "Well," she said, "you certainly have an alarming way of looking at a person!"

"That is the purest piece of rubbish—" he began. Then his scowl dissolved into an arrested expression. Merlin watched in fascination as his face transformed from its habitual cool intensity to a sudden grin. "Ah, yes," he said. "The Doomsday Look. A Falconer tradition."

She made a face. "Every day must be Doomsday in the Falconer family, then."

"Of course not. I only—" He looked at her. "Am I really so daunting?"

She nodded.

He worried his lower lip between his fingers. The brief moment of lightness faded into his usual cool intensity as he sat lost in thought and staring at her as if she were something midway between a particularly vexing conundrum and a bedbug.

"See?" she said.

"See what?"

"You're doing it now."

" 'It'?"

She picked up a silver platter, dumped the last crumbs of muffin onto her plate, and held it up before his nose. "There. Now do you see how you look? Hatchet-faced!"

For a long moment he was silent. At last from behind the platter he said in a strangely uneven voice, "Wiz?"

She peeked around it. "Yes?"

"*Please* marry me." He caught her wrist and drew the platter aside. "I need a dose of absurdity every morning at breakfast for the rest of my life."

His Doomsday frown had vanished. He was smiling at her in a way that made her throat feel squishy and peculiar. "Well," she said, and then couldn't think of anything else.

"I've never asked you properly, have I?" He kept hold of her wrist, and to her horror drew very close as he rose from his chair and set the platter aside. He went down on one knee at her feet. He bent over her hand so that all she could see of him was the powerful, elegant breadth of his shoulders and the thick brown hair brushed into merciless neatness. "Miss Lambourne—" She could feel his breath, warm on her fingers. "Pray do me the honor of becoming my wife."

"Oh," she squeaked. "Please get up!"

He let go of her hand and straightened, still bracing one knee on the floor. "Why, that was a most proper thing to say! I do believe you've read this book."

"No, I haven't. What book? Don't look at me like that!"

"What, am I being hatchet-faced?" He was still smiling up at her with a warmth that made her breathe too fast to think. "Save me, Wiz. I don't want to become a stiff-rumped old man."

Merlin's eyes widened, and she was tilting her head to survey the threatened part when he rose and pulled her up with him, backing away with a dancer's move and holding her so that she could only see the front of him. "Oh, no—none of your verbatim interpretations. I was speaking metaphorically, my dear."

Merlin touched her upper lip with her tongue. Ransom drew her closer, clasping her hands against his chest. She could feel the spark flare between them, see the quick blaze of passion in those eyes which had regarded her so coolly. He did not look cold now, but alive with feeling. His lips were full and curving in warm promise, his lashes half-closed in anticipation.

Very slowly, he lowered his head and skimmed her cheek, his skin smooth against hers: a tender, hot searching until he found her lips.

Deep in her throat, Merlin made a small humming note of accord. She opened her lips to his, her hands tightening over his clasped fingers. The morning breeze skipped and played around her skirts, blowing a stray wisp of her hair across their cheeks.

Ransom drew away and brushed it back, tucking it behind her ear. "Merlin," he whispered. "Marry me . . . marry me. I want you. It's been forever. I'm tired of stolen kisses in the breakfast room."

She looked up at him hazily. Always, this was tugging at the back of her mind, overwhelming her concentration, drawing her toward him on a relentless string. "I don't know," she mumbled. "Perhaps I—"

He waited. She traced the firm lines of his face with a dazzled gaze: the shape of his jaw and the decisive planes of his forehead and cheeks. There was nothing indefinite about him. Nothing soft or forgiving, but only this compelling power entwined and leashed in her hands.

"Merlin," he said, with laughing frustration in his voice. He twisted his hand free and caught her chin. "Finish your sentence, love. Like this. Yes"—he moved her pliant jaw up and down—"yes, yes, yes!" He kissed her nose. "Yes, I will marry you, Mr. Duke."

"But I—" She closed her eyes as he slid his palm behind her neck and bent to kiss her ear. "Oh, I . . . What were you . . . saying?"

"Wiz," he murmured in her ear as he rocked her. "Just one little word. One little yes, and I won't have to spend every blessed night staring at the damned canopy, going mad thinking about how you'd feel in my arms."

He chuckled, his breath a hot tickle in her ear. "Do you know what's embroidered on the underside of my canopy? The Falconer coat of arms. *Ad astra per aspera*, Merlin. Say yes. Marry me, and not only will it be yours, but you can read it every night of your life."

She drew back a little. A thought tugged at the back of her sluggish mind. "Every night?"

"Every night. All night." He nibbled her earlobe. "In your spare time."

Merlin stiffened. Her eyes flew open. "What?"

He smiled down at her lazily. "Never mind, Wiz. Concentrate on the question."

But whatever question he meant was lost in the ominous phrases that rang in her mind. *Every night. All night. In your spare time.*

"I can't!" She pushed her way out of his arms. "I can't possibly stay with you all night!"

He let her go. For a moment he stood looking at her. His eyes that had been golden and warm went slowly to arctic indifference. "I see," he said.

Merlin sincerely hoped that he did not. She regarded him warily.

He took a step away from her, grasping the scrolled and gilded cresting-rail that adorned the top of the caned-back chair. "Well. That does not affect my offer, of course. You would naturally have a bedchamber of your own. Although I desire an heir, I assure you I would not wish to impose upon your privacy any longer than necessary."

She looked up at him. "Necessary for what?"

His frown deepened into terrifying intensity. "I think if you put your mind to it, Miss Lambourne, you will recall the incident which occurred between us on the night that we met."

"Oh," Merlin said.

"I wish to marry you in any case, of course, since I've placed you in such a—such an untenable position. But I would like children, if you would not consider it too much of an imposition."

"Oh, no, I—I've quite come to like Woodrow. And the girls." She paused, and then added generously, "Even if there are two of them."

He looked down at his hand. His fingers tightened around the rail. "That runs in the family, you know. Twins. My first wife . . . there were twins . . ." He seemed to lose track of his thought and looked up. "But they died, you see," he said in a brusque tone. "We shall not dwell on that."

Merlin's mouth fell open. "You mean you've already *had* a wife?"

"Yes."

A little flare of jealousy sprang into her heart. "And why did you marry *her?* Was she in an untenable position?"

"Certainly not."

"Then why—"

"My grandfather arranged it. She was nothing but a child herself."

"Whereas *you* have always been an adult."

He looked at her sharply. Merlin became aware that she was clenching and unclenching her hands. She clasped them tightly together behind her back.

"I don't carry the willow for her, Merlin, if that is what disturbs you. I hardly had time to know her. She caught a chill which went to rheumatic fever shortly before her lying-in. It was a long time ago, Wiz. A very long time."

She bent her head and dropped a curtsy. "Please may I be dismissed?"

"Prettily done," he said dryly. "You've learned Woodrow's lessons better than he has. For God's sake, Merlin, you don't need my permission to leave the room."

"I don't?"

"Of course not. Woodrow is a child. You're a guest here."

"I thought I was a prisoner."

He gripped the back of his chair and smiled at her. "Merlin, I warn you. I am on the verge of losing my temper."

"Well, it doesn't make a bit of sense to me. If I'm not a prisoner, why do I have to eat breakfast with you and take riding lessons with you and do everything you say? Nobody else but Woodrow has to do so!"

"I told you. I wish you to learn how to go on in the world." He swept his arm out. "Do you think we go through all these exercises in polite conversation merely so that I can have the opportunity to exercise my tongue?"

Although that was exactly what Merlin did think, she decided in the face of his glower that it might be better not to say so.

"It has a purpose, Merlin. Woodrow must be able to talk sensibly to anyone, about anything, and it won't hurt you to learn to do so, either. If I sometimes ask difficult questions and expect a sharp answer, I have my reasons. This family doesn't languish in obscurity, Miss Lambourne, and neither will my nephew. It's not impossible that one day the fate of the Empire may ride on how well Woodrow can marshal his words and use his wits."

Merlin chewed her lip, dismayed at the idea of poor Woodrow with the fate of the Empire weighing on his slender shoulders. "Oh, dear. I'm afraid he may stammer rather dreadfully in that case."

"I'm speaking of the future. He will overcome the stammer."

"Oh, no. I've spoken to him about it. He's certain that it will afflict him always."

Ransom shrugged. "Nevertheless, I believe that he will conquer it."

This callousness brought a surge of protective anger to Merlin's breast. "I don't think you will be able to terrify him out of it with these awful lessons in conversation, if that is what you hope!"

"No, that is not what I hope, Miss Lambourne," he snapped. "I expect him to surmount the difficulty himself."

"But perhaps that isn't possible."

"It is quite possible, I assure you."

"What if it isn't? How do you know? Perhaps you think you know everything, Mr. Duke, but you can't possibly know how it feels to try to speak and have only a string of nonsense syllables come out of your mouth!''

"On the contrary," he said. His expression was impassive. "I know exactly how it feels."

Merlin blinked.

He said steadily, "I stammered. Until I was one and twenty years old."

She stared at him. Ransom—self-possessed, arrogant, autocratic Ransom. She could not conceive . . . In a small voice, she repeated, "You did?"

He nodded.

Merlin sat down, gazing up at him. "I can't imagine that."

He shrugged. "I don't wish you to do so. I only speak of it so that you won't encourage Woodrow to wallow in self-pity. I wish you will keep the confidence to yourself."

She stood up. There was a lump forming in the back of her throat which somehow made it imperative that she remove herself from Ransom's company as quickly as possible. "Oh, yes. Of course. But I must go now, Or I—I won't have time to change for riding!" She went as far as the door, and then paused with her hand on the knob. She glanced back at Ransom.

He stood there, looking just as he always looked: at ease, tall and elegant and impassive, with his hand resting on the rail of the chair. There was a large gold signet on his third finger. She noticed it for the first time because the skin around it was tight and flushed, and his knuckles showed dead-white against the metal and the ebony wood.

Merlin let go of the doorknob. She ran lightly across the room and slipped her hand over his, sliding her fingers beneath his palm to pull it free. She bent over and brushed a warm kiss above the gold signet. Then, because she didn't have a reason why or an answer to a question if he asked, she turned away without meeting his eyes and hurried out of the room.

Chapter 12

Ransom lounged in a wing chair in a secluded corner of the Godolphin Saloon, listening to Blythe playing the pianoforte for a group of houseguests gathered at the far side of the room. He stared at the back of his right hand. Behind him, Shelby and Jaqueline began the after-dinner bickering that seemed to have become a recent habit of theirs. He flexed his fingers, watching the candlelight move across his signet ring. It mellowed and warmed the gold, and made him think of the way the same light had caressed the curve of Merlin's cheek as she'd sat dutifully on the settee opposite him until a few moments earlier.

"Mamá," he said quietly, making sure the light, tinkling notes of Blythe's music would obscure his words from the other guests. "Do you think Miss Lambourne is ill?"

The Duchess May lifted her head from a book of Oriental poetry. "Why, no, dear," she said comfortably. "I don't believe I think that."

"She doesn't look as well as she did when she came here."

"Does she not?" Duchess May glanced around, her nose tilted up to support her spectacles, which gave her the appearance of a Blenheim spaniel testing the breeze. "Oh, she's gone up to bed already, hasn't she? Well, I daresay you would be the one to know, my love, if her looks were to go into a decline."

171

Ransom took a sip of port. "I fear—" He stopped, not quite ready to give his fears so concrete an expression as to say them aloud. He settled for: "It seems she isn't resting well."

His mother gave him a keen look. "And how are you resting, Damerell? You look a bit peaked yourself. I don't make a secret of it—I've always thought you would be more comfortable if you were to move out of those draft-ridden state chambers and into a cozy suite upstairs."

"I'm perfectly well, and you know it. It is Miss Lambourne who concerns me." He frowned into his glass. In a very low voice, he said, "You've never asked me why she is here, but you must have guessed that I'm forced to keep her—against her will, more or less. I'm doubly responsible for her. If she were to become ill . . ."

Again he left the sentence unfinished. Duchess May closed her book and laid it on the side table. She reached over and touched his hand. "What would you like me to do?"

Ransom lifted his eyes, grateful that she didn't question his motive. "Might you look in on her? Tonight."

She tilted her head. There was no emotion he could detect in the golden-green eyes that matched his own. On the other side of the room, Shelby made a sarcastic snipe at Jaqueline, and she instantly returned the comment with a well-aimed barb. Blythe increased the volume of her playing in a vain effort to cover their words.

The duchess glanced in that direction. "We *are* a civilized family, aren't we, Damerell?"

Ransom's mouth tightened. "Have no fear. I'll stay and see to it that no blood is spilled on the carpet."

"I believe they enjoy it," she said.

Ransom lifted his eyebrow, watching his younger brother launch into a tirade on Jaqueline's old circle of admirers. ". . . a bigger pack of scoundrels I've never seen," Shelby was exclaiming, his voice quite clear over Blythe's playing.

"This is nonsense you speak," Jaqueline snapped, her lovely face animated with color as she arched her brows and stared up at him. "Not old Coudry and Mr. Kettering?"

"Hah!" Shelby took a pace away from her and whirled back with a theatrical move that would have done Jaqueline herself justice. "What of that Italian devil, and—whatever was the ruffian's name—ah, yes . . . Winterbourne! Those two rascals ran tame in the drawing room, my lady. You won't deny it."

"I will! I do not even remember them, those two."

Shelby stopped his melodramatic pacing. "Among so many," he sneered. "What else could I expect?"

"Perhaps if you had *been* there, my lord, you might have seen there were not so many."

Blythe came to the end of her piece. Shelby flushed, and his voice carried with utter clarity throughout the room. "And when I was there, what did I hear? Endless questions. Where had I been? What was I doing? Who was I with? It was enough to drive any man out onto the street."

"If you had cared, you would not have gone," Jaqueline cried. "You would not have spent this time in gaming and—"

Blythe launched into a vigorous country tune. Ransom started to rise. He always intervened at this point, when the skirmish—which always seemed cattily playful when they began it—started to grow serious. Then he stayed near for the rest of the evening and deep into the night, playing referee, keeping them from one another's throats when they stubbornly showed no sign of a cease-fire. It was some strange phase in their turbulent relationship, he supposed—that since they had actually begun to speak to each other again they seemed compelled to air their soiled laundry in public this way. He would have thought they'd had enough of notoriety.

His mother caught his arm as he rose. "No," she said softly. "Do not interfere."

Ransom cast her a questioning frown. The Falconer name had already been dragged through the mud in Shelby's divorce. He could not believe his mother would approve of this renewed bitterness before her guests.

"And what else was I to do?" Shelby demanded above the bright, brittle sound of Blythe's rendition of the *schottische*. "Knowing I had no way to provide for you as I wished to do?"

"Lies, lies! Lies and excuses. You know you will not stop. You would never stop. Don't tell me that you gambled for me, for your family! Have you stopped it now? Now that your brother takes in the children that are yours? Now that *he* pays for your responsibilities?"

Ransom went still for an instant, not daring to look openly toward his brother. He busied himself with lighting another candle. Blythe gave up trying to cover the combat with music and rose, closing the keyboard and drawing the cloth over the pianoforte.

"Lady Harding," she exclaimed, approaching the matron whose ears had been pricked the hardest. "How *could* I have forgotten that just this morning dear Mr. Winston told me he so wished to have a game of chess with you! And here is the board—" She gestured to a pallid young gentleman, who quickly erased his sly smile. "If you would just move this table a bit closer to the fire, sir. It does grow chilly in the evenings even in the summer, does it not?"

Ransom glanced toward his brother. Shelby was standing over Jaqueline, talking in rapid, low tones. He had an unpleasant look on his face.

"Let me get you that volume of Tacitus that you were wishing for, Miss Montagu," Blythe said. "Mr. Lansdun shall read it to you, won't you, my dear? You have such a grasp of the classical historians."

The argument began to escalate again, and Jaqueline's voice carried over Blythe's in notes of vibrant passion. "I don't believe it! Never a moment's thought did you give to us!"

"That's not true, Jaqueline. Constantly, I swear it—" Shelby made a violent move with his hand. "But you wouldn't understand. You never try."

"Understand? What is there to understand about a man who gambles away his wife's inheritance—"

"A game of whist!" Blythe cried, as if the thought had struck her with blinding force. "That would be just the thing." She bustled about announcing that more card tables were being set up in the library. With her officious hospitality, a trait for which—for once—Ransom blessed her, she herded the rest of the unoccupied guests out of the saloon.

"You don't understand," Shelby said. "I was winning. You might have had half of Sheridan's Drury Lane!"

"And instead, he has *all* of *my* theater!"

Ransom nodded to several guests as they passed him, declining to join in a foursome. He kept his smile pleasant, refusing to acknowledge the existence of the quarrel that raged behind them.

"I'm sorry for that," Shelby said. His voice went lower, almost lost in the sound of Mr. Lansdun clearing his throat and beginning to read. "Oh, God, you don't know how sorry—"

Ransom closed the door to the library. He looked at his mother, a silent question, asking leave to put a stop to it. The duchess only smiled at him.

Jaqueline cried, "Sorry!" She stood up. Mr. Lansdun read louder. "Sorry," she hissed, a sound which carried even better than her normal voice. "You ruin my life; you gamble away my fortune, you set me aside for another woman. For this, I will never forgive you. Never."

They stood glaring at one another like Apollo and Diana—magnificent even amidst the wreckage. In the sudden silence, Mr. Lansdun's voice trailed off.

Shelby never took his eyes from Jaqueline. "I gamble," he said softly, "and I lost what was yours, and for that I will be ashamed until the day I die. But the rest . . . as for the rest: that I was false and unfaithful and put another in your place . . ." His finely shaped lips drew taut in an expression Ransom had only seen on them once, in a courtroom, in the defendant's chair six years before. "Jaqueline, there is one thing that I, too, can never forgive. You believed it."

He turned away, kicking the pianoforte's bench aside with a scrape of wood that rang in the quiet room. When the echo of the closing door subsided, Ransom turned to the shocked faces of Miss Montagu, Mr. Lansdun, and the chess players. "Pray continue, Mr. Lansdun," he said. "I'm afraid it appears that the second act will be postponed."

Amidst the others' uncertain smiles, Jaqueline gave him a look which would have done more credit to Othello than Desdemona in its violence. It lasted only an instant, and it was for Ransom alone. Then she shrugged and widened her lovely eyes at the huddle of guests. "Forgive me," she said with utter calm. "Have I disturbed your reading?"

Mr. Lansdun cleared his throat. "Indeed not, I—we were just preparing to begin."

Jaqueline gave him a spellbinding smile. "Then I will join you."

Ransom placed a chair for her. Just as she settled in with a liquid look toward Mr. Lansdun, the saloon door opened again. Blythe entered with Quin strolling behind her, a glass of port balanced between his first two fingers as he held the door.

"And where," he was saying, "would your fine Mr. Peale be languishin' at present?"

Blythe looked flustered, but she nodded at Mr. Lansdun, who had interrupted his reading once again. "Pray go on, Mr. Lansdun," she said. She pulled her hand away from where Quin had caught her fingers to detain her. "Mr. Peale prefers to do his daily meditation and devotions after dinner, I understand."

"Most obligin' of him." He smiled and touched Blythe's cheek, a move which turned into a mock-bow when she drew back in affront. "To leave the field clear."

"*Major* O'Shaughnessy," Blythe said in a tone which Ransom thought ought to be enough to give any man pause.

The major only slanted a look toward her, his eyes green and mischievous. "Dear lady?"

"I expect"—her small bosom rose—"to be addressed in a proper manner, Major O'Shaughnessy!"

"Dear Lady Blythe?" Quin revised.

Ransom started to look away, and then glanced back at his sister, mildly surprised to note that she was, in high looks tonight. Her rage at Quin's impudence seemed to lend color and an unfamiliar sparkling snap to her pale blue eyes, and the way she was pursing her lips made them look soft and full.

Not that it would do the fellow any good. Quin might be able to take the heat, but he wasn't going to get any nourishment from that particular kitchen.

Unfortunately, Ransom's candidate didn't seem to be doing much better. Ransom wondered, irritably, why Peale had taken to wandering off after dinner instead of engaging in a little judicious flirting. Ransom hoped the reverend wasn't stupid enough to be put off his stride by Quin's outrageous brand of lovemaking. Anyone could see that the handsome officer was only amusing himself— probably even had some guineas resting on whether he could coax a smile out of Bloodless Blythe.

Ransom wouldn't put it past Shelby to have taken the major up smartly on odds as long as that. Blood 'n' hounds, Ransom thought with an inner grin, he would have laid fifty pounds on that wager himself.

Duchess May appeared silently at Ransom's side. "I shall go to see to Miss Lambourne now," she murmured.

He looked down at her. "Thank you," he said.

She squeezed his hand, which touched an absurd soft place inside of him. It was a shame, he thought as he watched her leave, that his sister had not inherited any of that wise, feminine warmth that their mother had in such lively abundance. But Blythe—first-born—lusted after greater things than a daughter's place. If there was not real bitterness in her over the accident of her sex, it was only because she lived the Duke of Damerell's life as nearly as possible through her constant intrusion into Ransom's affairs.

"I've found a new rose in the garden, dear lady," Quin said, and then added belatedly, "Blythe!" when she gave him an icy glance. "Come walkin' with me tomorrow in the morning, and show it to you I will."

Blythe turned partially away, as if to move around him. "Thank you, but I expect it will rain in the morning, Major O'Shaughnessy."

"In the afternoon, then."

She looked impatiently beyond his broad shoulder. "I fear I shall be quite busy tomorrow afternoon."

He opened his mouth as if to press her again. Before the coaxing words emerged, he caught Ransom's steady observation. The look held between them an instant, and then Quin glanced away with a wry lift of his brow. Message taken. Ransom watched as the other man made a polite expression of his everlasting disappointment and moved back, allowing Blythe free passage past him.

Quin scanned the room and sauntered over to Ransom. "Good evenin', Your Grace."

Ransom inclined his head.

"The room seems thin of company tonight."

"Miss Lambourne has gone up to bed."

The officer glanced at Ransom. His green eyes narrowed in acknowledgment. "Yes. I keep good track of *her*, of that you may be sure."

"I'm relieved. There are so many . . . distractions here about."

Quin maintained his impudent grin, though there was a dark flush at his collar. He took a gulp of brandy. "I'm after missin' my Lord Shelby tonight. Has he retired so soon?"

"A few minutes past."

Quin sighed. "And so—am I deprived of all recreation this evening?" He looked toward the library door with a disgusted expression. "By the Powers, not even a hand of whist to be had for more than ha'penny a point!"

Ransom half-smiled, amused in spite of himself at the incorrigible character of Quin O'Shaughnessy. He gave a thought to what the real man might be like, and what combination of temperament and duty would bring him to this work, which most of his fellow officers thought debased beyond comprehension. Ransom held no such prejudices, but neither was he naive. Just as any loyal soldier might prove a coward under fire, so might a man who worked secretly for one side be "persuaded" to work secretly for another. Castlereagh had sent Quin, and Ransom would trust him just that far . . . which was considerably farther than he would trust any other untried agent.

After a final swallow of port, a manufactured yawn, and another rueful lift of his eyebrows, Quin wandered off, flirting with Jaqueline for a few minutes before he let himself out of the room. Ransom frowned a moment later when his brother's former wife rose and made her excuses—and drifted through the door after Quin.

"It's no use," Merlin said, tossing the tangle of wires and metal back in the wooden box. "It must be exactly the right dimensions. I'll have to dismantle every clock in the house!"

She slumped back against the mantelpiece, staring hopelessly at Mr. Peale and Woodrow, who stared back with no solutions. They all turned sharply at the click of a key from the gloom that hid the ballroom doors. The pages of a book lying open on the floor lifted in a draft. A soft, echoing boom followed as the double doors shut again. There was a collective rustle of relaxation as a golden blob that could only be Shelby's bright mane of hair materialized out of the shadows where candlelight did not reach.

"Dismantling clocks?" he asked, with a brittle-sounding laugh. "Poor Damerell will be fortunate to have a home left by the time you're through, Merlin."

She lifted a handful of metal and let it dribble from her fingers with a mournful tinkle. "I can't find a three-sixty-fourths-inch Vaucanson helical pinion gear," she said tragically.

"No!" Shelby's face lost some of its odd tension as he pressed his forehead in a dramatic gesture. "Are we doomed?"

"Woodrow thought perhaps a clock, or the wind vane in the Great Hall, might have one."

Shelby caught Woodrow and held his forearm across the boy's neck in mock-threat. "Hold there, you band of cutthroats! You can't go about murdering innocent clocks in the dead of night. What if the housekeeper reports the dead bodies?"

Woodrow giggled.

"I'll put them back together," Merlin said indignantly.

"Ah, but will they tell the time?"

Merlin shrugged. "I'm sure they will," she said. "One, at least. I'm not very good at clocks. And I don't see why one house needs so many clocks in any—"

"Sh-sh-*shush!*" Woodrow whispered.

They all looked again toward the ballroom door. It swung slowly open. Merlin stood up straight, clutching her hands together as a single candle appeared, outlining the tiny, upright figure of Duchess May.

"Mamá," Shelby said in soft rue.

"Good evening, Woodrow," the duchess said. "Miss Lambourne. Mr. Peale."

Mr. Peale cleared his throat. Before he could speak, Duchess May glided forward, avoiding the tools and scattered scraps on the floor without even glancing down at them. "Don't disturb yourself, Mr. Peale," she said. "I'm merely looking in."

The four of them just stared at her, caught out in the forbidden ballroom completely red-handed.

She approached Merlin. "Are you feeling quite well, my dear?"

"Oh, yes," Merlin said. "Of course."

The duchess pressed the back of her palm lightly against Merlin's forehead. "Good. I told Ransom so, but he worries for you, you know."

"Will you—Oh—" Merlin wrung her hands. "What will you tell him?"

The older woman smiled. "Why, I shall tell him the truth, dear. You are feeling just the thing. You *are,* are you not?"

"Yes, but—"

"That should be sufficient to ease his mind. Good night, Miss—Or would you give me leave to call you Merlin?"

Merlin dropped an awkward curtsy. "Yes, Duchess May. Please do."

"Thank you. Such a pretty name: Merlin. It makes me think of all sorts of nice things. Good night, Merlin. Sleep well."

She left them and walked silently to the door. Just before she reached it, she stopped and turned. "Is it not past your bedtime, Woodrow?"

"Yes, Ga-Ga-Ga . . . Grandmamá," Woodrow said in a thin voice.

She smiled at him and held the candle out.

He swallowed. With a miserable glance at Merlin, he gathered his nightdress around him and shuffled on slippered feet after the duchess. She stroked his hair briefly, then took his hand and led him through the door.

Shelby rolled his eyes. "A narrow escape."

"Will she tell him?" Merlin gasped.

"No, of course not," Shelby said. "She so much as said so."

"Poor Woodrow," she moaned. "He said they would confine him to his room if anyone found out."

"Well, not Mamá, you may be sure. She don't hold with that sort of thing. She just looks at you"—Shelby made a face—"and you suddenly feel like the scurviest wretch alive."

"I agree that our secret appears to be safe with the duchess," Mr. Peale intoned. "But what of the necessary gear? Let us—"

"An' what gear would that be, me gentle friends?"

Merlin didn't even jump. She was becoming used to Quin's ability to appear silently out of the dark. She brightened hopefully at the resourceful Irishman's entry. "A three-sixty-fourths-inch Vaucanson helical pinion gear."

"Ah," Quin said.

Shelby leaned against the mantel, arms crossed. ''Don't happen to have one on you, do you, old man?''

Quin's green eyes went wide. ''*I*, my lord? I'm just a poor peasant, I am.''

''Oh, but you can *find* things so well,'' Merlin exclaimed. ''There was the bottle-jack you located for me, and that cleverly shaped piece of metal from the fireplace tongs in Lady Blythe's bedroom—''

''Lady Blythe's *bedroom!*'' Mr. Peale stiffened. ''Now see here, Major!''

''She weren't in it at the time, my jewel,'' Quin said. '''Twas a scoutin' mission, merely. On Miss Merlin's account.''

Shelby snorted in disgust. ''Good God. That my brother allows you to slink about the house in such a way absolutely defies comprehension!''

Quin shrugged and smiled sweetly. ''Will you be after askin' him to toss me on me ear, my lord?''

''I did.'' Even in the candlelight, Shelby's reddening was visible. ''And he wouldn't, as you well know.''

''I believe His Grace was quite proper in what he told you, Lord Shelby,'' Mr. Peale admonished. ''You owe Major O'Shaughnessy a gambling debt. For myself, as a student of both the classics and Christian theology, I found the duke's description of Major O'Shaughnessy as your 'nemesis' most intriguing. As His Grace pointed out, retribution for one's sins can sometimes be visited in strange forms.''

''Oh, yes, my brother's a knowing one, ain't he?'' Shelby rolled his eyes. ''I only hope his ingenious sense of humor holds so well when he finds the family jewels gone missing!''

The dull sound of the ballroom door caught their attention again. Jaqueline came to stand by Quin, taking his arm.

''Do you have a three-sixty-fourths-inch Vaucanson helical pinion gear, me dearest?'' he asked, patting her hand and lifting it to his lips.

Jaqueline raised her fine eyebrows. ''A moment. I must have a moment to think.''

"Think an hour, Jaqueline me love." He slipped his arm around her waist and pressed her against him while Shelby turned from red to white. "I'll stay right here to help."

"Never mind," Merlin said glumly. "I know she won't have one. *Nobody* has one. I might as well give up on beating Mr. Pemminey right now."

The Duchess May returned to the saloon after all the other guests had retired. Ransom stood gazing down into the coals of the fire, waiting for her. He looked up at her entry.

"Miss Lambourne is quite in good health," his mother said, seating herself near him.

He stirred at the coals. Long shadows danced across the portraits and heavy draperies. "Is she? You're certain of that?"

"Very certain, my dear."

"Then why—" Ransom began, and left off, staring moodily into the red glow.

"I agree that she seems overly tired. Perhaps she's pining for her home."

He slanted a sharp look toward her. "Did she say so?"

"No. Not to me."

"I suppose you think it is because I've forbidden her that damn—excuse me—that cursed flying machine."

"Yes." She tilted her head. "I believe that might have something to do with her distress."

He stabbed at the charred end of a log, and then thrust the tongs aside with a clatter.

In a quiet voice the duchess added, "It was not the most diplomatic thing you've ever done, Damerell."

"She'll kill herself," he said savagely.

His mother folded her hands and watched him.

"What else should I have done?" he demanded. "I can't send her home—her life would almost certainly be forfeit. I don't need to explain the details for you to believe me when I say so! And this flying machine . . . for God's sake, I've not brought her here for her protection, only to have her break her head with that lunacy."

"I can't really see the difficulty. Why haven't you let her continue her work? Simply forbid her to try to actually fly the thing while she's here."

Ransom thought of the cat's seat, thirty feet above the floor. He repressed a shudder. "It is out of the question. She cannot work on it."

"But eventually she will go home, will she not? You cannot stop her then."

He made a sound of denial deep in his throat.

"You still wish to marry her?"

He looked at her with narrowed eyes. "You know very well that I must."

She lifted her shoulders. "But surely anyone must feel you have done all that is humanly possible to rectify your . . . lapse of honor. You have attempted to fulfill the obligation you incurred as best you can. She has turned you down—more than once, has she not?"

"She is a child. She does not understand."

"Understand what?"

He whirled on her. "How can you ask? She doesn't understand that I've ruined her. That she cannot hope to marry as her station should deserve. That she'll spend her life locked away from good society. In seclusion. As if she were a nun in a damned nunnery, with no prospects of a husband and a family and a future of her own!"

The fire popped softly in the silence.

"Ransom." His mother sighed. "Can you honestly believe it was ever different for her?"

He turned away. "That doesn't matter."

"Ah." Her skirt rustled as she smoothed it in her lap. "You are not often so inexpedient."

"I don't often have a well-bred female's innocence on my conscience."

"No?" she asked with a soft chuckle. "What of the ill-bred ones?"

His lip curled. "Don't mock me. Not over this."

"*Dedeo!*" she murmured.

Ransom realized his fists were clenched. He relaxed them with an effort. "Oh—you yield, do you? Long-suffering duchess. Forgive me," he said. "I don't wish to pull your hair."

"And I should not tease you. You are such an admirable son. I sometimes forget that the offspring of a lion must have claws."

He gave her a rueful, sideways grin. "Do you think I am admirable, Mamá? While I pride myself on my infamy!"

She nodded judiciously. "That would be your grandfather in you. But tell me, Ransom. Are you in love with Miss Lambourne?"

"Am I—" He thrust his hands in his pockets and lifted his eyes to the ceiling. "Oh, it's to be a romance now, is it? Don't be a mooncalf. How could I conceivably be in love with someone like Miss Lambourne?"

"It does seem out of character."

"Extremely so. I haven't been 'in love' with a woman since—"

His mother raised her eyebrows expectantly when he broke off. Ransom cleared his throat and turned back to the fire.

"I know!" the duchess exclaimed when he did not go on. "It was that summer you turned fourteen, was it not? I remember it well. That lovely woman . . . what was her name?"

"Leave off, Mamá. This discussion is nonsense."

"But what was her name? I can't recall . . ."

Ransom scowled down into the fire.

"Oh, this will plague me now all night! I can see her face as if she stood in front of me—so beautiful and calm—"

"Lady Claresta," he snapped. "As if you didn't know full well! It was a schoolboy infatuation, and a monumental coincidence that her daughter is Miss Lambourne, I assure you."

"I'm only trying to understand why you are so determined to marry the poor child," the duchess said reproachfully. "I can't think of a more mismatched couple."

"Certainly it's not because I'm 'in love' with her."

"Then I cannot understand why you are being so stubborn about it."

Ransom drew in a sharp breath and faced his mother. "You want to know why? You truly wish to know?" He threw out his hands in a violent move. "Because your oh-so-admirable son *lusts* after her, that's why. Because I'm going crazy with it. Because I can't work and I can't eat and I can't sleep, and I'm bloody well pushing the end of my endurance! Is that a satisfactory explanation for you?"

But he did not wait for an answer. With his face flaming, he shoved himself away from the fireplace and strode to the door.

A moment before it closed behind him, he heard the duchess murmur in her imperturbable voice, "Really, Ransom. What a topic to bring up with your mother!"

Chapter 13

Merlin was nervous.

She became very foolish when she was nervous. She knew it. She'd tried to tell Shelby that, but he'd just waved his hand and said "Poo!," which was kind but not very reassuring. When she was nervous, her heart did funny things, and it seemed to interfere with the normal processes of her brain.

She and Shelby had agreed to act out their scene in the Great Hall, where Ransom always passed on his return from his morning ride. Merlin had to calculate the time of her morning trek to the Blue Room for breakfast just at nine o'clock, so that she and Shelby and Ransom would all meet in the Great Hall as if by accident.

She was early. She squinted up at the huge clock face imbedded in the stone wall, and hastened back into the side corridor when she heard Ransom's voice, carried from outside on the clear summer air through the open windows. Fortunately, he seemed to be lingering out there, engaged in some conversation with the groom over the shoeing of a favorite hunter.

She chewed on her finger, straining to hear the sound of his footsteps on the stairs. Inside her apron pocket, the hedgehog squirmed. She absently patted the outer fabric, wincing and then sucking her finger when a stray spine pricked through the rough cotton.

To her relief, she heard a ring of hooves in the courtyard, and then Shelby's own voice, raised in morning greeting.

The monumental doors swung open on their silent brass wheels and tracks. Hanging back in the alcove, Merlin peered around the corner. Through the tall window, she could see Shelby vault easily from his bay stallion. He tossed the reins to the groom, who led the animals off.

The brothers mounted the steps and came through the door together, talking horses. Shelby was spinning his top hat on the end of his riding crop. Merlin hesitated with a mental moan of trepidation, and then flung herself forward.

"Ho, there!" Shelby's laughing exclamation echoed in the domed hall as he caught her arm. "Where are you off to in such a hurry, miss?"

Merlin looked up into his blue eyes, and took a deep breath. "Good morning!" she said—the only line she could remember out of all she had rehearsed.

"Good morning," the duke said, removing his hat.

Still caught in Shelby's hold, Merlin met Ransom's faint smile. His deep brown hair was tousled, his golden-green eyes keen beneath the faintly inquiring lift of strong brows. They were brothers, but where Shelby's face was laughing and beautiful, Ransom's face was always a little fierce—handsome and inflexible even in a moment of relaxation.

She managed a nod.

"Ask me where I've been this morning," Shelby suggested gaily—which was what she was supposed to have asked without prompting.

"Oh!" Merlin said. "Oh, yes. Where have you been?"

He reached beneath his coat and drew out a tumbling cascade of colored ribbons. "Buying pretties for the ladies."

Ransom eyed the satin tangle. He tucked his top hat under his arm. "I wondered what could force you out and about so unfashionably early. A new inamorata?"

"Two of 'em!" Shelby rolled his eyes comically. "They're both a bit short for my taste, but a man must keep an eye to the future, y'see."

Ransom grinned. "Aye. Best to bribe that pair into compliance early. You'll have a matching set of diamonds on your hands in a few years.'' He seemed to be in unusual charity with Shelby this morning, and Merlin took heart a little.

"How beautiful,'' she said, poking at the ribbons in Shelby's hand.

His fingers closed over them. He held them away. "Oh, no! I know you females and your love of fripperies. These are already spoken for.''

"Um—'' Merlin twisted her hands together, trying to ignore Ransom's interested gaze. "Are they?''

"Yes, they are. And you needn't look so innocent—I see the covetous light of greed in your eyes, Miss Lambourne!''

"I—uh—I only thought . . . they're very pretty, you see . . . and—well . . . and I thought I might have some for—'' She stumbled to a halt. Oh, what was it she was supposed to want the stupid ribbons for? What *would* one want them for? She stared at them, frowning—but all she could think of was that if she didn't remember, she would lose her chance to escape Mount Falcon with Shelby and purchase a Vaucanson pinion gear. And she'd already fallen another week behind, because Mr. Pemminey's aluminium wire had not been satisfactory at all, and she'd had to take it all down and string catgut again.

"Developing a taste for fashion, Miss Lambourne?'' Ransom gave her an approving smile that made all thoughts of ribbons and gears vanish. "You needn't worry. You shall have as many trimmings as you could wish. I'll have Duchess May's couturiere attend you and the other ladies at tea.'' His keen glance traveled over her, taking in the well-worn skirt and bulging pocket of her apron. "Perhaps she could begin on an entirely new wardrobe for you.''

Merlin opened her mouth and shut it again. That was not at all what he was supposed to say! She looked at Shelby, who—with his face turned away from his brother's—was silently mouthing some instruction. He lifted his hand, moving his eyes rapidly back and forth between Merlin's face and the ribbons.

"Oh! Oh—uh—but *these* . . ." she exclaimed. "I like these."

Ransom waved a dismissive hand. "They're only tinker's goods," he said, and began to walk toward the corridor that led off to the breakfast room. Merlin and Shelby trailed along. "The twins will be delighted with them, but you must have something finer."

Merlin frowned. "I don't want something finer."

"Wait until you've had a chance to compare," he said with an easy confidence that made Merlin want to stamp her foot. "If you order new dresses, you'll want trimmings to match."

"I'd rather have some of these."

"And you shall have them!" Shelby patted her arm. "I'll take you as soon as you've finished breakfast."

"Take her where?" Ransom asked instantly.

"To the tinker."

"There's no need for that." He threw his gloves into his hat and handed it to a footman as they passed. "Besides, I don't wish Merlin to leave the estate."

"For God's sake, the fellow's camped just outside the Sunderland Gate. Ease up a bit, brother."

Ransom stopped. "I don't need your advice."

Merlin saw something flicker in Shelby's face, an instant of darkness that disappeared into a rueful smile. He tucked the handful of ribbons beneath his coat. "Whatever made me think so?"

"And *I* don't need *yours*," Merlin said, turning on Ransom. "Why do you always have to bully everyone?"

"I don't bully everyone," he said in exasperation.

"Then let me pick my own ribbons."

"Of course you can pick your own. I only meant for you to choose from among the pretty ones."

"I think these are pretty ones."

He waved his hand. "Merlin, these are just cheap pedlar's trinkets."

"I like them."

"Only because you've never even seen any of quality, I'll wager."

"I don't need to see any of quality. I know what I like."

He sighed and walked on. "I can't see why—"

"Of course you can't see why!" She planted herself in front of him. "You can't see anything. Supposing I like cheap pedlar's trinkets. Supposing I think they're pretty. Why should you say they aren't?"

"I didn't say—"

She reached out and flattened her hand against his chest, shoving at him. "Don't try to mix me up with what you didn't say!" she cried as he took a step backward under the unexpected push. "I know what you said. I want ribbons like Shelby's. I don't need you to tell me which ones are pretty."

He looked down at her as if he hadn't even seen her standing there until just then. "Merlin—there's no need to upset yourself."

"I shall if I please!" She was nearly shouting by now, her voice echoing off the stone walls. "Why should you stop me? I'm tired of it, do you hear—"

"Go get the ribbons, then."

"No! I won't *take* any more orders from you. First you drag me here, then you steal my flying machine, then you have to tell me what to do with every instant of my—"

"Merlin," Shelby said.

"—of my *life!* I want *those* ribbons. I don't want any silly, stupid, horrid *quality* ribbons. I suppose Lady Blythe wears quality ribbons, but I don't! I wear just—"

"Oh *Mer*-lin."

"—what I please, and no one, least of all you, Mr. Duke, is going to— Ow!"

Shelby's hard grip towed her backward. "Let's quit while we're ahead, shall we? Good day to you, brother. I do believe Miss Lambourne wishes to take a walk."

She was half-dragged down the corridor, stumbling to keep up with Shelby's enthusiastic pace. Glancing over her shoulder, she saw Ransom standing alone where they'd left him.

He wasn't frowning, but he wasn't smiling, either. "The Sunderland Gate," he snapped after them. "Not one step farther."

"Right-o!" Shelby lifted his hand in salute. Then they were out the front door, and Ransom was gone from view.

They had passed through the huge court and under the east arch and out of the stableyard before Shelby slowed down enough to speak again.

"I say, Merlin, you certainly can't be accused of an overabundance of diplomacy, can you?"

"I'm an inventor," she said, shaking off his hand and rubbing her bruised elbow. "I don't need diplomacy."

"That's a damned lucky thing. Here, we'll take this path through the park—it cuts a half mile off the drive."

She followed him into the tall, unscythed grass at the edge of the manicured lawns, picking a fuzzy caterpillar from a green stem and dropping it into her pocket for the hedgehog. "Do you really think this tinker will have a proper gear?"

He shrugged. "You'll just have to look and see. He told me he did, but then I wouldn't know a helical pinion gear if it came up and asked me for a waltz."

"I'll bet he doesn't," she said glumly. "It's too good to be true. I couldn't believe it when you said you found him yesterday, camped right outside the gate."

"Worth the walk, anyway. Just to see."

"I suppose so."

He came to a halt and looked at her. "What's this? Losing interest at the prospect of a bit of exercise?"

Merlin tugged at a weed. She frowned and walked on past him, shaking her head.

"What, then? By God, I thought you were *living* for an opportunity to find this blasted gear."

"Now *you're* angry with me, too."

He sighed. "I'm not angry, Merlin. Just puzzled."

They walked along a few moments, the only sound the swish and slap of grass against Shelby's boots.

"Why does he want to change me so much?" she cried suddenly. "Aren't I good enough as I am?"

Shelby looked toward her. She bit down on her lip, quickening her pace. The path left the open meadow, entering a tangle of woods.

"Merlin."

"Never mind!" The path took a sudden turn, passing between two ancient yews, and broke out into a slash of sunlight. The footway wound down a long, unnaturally straight avenue flanked by overgrown shrubberies and choked with weeds and wildflowers.

Shelby caught her arm. "Merlin," he repeated.

She shook free. "What do I need with a new wardrobe? I hate new clothes. They itch!"

Shelby smiled.

She glared at him. "Yes. Laugh at me. Everyone laughs at me. They think I don't notice. Well, I notice. I just don't have time to . . . to . . ."

"Murder them?"

She swung her arm. "What's wrong with my dress? What's wrong with my hair? What's wrong with my conversation? I don't want to learn how to go on in the world."

The abandoned avenue ended at a crumbling edifice, a little round temple half-eaten by vines. Shelby put an arm around her shoulders and drew her close to his side. "Don't cry."

"I'm not crying!"

He touched her cheek, tracing a damp path downward. "Oh," she said.

He pressed her down onto one of the stone slabs that flanked the temple's steps and knelt in front of her, offering a handkerchief. Merlin blew her nose.

Shelby cocked his head, watching her.

"I want him to like me," she said.

"I know."

She touched her lower lip with her forefinger. "It's useless, isn't it? He never will."

The corners of his mouth turned up just a little. "Oh . . . I don't know about that."

"Mr. Collett and I are almost finished with the speaking box. I just have one more test to make. Maybe I can go home soon."

Shelby looked up at her. "Won't you be lonely at home?"

Merlin's throat closed on a sudden rush of fresh tears. She nodded, burying her nose in the handkerchief's crisp folds.

"Don't go, then," he said softly. "We'd miss you here. All of us." He paused, and then added with a little grimace, "My brother included. My stupid clunch of a brother most of all, I think."

"Yes," Merlin agreed. "He is a s-stupid clunch."

Shelby rose to his feet and held out his hand with a grin. "One of the stupidest. Come along, Miss Merlin the Inventress, or that stupid clunch will have his stupid minions out to hunt us down before we can obtain this most necessary gear."

She slid off the stone slab, feeling somehow better, even though nothing was different. Shelby always managed to make her smile.

She followed him along the path, skirting the odd little temple that sat silently in its clearing in the midst of the tangled woods. The ancient trees closed around them again, but soon they broke free, emerging just a few feet from the great stone wall that surrounded the duke's vast park. Ahead lay a neatly raked drive and a pair of iron gates.

The gates were closed and locked. Unlike Mount Falcon's main entrance, with its triumphal arch and liveried guards, this gate was unmanned. Shelby produced a cumbersome iron key and waved Merlin through, locking the chain behind them.

She spotted the tinker immediately, only a little distance away, his wagon decorated with examples of the gaily colored ribbons and a collection of copper pots. He was sitting on a log outside a lean-to that had been erected against the estate's wall, tapping with even strokes at the iron handle of a coffee mill. There was no one else nearby—the gravel drive from Mount Falcon's park seemed to end at the disused gate, dying out to a dirt track surrounded by woods. The tinker looked up as Shelby and Merlin approached.

" 'Mornin'. " He came to his feet with a grunt, a tall, skinny man with a streak of silver-gray in his hair. "Ma'am. Sir. Top o' the mornin' to you."

"Papa? Is that . . ." A young woman poked her head from the lean-to. "Oh, yes. The man who bought ribbons." She swept the canvas back and stood straight, her slender figure accentuated by the generous exposure of pale bosom above her bodice. She wore her black hair loose, which made its streak of silver-gray that matched her father's appear quite striking. Merlin thought she was very pretty.

"Susanna," Shelby said. "A pleasure to see you again so soon."

"M'lord." She dropped a curtsy, making it more playful than respectful, and whisked across the grass to the wagon. "More ribbons for your lady, m'lord?"

"Nay!" He laughed. "You talked me into three dozen beyond what I wanted the first time."

Susanna cast down her eyes as he ambled past the pedlar and leaned against the wagon near her. " 'Twas your own choice, m'lord. They were all so pretty, you said."

"I said they all were so pretty on *you*."

Susanna rubbed the peeling paint on the wagon with her finger, looking under her eyelashes toward Merlin.

"Miss Lambourne has come to see if you have the pinion gear I asked you about," Shelby said.

"Aye." The tinker gathered his lanky frame into action. "I'll get out what I have directly." He disappeared around the wagon.

Shelby looked back at Susanna. His golden lashes lowered, and he gave her a smile. "Have you done your chores, Susanna?"

She continued rubbing at the patch of weathered paint. After a moment, she nodded. Shelby reached out and chucked her under the chin.

"A glass of that Portuguese wine would go well."

The girl tilted her head in a move that even Merlin recognized as coyly enticing. "Would it now, m'lord? And the lady?"

"No, thank you," Merlin said.

Susanna turned in a whirl of dark skirts and disappeared again inside the lean-to. Shelby stood looking after her with that particular smile still lingering on his lips.

Merlin frowned. Susanna was pretty, but Jaqueline was beautiful. The spark of interest in Shelby's blue eyes when he gazed after the tinker's daughter caused Merlin a surge of annoyance. She moved closer and pretended to examine a dented pot that hung from the wagon.

"Do you like her?" she asked nonchalantly, her voice covered by the clatter and scrape of the pedlar's wares as he rummaged on the other side of the wagon.

Shelby looked around with a grin. "I'm completely besotted, I'm afraid."

"She isn't very nice."

"No?"

"She didn't even say good morning to me."

"Ah." He leaned his elbow on the wagon. "But it wasn't her manners that impressed me, you see."

"Jacqueline is much nicer."

Shelby gave her a dry look. "To you, perhaps."

"Much prettier, too."

He shot her a damping frown as Susanna emerged again from the lean-to, carrying a bottle and a pair of earthenware mugs. The pedlar's girl stopped at the corner of the wagon and leaned against the side, her hair falling across her face. "Come round here, m'lord," she murmured, "whilst Papa shows m'lady her trinkets."

Shelby moved willingly, hesitating only when Merlin said under her breath, "Stupid clunch." She saw his shoulders stiffen for an instant, but then he slid his arm playfully around Susanna's waist.

"My wine, love," he said, reaching for a mug.

But Susanna held her hand away. "Greedy, m'lord," she said huskily, turning just enough so that her midnight hair fell across Shelby's shoulder. As Merlin watched in disgust, he bent and nipped at Susanna's white throat as he reached again for the mug. His hand closed over hers.

"Aye," he growled. "Greedy."

Merlin made a face. She heard the tinker come around the other way, the box he carried rattling with each step. The man ignored the outrageous flirting occurring behind the wagon and hefted the box, loosening one of the wooden panels on the wagon. It dropped with a squeak and a thump, creating a platform of convenient height. He shoved the box full of metal scraps on top and stood back.

Merlin listened to Susanna giggle and looked reproachfully at the tinker. The man looked back at her with bland eyes and jerked his head toward the box.

"If ye want it, I got it there," he said.

Merlin gave the tangle of junk a dubious look. "I need a three-sixty-fourths-inch Vaucanson helical pinion gear."

"Yeah," he said. "I got one o' them. Mebbe a couple."

She waited for a moment, expecting him to produce the requested object. When it became clear that he was going to do nothing but stand over her shoulder smelling of stale tobacco, she squared her shoulders and began pulling items out of the box.

Merlin was used to junk, but that was *her* junk. She found it quite irritating to have to deal with someone else's junk. After beginning by laying things out in neat rows on the wooden shelf, she saw that she would be all day at that rate. She started to haul things out by the handful and paw her way through them, dropping the discarded items in a pile on the ground.

"Hey—" the pedlar snarled. "Don't be throwin' it all down like that. How d'you figure I'll get it up again?"

"Get me an empty box, then," Merlin ordered.

He grimaced and walked away around the wagon. Merlin looked over to Shelby and his new sweetheart. She could just see them around the tail of the vehicle. Shelby was embracing the girl, leaning heavily against her as he upended his mug. He threw it down on the grass and bent to kiss her, full on the mouth. His blond hair flashed gold in the sun, and his hand slid up her arm to her breast. Susanna lifted her hand, as if to stop him, but instead her fingers only curved around his wrist and held there.

Merlin rolled her eyes and looked back at the box. She poked at a small tin container. The lid fell off, spewing conical-shaped objects into her hand. "Here!" she cried. "Oh, look—here they *are!* The pinion gears!"

She lifted her head, expecting to see that she'd caught Shelby's attention at last.

But she hadn't.

Shelby wasn't looking at her. He wasn't looking anywhere. He was falling, a strange, slow crumpling of his knees. He seemed to slide down Susanna's side and lay still on the ground at her feet.

Merlin stuck the pinion gears in her pocket. She opened her mouth. Her nostrils filled with a sweet, sickening scent. Something hit her mouth with bruising impact, and she staggered backward into a tight embrace. A heavy cloth pressed her face. She flung her arms, fighting wildly, gagging on the smell of ether.

Oh, no. It was the last thought she had before the darkness devoured her. *Oh no, oh no. Not again.*

Chapter 14

The Gray Gelding moved at an easy canter across the park. Ransom kept his hands very light on his favorite hunter's bit—with careful self-discipline for his rising fury at Merlin and Shelby's foolhardy tardiness. The long grass parted beneath the horse's hooves as Ransom passed along the edge of The Wilderness, where his seventeenth- and eighteenth-century ancestors had once sought relief from the geometric precision of Mount Falcon's formal gardens.

It was a true wilderness now, not a tamed and pampered one. It had been left to go its own way half a century before, when Capability Brown had attacked the park and reshaped it, drawing the focus to the artfully designed lawns and cascades that provided the glorious prospects viewed from Mount Falcon's windows. The former Wilderness had become a forgotten tangle, used only by adventurous children as a splendidly spooky place to carry on childish pursuits.

He rocked the gelding back to a trot, skirting the last outlying elms at the edge of the Sunderland drive. Beyond lay the gate itself, closed and locked. Ransom dismounted, worked the rusty chain open, and led his horse through.

It had been years since he'd come through the Sunderland Gate. The road beyond had not been in use in his lifetime. He slapped lightly at the gelding's nose with his riding crop when the animal dropped its head to grab at the lush grass in the clearing just outside the gate.

There was nothing human in sight. The grass beneath his boots was crushed, and clear wagon tracks led off to the overgrown ruts that passed for a road. But Shelby's tinker had disappeared.

Ransom sighed. "What do you think?" he asked the horse. " 'No farther than the Sunderland Gate,' I said. You see how I rule with an iron hand." He flicked the crop as the animal lipped at the grass again. "Leave off with that. I'd as lief you didn't foul a good copper snaffle-bit, you oat-burning—"

The gray hunter pricked its ears. Ransom stopped speaking as the animal threw up its head and stared off into the woods, its nostrils flaring.

He hesitated. The gelding stretched out its neck and whickered as Ransom walked forward a few steps. The horse followed, and then stopped suddenly, shying back and prancing.

He searched the wall of undergrowth where the animal was looking. "Hullo," he called. "Who's there?"

The gelding sidled against him, breathing in loud, nervous gusts. Ransom took another step, and then he saw it.

In the shadow behind a low-hanging laurel, a gleam of gold caught the sun.

"Oh, God." Ransom recognized it instantly. "Oh, God—Shelby—"

He dropped the hunter's reins, shoving aside the undergrowth. His brother lay bound and gagged, his head lolling helplessly when Ransom tried to raise it. He tore off the loose, lacy scrap of a gag, and threw himself down, listening for a heartbeat.

It was there, steady and strong. Ransom pressed his hand over his eyes and took a deep, gulping breath of thanks. He felt over Shelby's body for blood or injury, but there was nothing to be seen—only a slow, stentorous snore now that the gag had been removed.

Ransom worked the bindings free. They required no more effort than the gag. He grabbed Shelby under the shoulders and hauled him backward, out of the bushes, ignoring the way the snores turned into a groan.

Wrestling Shelby's limp torso upright, Ransom propped his brother against his bent knee. He ripped up a handful of grass and drew a long, fuzzy stem under Shelby's nose.

His brother snorted and moaned, tilting his head back. His eyes fluttered open and rolled closed again. Ransom whacked Shelby's cheek with the back of his hand, in no mood for compassion.

"Where's Merlin? Wake up, damn your worthless hide, and tell me what happened."

"Hul—" Shelby muttered and groaned again. Ransom shook him. The blue eyes opened blearily. "Hull . . . ohh."

"Where's Merlin?" Ransom gripped his brother's jaw and tilted his head up. "Where is she?"

"Rrr— Wai . . ." Shelby's head lolled. "Wait, I . . . what?"

Ransom whacked him again.

The blond head snapped back. "What?" Shelby groaned. "What . . . y'want?"

"Wake up." Ransom's mouth was drawn back in a grimace.

Shelby lifted a shaky hand and rubbed at his eyes. He licked his lips. "Ransom," he said hoarsely.

"Where—is—Miss—Lambourne?"

"What . . . happened?"

Ransom shook him in disgust. "You've been so doped you can't stand up."

Shelby swallowed. He worked his way onto his elbows and looked around.

"Where's Merlin?" Ransom asked again.

"Merlin." Shelby frowned. He lifted one eyebrow and surveyed the clearing. Ransom saw a slow change come in his brother's expression. "Merlin," Shelby said again, and closed his eyes. "The—tinker. Oh, God . . . Ransom." His croaking voice fell to a whisper. "Ransom. I'm . . . sorry."

Ransom let go of his brother so suddenly that Shelby dropped to his back with a thud. He groaned and rolled to his side, covering his mouth while his body jerked in a dry retch.

Ransom stood up and walked away, swinging up onto the gray gelding. All his instincts clamored for action, for a wild, pounding pursuit down those silent wagon tracks.

Seven hours, at least, since Merlin and Shelby had left the house. Seven hours. A tinker's wagon might have traveled twenty miles—but Ransom had no hope they'd be stupid enough to journey so conspicuously. No, the wagon would be found abandoned, probably not two miles away.

He spent one passionate instant staring at the rutted tracks, his jaw clenched and his soul in turmoil, wanting to fling himself into full-out chase.

But his reason knew better. He gave Shelby a disgusted look. "I think you can walk home, dearest brother," he said with silken scorn. "When you're feeling more the thing."

He spurred the gelding around and cracked it once across the rump, driving the animal back through the gate at a gallop.

Within two days, Ransom's organized search had covered every yard of ground from Mount Falcon to forty miles beyond, in an ever-expanding radius.

She was nowhere to be found.

The wagon had been located—abandoned, of course—on the edge of the woods beyond the Sunderland Gate. The hounds had milled about it in confusion, crying off in five different directions. Eventually, it was clear that they were just backtracking until they came to the solid park wall of Mount Falcon itself and ranged along it in futile excitement. Ransom cursed the seven hours' lead and the decoy scents that had been spread so cleverly.

He did not raise his voice when the reports came in. He issued orders calmly, despatched messages, doubled the searchers, sent them out again.

But in his heart, he was growing frantic.

He was in the library, leaning over his desk to mark a map when the footman announced Quin O'Shaughnessy. Ransom looked up and nodded.

The servant closed the door. Quin hesitated near it for a moment, and then came to stand in front of Ransom's desk.

In a soft voice, without a trace of the Irish brogue, he said, "I ask of you, sir—if you intend to furlough me from my duties, I hope you will do it now."

Ransom straightened. He gave Quin a level look. "Why should I intend to do that?"

The other man's mouth hardened. "I've failed to provide protection for Miss Lambourne. You've asked for nothing but information from me in your efforts to recover her. I can only conclude, sir, that you feel I've failed my trust and am not fit for more active duty."

"Nothing would give me more pleasure than to find a scapegoat, Major O'Shaughnessy." Ransom lifted his eyebrows. "Are you volunteering?"

Quin's neck turned red, but he kept his eyes steady. "I've failed. I have no excuse to offer for it."

"I'm perfectly aware of the circumstances under which Miss Lambourne left the estate. It was with my permission."

"I should have gone with her."

"My brother went with her, as you know. It was my own error in judgment not to foresee that Shelby wouldn't be equipped to anticipate or handle a confrontation."

Something subtle changed in Quin's face. His green eyes faltered for a moment, and then held steady again. "If you don't reproach me for my negligence, Your Grace, you are too generous."

"Not at all generous. Pray don't leap to the erroneous conclusion that you stand high in my estimation just now."

Quin shifted his legs apart, clasping his hands behind his back. "Sir?"

"You say I've asked for nothing from you but a report on your recent observations here. To be blunt, Major O'Shaughnessy, the reason is that I had an impression from that report that you weren't imparting all you know."

Quin took a deep breath. "I answered your questions to the best of my ability."

"Major O'Shaughnessy," Ransom said slowly, "I don't split hairs about notions such as truth and honor, but I really dislike dealing with hypocrites."

The flush that had been lingering above Quin's collar spread to his cheeks. He shifted his weight and stared at the desk between them for a long moment before he lifted his eyes again. "I'm under certain orders, Your Grace."

"Are you? Are you indeed? And do they include trying to bamboozle me? I shall have to have a talk with your excellent commander, if that is the case."

The flush gave way to white under Quin's freckles. He managed without moving a muscle to look utterly miserable. After a long moment, he said stiffly, "Are you giving me a directive, Your Grace?"

"Yes." Ransom lifted the map and rolled it, fully aware that he had the officer in a corner between Castlereagh's mysterious orders and his own demands. The war secretary's direct commands took precedence, of course, and both of them knew it. But Ransom had his own strings to pull, and both of them knew that, too. He decided that he'd made Quin uncomfortable enough, and eased up a fraction. "As far as it doesn't countermand your explicit orders, I want to know everything you can tell me concerning Miss Lambourne's disappearance."

"I have given you all the facts I know about her disappearance."

Ransom caught the hint instantly. "Then give me your suspicions, Major."

Quin dropped his eyes. He turned aside, and Ransom saw his hands clench behind his back. "Your Grace. This is—very difficult."

Ransom waited.

The officer turned back suddenly. "I believe I should tell you what my orders are, sir. Then perhaps you will understand better."

"Out with it, Major. Before I collapse from trepidation."

"I'm sorry, sir." Quin looked at the floor and began to speak in a rush. "You've told me how you feel about hypocrisy. I honor that. I've seen in the past weeks the kind of man you are—that you don't sneer at fellows like me, who have an odd talent that gets them put to use in what some might call . . . a sordid task." He lifted his head with a proud, brief jerk of his chin. "I'm not usually ashamed of it, but I didn't wish for this assignment, Your Grace; I didn't like it at the first and I like it less now, having come to know you and your family. And that is God's truth. There's no hypocrisy in it."

With a controlled motion, Ransom laid down the map. "Exactly what are your orders, Major?"

"In addition to providing protection for Miss Lambourne . . . Your Grace . . . sir . . ?" He trailed off, and his mouth grew bitter and hard. "I was sent down to continue my investigation of Lord Shelby, sir. On suspicion of his dealings with a known French agent in London."

Ransom stared at the officer. "Were you, by God," he hissed.

"Yes, sir. I'm sorry, sir."

Ransom realized his fingers had closed around the map and crushed it. Slowly, he relaxed his hand. "What kind of dealings?"

"He is in debt to this man. Alfred Rule, sir. Sixty thousand guineas."

Ransom closed his eyes. He leaned a moment on the desk. Beneath his palms, the inlaid leather surface of the desk grew warm with the fury that burned through his veins, with his rage at this allegation and the desire to beat Quin's handsome face to a bleeding pulp for bringing it.

After a long silence, Ransom straightened. "Major O'Shaughnessy, I've no doubt my brother is fool enough to get himself in hock to a French spy who intended to use him to reach me. But understand this"—he glared into Quin's unhappy face—"there is no question of Lord Shelby's loyalty—to his country and to his family. None whatsoever. If you have any solid evidence to the contrary, lay it before me now or hold your peace forever.''

Quin looked unhappier still. "I have no more solid evidence, Your Grace."

"Then you have a choice. You may take your suspicions back to your commander, along with a note telling him what I think of them, or you may accept what I tell you about my brother and stay here to assist me in rescuing Miss Lambourne."

Quin glanced away. His shoulders rose in a deep breath. "You know that if I remain under those terms, I violate my orders."

"I offer you the choice, Major." Ransom sat down and took up the map again, deliberately leaving Quin to stand. "I don't tell you what to do."

Quin's jaw worked. Ransom could see the faint quiver at the corners of the officer's taut lips. It was really no decision at all. Any man with a particle of sense would carry out his orders or return to explain why he'd failed.

In a voice barely above a whisper, Quin said at last, "I'll stay, then, sir."

Ransom lifted his brows. "My terms."

"On your terms, sir."

"If I discover you deliberately looking for evidence of treason against my brother, you'll find yourself in an infantry ditch with your shoulders stripped before you have time to say your last prayers."

"Yes, sir."

Ransom narrowed his eyes. "I can do that, Major. Don't think Castlereagh can protect you."

"No, sir."

He sat back in the chair, rubbing his jaw as he looked at the officer. "I don't know if I'm dealing with a brave man or a fool."

Quin's green eyes held steady. "A fool, I think, sir." He gave a little bow. "I'd like to join the search party, with your permission. If you would excuse me, Your Grace?"

* * *

An hour later Shelby strode into the library, his golden hair dark with sweat and the smell of horses still on him. "What is it, Ransom? News?"

"No."

Shelby's anxious expression darkened. He frowned toward the window where Ransom stood. "What the devil do you want, then? I was trying to head up that foot search on Potter's Hill." He dragged a handkerchief from his pocket and wiped at his hands. "Lord, I near shot my bay's wind to get back in such a hurry."

"Sit down."

"The only decent mount I've been able to keep my hands on," Shelby grumbled. "And a stud, too. I'll have some racing stock from him, you mark my—"

"Sit down."

Shelby looked up, his eyebrows lifted. After an instant's balk, he shrugged and sat.

"There's a bank draft on the desk," Ransom said. "Sixty thousand pounds."

Shelby jerked around in the chair. *"What?"*

"Made out to the order of Mr. Alfred Rule."

Ransom saw the effect that name had on Shelby—a moment's blankness and then recognition, and after that a dawning horror.

His brother sprang up from the chair. "He hasn't— Good God, that fool's never brought his damned notes to *you* for payment?"

Ransom looked at Shelby. Hard. And all he saw was his brother—wild and brilliant and fiercely loved.

He walked over and stopped, so close to Shelby he could smell the sheen of dust and perspiration on his brother's skin. "Pay him off. Don't wait a day. Don't wait an hour. Take that draft and get out of here, and don't come back until you have the notes."

Shelby's chest rose and fell. For a moment Ransom thought he would argue. Never—never once had Shelby let his older brother pay his debts. Not once had he asked or accepted rescue from the disaster he'd made of his life. It was some crazy point of honor with him, a quirk that made Ransom alternately proud and exasperated.

But this time . . . this time Shelby's blue eyes held Ransom's and then faltered. He set his mouth and looked away.

"All right," he said. "I'll pay him off." He turned around and swept the sealed paper from the desk, not glancing back as he strode to the door.

A thought struck Ransom just as his brother reached for the doorknob. "Shelby," he said sharply. "Don't meet with Rule yourself. Don't go near him. Send your man with the draft and a pistol to get back those notes."

Shelby stood motionless by the door for an instant. His expression did not change. "As you wish," he said curtly, and was gone.

It was early twilight, but the ancient trees already cast thick shadows against the pillars of the little vine-clad temple. Ransom paused in his aimless walking and gazed at the columns, where lichen-stained crusts flaked off the decaying stone.

He sat down on a flat sandstone slab that bordered the stairs, resting his boots on the two lowest steps. The forest was quiet. Only the distant baying of a hound carried on the still air. He listened to the silence, to the hush that was so deep he could hear the subtle hum of his own blood in his veins.

Detachment was what he sought. He needed to *not care,* to set aside his trammelled emotions and find the threads of logic that he knew were there. He was furious at the situation—at Merlin and Shelby and himself—and straining under the weight of a dread that seemed to have gone all the way to his bones.

In the cool light of evening, he stared at the play of rosy gold color on the stone. As a child he had come here to hide and dream, safe in this secret place from tutors and dancing masters and instructors of elocution. They might have followed him here, those plagues of his childhood, but they never found him. For those with the key, the innocent little temple in its sylvan glade was an impenetrable fortress.

He smiled to himself, recalling the beginning of that half-forgotten oath. *A swallow-flight, a fair wind's run; five steps to the setting sun . . .*

Too many decades of adult concerns obscured his memory of more. Perhaps Shelby recalled the rest of it. Ransom hoped so. It was Shelby's to pass along to his son. Woodrow was twelve already—he should have been given that gift years ago.

Ransom's half-smile faded. He'd find out if Woodrow had been told of the temple and the oath as soon as Shelby returned. It was a silly thing, maybe, but The Wilderness and the temple were precious in odd ways. It was the trust implicit in that shared secret, perhaps: the assurance of unbending loyalty. Ransom, Shelby—even Blythe: their oath was a bond of blood and faith in one another.

As the sun began to set, the orange rays pierced a glowing slice between the columns of the small, round structure. *Five steps to the setting sun,* Ransom thought. *The snow, the spring, the circle closed . . .*

He looked over his shoulder into the smooth-floored interior. The small night creatures of The Wilderness were already beginning to emerge and forage: there was a flash of movement as a field mouse scuttled across the stone, and a hedgehog rummaged among the pile of moulding leaves at the base of a pillar.

Ransom turned back, steepling his hands and resting his chin on them. His only comfort was that the speaking box and her notebooks about it were still safely locked in the vault at Mount Falcon. That meant that the kidnappers needed Merlin. Her life was assured, as long as that need lasted. As long as she did not tell them what they wanted to know.

But his blood ran cold when he thought of the kind of "persuasion" she might encounter.

Time was inexorably against him. The net of men and dogs he'd flung out in two days' hard ride in all directions had closed on nothing. She would either speak and then be murdered, or hold her tongue and suffer the consequences. And he doubted the French agents who'd taken her were men who'd be willing to listen long to Merlin's idea of rational conversation.

He locked his fists and chewed on his knuckle. He knew what would happen. He could see it. They would think she was trying to confuse them with nonsense, and retaliate by . . .

He made a vicious sound in his throat.

All right. Enough. Enough of that. He closed his eyes and refused to be drawn into a circle of thought that would only lead him to a helpless frenzy.

Deliberately, he made his mind blank again, trying to recapture the moments of calm he'd known before. He stared at the temple steps.

The leaves rustled behind him. Ransom turned a little, and saw the hedgehog trundle across the temple floor, stopping occasionally to examine cracks and likely crevices for food.

He watched it idly. The temple grew dimmer. Like an annoying bit of song, that half-forgotten childhood oath went around and around in his mind: *The snow, the spring, the circle closed—then opened for the one who knows.*

The hedgehog snuffled through one last chink and ambled over to the steps, nosing out along the sandstone slab where Ransom sat. It came to his hand and stopped, lifting its black, buttony nose and weaving it back and forth in the air.

He frowned at it.

The small, spiky beast lowered its head and turned around, waddling back into the temple.

Ransom stood up. "Good God," he whispered.

A swallow-flight, a fair wind's run; five steps to the setting sun . . .

He found himself at the center of the symmetrical building, counting steps. Only three brought him to the western pillar, but he'd been smaller then. *The snow,* for one pillar north; *the spring,* for the little alcove where a statue of Persephone had long since vanished; *the circle closed* . . .

He reached up, sliding his palms down the stone curve of the alcove, seeking the faint indentations for his fingers. It took him a moment to find them—another shock, to see how low they were; how they seemed too small for a man's broad hand. He fitted the heels of his palms against the stone, his feet spread in a long-remembered stance, until his arms and the wall of the alcove formed a circle.

He took a breath, blinking at the featureless wall in front of him. *A swallow-flight, a fair wind's run; five steps to the setting sun. The snow, the spring, the circle closed—then opened for the one who knows. I keep this rhyme for future times, for I and mine, not thee and thine. My line and name I never fail; I swear by blood I will not tell.*

He shifted his weight. Without even a squeal of protest, the false wall gave beneath his push, swinging silently aside in an arc to reveal the narrow doorway in the stone behind. Damp, mossy air moved past him in a light breeze.

He did something stupid, then. He bent over and plunged into the black doorway, and he was halfway down the familiar, spiraling stairs before he realized just how asinine a move it was for an unarmed, unprepared man who was making all the noise it was probably possible to make. He stopped on the fourth step, exclaiming, *"Drop your weapon!"* in a commanding voice, and knowing he was going to feel exceedingly foolish when it turned out there'd been no one in the hidden chamber for years.

Utter silence met his words. He could just see the stairs in what was left of daylight, but the stone newel hid the room itself from his view.

"Ransom?" came a very small voice from the dark.

He let out a huge, harsh breath. "Merlin! Thank—"

Then he almost made the same mistake again, throwing himself down the stairs blind. With a silent curse, he caught himself, hanging on the stairs in sudden realization that an ill-conceived move could cost both their lives if one of the kidnappers was waiting out of sight for him below.

Silence reigned again while he racked his brain for a plan.

There was a faint rustling noise from below. He went still and tense, gathering himself for a spring.

A sad little sneeze sounded in the dark. "Ransom?" she asked in that small, wistful voice. "Aren't you going to rescue me?"

His muscles relaxed. "You're alone?"

"Yes." The rustling came again. "My hedgehog got away."

He descended the last four stairs, squinting into the dimness. A very faint, green-tinged light came from a moss-lined crack in the ceiling. She was sitting on the stone floor, her hands manacled by two feet of light chain, fastened in turn to a length of far heavier steel that was padlocked to the wooden handle of a huge, ancient chest. The rest of the circular room was empty except for some dusty chairs and abandoned toys that were streaked with age and chipping paint.

"God damn," he hissed, striding to her side. "I'll kill them."

With one savage kick, he smashed the handle from the chest. The chain fell free with an echoing clatter.

He picked it up, and the weight of the thick links sent red fury through his veins. "Come on." He hauled her to her feet by the elbow and pushed her toward the stairs, looping the heavy shackles in his hand.

She went up in front of him, turning awkwardly as he carried the end of the chain behind her. He came out of the hidden entrance and straightened, catching her arm again, moving as fast as possible with the weighty encumbrance of the steel. He'd not had time to think through the logic of where he'd found her and why she'd been there and how it was possible—he knew only that he wanted to be out of there and back in the safety of the house immediately.

They were down the steps when Merlin cried, "Wait! Wait a moment. My hedgehog—"

Her sudden stop made the chain go taut. Instinctively, Ransom swung his arm back, letting go of a loop rather than allowing it to jerk her forward. But Merlin had braced for the tug. The slack sent her toppling backward onto the lowest step. There was a loud crack, a puff of lichen and sandstone, and a blow to Ransom's upper arm that made him stagger sideways.

For an instant he stared stupidly at the chain still in his hand with a confused idea that a link had popped. He'd seen that happen once, on a towing barge. The recoil had killed a cow standing eighteen feet away on the bank.

But the chain seemed whole. As he stood there looking at it, Merlin scrambled up and turned away, pulling it after her.

"Merlin—never mind that." He frowned at the stone step, where a fresh slash showed white through the weathered surface. He looked up at her. "Come on."

She ignored him. The chain reached its full length and lifted between them. It seemed suddenly even heavier than before—so heavy that his hand would not take the weight. It slid from his fingers. Ransom stepped forward to catch it, but Merlin was already dragging it toward her with a loud clatter, looping it as she went.

He straightened, blinking at the link that bounced crazily along at the end of the chain. The movement woke a tiny, peculiar curl of nausea in the back of his throat. "Hurry up," he said.

"Just a . . ." She was stooping in the shadows of the temple. The steel clanked. ". . . minute."

He squinted into the little building. The evening contrast made his eyes do odd things, causing the shadows to waver and slide. She straightened and bent over again, and the late sun flashed a moment on the links of steel. He kept trying to think how the chain might have snapped, and then remembered that it had not. The sequence went around in his head like a revolving wheel.

"Merlin." He swallowed. There was a bitter taste in his mouth. "I'll send someone back for the hedgehog."

The temple echoed with the sudden rattle of metal. "There!" she said. "Got you." Much clinking and rustling followed.

Ransom squinted and swallowed again, trying to compensate for the strange things the twilight seemed to be doing to his vision.

Merlin came out of the temple, carrying the looped chain in both hands. "He's in my pocket," she said, as if that would be the foremost question on Ransom's mind. She stopped when she reached him. "Here."

Ransom moved to receive the chain as she dumped it. The weight of it hit his arm, and dropped right through his hands.

Bewildered, he watched it go down, just managing to catch the tail end. He heard the clatter as steel hit the steps again. He felt peculiar. Sick. As he stood there trying to make sense of the scene, something wet slid between his fingers. He turned his palm. In the last glow of daylight, brilliant copious streams of red flowed down his hand and soaked his cuff.

"The devil," he said vaguely.

A sharp burst of sound exploded in the quiet air, matching the first one. But this time there was no chain falling to the stone that might have caused it. He blinked.

"What was that?" Merlin exclaimed.

Ransom wasn't really listening. He was still looking in bafflement down at his palm. And at his coat, torn wide open across the underside of his arm, and the bright blood that seeped rapidly through it. There seemed to be crimson everywhere: on his shirt, on his breeches, dripping off his hand, and puddling on the lichened stone at his feet.

"He's shooting at us!" She sat down suddenly on the step.

The numb place on his arm began to burn.

"Get down!" Merlin gave her end of the chain a tug.

The jerk sent a burst of pain through his arm as he stumbled and went to his knees. Then, because it seemed too difficult just at that moment to straighten up, he leaned his forehead on the second step and lay there, trying to catch his breath. He heard another loud crack. Merlin whimpered.

He managed to turn his head. The world seemed to go unbalanced around him. "All right?" He groped toward her with his good hand. "Merlin . . ."

"Yes, I'm all right," she whispered. From his sideways view with his cheek pressed to the stone, he saw her turn to him. "Quick, move closer over here!" The chain clattered as she tugged at his hand, trying to pull him with her into the shelter of the sandstone slab that flanked the stairs.

"Shooting," he mumbled, trying to think through the dizziness. He took a panting breath and swallowed. "Shooting . . ."

"Oh, my God."

Suddenly she was pulling on him bodily, trying to make him roll toward her. The pressure sent pain rocketing through his arm and shoulder. "Don't—" He couldn't seem to get enough air in his lungs to speak.

"You're shot! Where are you shot?" She sounded a little breathless herself.

"Arm," he panted. "Scratch . . ."

He felt her leaning over him. She circled his chest and dragged him into a clumsy roll that forced a strangled groan from his throat. He hit his back and bit into his lower lip, wanting badly to retch and too dizzy to manage it.

"That's an artery," she said, just as another cracking explosion sent a splatter of stone and lichen into the air over their heads.

"Merlin," Ransom croaked, and tried to reach for her.

"Yes, yes, I'm all right." She sounded suddenly impatient. "Don't talk to me now."

He heard the chain clatter. It fell across his arm, and he winced. Then she was working away at him, the sound of scissors slicing through fabric mingling with the quick chink-chink of the manacles. He looked up at her face through his eyelashes. There was a familiar crease between her brows and that look of utter concentration in her gray eyes.

She pulled the sleeve away from his arm. The chain clanked with every move she made. He closed his eyes, and when he opened them, she was tying his arm above the wound with a pair of the gaudy tinker's ribbons.

She moved away, sitting up a little, digging her chained hands into the bulging pocket of her apron as the hedgehog tumbled out. A fourth shot made her duck down swiftly, but she kept feeling in her apron. "He's coming closer."

"Naturally," Ransom whispered. His voice was hoarse. He lifted his head to see if he was still bleeding, and giddy nausea surged into his throat. "Go . . . back in the . . . temple." He wet his lips. "Lock the . . ." God, he was so dizzy. "You can . . . lock the door."

She shook her head, drawing something out of her pocket. "You've already bled too much. You'll fall down if you try to get up."

"*You,*" he said, breathing hard to keep his head clear.

"I have to fix you," she said calmly. From the corner of his eye, he could see her opening a tin box and unwrapping a bulky little package.

"Merlin, for the love of . . . We've no way . . . He'll walk—right up here . . ."

"No, he won't. He's going to think we have a gun, too." She tapped the package with a self-satisfied smile. "I've been making rockets."

He stared up at her blearily. His arm throbbed in swollen agony. The deep evening sky seemed to fade and brighten again every time he moved his head.

"I'll set them off in the drainpipe," she said. "That should make a nice bang." She shifted out of his line of vision, sliding up the steps, the chain slinking along with her. Through a faint singing rush in his ears, he heard rustling and tapping movements, and then the unmistakeable scrape and snap of a flint.

She moved back suddenly, throwing herself against him, her torso half-curled around his head and shoulders. Ransom bit back light-headed sickness at being jostled.

Something above them exploded with a report that made his whole body snap to convulsive attention.

Merlin's arm tightened around his throat, and then she was gone, scooting back up again to rustle and strike the flint. Another sharp explosion cracked in his ears just as she threw herself against him again. It was followed by a shot from their attacker, and then the sound of movement through the underbrush.

Ransom went stiff, trying to gather himself to rise. But he was fading, and he knew it.

"Coward," Merlin said.

It took him a long time to realize she meant their attacker and not him, and that the crash of noisy passage was receding. Merlin set off another rocket. As the echoes died away, he could just hear the sound of retreat in the distance. Spurred by the disgust in her voice for the other man, he tried again to sit up.

"Lie down," she ordered. "You aren't fixed yet."

She held his arm, loosening the tourniquet. He smelled his own blood with every breath, a thick, heady, rusted sort of smell that he associated with butchers' shops and the nicks he always got when he shaved himself. As she turned away and searched in her pocket again, he attempted to lift his shoulders. When she saw what he was doing, she pushed him down.

He allowed it, not having much choice, since his head rang like the inside of a parish bell. "Merlin," he said weakly. "*Why* . . . do you have . . . rockets . . . on your person?"

She was leaning over his arm. At that, she glanced up at his face. Ransom could barely see her, but he thought her expression looked guilty. "I told you," she said. "I made them."

She turned back to his arm and bent over, tightening the tourniquet and then doing something to the wound that brought a shuddering sob of pain from his throat.

"Made . . . 'em," he gasped, trying to keep his mind from whatever torture she was practicing on his arm. "Why?"

"There's no saying when one might need a rocket." Her voice held a touch of annoyance. "I told you not to talk to me."

He was silent then, drifting from anguish to darkness and back again. He thought he heard her say something, but the words slipped past him, meaningless.

"What," he mumbled finally, coming to precarious consciousness and finding that she'd left off the torture and was looking down at him. He could see her more clearly, but the light was flickering, a mellow color that danced and cast shadows on her face. "What . . . di' you do?"

"Fixed you," she said. "They're bringing Theo's doctor."

"Thirsty." He took a breath and wet his lips. "Who's bringing . . ."

"Quin found us." A trace of accusation. "Ransom, you didn't tell me we were right here at Mount Falcon!"

He tried to smile, but it didn't seem to work. It occurred to him that perhaps he was dying from this ridiculously minor wound. He supposed, vaguely, that if one could die from slit wrists, a slit arm was not very different. But it seemed an absurd and undignified way to go, to just lie down and trickle away.

Merlin was still looking down at him. He became aware that she was holding his hand, and that something softer than the stone step was under his head. The chain that bound her hands together was draped across his chest.

He wanted to ask her if he was dying, but he thought it would sound ridiculous. It seemed as if he ought to know that himself, one way or the other. Finally, having considered it from several foggy directions, he murmured, "Fixed me, Wiz?"

"Of course," she said promptly.

He looked up at her, and got lost in a tangle of how pretty she was in the flickering light and how clever she'd been to chase off the kidnapper with her rockets and how he wished she would lean down close enough that he could kiss her. Something warm and sloppy seemed to make a hazy glow in his chest. "Merlin—" He swallowed. "Everything . . . y'did—" He closed his hand on hers. A long time seemed to pass, and then he remembered what he was saying. "Good girl," he mumbled. "Good girl."

She nodded, with a little smile, and the chain clinked as she stroked his forehead gently.

That worried him. It didn't seem like the kind of gesture anybody would normally make over His Grace the Duke of Damerell. Then she sniffed. He saw something glisten on her face, and that really worried him. He struggled against the encroaching darkness. He still could not bring himself to ask, but . . . just in case . . . there was something he wanted to . . .

"Merlin," he murmured, tightening his hand. He waited until she was looking into his eyes again. A dark lock of hair had fallen loose from her pins and hung in a graceful curve over her shoulder.

"Yes?" she said.

He quirked his lips up a little—the best he could manage as a smile. "Love you . . . Wiz," he whispered. He rubbed his thumb across her knuckles. ". . . all my heart . . ."

Just in case . . . just in case . . . just in case . . .

Chapter 15

At three a.m., Merlin paused outside the gilt-trimmed door to Ransom's chamber. She touched her lower lip, frowning at the door carving that reflected gold and shadow from her shielded candle.

He'd be asleep, of course.

She just wanted to see him. Just for a little while.

She was feeling guilty. It was one thing to sneak about and evade Ransom's odious orders when he might appear at any moment and take her to task for it. It seemed like another thing entirely when he'd come so near to not being there at all. Even though the doctor and Thaddeus had virtually poured a dose of laudanum down her throat and tossed her in bed as soon as it was clear Ransom was out of danger, she felt reprehensible for sleeping all day through her schedule of lessons.

Worse, the six nocturnal hours she'd just spent installing the pinion gear weighed like iron on her conscience. And after two days in chains, she had a pretty good notion of just how heavy iron could be.

The night nurse was an old governess of Shelby's. He called her Prune-Face, which Merlin was fairly sure was not her real name. So Merlin hadn't used any name in particular when she'd woken the woman in her bed in the adjoining room a few moments earlier. The old governess had roused only long enough to snort and nod when Merlin said she'd take over for an hour.

After glancing at the little bottle half-concealed by the nurse's pillow, and taking a sniff in the earthenware water pitcher, Merlin had decided that the nurse would be fortunate to rise before noon, having helped herself so liberally to Ransom's medicine and spirits.

Merlin let herself into his room as quietly as she could. Stuffy warmth hit her. There was another candle, guttering very low in the far corner, and a coal fire that seemed to be radiating enough heat to fill several rooms.

Underneath the gigantic canopy, Ransom lay on his side, turned away from her. Candlelight and shadow slid over his bare skin above the sheet, making the bandaged poultice around his upper arm stand out in glowing white.

She set down her candle and moved around the bed.

He was awake, his good arm curled under his head. He made no attempt to turn toward her, but waited until she came within his range of vision.

"Wiz," he said softly.

Merlin nodded.

He smiled without moving, a dreamy lift of his lips. "Thought it would be Prune-Face."

"No." Merlin hung a few feet away. She felt suddenly shy. "I told her to sleep."

"Mmm. Good idea. I much prefer the present company."

"You should be asleep, too."

He made a low, amused sound. "In this oven? I just lie here and bake, Wiz. I hope you're not offended by my informal attire."

Her gaze slid over his arm and the curved, shadowed muscles of his chest, warm ivory in the candlelight. On the floor next to the bed, his nightcap made a puddle of cotton.

He saw her glance at it and smiled again without moving. "Rebellious patient. I've already driven my nurse to drink."

She nodded. "I know."

A long silence engulfed them. Merlin stood fingering her skirt, wondering what to say. She hadn't expected him to be awake. She'd just wanted to see that he was safe and comfortable. The doctor had said as much, but—she'd wanted to see for herself.

"Come here," he said.

She moved forward.

"Closer."

She went all the way to the edge of the bed.

"Down here," he said, without turning to look up at her. "So I can see your face."

She gathered her skirt and knelt, where she was at eye level with him.

"That's better." His golden-green hawk's eyes seemed soft and unfocused under the heavy, dark lashes. "I get a little dizzy when I try to sit up, you see."

"You should rest."

He sighed. "I'm afraid there isn't much choice for a man who falls down if he tries to stand up."

"Is it very painful?"

"No." His mouth flattened. "Not at all. This is an embarrassingly unheroic injury, my dear. Half an inch long, clean cut, a few stitches, no fever . . ." He closed his eyes. "I just managed to stand about bleeding a bit too long."

Merlin lowered her gaze. Those terrifying minutes when she'd worked to stop the crimson flow were all too clear in her memory. She looked at the even rise and fall of his chest, watching the candles dance red highlights off smooth skin and the sprinkling of hair on his forearm.

"You fixed me, Wiz," he said quietly.

The gentle depth of his voice brought a lump to her throat. She shook her head, still looking down.

"Doctor told me." The bedclothes rustled as he shifted a little. "Where did you learn that?"

"Learn what?" She was watching the gold signet ring on his hand, trying to make the blur in her eyes go away.

"I don't think many well-bred young ladies would know how to tie off a hemorrhaging artery."

"Oh." She shrugged a little. "Uncle Dorian taught me."

Ransom smiled. "Bless the queer old nibs."

"He made me do anatomy. I didn't like it much."

He reached out, moving his injured arm with slow care, and laid his palm against her face. He slid his thumb back and forth across her cheekbone.

"Ransom?" she asked.

"Mmm?"

"Do you remember . . ." Her voice was trembling a little, and she swallowed. "Do you remember what you said to me last night?"

His fingers spread, sliding into her hair. "I was in and out, Wiz. I might not remember all of it."

She took a deep breath. "You said you loved me. With all your heart."

"Ah." With a light pressure, he drew her toward him. "Yes. I remember that. You see, I was afraid I might not be here to tell you later." The lazy pull brought her closer, until her breasts pressed into the down mattress. "I thought you might want to know."

"Ransom," she whispered, "I love you, too."

He smiled with half-closed eyes. "That's a good thing, Wiz. That's a very good thing. Because I think, if you'll come a little closer, that I'm going to kiss you."

She parted her lips, giving way to the guiding pressure of his hand. He turned a little, pulling her down until she met him. His solid warmth engulfed her instantly, though it was only his hand and his mouth that touched her. He held her in a long, long kiss; a sweet, deep exploration that made her ache for remembered sensations, for his body pressed along hers, his weight in the hot darkness.

He eased his hold, relaxing his head back. "Dizzy," he whispered against her skin. "Mmm, no . . . don't go," he said when she tried to move away.

She looked down at him. His eyes were almost closed, his mouth curved in that dreamy smile.

"Bad luck, Wiz," he murmured. "Have the lady I love in my bedroom, and I can't even lift my head."

She moved her fingertips over his face, tracing the strong line of his cheekbone, the curve of his brow. "What would you do with her if you could lift your head?"

"This. Just . . . this." He made a luxurious low sound in his throat as her fingers caressed him. "All . . . over."

"I can do that."

The smile turned into a slow grin. "Have at it, Wiz."

She stood up, touching her lower lip as she studied him and the bed. "I think it would be more practical if I sat beside you on the mattress."

"By all means, let us be practical."

She tested the down. It gave deeply under her hand.

"You'll slide off," he said. "Perhaps I should move over."

"No. No, I don't want you to move. I'll go round to the other side."

She skirted the huge bed, kicked off her shoes, and hiked up her skirt, climbing into the down and scooting across until she was close to him. He lay on his back, his uninjured arm behind his head, watching her.

"Do you know," he said with a languid, sliding glance down her body to her bared stockings, "I believe you'll make an excellent nurse."

"Of course. Thaddeus and I nursed Uncle Dorian, and Theo, too."

"Fortunate fellows."

"They were much more ill than you are, too."

"I'm not ill at all. Only a little giddy." He closed his eyes as she touched his chest, running her palm across the smooth skin in a soft stroke. "Becoming giddier by the moment."

She lifted her hand. "I don't want that."

"Don't stop," he murmured. "I'll expire instantly if you stop."

She frowned at him. "Are you bamming me?"

"No, no," he said. He sought her hand where it was braced against the mattress, curving his fingers around her wrist. "I'm seducing you."

She lifted her eyebrows. "To do what?"

"I'll think of something, Wiz."

Merlin bit her lip. "I suppose you mean—you want to do what we did at my house, when you first came."

"Oh, God . . . yes," he murmured. He closed his eyes and tilted his head back, caressing the inside of her wrist with his fingertips. "Let's do what we did at your house."

"You *are* giddy. Don't you think that's a bit too much excitement for you just now?"

He grinned without opening his eyes.

Merlin looked at him suspiciously. "I thought you said you couldn't even stand up."

"You can do all the work."

She put her hand on his chest again, sliding it downward and up. Beneath her palm, he felt warm and alive. He took a deep breath, and his soft sound of pleasure vibrated against her hand. "I'll do this for a while," she said. "Until you go to sleep."

"Mmm." With a little grimace, he shifted his injured arm, bending it up so that the wounded underside didn't press on the bed. The move emphasized the curve of his muscles, throwing shadows across his skin. Against that easy, powerful flex, the stark white slash of the armband made him look both very male and very vulnerable.

She allowed her fingers to drift across him, learning his shape and contours. He seemed to be going to sleep already, his breathing soft and even, his eyes closed and his lips slightly parted.

For once, the relentless severity of his features had eased, revealing a surprising beauty to his face. In repose, without the dark intensity that marked his usual expression, he was equally as perfect of countenance as Shelby. It was odd, Merlin thought, that no one ever noticed that. They all said Shelby was the handsome one, the *beau ideal*—the beauty of the family.

She smiled down at Ransom, feeling like she had discovered a secret that no one else knew.

He opened his eyes lazily. "Have I swept you off your feet yet?"

She tilted her head in question.

"Kissed you into submission? Caused you to swoon with my passionate embrace?" He gave a velvety sigh.

"This is by far the most splendid seduction I've ever attempted. I don't want to miss anything."

"I've only been rubbing your chest."

"Oh. Is that all the farther we've come? When will I progress to nibbling your delicate earlobe, do you think?"

She tried to press the smile out of her lips. "Perhaps when you're man enough to sit up and reach it."

He moved his injured arm with unexpected swiftness, grabbing her wrist and pulling the support out from under her. Merlin collapsed into the down mattress beside him. "Problem solved," he said.

She scrambled to raise herself, but he trapped her shoulders, exerting easy strength to hold her.

"I thought your arm was hurt," she protested, trying to break out of his grip.

"Yes, and if you wish for me to start bleeding again, thrashing about like a freshly landed turbot is an excellent way to achieve it."

She stilled instantly.

He turned his head, brushing his lips against her temple. "Good. I like a girl who's easily subdued."

Merlin closed her eyes. She allowed her head to rest lightly on his shoulder, careful to avoid the bandage. "Don't you want me to rub you some more?"

"What kind of improper suggestion is that? I'm the seducer here, if you please." He was pressing delicate kisses over her forehead and eyes. "Don't rush me. I'll faint."

She lifted her chin, and he kissed her mouth for a very long time. When finally he broke away, he was breathing hard and deep.

"I think I am going to faint," he muttered.

Merlin raised herself quickly onto her elbow, frowning down at him.

He blinked at her. "All right," he said a little breathlessly. "I'm all right now."

"I shouldn't be letting you do this."

He caught at her hand as she moved away. "That's what all innocent young ladies say as they're being debauched. But they love it, really."

"You're ridiculous."

"Let's call it delirious." He slid his hand up her arm and rested his palm there. "That sounds so much more suitable for a sick person."

Merlin hesitated. But she liked lying beside him; she liked the feel of his body against the length of hers, and the way she fitted into the space beneath his shoulder. After a moment, she settled back into place. He spread his fingers in her hair.

"No kissing, I think," he said judiciously. "There seems to be a minor but insurmountable difficulty. Lack of air. It makes my ears ring."

"It is not lack of air. It is loss of blood."

"That, too."

She drew her fingers across his chest, making circular patterns on the firm plane of his torso, pushing the sheet idly back and forth.

"Ahh . . . Merlin . . ." he breathed. With his free arm he nudged her hand lower.

The bedclothes gathered and slid away. Merlin closed her eyes, savoring the texture of his skin, the unexpected silken smoothness in the places she'd never seen or touched since that night in her great-uncle's musty bed. Here, there was no dusty smell of neglect; the scent of Ransom filled her, tangy and warm with the heat in the room. She spread her hand and explored him more freely, pressing a little closer as a melting urgency began to spread inside her.

Suddenly she jerked her hand away and sat up. "You aren't wearing anything!"

He smiled drowsily. "Yes. Shocking, isn't it?"

"Ransom!" She squeaked, staring down at him. "What's happening to you?"

He said calmly, "It's your fault, you know, Wiz. You can't lie down with a man and do what you've been doing and expect he won't react."

She put her finger to her lower lip, chewing.

"Really, Merlin," he said, with a patient chuckle. "How do you think it worked the first time?"

"The first time? Oh, you mean . . ." She took a deep breath. "I don't actually remember. I'm not very good at details if I don't write them down."

He cleared his throat with a peculiar choking sort of sound. When she looked at him, his mouth was twisted oddly. "I'd be happy to remind you," he said.

"Oh, my." She pulled up the sheet and buried her face against his belly. "This is embarrassing."

He smoothed her hair, toying with a loose strand. Merlin felt him pull a hairpin free.

She brushed at the thick curl that fell in her eyes as she turned to look up at his face. "Really, I don't think we should be doing this."

He pulled another pin free, and her hair fell down over her shoulders. His fingers searched through it and worked at the first tiny button on the back of her bodice.

"What if you faint?" she said. "What would I do?"

He just went on unbuttoning buttons, with that subtle, musing smile.

"Ransom," she wailed. "If we do that—if something happens to you—"

He stroked her skin lightly between the loosened buttons. "If something happens to me?" he prompted.

"It would be my fault! You said it would."

"Ah, well. There are a few Whigs I know who'd congratulate you for putting me out of commission." He tugged at the bow on her sash. It came untied. He began pushing the dress off her shoulders in small, caressing moves.

"I'd die if I did something to hurt you," she said fiercely.

He paused. His fingers rested on her bare skin. "That's gratifying."

The freed bodice drooped down to her waist.

"Merlin," he said. "Oh, Merlin."

She swallowed.

"Come here," he whispered, fingering the edge of her loosened dress. "Take that off."

Still she hesitated.

He said, "I'll be all right. I swear it. Merlin, you'll drive me mad."

"I just don't think—"

He shoved the bedclothes down before she could finish, turning to reach for her. She saw the quick tightening of his lips as his injured arm hit the pillow. Then he caught her, pulling her down beside him as he buried his face in the thick fall of chestnut hair that curled at her breasts.

It was unexpected. He'd seemed so hazy and languid, yet there was sudden crushing strength in his hand as he turned to his side, trapping her wrists behind her and arching the whole firm length of his body into hers. Imprisoned by his hard arm around her waist and by her fear of hurting him, she lay rigid, her mouth and nose pressed into the warm, raw-silk tickle of his hair.

He didn't do anything for a moment, just held her there. She suspected that it was another wave of dizziness he fought.

Then his arm loosened a little, and he heaved a sigh. "Exactly," he said into her hair, "where I wanted to be."

Merlin gave an exasperated sniff. "And you always get what you want, don't you?"

"Always."

She relaxed somewhat, seeing that no ill effects seemed to have followed the change in position. "Thaddeus says you're a spoiled brat."

"But a well-mannered one. Much too polite to tell you what I think of Thaddeus." He hooked his fingers in the opened back of her bodice and kissed the deep curve between her breasts. "You smell wonderful," he murmured. "Where's your hedgehog?"

She shrugged. He took advantage of the move to turn his head and draw a lingering kiss across the swelling shape beneath his cheek. Merlin parted her lips and arched slightly. Her fingers curled around his arm.

He drew down on the bodice, exerting pressure that made Merlin shift and turn a fraction away, allowing the persistent pull to drag her dress all the way to her waist.

Instantly, she felt the rough, warm stroke of his tongue on her nipple.

She made a small sound of agitation. But he would not let her pull away; he held her still, his fingers sprawled across her bared back, the tips pressed into her skin as he caressed and fondled and tugged at her. Her breath came shorter. She drew her leg up, sliding it along his.

"Oh, my," she said. "Oh, my."

He hugged her closer. "The dress." His voice was husky, muffled against her skin. "Take it . . . off."

She lifted herself, feeling his fist gather fabric and slide it down over her back and hips. The dress collected in a loose bunch around her lower thighs. He left it there at the limits of his reach, smoothing his open palm up the curve of her body as he returned to kiss and suckle.

Merlin whimpered. She was beginning to lose focus, to tumble into the net of sensation he spread around her. She slid her arms around his shoulders, crossing her wrists and spreading her fingers into his hair. The slight arch of her body brought him against her, a thrusting heat as he kicked the dress free and tangled his legs with hers.

She pressed into him, asking for more. Ransom groaned. He was breathing hard as he pulled her across him and rolled onto his back. The bandage flashed white against his skin. The room seemed to have grown unbearably hot, but she wanted nothing more than the heat of his body against her.

She remembered everything now; all the particulars had come flooding back in one lightning rush of passion. Easily, so easily, she answered the urgent demand and joined with him. He was looking up at her, saying her name, tilting his head back with an expression that would have frightened her if she had not felt the same dark whirl of pleasure and agony dragging her into its heart.

He clasped his hands at her hips, moving in time, his fingers pressing deeper and deeper. Beneath her his body was glowing with a faint sheen of perspiration, his muscles tense and flowing in the shadows. She could see the pulse beating hard in his throat. She moved to come closer, to drink in all of the sweet, hot electricity that surged between them.

"Merlin," he gasped. He turned his head to the side. His hands gripped her convulsively for an instant as he made a strange, low sound, a whimper in his throat.

Without warning, his eyes slid shut. His fingers dropped passively and his whole body went lax beneath her.

Merlin clutched at him, the charge of passion transformed instantly into fear. But before she could even cry out, his eyelashes trembled. He swallowed and took a deep breath.

"Damn," he muttered. "I missed it, didn't I?"

She threw herself down on his chest. "Ransom! Oh, Ransom, you frightened me to death!"

He lay beneath her, still breathing deeply. "Sorry, Wiz." He brushed her back. "I didn't mean to do that."

She pressed her cheek against him. His heartbeat was hard and regular in her ear. She listened to it, feeling her own pulse subside as his did. He patted and caressed her shoulder blade with a comforting rhythm. It faltered once, and she lifted her chin sharply. But he was already blinking away the instant of oblivion.

He looked down at her with a rueful smile. "Possibly I've been a bit premature in my choice of exercise."

"It's my fault," Merlin said miserably. "What if you'd died?"

He slid his hand down and patted her bottom. "I assure you, my love, a man could not possibly choose a more delightful demise."

She scrambled off of him, in spite of his efforts to the contrary. "Laugh if you will," she said. "The doctor said if you went into too deep a faint, your system could not stand the shock." She sat up, wrapping the sheet around her in disgust. "I knew you shouldn't have any excitement. I knew it. I always let you befuddle me."

He caressed her hand with the back of his wrist. "Don't be too hard on yourself. I've befuddled better men than you, Wiz."

"Yes, I imagine you have." She glared at him. "And you think you're exceedingly clever, don't you? Just wait till you're dead, and see where it gets you."

He lay grinning up at her. "I always enjoy conversing with you, Miss Lambourne. You make your points with such precision."

She snorted.

He drew a soft pattern on the back of her hand. "'Love you, Wiz," he said softly.

"With all your heart," she prompted.

"Every black inch."

"Good."

"You love me, too?"

"Yes."

His lips curved in a satisfied smile. He looked like a cat with cream on its whiskers. He rested his head back and sighed extravagantly. "And now—*now* will you marry me?"

"Marry you?"

He turned to look at her. "Yes, I believe that's what I said."

She gazed into his golden-green eyes, stroking his arm with complaisant affection. "No, Ransom," she murmured. "I won't."

Chapter 16

"I'm getting up," Ransom snapped.

He already had the bedclothes thrown aside. There was a rush and a scramble as his feet touched the floor, and the doctor and Shelby both grabbed for him. The doctor grappled with his injured arm, and Ransom clenched his teeth on a grunt of pain. Darkness swam in his vision; in the next moment that came clear he wasn't standing up any longer—he was sitting on the edge of the bed with his head between his knees and all the bells of Westminster pealing in his ears.

"Hell and the devil," he muttered to his bare leg.

"Slowly, Your Grace," the doctor said. "We'll support you if you wish to sit up."

Ransom took a few deep breaths. He lifted his shoulders, taking the doctor's advice this time. For an instant, giddy cotton seemed to fill his head, and then it evaporated sluggishly. He kept breathing in deep, deliberate rhythm.

"Very good, Your Grace. This will pass. In a few weeks you will be as fit·as ever."

"A few weeks! A few weeks be damned." He leaned on Shelby's hand, lifting his head. "I'll not lie in this bed for another day. And open the window. It feels like the seventh level of Hell in here."

"I'm afraid that would be courting a chill, Your—"

"Open the window," Ransom snarled. "It's no wonder I can't stand up—I'm suffocating, for God's sake." He sat up straight, setting his jaw against the giddiness.

"You may go," he said to the doctor. "I wish to speak to Lord Shelby."

When they were alone, Shelby crossed his arms and leaned his shoulder against the tall door of a carved and inlaid wardrobe. The room became silent, only the new, light draft from the opened transom moving to flutter the embroidered hangings on the bed.

"Ransom," Shelby said suddenly, "if you ever have the audacity to stick your spoon in the wall and leave me to be duke, I'll—"

"Yes?" Ransom asked, after Shelby seemed at a loss for suitable words.

"Dig up your grave and toss you to the dogs, at the very least. What in God's kingdom were you about, taking on those villains without even a decent sword at your side?"

Ransom tilted his head back, resting it in an unsuccessful attempt to ease the ache. "I didn't go out intending to take on anyone," he said. "It was supposed to be nothing but a mild ramble through the woods. Did you get back those notes from Rule?"

Shelby reached into his coat and took out a packet. He tossed it onto the table in front of Ransom.

Ransom picked it up, running his thumb up the edge. The bundle of papers flipped along his finger. He put the packet down again, unopened. "The man's a French agent."

"Yes," Shelby said with a trace of bitterness. "I managed to puzzle out that much."

"I'm sorry."

"Why? Because sixty thousand of your money had to go to my debts? I'll pay up, brother. You may take it out of my allowance."

Ransom made a low sound of amusement. "I'll indeed have passed on to a better world before I see it back at that rate."

Shelby scowled.

"Don't be a slowtop," Ransom said wearily. "The money's nothing. It was a set trap. Not your fault."

"No one forced me to sit down at a game table with the man. I should have seen it."

"If you had, and not done as they wanted, you'd be dead by now. A conveniently arranged affair of honor, most likely."

Shelby chewed his lower lip. He looked up at Ransom. "So. How did you figure out where Merlin was hidden?"

"Nothing but the devil's own luck. I was just sitting on the temple steps, musing, when her damned hedgehog walked up and announced itself."

"But how did they find out about the temple?" Shelby asked. "I thought no one alive but the three of us knew of that old verse."

Ransom tilted his head, watching his brother. After a moment, he shrugged. "I've never told anyone."

"Nor I. Blythe wouldn't, do you think?"

"It might have been anyone. An accident. The servants may have known of it for years. Who can say?"

Shelby looked troubled. "I'll tell you something, Ransom. Since you found out about Rule, I've been thinking. This fellow O'Shaughnessy. He's gone out of his way to put himself in my path, too. Just like Rule." He grimaced. "I owe money in that quarter, too. I think—"

"Ho there—rein in. You won't be able to blame all your debts on French agents, my dear, dissolute brother. I have no reason to suspect Major O'Shaughnessy."

Shelby's mouth tightened. "Aye, I can see that, the way you let the dog run tame in the house! I say to you, Ransom, it wouldn't surprise me at all if he's not your man. Someone inside Mount Falcon arranged this kidnapping."

Ransom lifted his eyebrows, but he was growing tired. His mind was not as clear as it might have been, he knew. "What makes you think so?"

"Look at the coincidences. It was someone who knew I always use the Sunderland Gate when I go into town. Someone who knew that I'd pass by and see the tinker. Someone who knew about the temple. Someone who made sure the tinker had what Merlin was—" He stopped suddenly and looked uncomfortable.

Ransom rubbed his forehead. Waves of sound came and went in his ears. "Go on."

Shelby shoved his hands in his pockets. "Nothing. It just seems odd to me that they could count on Merlin coming out to the wagon in person."

"As I recall, you had a pretty active hand in her going yourself."

Shelby kept his eyes lowered. "Well—she wanted the damned ribbons. I didn't mind taking her. I feel like ten kinds of a criminal fool, and you know it."

Ransom rested his cheek on his palm. He sighed. "Perhaps it wasn't so finely planned. Perhaps they just hoped to catch her, and got lucky."

His brother's blue eyes narrowed. He slanted a look at Ransom. "Are you feeling well?"

"Tired."

"I'll come back later."

Ransom started to object, and then lifted his hand in dismissal. "Forgive me, Shelby. You find me with my brain in a sorry state just now."

The look on his brother's face brought a sudden rush of weakness in Ransom's chest. It seemed to have become disgustingly common with him, this cursed euphoric emotionalism, ever since he'd woken in Merlin's arms on the temple steps. He tightened his jaw to hide the embarrassing quiver at the corner of his mouth. "Just do me a favor, Shelby, and don't become embroiled in any of your devil bedamned scrapes and rows for a while."

Shelby stood away from the wardrobe. He stopped by Ransom's chair and gave his brother's ear a gentle cuff. "You know," he said, "There aren't any words to say how glad I am that you're still around to plague me."

When Ransom next awoke, his nurse informed him that his mother and Miss Lambourne had visited him while he slept.

"Why didn't you wake me?" he demanded irritably.

"Her Grace wouldn't hear of it."

"Send Collett and O'Shaughnessy in here." He pushed away the glass the nurse was holding to his lips. "For God's sake, do you think I can't hold on to a glass of wine? Put it there on the table and be off with you. Must you act as if I'm two years old?"

Prune-Face lifted her iron-gray eyebrows. "I shall resist taking you up on that question, Your Grace." She cleared her throat and left the room. The secretary and Quin appeared before Ransom had even managed to finish the wine.

"I want you to organize a search of the grounds, Major," he said without preamble. "For evidence of these tinkers and who they are."

"By your leave, Your Grace," Quin said. "I've already done so."

Ransom lifted his eyebrows. "And?"

"We've found nothing of real interest, sir. A few spent powder-wads and tracks through the woods. They seem to go over the wall, but there's quite a bit of confusion. It's even possible your—uh—your attacker circled back around the house before escaping."

"You saw nothing when you came to the temple?"

"I'm sorry, sir. It took me a good twenty minutes to locate the source of the gunshots when I heard them—by the time I arrived, the man was well gone, and . . ." He paused, looking embarrassed. "I felt at the moment that my first concern was to see that you had medical attention and Miss Lambourne was escorted to safety. I went back as soon as you were both in the house, but in the dark . . ." He shrugged.

"Yes—I see that you did what you could." Ransom grimaced, poking at the fish on his tray. "Damned stupid of me, wasn't it? Stand there and be shot and then bleed like a pig."

"Line of duty, sir," Quin said. But there was a twist to his mouth that made Ransom stare at him blackly.

"Continue your investigation, Major. And you may pretty well be sure I'll have your head if anything else happens to Miss Lambourne."

"Yes, Your Grace."

"You may go. Collett, I want to speak to you a moment."

Quin bowed and left the room. The secretary frowned after him. "Excuse me, Your Grace," he said. "I thought Major O'Shaughnessy was an Irishman. He seems to have lost his brogue."

"God knows what he is." Ransom closed his eyes, feeling his strength on a slow drain. "You're under his orders until I can get out of this cursed bed by myself. His *reasonable* orders. I want to hear of any peculiarities."

"Yes, Your Grace."

Ransom opened his eyes. "I trust you, Collett. If I hear any faradiddle about how I was too weak to be kept informed, I'll . . ."

"I understand, Your Grace," Collett said while Ransom was still searching his sluggish brain for a suitable threat.

Ransom nodded. He drew a deep breath. "That's all. You may tell that female creature she can return in a quarter hour and remove this wine."

"Yes, Your Grace."

Prune-Face elected to ignore the hint and came into the room as soon as Collett left. Ransom lifted his eyebrows at her, but he reserved energy and expressed his opinion of her company by scowling silence. He was exhausted, and wanted nothing more than to lie back and hope the roaring in his ears would subside. But he sat up straighter as the old woman took the glass. "I wish to see Miss Lambourne," he said. "Go and fetch her."

"In a moment, Your Grace." The nurse laid her hand against his forehead, and checked the poultice on his arm. "Are you in any pain?"

"Not in nearly so much as you will be, if you don't comply with my instructions."

"I can give you laudanum, if you wish it."

"Fetch Miss Lambourne," he ordered. "Now."

Prune-Face nodded. "Certainly, Your Grace." She fiddled with the bandage a moment more, just to show him that she could, probably, and then marched out of the room.

Ransom sank back into the pillows. He lay very still, cursing his evaporating strength.

The door opened a long time later. "Miss Lambourne refuses to see you," Prune-Face informed him briskly. She began arranging the wrinkled bedclothes across his legs and chest. "The young lady also asked me to tell you on her behalf that she will not marry you, and you are not to think that you can plague her into doing it."

Ransom dropped his head back. He wet his lips and stared up at the canopy.

Prune-Face made a final tuck and looked at him with a little sympathy. "Will you take some laudanum now?"

"Yes," he said dully.

Glass chinked. A spoon appeared. He put his good arm behind his head long enough to take the bittersweet syrup and then lay back again, gazing moodily at nothing. Prune-Face unwrapped the bandage, renewed the poultice, and changed the strips of cotton.

Ransom felt the medicine begin to fog his brain. The annoying buzz in his ears receded. His eyelids drooped.

"Damn her," he said softly. "Damn her."

Cool, efficient hands sponged the sweat from his forehead and patted his shoulder. "Just go to sleep now, Your Grace. She's a very foolish young lady, but you'll bring her 'round. No one doubts that for a moment."

He was doubting it, himself. A day later he sat in a slip-covered, wing-backed chair in the Godolphin Saloon, like some decrepit old man, his feet propped up on a stool and a rug across his knees. Rain slid down the tall windows in sluggish currents, blurring the green and blue-gray world outside.

She wouldn't talk to him. She wouldn't even see him. It made him want to rage and throw things, to be tied to this chair and unable to track her down and corner her and kiss her into submission. He did well enough now— his head didn't throb and his ears no longer rang, but if he tried to stand up, he was as liable to faint as to walk.

The door opened behind him. He felt his heart begin to pound and had to fight a familiar wave of light-headedness. It passed quickly, and he turned.

Mr. Peale was brushing a few drops of rain off his cuff, a hat tucked under one arm and another in his hand. Both headpieces glistened with a dewy sheen.

"Your Grace," he said, with a trace of surprise. He walked forward eagerly. "Your Grace, I'm so pleased to see you up and about! I'd not have expected you to leave your bed for several weeks after such a debilitating injury. Are you certain it's quite wise, to exert yourself so soon?"

"I'm perfectly fit," Ransom said. He had an irritable urge to stand up and try to prove it. Only the mortifying memory of having attempted exactly that with his mother—and ending up on the floor at her feet—kept him in his chair. Instead, he said, "How are you going on yourself, Mr. Peale?"

The young clergyman looked uncomfortable. "Quite well, Your Grace. Quite well, thank you."

Ransom rubbed his chin. He was wondering what had come of the marriage suit, but he wasn't going to ask, and Peale knew it. But the other man seemed to have no intention of imparting any information.

It obviously wasn't going well, then. Which came as no surprise. Ransom felt a renewed surge of annoyance. "Forgive me, Mr. Peale," he said when the silence had become too long. "But I can't help puzzling over your reason for carrying two hats."

Peale looked down. "Oh—of course." He smiled self-consciously. "That does look queer, does it not? I've just been for a bit of a stroll. I found this lying at the edge of the woods—The Wilderness, do you call it? I thought perhaps one of your guests had lost it."

"A poor morning for a walk," Ransom said.

Mr. Peale shook his head. "I find much to appreciate and meditate upon in such weather."

Ransom held out his hand. "You found it near The Wilderness, you say?"

"Yes. Not far from that gate where poor Miss Lambourne was taken. Actually, I found it quite *in* the woods themselves. There is a path that's a shortcut. It's rather overgrown. But you'll know that, of course, Your Grace. I don't wish to seem familiar by presuming to tell you about your own property! Lord Shelby showed the way to me not long ago." He handed the hat to Ransom. "I fear the thing is past recall, wet as it is. For its original owner, anyway. The housekeeper might dry it out and put it in the charity box."

Ransom turned the sodden hat in his hands, looking at the dove-gray silk that lined it. It was a well-made hat; a gentleman's hat. The maker's name was stamped in gold on the lining.

"I'll keep it, if you don't mind," he said. "The twins were just looking for an old hat for one of their games."

"Oh, yes, do give it to them, Your Grace. I should like to think I'd brought a bit of sunshine to them on a rainy day."

"A commendable sentiment."

Peale bobbed a little bow. "Thank you, Your Grace." He stood a moment longer and cracked his knuckles. "I'd best leave you to rest now. If you'll excuse me?"

"Certainly."

"Thank you, Your Grace," he said again. Then he paused, clearing his throat. "I—uh—I have not yet found an . . . appropriate moment . . . to speak to Lady Blythe. But I hope to do so in the very near future, Your Grace."

"In your own good time, Mr. Peale."

"Ah—yes. Well, I thank you for your patient hospitality. I fear I—that is, you see . . . I'm not a clever man with words, Your Grace. I don't wish to prejudice my chances by—speaking precipitously."

"Of course not."

Mr. Peale looked vastly relieved. "Thank you, Your Grace. Thank you. I shall pray for your recovery."

Ransom watched Peale leave, and decided that he himself would be praying for the man's early removal from the premises. Mr. Peale was becoming something of an albatross around Ransom's neck.

He turned the damp hat in his hands, frowning down at it. The chill of the day outside soaked into his fingertips. He set the hat on the table at his side and rested his head against the chair wing, cursing the drowsiness that still plagued him.

The saloon door opened and closed quietly. He opened his eyes and blinked, not sure if he had been asleep.

"Merlin!" he said.

She jerked around from the bookshelf she'd been perusing, clasping her hands behind her back. "Oh! Hullo."

"Merlin," he said again, at a sudden foolish loss for words.

"I didn't know you were here."

"Didn't you?" He felt a rush of bitterness. "And I suppose you wouldn't have come, if you'd known."

She looked at him suspiciously. "Aren't you supposed to be in bed?"

"I assure you, I have full permission to be sitting here. No, you don't have to ring for anyone—Merlin, wait, I—" As she moved toward the door, he grabbed the arms of the chair and thrust himself out of it. "Wait." He took a step, gulping for air as the blackness closed in. "Ah, no . . . damn it, damn . . ." He didn't quite lose consciousness—as soon as his legs collapsed from under him and he was kneeling with his forehead pressed against the chair, the dimness began to ebb. "Merlin," he said, not able to lift his head to see if she was still there. "Please stay. Just for a . . . moment. Please."

When he managed to turn his head, he found a skirt hem, a pair of black-shod toes, and a space of colorful East India carpet within the range of his vision. He took a deep breath. "Thank you."

He hid his face an instant longer against the striped cotton that covered the upholstered arm—a small retreat into pure embarrassment. It was enough to make a grown man weep, this dizzy weakness that no amount of determination could seem to overcome.

Merlin said nothing, for which he was grateful. He thought if he had to protest that he was perfectly fit one more time, he *would* weep.

"Do you object to sitting on the floor?" he asked, a muffled attempt at humor.

"Not at all."

He heard her skirts rustle. With a slow, careful shift, he turned around and eased himself down, his back braced against the side of the chair. Merlin was watching him, sitting cross-legged on the India carpet. Her casual, open posture—not at all what he was used to among the finer ladies of his acquaintance—brought a suggestive warmth to his loins.

She looked at him expectantly.

"Merlin," he said, clearing his throat, "we must talk."

"Not about getting married," she said immediately.

He held back the instant argument that wanted to rush out. "All right." He raised one knee and brushed indigo carpet lint from his pale gray trousers. "Then . . . tell me, what have you been doing the past few days?"

Her misty eyes widened a little. "Nothing special," she said.

"I heard that you came to see me when I was asleep."

She clasped her hands in her lap. "Well. I wanted to know how you were."

"Why didn't you come when I was awake?"

She shrugged, staring down at her fingers.

"I wanted to see you, Wiz. I missed you."

Her slender hands squeezed and unsqueezed restlessly.

"It was wonderful," he said, "when you came that first night. I was so . . ." He paused, taking a moment to overcome another of the flooding surges of emotion that swamped him so often now. "I was happy, Wiz. Even if I was a bit . . . light-headed."

Still she didn't say anything, just sat looking down at her hands.

He began to feel a little desperate. It had been such a revelation to him, there on the temple steps—this discovery that he really did, in all truth and honesty, love her.

A brush with mortality could do that, he supposed—shock one into recognizing truths so simple they'd been lost in the relentless cycles and confusions of daily living. He'd thought his offer of marriage was a matter of duty, of taking responsibility for errors committed—and never questioned why he'd persisted in it past all reason and rebuff.

Well, now he knew why. The explanation sat patiently on the carpet in front of him, with chestnut hair and cloudy gray eyes and skin that glowed like soft midsummer moonlight. He loved her; he wanted to stand beside her forever, be the man she turned to for comfort and companionship; the one she went to first with those crazy, clever notions of hers; the one who listened and smiled and knew when to laugh—who recognized the difference between her accidental absurdities and the rare times she made an authentic quip in that quiet, ingenious way she had.

He tapped his fingers on the side of his knee and rubbed at an imaginary spot there. He wished she would say something—make some response—*anything* that indicated she felt as he did. He was beginning to believe he had dreamed those moments in his canopied bed.

At his age, with all of his position and advantages and experience, the awful possibility that he might have given his heart where it wasn't wanted precipitated an unpleasant sinking sensation in his chest.

So he sat there, contemplating his knee. After a while, looking down, carefully casual and steady, he murmured, "Still love me, Wiz?"

"Oh, yes," she said. "Of course I do."

He closed his eyes. Relief that he managed to hide rushed through him. He said, "I love you, too."

It was preposterously difficult to keep his voice from cracking.

He ventured a look beneath his eyelashes. She was smiling at him fondly. He began to feel better. But he had to tread softly—that he knew. Taking an oblique tack, he said, "I'll be conveying your speaking box to London soon."

She nodded. "I hope it works properly."

"I think it will. You've done beautifully with it. The Admiralty will be most impressed." He gave her a wry smile. "In all likelihood, the poor old codgers will be utterly confounded."

She looked at him dubiously. "But it's quite simple to operate. Are the admirals very stupid, do you think?"

"I believe I can explain everything to them adequately. And if the tests work as I hope they will, the speaking boxes will be placed on every British ship over the next year. Within the range of the boxes, we'll have instant communication, even in the thickest weather. You'll be responsible for saving many a loyal seaman's life, Merlin."

"Yes. I'm becoming rather good at that, aren't I?" She smiled, peering at him sideways with a sly tilt to her chin. "The doctor said I saved your life."

"Undoubtedly. But then you might keep in mind that I was injured in the process of rescuing you, ungrateful wretch."

"Well, that is your avocation, is it not?"

"What, rescuing ungrateful wretches? Certainly not." He leaned his head back and watched her out of narrowed eyes. "I expect a full measure of gratitude from every wretch I rescue. And I don't believe I've received a bit of yours, young lady."

"You fainted away in the midst of it and have forgotten."

He did not try to hide the grin that crept across his face. "I demand an encore, then."

She looked at him, an age-old look beneath her lashes, which must have come to her by instinct. He could not imagine, with Merlin, that it was meant as a deliberate flirt. But the effect was the same either way.

His heart began to quicken. Beneath the simple dress she wore, he could easily find the soft outlines of her body. He swallowed, wanting to shake his head and clear away the resonating hum in his ears.

With the easy trust of a friendly puppy, she uncrossed her legs and slid nearer, nestling into the curve of his arm and laying her cheek against his shoulder. "Yes," she said, resting her hand in a place on his thigh that made him go hot and dizzy, "I should like to do an encore with you."

Ransom sat there a moment, trying to gather his ringing wits.

Finally, he said unsteadily, "Not on the saloon floor, I think."

"Of course not. When you're better. In a few weeks, the doctor said."

Ransom hoped she had not asked the doctor for that information point-blank. But he curved his arm around her shoulders and caressed her cheek. The comment had given him the opening he'd needed. He bent his head a little, brushing his lips against her temple. "You know, Wiz," he murmured, "I'll miss you when you aren't close anymore."

She patted his thigh. "Oh, well—you will be back from London very soon. And then we shall have our encore."

Ransom laced his fingers with hers, as much to limit the distracting stroke of her hand in touchy places as to command her attention.

"But you won't be here when I come back from London, you know," he said. "You will have gone home."

The announcement had all the effect he could have hoped. She sat up straight and stared at him in dismay. "You're going to send me home?"

He looked into her eyes and mixed lies and truth without compunction. "Of course. The speaking box is finished. You'll be safe enough from foreign interests when it's transferred to the Admiralty. And I can't keep you here indefinitely. People have already begun to talk."

"Talk about what?"

"You've been here over two months, Merlin. There's no particular connection between our families to account for it; I'm not your guardian, nor related to you at all. As long as my mother and sister are here, it's permissible"—he paused—"if a bit odd, in the eyes of society. But Bonaparte's withdrawn from the French coast, and it's safe enough to visit Brighton. They say the company is brilliant there this season. The duchess and Blythe are wild to be off. They'll be leaving for the shore quite soon, and then you must either go with them . . . or go home.''

''Oh.'' She touched her lower lip. ''Are you going with them?''

''No, indeed. Do you think I have time to while away at sea-bathing? I shall be traveling between here and London. We'll close up most of the house until autumn, except for my wing.''

''Oh,'' Merlin said again. It was a rather small ''oh'' at that.

Ransom followed up his advantage. He drew her back against him. ''I'll miss you, Wiz,'' he repeated, a soft whisper into her silky hair. ''I love you.''

''But—can't you come visit me? I know that you'll be very busy, but . . .'' She sat up, brightening. ''You could come to my house instead of here when you don't have to be in London.''

He shook his head. ''I'm afraid that would be quite ineligible, Wiz. A bachelor visiting an unchaperoned young lady—it just isn't done.''

The familiar crease appeared between her eyebrows. It did peculiar things to his heart: the miserable, anxious way she looked at him.

''Do you mean that I'll never see you again?'' she asked.

Gratification flooded him, but he had no intention of showing it. ''Next year, perhaps. You could come again next summer, as my mother's guest.''

''Next year,'' she said in faint shock.

He touched her cheek. The manufactured threat of this impending separation seemed to seize him, too, entangling Ransom in his own strategy. He could not stand the thought of it, of her going away where he could not reach. He pulled her toward him and sought her lips—a fervent, possessive move, his hands tight around her upper arms, his mouth hard against the sweet, yielding velvet of hers. He kissed her; he held her and tasted her and owned her until the darkness roared in his ears and burned behind his eyes, and then, just before it claimed him, he pulled away.

Still holding her, he dropped his head back against the chair, seeking air in great gulps. "Merlin," he said, between harsh breaths. His head was spinning, thoughts and tactics and need tumbling together in disarray. "Marry me. Marry me, and"—he tightened his hold on her arms—"then you won't have to go."

From beneath his half-closed eyelids he saw her face change. The dreamy confusion of the kiss gathered into a frown. She disengaged his weakened fingers from her arms.

Even through his dizziness he saw his mistake. Her gray eyes had gone dark with suspicion; she swept back a loosened fall of hair and tossed her head. She was on her feet before he could reach to stop her. "I told you," she said. "I won't talk with you about that."

Then she was gone, leaving him helpless on the floor. He clenched his hands into fists, hitting the India carpet with a thud of futile rage. "I don't understand," he shouted after her. "Damn you! I love you, Merlin. I don't understand."

She paused at the door. "If I marry you, will you let me work on my flying machine?"

He looked up at her, caught by surprise. He tried to think, tried to make sense out of the light-headed buzz in his mind. "Is that your condition? You want me to promise I'll let you work on it?"

" 'Promise,' " she said scathingly. "You've already told me what your promises are worth."

He was desperate. "A bargain, then. Call it that."

"You would find some way out."

"Merlin—" Renewed fury sent sparkling color and darkness dancing in front of his eyes. "Is this the reason? Is this why you won't have me—because of that thrice-damned, spawned-by-the-devil flying contraption?"

She stood silently by the door a moment. Then she said, "Yes. I suppose it is."

He grabbed the arm of the chair, and with painful slowness levered himself to his feet. He leaned with both hands on the chairback, bending over it a little, willing away the dark. "You say you love me," he said, hearing all the anger and bafflement and hurt in his own words. "And you choose that thing over me."

She answered slowly, "You say you love me, and you want to take it away."

"I don't want to take anything away!" He turned his head, managed to straighten with a deep breath. "I don't want you to kill yourself. Why can't you see that? It's *because* I love you, Merlin. Let a thousand bird-witted inventors jump off bell-towers and flap their arms and be smashed all over the churchyard; I don't give a tinker's damn!" He gripped the chair and closed his eyes. "But not you, Wiz. Not you."

"Then you *will* take it away if I marry you."

"We'll talk about it." It was the best he could do, and an obvious lie. "We'll find a compromise."

"Jaqueline told me—she said if I married you, you could force me to obey you. That you could do whatever you wished with what's mine."

"I love you. How can you talk of force?"

"But is it true? Is that the law?"

He clenched his jaw. "For your protection," he exclaimed. "Yes, if you marry me you pledge to obey me. And I pledge to love and honor and cherish you—to take care of you. I give you my home, my name—everything I have I give to you gladly; all the happiness I can humanly make for you. I want to do that. I want you with me; in my arms at night and in my house. Merlin . . . I don't know what else I can . . ." He stopped, swallowing emotion. His knees were turning to water underneath him. "Everything—" He moved his hand in a weak sweep, leaning hard on the chair. "It's all yours, Merlin . . . my home, my life . . . all the years that God grants me on earth . . ."

He heard her take a shuddering breath. "It shouldn't be a choice," she cried. "I love you—I do love you—but I shouldn't have to choose."

"What choice?" It was hard to see her through the haze. He felt befuddlement overtaking him. "What

choice? I won't allow it. I want you, Merlin. You can't
. . . leave me.''

He said the last words to the back of the chair, with
his face buried in his arms. It all kept spinning . . . It
made no sense . . . a flying machine, a damned flying
machine . . . What did she want?

He found himself on his knees. What could he promise? But no, no promises, she would not believe him . . .
but he could not think . . . everything just kept spinning,
and he could not think . . .

''The doctor feels he must be kept under sedation,''
Duchess May said, taking a seat by the fire. Rain still
thrummed against the windows of the Godolphin Saloon.
''He hasn't been a very good patient, I'm afraid.''

''I'm sorry, Duchess,'' Merlin said miserably. ''I'm so
sorry.''

''Well, it is done. I should have known he would be
provoking altercations the moment he was allowed out of
bed. He's come to no real harm, the doctor assures me.
But it is a very great strain on his heart, to become excited so soon after losing so much blood.''

''I'm sorry,'' Merlin said again. ''I tried to leave without talking to him. But he stood up, you see, and then
he looked so very—'' Her eyes began to blur, and she
quickly looked down at her lap. ''It's all my fault.''

''I doubt that,'' the duchess said.

''I think I should go home. Ransom said it would be
safe now, and you and Lady Blythe will be going to
Brighton soon.''

The duchess made a moue of distaste. ''Going to
Brighton? My dear, wherever did you come by that notion? 'Tis only the prince's set who frequent Brighton.''

Merlin looked up. ''Ransom told me.''

''Did he? I expect he was trying to flummox you.''

''But he said—'' Merlin chewed her finger. She
frowned, and then frowned harder. After a moment, she
exclaimed, ''Then he lied. He lied to me!''

The duchess regarded her wisely. ''I suspected this ep-
isode wasn't your fault.''

"I knew it!" Merlin sprang up and began to pace, her skirts swishing on the India rug. "He'll say anything to get his way."

"He isn't very scrupulous," the duchess agreed. "He has it from his late grandfather, I'm afraid. That man would have perjured himself to increase the collection in the plate at Sunday service."

Merlin was hardly listening. "I could never marry him. Never. No matter if he promised me a hundred times that he'd let me fly. He'd force me to do whatever he pleased the instant I gave him authority over me."

"Oh," the duchess asked mildly, "were you thinking of marrying my son?"

"How can I not think of it? He plagues me with it constantly. And the way he looks at me . . . the things he says . . . about . . . about—" She turned to the older woman, her face going crumpled and out of her control. "Do you know what he said, Duchess? Do you know? 'All the years that God grants him on earth' . . . He *said* that; he wanted to give them to m-me. His whole *life,* when he is so splendid and I'm such a maggoty-brained clunch! And I don't believe it, either. It's just another of his flummeries. If he cared about me so much, why would he take away my . . . f-flying machine, which is the only thing I've ever . . . d-done . . . in my life that's going to be . . . *worth* something?"

The duchess listened to this speech, which became progressively more broken and tearier as it went along. She drew a handkerchief from her bodice. Merlin blew her nose and hiccoughed.

"Merlin, dear," the duchess asked, "have you ever been afraid of anything?"

"W-what?"

"Are you afraid to go up in the air in your flying machine, for instance?"

"No," Merlin said into the handkerchief. She wiped her eyes and crushed the lacy linen in her hand. "Of course not. It's not at all a matter of jumping off a cliff, as Ransom thinks. I've worked out all the equations, and tested everything, and I know exactly how it will work. I won't try it until I'm perfectly sure it's ready.''

"You are in control of it.''

"Well . . . yes, I suppose so.''

"And nothing else has ever frightened you? You've never been very afraid that something terrible was going to happen? Were you not afraid when you were kidnapped?''

Merlin waved her hand, dismissing that. "I knew Ransom would rescue me. He always does.''

"Does he? How very fortunate for you, my dear. So you've never been a bit afraid of anything?''

"Oh, no, you must not think—of course I have! When Ransom was shot—I was . . . oh—I was terrified!''

"Why?''

"Why! Because I was afraid he would die.''

The duchess smoothed her skirt in her lap. "But you were there to save him.''

"Yes, but what if I hadn't been able to?''

"Indeed. What if you hadn't? What if—when you'd tried to treat his wound—he'd fought you off and prevented you?''

Merlin's eyes widened in horror at the thought. "If he had prevented me? I would have *made* him let me treat him. Besides, he was so weak; he could not have stopped me.''

Duchess May nodded. "Yes. You had the power, in that instance. And you would have wielded it against his wishes if necessary.'' She smiled placidly. "For his sake. To protect him.''

"Well, of course I would have.''

The duchess tilted her head and watched Merlin, still with that calm smile.

Merlin clasped the handkerchief between her hands, frowning down at it. "You are saying that he feels the same about my flying machine.''

"You might give that notion some consideration.''

"It is not the same,'' she said. But her voice had lost some of its assurance.

"Not from your point of view, perhaps.''

"It isn't the same! It cannot be. It didn't take anything away from him when I treated his wound. It didn't make him any less the person that he is."

"Oh, Merlin, you don't really think that losing your flying machine would lessen you?"

Merlin turned on her. "You don't understand, Duchess. No one here understands!"

"I understand the difference between a person's own worth and the things that person is trying to accomplish. Achievements are *things,* Merlin—they're not the heart and soul that make you who you are."

"How can you say that?" Merlin cried. She spread her arms wildly and began to pace again. "Duchess May, have you never dreamed? Have you never wished to see what even the smallest bird can see? To take the gift—to learn the secret that's been right before our eyes since the world began!" She crushed her hands into fists and lowered her voice to passionate softness, staring into the fire. "It *is* what I am. The machine in the east ballroom will fly. I know it will. I've spent all my life building it. It is *my* heart and *my* soul, Duchess. And no one . . . *no one* is going to take it away from me."

Chapter 17

Ransom sanded the last of his letters a little more hurriedly than usual. A smile played around the corners of his mouth, though he tried to maintain a dignified gravity as long as Collett still lingered for the out-going correspondence.

After a fortnight's absence, there was an impressive pile of work waiting. One week had been wasted while he'd been dosed into oblivion by his well-meaning but half-witted physician and relatives. The next week—after he'd shaken off the effects of the opiate—he'd gone directly to London, not taking any chances on further delay with the speaking box. The secret briefings had proceeded quite satisfactorily, and Ransom was in an exultant mood.

As a self-disciplinary measure, directly after breakfast this morning he had come to his study to deal with the most pressing matters, only slightly disappointed that Merlin had slept late and missed the morning meal. He'd been looking forward to surprising her with his pre-dawn return.

It was just as well, he thought. At least he knew she was getting her proper rest and not driving herself to exhaustion over that damned flying folly of hers.

He smiled. Not that the aviation machine would be a problem between them any longer. The answer had come to him somewhere in those narcotic dreams, though it had taken Ransom several days of clear-headed thinking in London to realize it.

He would let her finish her flying machine. He would encourage it. And when she was ready, he would hire someone else to fly it.

It was so simple.

At breakfast, the table had been empty except for Ransom. Not even Woodrow, who was usually up and about quite early enough to breakfast with his uncle. Ransom shook his head. His mouth twisted in rue. Travelers who arrived home a day early should not expect a rousing welcome. What matter if his throat hurt from a full day's arguing at Whitehall and his mouth still tasted of road dust and his eyes felt gritty and his back ached from driving until four a.m.? The horses in the stable probably felt better than he did.

But the smile still tugged at the corner of his mouth, widening when a beady black nose and a pair of solemn eyes regarded him from inside the deep-sided stationery box as he lifted the lid. "Good morning," he said. "How do you do?" He nodded at the hedgehog that huddled in the depths of the box. "Why, yes indeed, I had quite a successful trip, thank you! And I quite agree, the road south of Sevenoaks is atrocious. I've written a letter to the commissioners just this morning. Oh, you'd like to sign it, would you? Come out then—careful there, we don't want another unfortunate incident, do we? Now— paw in the inkwell. Quite. Just there. Excellent, excellent. That should command their attention immediately. And Collett undoubtedly has a handkerchief available if you'd like to clean off the ink."

"Will you be retiring for a rest, Your Grace?" The secretary extended a square of plain white linen. "I fear you're exhausted from the journey."

"No, whatever makes you think so?" Ransom grinned, flexing his arm. Some soreness still lingered. The plaguey dizziness had vanished, leaving only a slight tendency to tire more easily than he ought. But this morning that trace of fatigue meant nothing. He stood up and walked to the door, pausing with his hand on the knob. Collett tarried by the desk, examining his ink-stained handkerchief.

"The housekeeper will have a replacement for you, I'm sure," Ransom said. "And when you've copied and posted all this, why don't you take a week's holiday, my man? We both need the rest."

Collett looked up. "Your Grace?"

"Oh, I'm quite serious. A week should do nicely, but if you'll leave your direction with Mrs. Tidwell I'll have her notify you if I decide to extend it to a fortnight. With full compensation for you, of course."

Collett cleared his throat, not quite managing to sound as if being given a week-long paid holiday on a moment's notice was an everyday commonplace in Ransom's employ. "Certainly, Your Grace. I will make sure to do so."

"Good day to you, then."

Ransom strolled out into the corridor, feeling rather like a child who had just given himself the day off from school. He stuck his hand in his pocket and stroked the small velvety box there, tracing the embossed name of London's finest jeweler. He visualized for the thousandth time a face with a dreamy, sweet smile. He was being foolish, he knew—foolish and besotted and enormously pleased with himself for falling in love with a muddled miss and her preposterous ways.

He paused at the foot of the staircase. It was after eleven. He'd left word with the head footman to send her to him when she came down to breakfast. He pursed his lips, feeling impatient, wondering if it would be too obviously fatuous to have a maid sent up to wake her.

It was hard, being a grown man with suddenly juvenile impulses. He crushed the desire to yell up the stairs a loud demand for her to appear immediately, bedamned to her state of dress. Or undress.

He grinned to himself. Really, the less dress the better. He drummed his fingers on the carved newelpost and sauntered into the hall, feeling about seventeen years old.

His boots echoed on the marble floor, loud in the churchlike silence. He stopped in the center, looking around at the huge stands of candelabra—taller by far than he was—and at the laughing statues of nymphs and satyrs lined along the wall. Where the bloody hell had everyone gone? Two footmen stood at attention beside the great front doors, but Ransom was damned if he was going to ask his servants where all his family and guests had got off to.

It was as he stood there in the massive silence of the Great Hall that he heard the first faint shouts. He turned his head toward the doors.

The footmen stood unmoving, eyes cast down. Ransom saw one of them tilt his head a little, sliding a glance toward the open window to his right. The shouting came again, louder. Ransom strode to the window.

Outside, the immense courtyard was empty. But people were shouting, somewhere. He could hear them, long, joyous cheers that floated closer and closer. Suddenly, out on the lawns beyond the court, where the ground sloped gently down to a stream and then pitched up again to the sharp brow of a hill, figures appeared at the top of the rise.

They were running toward the house, still too far away to recognize, mostly men, with a scattering of ladies in hiked-up skirts. A pony—Ransom identified Woodrow's little gray gelding—cantered gaily through the crowd, its rider turned back and waving a tricorne.

Ransom squinted, caught between a frown and a smile at this strange procession. He was about to turn away toward the door when the crowd split into two groups and opened a wide path for a horse and rider that burst over the crown of the hill.

It was Shelby, his blaze of hair and his powerful blood-bay stallion unmistakeable, racing hellbent across the summit and down the steep hillside. And behind him . . .

Behind him rose an apparition Ransom could never have imagined in his deepest, deluded fantasies.

Like a monstrous white bird it appeared, dwarfing Shelby and the crowd below it, an immense pale shape that loomed for an instant on the horizon and then resolved into wings as the thing exploded into full view, launched from the hill's crest to mount the air.

Ransom made a wordless sound of horror. He did not wait for the footmen, but threw the window wide and vaulted the low sill, hitting the stone pavement at a run.

The enormous object was climbing into the air at a wild pitch. It seemed to hover, like a monstrous demonic angel, casting a shadow that rippled over the crowd and sailed across the trees and lawn. A taut rope, a flimsy string at this distance, connected it for another moment with Shelby's racing mount, and then that fell loose, leaving the thing free to soar as the stallion shied and came to a lathered halt.

Ransom halted on the top step, frozen, staring at the flying machine as it rose and tilted in a graceful sweep over the stream, angling to pass south of the house. He could see Merlin, suspended between the wings, her skirts pressed against her legs by the wind and her features barely discernable. He lifted his arms, shouting.

The apparatus tilted again in the other direction, soaring back toward the house, well clear of the tall chimneys that lined the roof. She was close enough now that he could hear her voice. She was laughing. Laughing! Ransom shouted at her again and again. He could not see her face for the tears of panic in his eyes.

He was still shouting when she was almost overhead; still shouting when it happened—the steady wind gusted sharply and the machine slewed sideways. He heard a loud pop, and the great spread of wing collapsed. He watched it turn over in the air like a broken bird catapulted in a strange, slow tumble. It dropped. A tangle of canvas and wood hit the court in front of him with a sound he knew would echo through his blackest nightmares every night for the rest of his life.

He heard what he had been crying then, heard his own shouts turned into sobs: *No no no come down come down*—a litany that rasped in his throat as he ran in a dream toward the wreckage of wire and cloth that lay on the gravel court.

He reached her first, before anyone else, lying as she was with her eyes closed and her face all bloody from the streaming cut above her temple. "No," he was saying, "no, no . . ." He could not seem to stop himself. All through it, through stauching the bright blood with the cravat he ripped from around his throat; through lifting her hand and finding her pulse, weak and irregular; through checking her arms and legs and cradling her head on his knees. *No no no . . .*

Someone was talking to him, hands on his shoulders, pulling him away. He resisted, throwing them off fiercely, recognizing Shelby's appalled face like an afterthought. Ransom turned away from his brother and bent over Merlin's limp form, still crooning his endless denial like a broken lullaby. *No no no this has not happened this is not real come down come down come back to me.*

There was the doctor then, and something to carry her on—a crowd of shocked faces that parted before them. Ransom held her hand. He clung to it. It felt small in his, and cold. Ice-cold. He snarled like an animal at anyone who touched him or tried to coax him away.

They took her to his bed and laid her there, a small, feeble shape under the towering canopy of state. He had a vague idea that he had issued the orders himself, that they'd wanted to take her upstairs where he could not go. At this moment, it would have made him retch to climb even as high as the first landing that overlooked the hall. He felt near to being sick anyway; he had to breathe in short, harsh gulps to keep himself standing on his own feet.

He held on to Merlin's hand. He was afraid to let go, afraid that when he lifted it again there would be no fluttering pulse at all. His mother's face swam out of the crowd around the bed. She was speaking to him, frowning up into his eyes, but the words seemed soundless, as if there were a glass wall between him and everything real.

"She's alive," he said to his mother's image through the wall. "She's alive. I can feel her pulse."

". . . the doctor . . . make room . . . let go . . ."

The disjointed pleading came to him in waves, like roaring oscillations with silence in between. "No," he

said. His own voice seemed so far away. "I won't let
go."

"Let Ransom . . . hold her . . . God's sake . . ."

That was Shelby. The scene seemed to break up into
kaleidoscope pieces, and re-formed with Ransom on the
edge of the bed and the doctor on the other side, leaning
over Merlin like a black-coated spider. There was a hand
on Ransom's shoulder, a pressure and a presence at his
back that was solid and real. He focused on that, knew
somehow it was his brother though he could not see Shelby's face. It kept Ransom anchored, kept him from falling into shattered fragments when he lost the thread of
Merlin's pulse for a long instant and then found it again.

"Dislocated shoulder," the doctor said.

"Is that all? Then she'll be all right?" Their mother's
voice was thin and trembling.

The man said nothing. He leaned over and lifted Merlin's eyelids, one at a time. He laid the back of his hand
against her cheek and then took a small pinch of her pale
skin, watching it as he let go. He held sal volatile beneath her nose, so pungent that Ransom's lips curled from
two feet away. He asked for water and sprinkled it over
her face. He slapped her cheek lightly and spoke her
name in a loud, questioning voice, asking her to wake up,
to open her eyes and answer him. In the silence that followed, he pressed his fingers beneath her jaw and slipped
a timepiece from his pocket. After a full minute, he
looked up. He shook his head slowly. "Your Grace, I
would advise you to send for her relatives as quickly as
possible."

A dark well seemed to open up in front of Ransom's
eyes, a spinning blackness. He sat very still, bracing
himself against his brother's hand.

"Ransom?" Shelby prompted softly.

"No," he said. His voice sounded strange even to
himself. "No, we won't do that."

There was a little pause. He was aware that everyone
in the room was looking at him. The blackness wheeled
before his eyes, a spiraling void with the room and the

audience around the edges, as if they peered at him down a long tunnel. He clutched Merlin's hand.

". . . severe concussion of the brain," the doctor was saying. "Amazing if there is no skull fracture. With an injury this debilitating . . . there is commonly a profound depression of the vital processes—the brain subsides into fatal torpor, the blood volume is reduced, the breathing is shallow, the body grows clammy. I could profess to have a cure; I could bleed her or mix an ammoniac solution to rub on her forehead, but I will not misrepresent our state of knowledge in cases of this sort. In truth—" He looked around the room. "I'm sorry. Very sorry. There is absolutely nothing useful I or any other medical gentleman can do."

"She's alive," Ransom repeated dully.

"Yes, Your Grace. She is. But to fall from such a height . . . I cannot hold out hope to you that she will ever wake again."

His brother's fingers closed on his shoulder in a hard grip. Ransom looked toward Merlin, and found the blackness giving way to her face: blank, comatose, her forehead covered with his knotted, scarlet-soaked cravat and a raw scrape across one cheek that trickled blood in a dark web against the shocking white of her skin.

Out of his deadened emotion, anger began to grow—a cold power, a force that expanded inside of him and gave him mastery of his own limbs again. He took a deep breath and stood up, shaking off Shelby's hand. "Where is Collett?"

Someone opened the door. There was a small commotion, and a moment later the secretary stepped through. He glanced at the figure on the bed and then at Ransom, his lips white.

"In the courtyard," Ransom said. "The thing in the courtyard. I want everything cleared out of the ballroom and placed with it. Everything. Notes, models, tools, scraps . . . everything."

Mr. Collett drew a breath. "Yes, Your Grace."

Ransom waited. When Collett did not move, he said, "Immediately, Mr. Collett."

"Yes, Your Grace. And—and what shall I do when it is all placed there, Your Grace?"

Ransom felt his rage do subtle work on his features, felt his mouth curl and his jaw grow tight. Something vicious rose in him, an inner roar of grief and fury that swelled and swelled until it made a rushing sound in his ears. He heard his own voice through it, like ice in the maelstrom.

"Burn it," he said. "Burn it, Mr. Collett."

Shelby came to him on the fourth day. Ransom was sitting near the shuttered windows in his room beneath the elaborate, aging curtains, staring at nothing.

His brother paused, looking down at the still figure on the bed. He said nothing. After a long moment, he lifted his head and turned to Ransom.

"Yes," Ransom said in answer to the unspoken question on his brother's face. "She's dying."

Shelby drew a breath and opened his mouth.

Ransom interrupted. "It's not your fault."

His gaze lingered on Merlin, on the sunken cheeks and eyes; the faint, faint rise and fall of her chest. At first there had still been hope. At first, there had been some small chance that she might recover, that the miraculous processes of nature might spontaneously overcome the concussion to her brain. It was not utterly impossible, the doctor said. He had heard of such. But it had been four days. Four days . . . and she was dying now, not of the injury to her head, but from lack of the fluids and food her body needed.

"It's my failing," Ransom said. "My fault."

Shelby came to the window. He leaned against the carved trim. "That is a pack of rubbish."

Ransom closed his eyes. He felt dull, unable to face the blue intensity in his brother's eyes. "It doesn't matter."

Shelby laughed harshly. " 'It doesn't matter,' " he repeated. "Yes. I can see that you couldn't care less."

"I don't blame you."

"Look at me and say that."

Ransom lifted his eyes. He tried to look at Shelby. He tried. But all he saw was the image of those great, white demon wings rising over the hill behind his brother's stallion. "Damn us both to hell," he muttered, and looked out the window. "I should have known. I should have stopped her."

"I did know, and I didn't even try to stop her. I helped in every way I could."

Why? Ransom asked in silence. *Why? Why? Why?*

In uncanny answer, Shelby said, "Because I wanted to cross you. Because I always want to battle you. Oh, God . . ." His voice began to shake. "Ransom . . ."

Don't, Ransom thought. *Don't do this to me, Shelby.* He closed his eyes again, because he was afraid that if he looked at his brother, the terrible suffocation in his throat would dissolve. He would break. He felt himself that close to it: that one look or one word would bring him to his knees and release the agony that pressed with hot, prickling warning behind his eyes.

He heard Shelby move. The footsteps went away toward the bed and stopped. When Ransom looked again, his brother was standing over Merlin with a bleak frown.

"Too bad she's not a damned horse," Shelby snapped. "When it was my prize stallion down, my groom shoved a bleeding length of tubing down his throat before he let him lie there and fade away."

He jerked open the door. It shut behind him with a hollow thump.

The doctor shook his head. "It would not be for the best, Your Grace," he said kindly, leaning forward and placing a bony hand on the edge of Ransom's desk. "Better to let her slip away quietly than to—"

The doctor shut his mouth abruptly, dropping his eyes before the saber-silence of Ransom's cold stare.

"Is it possible?" Ransom asked.

"Well, yes, I— It is not *im*possible, Your Grace. But I should not like to be responsible—there is the gagging reflex, the shock of food delivered directly to the digestive tract—should she choke now, while insensible—Oh,

I should not like to be responsible, Your Grace. It would kill her immediately.''

"Do it.''

"But—Your Grace! It would not be a cure. Yes, we might keep her alive longer, but the chances of recovery are absolutely negligible.''

"If she dies,'' Ransom said, "they are absolutely non-existent.''

"Your Grace.'' The doctor shifted uncomfortably in his chair. "Your Grace, we have not discussed the possibility, but—you must understand. Even if she were to wake . . .''

Ransom flexed his hand around the arm of his chair, feeling a lump of ice begin to form in the pit of his stomach. "Yes. Go on.''

"I cannot promise . . . It seems most likely . . . that is—'' The doctor rubbed his upper lip in little, jerky moves. "Even if she woke, you see—we cannot expect that she will be . . . *herself.*''

"And who,'' Ransom said with deadly leisure, "will she be?''

"Your G-Grace—pray don't look at me so! I have used all my professional skill in this case! It is in our good Lord's hands now. Not mine!''

Ransom stood up and reached for the bellrope. "You've come to the end of your professional skill. Very well. You are dismissed.'' He glanced at the footman who opened the door. "Conduct this gentleman to Mr. Collett, and send my brother to me. Instantly.''

When Shelby appeared only a few moments later, Ransom left his desk and strode toward the door, catching his brother by the arm and pulling him along. "Find me your groom,'' he said. "It's bloody well time for a man with some horse sense.''

Three days later, Ransom frowned down at the fading bruise on Merlin's temple. She no longer looked as if she might breathe her last at any moment. Her hands, so still against the bedclothes, were achingly frail, but her cheeks

were full, her skin smooth and supple. She seemed un-
hurt. She simply lay there as if in a deep, quiet sleep.

The salty, strong broth that the groom and Thaddeus
managed to force into her with their untutored methods
had saved her life. It had not, as the grim predictions had
promised, brought her to conciousness.

So Ransom waited for a miracle.

He opened the cabinet beneath his bookcase and drew
out a decanter. He poured malt whiskey into a glass,
tossed it back, and poured again. Then he put down the
glass with the malt still in it.

"Merlin," he whispered. "Little wizard. Come back
to me."

She lay still, not a sound or a flicker, no movement but
the even rise and fall of her breasts.

He pulled the ring from his pocket, turning it over in
his hands. He read the engraving to her once and then
again. Louder. *Ad astra per aspera.*

Her long lashes rested without motion against her pale
skin.

He moved to the bed and lifted her hand, carefully
sliding the diamond onto her finger. It wobbled and
slipped sideways, too large for the slender bone and
wasted flesh. The knot in Ransom's throat swelled until
he could not swallow past it.

He laid her hand down on the coverlet, arranging the
pliant fingers, trying to make the pose look natural instead of the stiff arrangement of a corpse. He spent a long
time over that, because his own hands were shaking and
the ring would not stay upright, and sometimes the room
and the bed and her face got lost in a blurry darkness that
came and went behind his eyes.

Finally he abandoned his inane efforts, vaguely recognizing that it made no difference, that it was mostly just
because he wanted a reason to touch her. He gripped her
hand, ruining his careful arrangement, and leaned down
until his cheek brushed the cool skin of hers. "Come back
to me," he said, his voice muffled in the cloud of her
loosened hair. "Merlin, I love you. I love you. Do you
believe me?"

The ring felt hard and cold beneath his fingers, drawing no warmth from her still figure. He straightened, disentangling his fingers from hers. For a long moment he sat looking down at her pale hand and the diamond that sparkled there.

With a little plunk, the ring slipped down and hit the satin cover.

Ransom stood up abruptly. He strode away to the window, and then whirled and looked back at her. In the great bed she was a child, a tiny doll, a mere ripple in the bedclothes beneath the giant canopy.

"Wake up!" he shouted. *"Wake up,* damn your eyes!"

He grabbed the whiskey glass and flung it. Crystal shattered at the foot of the bed, spraying liquid across the needlework that adorned the footboard.

Ransom did not wait to watch it soak into the fabric. He hurled himself out of the room, unable to bear the answering silence any longer.

Chapter 18

The voice came pounding out of a dream, thudding over and over in his aching head. He groaned. He did not want to wake up; his eyes hurt, and his mind, and his heart. He threw his arm across his eyes and opened them on streaking patterns of light and dark.

"I'm here," he mumbled. "What . . . ."

An ungentle grip tore the protecting arm from his face. Ransom scowled, trying to force his eyes open past the gritty pain that seemed to seal his lids closed. He gathered his body and rolled, bringing himself upright in one dizzying motion. His feet touched the floor and he sat, recovering.

"Awake?" Shelby asked.

Ransom drew a shaky breath. He put his hands over his eyes and rested his elbows on his knees. He shook his head slightly.

Shelby's footsteps moved away. There was a chink of glassware and a splash. Shelby came back. "Here. Drink."

Supporting his head with one hand, Ransom took the glass and upended it without looking. He had expected strong spirits. What he got was lukewarm water. He spluttered, and then swallowed a gulp. His insides trembled.

Shelby took the glass back. Ransom managed to open his eyes just enough to see the pale light of a single candle that lit the small gentleman's bedroom where he'd been sleeping. His lashes clung together, his eyelids too swollen to open more. He stood up, groping for the curved wooden head of the narrow campaign bed.

"You look like hell," Shelby said. "Been drinking?"

"No."

Shelby frowned. Ransom stared at his brother from beneath half-closed lids.

"What is it?" Ransom said. His head throbbed. He sniffed. He felt in the pocket of his rumpled coat for a handkerchief and blew his nose.

Shelby just stood, looking at him in that peculiar way.

"What's the problem?" Ransom shifted with a show of impatience, turning away from his brother's gaze. He pretended to examine his slept-in coat for damage.

"No problem," Shelby said softly. "I just didn't believe you had tears in you anymore, big brother."

"Go to the devil," Ransom snarled. "You never woke me up to say that."

A little smile curled at the corner of Shelby's fine mouth. "No. Of course not. It's Merlin—"

Ransom stiffened.

"*Don't,*" Shelby said, reaching out. "Don't panic. There's no change for the worse."

"What, then?"

"She's been moving. She shifts her hands when someone speaks to her."

It seemed to Ransom that he swept upward while he was standing still, carried on a sickening surge of hope and despair. He felt his stammer hovering behind his tongue, and remained silent for an unbearable instant to control it. After a pause, he managed: "I . . . *should* . . . I want to . . . *be* there."

Thaddeus had the room in a blaze of candle and firelight, reflecting deep velvet blues and crimson embroideries from the gilded mirrors and picture frames.

"Lookat 'ere, Miss Merlin," he said from the end of the bed. "If it ain't his fancy lordship, come to see ye."

Ransom glanced at the old man, but his eyes were drawn away instantly to Merlin's frail figure. Her fingers curled, as if to clutch at the setting of the ring which had slipped inside her palm. She turned her head a fraction of an inch.

Ransom stopped breathing. It felt as if someone had delivered a heavy blow to his chest: the wave of shock and dizzy hope. He strode over to the bed and clutched her hand. "Merlin," he said. "Can you hear me?"

Her fingers curled, an unmistakeable pressure on his own.

"Oh, God," he said, staring at her still face.

"'Bout time to rise 'n' shine, lazy miss!" Thaddeus said. "I'm tired enough o' doin' fer ye, I'll say that. Runnin' me to a nub, ye are, 'twixt you an' that slugabed Theo."

If Ransom had not been staring at her face, he would have missed the tiny quiver of her lashes. "Thaddeus," he exclaimed. "Her eyes!"

"Aye," the old servant said in gruff agreement.

An odd panic struck Ransom, that she would open her eyes and the first thing she would see was him—like this: rumpled and unshaven and wild-looking, with his hair in tangles and his cravat pulled free and dragging. He let go of her hastily and stood back. "I'm going to clean myself," he said. "I won't be long."

Thaddeus gave him a jaundiced look. "Nay, ye won't want her to catch ye with a wrinkle in yer hankie."

"Leave off, you old makebate," Ransom snapped, swinging open the door. "Like as not she wouldn't even recognize me like this."

Thaddeus chuckled. "What, a dukely fellow like yerself? Nay, nay, who could not?" He gave Ransom a toothless grin. "But best bring one o' them callin' cards back wi' ye."

Ransom closed the door with a thump.

He rushed through his ablutions with all the haste and anxiety of a green girl preparing for her London debut. It was stupid, Ransom knew that; he wasn't even certain if she would really wake. But there was hope, and that was something he had not had for days that seemed endless.

When he reached the state bedroom again, he paused in front of the paneled door. What if she was awake already? What if he walked in and she was sitting up in bed? What should he say? What should he do?

He felt the stammer threaten for an instant, and drew a breath, reasoning consciously with himself. Even if it were true that these signs meant recovery, like as not it would take hours for her to come fully to awareness.

He opened the door.

"Un . . . cle?"

Ransom froze at the faint, querulous sound of her voice.

"Uncle Dor . . ."

The word drifted off. Ransom stood by the door, his heart pounding.

"Mr. Dorian ain't here," Thaddeus said in a kind, rough tone. He leaned over her where she lay propped up on several pillows. "Open them peepers, Miss Merlin, now. Time you woke up."

"Tired . . ." The word was a whisper. "So . . . tire . . ."

She lay still again, her hand relaxing on the coverlet. Thaddeus looked up and shook his head.

"I dunno," he said. "She won't wake up 'nuff to feed her. An' now, half-driftin' this way, she's like to choke if I try to put that blasted piping down 'er throat."

"Wait a bit, can't you?"

Thaddeus touched her forehead. "Fever. I ain't been able to get nothing down 'er for eight hours. I don't like it none, I tell you. She's dryin' up, like she were before when she went that time wi' no water." He looked down at her gloomily. "We was better off the other way."

"The devil we were." Ransom strode over to the bed, grabbing the whiskey decanter from its little Pembroke table as he passed. He pulled his handkerchief from his pocket and wet it with the golden malt. At the touch of the burning liquid on her lips and tongue, her fingers curled.

"*Miss Lambourne,*" the duke said in his most biting autocratic tone. "Miss Lambourne, open your eyes! I'm in no mood for trifling, I warn you."

"Mmm . . ." She turned her head, as if to evade him.

"*Miss* Lambourne." Ransom took her chin between his fingers and leaned down close to her face. "Have you heard what I said? Open your eyes."

She whimpered. Her lashes fluttered and sagged. Ransom tightened his grip on her chin.

"Do you know who I am, Miss Lambourne?" he demanded through clenched teeth. "Do you know what will happen if you don't obey me? Open your eyes! I warn you, Merlin. You cross me, and you won't like it."

Her breasts rose and fell rapidly, and a series of agitated moans came from deep in her throat.

"Wake up," he commanded. "*Now.*"

With a trembling breath, she lifted her eyelids.

"Oh, no you don't," Ransom warned when they threatened to slip closed again. "Look at me!"

She groaned. "Uncle . . ." Her eyes came full open, and she stared with blank weariness at Ransom. Thaddeus sat down on the other side of the bed, and she followed that movement. A slow focus came into her face. "Thaddeus," she murmured hoarsely.

"Aye. I'm right by, I am. Are ye thirsty, miss?"

Her brow wrinkled slightly. "Uncle . . ."

"Nay, yer Uncle Dorian ain't here. He's gone, Miss Merlin. Gone these five years an' more."

She closed her eyes, but they came open again almost immediately. "Died. Yes, I . . ." Her husky voice drifted. ". . . miss . . ." The heavy-lidded glance slid to Ransom. She stared at him again.

Thaddeus lifted a kettle from a tripod by the fire. He poured hot broth into a bowl and lifted a spoonful, testing it against the back of his gnarled hand. "'Ere ye go, Miss Merlin. Open the hatch."

Obediently, she let Thaddeus spoon liquid into her mouth and swallowed, her eyes never leaving Ransom's face.

Ransom smiled at her tentatively. "Good girl."

She simply looked at him.

Thaddeus offered another spoonful. She swallowed it, and her eyes sank closed again. She seemed to lapse back into stupor. Thaddeus's third spoonful hovered uselessly at her lips.

Ransom frowned. "Merlin!" he ordered sharply. "Wake up. This instant!"

Her eyes rolled open. She looked at Thaddeus and sipped the broth. And they went on like that, with Merlin drifting off after each few swallows and Ransom barking commands at her to open her eyes—until Thaddeus was satisfied that she had consumed enough.

She kept her heavy lids open a few more moments, blinking at Ransom. He smiled at her. A small frown creased her brow. Her eyes closed, and she took a deep, peaceful breath. Her head nestled on the pillow.

"Merlin!" he demanded, afraid each time she shut her eyes that words might not bring her back again.

Her body jerked at the sound. Her long lashes snapped open.

She looked at Ransom as if she could not quite understand why he was there, and then at Thaddeus. "Up," she whispered, and began to move, pressing down with her arms.

Both Thaddeus and Ransom jumped to support her. Thaddeus took her weight and gently pushed her down. "Nay, Miss Merlin, not just as yet. Ye've been sick a mite, if y'know what I'm saying."

"Thaddeus. I need to . . . get up."

"Like as not y'do, but ye ain't going to be using the chamber pot on yer own for a while," the old servant said inelegantly.

"But I . . ." Her glance slid to Ransom. The faint frown returned.

"Aye, I know," Thaddeus said. "His Gracefulness ain't much at takin' a hint."

Ransom sat up straight. He cleared his throat and stood up. "I'll wait outside."

"Good idea," Thaddeus said. "What a noggin the man's got on 'is shoulders."

"Excuse me." Ransom bowed, absurdly self-conscious beneath Merlin's solemn gray gaze. "I'll—um—return later." He tugged at his cuff, aware that she watched him all the way to the door.

He'd opened it and started out when he heard her thin voice behind him.

"Who is he, Thaddeus?" she asked in a plaintive tone. "Was that the doctor?"

"If she's still very disoriented," Duchess May said to a crestfallen pair of twins, "then perhaps we should give her a few more days to recover before you visit."

"Yes," Woodrow added. "Uncle says we ma-ma-ma-must ba-ba-*be* very ka-ka-ka-kind and ka-*quiet!*"

"But I want to give her *this*," Augusta cried, holding up a small, perfectly shaped wren's nest.

"And this!" Her twin dug inside the pocket of her smock and brought out a limp and much-folded mulberry leaf. "Nurse was going to put it on the dustheap, but I *saved* it for Miss Merlin!"

Ransom pushed his chair back from the breakfast table. "May I take them to her, and tell her that they are especially from Augusta and Aurelia?"

With breathless agreement, the bird's nest and leaf were placed reverently in his offered hand.

"Wait, pa-pa-please—Uncle, ca-ca-ca-*could* you wait? I have something, ta-ta-ta . . . *too*."

"Certainly." He leaned back in his chair, smiling at his mother and Jaqueline as Woodrow and the twins raced out of the room. The door opened again a moment later. The butler walked in with a small bandbox and a huge spray of pink and yellow roses.

"The items you requested, Your Grace." He placed them on the table next to Ransom with a stilted bow.

Ransom nodded, hoping that the females would not notice either the twitch at the corner of the butler's mouth or the flush Ransom felt growing in his own cheeks.

"How sweet," Duchess May said serenely. "Roses."

"*Tres bon,*" Jaqueline agreed. "You become a romantic, Duke."

Ransom rubbed the bridge of his nose with a forefinger. "To brighten things up in the sickroom," he said, trying to sound nonchalant.

The lid on the bandbox lifted and dropped with a soft bump.

Jaqueline eyed it. "No," she said resolutely. "I do not ask."

The door burst open, and Woodrow flew in. "H-h-here. *Here* it is, Uncle!" He stopped short at the sight of the profusion of dewy roses, and looked down at the drooping posy of violets and strawflowers in his hand. "Oh. You already have sa-sa-sa-some."

"Your grandmamá wished to put roses in the Godolphin Saloon," Ransom said smoothly. "Have you picked these for Miss Lambourne?"

Woodrow nodded, brightening.

"A very handsome gesture! Here, shall we put them in this vase for me to carry?"

Woodrow's face broke into an eager smile.

So it was that Ransom entered the sickroom a half hour later laden with a bird's nest, a wrinkled and oft-folded leaf, a handful of wilting wildflowers, and a hedgehog in a bandbox. He was prey to a strange combination of sheepish elation and anxiousness—a set of feelings he had not experienced in a very long while.

Merlin was sitting upright in bed. Ransom had not expected that so soon. He paused in the doorway.

In the six hours since she had regained consciousness, she'd undergone a startling transformation. No longer did her eyelids droop in lassitude, or her hands lie still as death against the bedclothes. Instead, she was sipping at a steaming cup, and finishing the last of a toasted crumpet from a tray in her lap.

She looked up. Ransom summoned a smile.

"I'm glad to see you looking so well," he said. "How do you feel?"

She set down the cup. Her answering smile was polite but wary. "Better, I think. Thank you." She blinked at Ransom, and then looked toward Thaddeus uncertainly.

The old man leaned over and removed the tray. Without glancing up, he said brusquely, "That there's the duke." Then he turned away.

"Oh." Merlin turned back to Ransom. "You are the one who is to tell me everything, then."

He caught himself beginning to frown, and made a conscious effort to lighten his features. "What is it that you wish to know?"

"Everything. Where I am. How I got here. What happened to me. Thaddeus says you will tell me."

Something icy coiled and grew in Ransom's chest. "You are in the state bedroom," he said in an even tone. "It is mine, normally, but I have vacated it temporarily."

"Yes, but—"

"May I give you these things first?" Ransom asked. "I've brought some gifts for you. From your friends."

She tilted her head like a curious sparrow. Ransom took that as approval and moved near the bed. "These are from Woodrow. He says that you will know exactly where he picked them."

She took the flowers. Ransom waited. After looking at them for a moment, she said, "They're very pretty," and held them out to where Thaddeus stood on the other side of the bed. The old man took the vase and set it on a table.

Ransom took a deep breath. "From Augusta," he said, laying the little bird's nest on the coverlet near her hand. "And Aurelia." He smoothed the mulberry leaf open and placed it by the nest.

Merlin looked at them. The familiar crease appeared between her eyebrows. At the blank puzzlement in her eyes, a shaft of bright pain went through Ransom's heart.

"And this"—he put the bandbox on the bed and lifted the lid—"is courtesy of myself."

A round black nose appeared at the rim of the box, twitching. It disappeared again.

"Oh," Merlin exclaimed. "My hedgehog!" She reached for the bandbox and drew it toward her. "Thank you so much. Where did you find him?"

"In my stationery box."

"I can't imagine what he was doing there. Why would he be in your stationery box?"

"I confess myself equally baffled."

She lifted the hedgehog out and set it on the satin coverlet. It began to trundle away, scrabbling at the slick material, but she grabbed the bandbox and turned it over on top of the animal. The box scratched along a few inches and stopped.

"There," she said. "Is that all you have for me?"

"For the moment."

"Then you will tell me where I am, if you please, Mr. Duke."

Ransom glanced at her sharply, his spirit lifting at the familiar misnomer. "As I said, you are in my . . . in the state bedroom."

She nodded, as if that were part of a lesson already learned. "Yes, I understand that. But where is this state bedroom?"

"We are at Mount Falcon, of course."

"And where is Mount Falcon?"

Ransom looked away, staring at the intricate blue and gold embroidery while he tried to gain control of the painful plunge of his emotions. "Mount Falcon is in Kent, Miss Lambourne," he said tonelessly. "It is the seat of the Dukes of Damerell, of which I am the fourth. My given name is Ransom. My surname is Falconer. Do you remember none of this?"

She had been gazing at him with wide eyes. At the abrupt question, she ducked her head in a gesture that was so familiar that a new knot formed in the back of his throat. "No. No, I don't think I knew any of those things."

"What is *your* name?" he asked suddenly.

She raised her head. "Oh, has no one told you? I'm Merlin Lambourne. And this is Thaddeus Flowerdew, who has been with my great-uncle for . . . oh, for lifetimes! He and his brother Theo. They're twins, you see. But Theo has been rather ill lately, and so Thaddeus must do all the work. He doesn't like that much, I'm afraid. Do you, Thaddeus?''

"Nay, Miss Merlin, I don't. I'd a sight rather lay aboot the place and drink tea wi' me pinkie in the air, like they does here, I'll tell you that.''

Thaddeus's voice was its usual grumpy grate, but he met Ransom's eyes across the bed with reluctance. After a moment, he shrugged helplessly and looked down.

"Well," Merlin said. "I'm very sorry for falling ill on you, and I think it's excessively kind of Mr. Duke to take us in, especially considering that he didn't even know my name, but I'm feeling much better now, I assure you. I think I should like to go home as soon as I may.''

Ransom started to push his fingers through his hair, before he remembered how carefully he had insisted his valet trim and brush it earlier that morning. He cleared his throat. "You don't recall your accident?''

The crease appeared between her eyebrows. Slowly, she shook her head.

"Can you tell me," he asked softly, "what it *is* that you last remember, before you woke up?''

She bit her lip. "Someone shouting at me—to open my eyes.''

"Before that, Miss Lambourne. Before that.''

She frowned deeply, lifting her finger to touch her lower lip. Her face seemed to screw up and then turn petulant. "Thaddeus," she whimpered. "My head aches.''

"Serves ye right, miss. Mebbe ye'd best answer the old duke here.''

"But—''

"Nay, Miss Merlin, don't fishtail aboot. He's took a sight o' care for ye, and ye kin answer an honest question.''

She worried at her lower lip, all painful concentration. It made Ransom want to gather her up in his arms like a child.

"I don't know, really. Nothing . . . special," she said at last in a small voice. "Just being at home. Working on my wing design.'' She looked up at Ransom. ''I'm inventing a flying machine, you see, Mr. Duke. Perhaps you would like to look at the plans?''

In his memory's eye he could see her—with just that same look of shy hope on her face, standing in the dusty passage of her home, saying to him: ''. . . you may have as many copies as you like . . .''

''I know!'' she exclaimed suddenly. ''That scaffolding in the barn fell on me, didn't it? I *knew* I should have dismantled it when you told me to, Thaddeus. What a whopstraw I can be!''

''Aye,'' Thaddeus said gloomily as he met Ransom's bitter smile. ''Ye kin certainly be that, miss.''

''But I still don't know why I'm here in Mr. Duke's house,'' she added with a timid glance at Ransom. ''Though it was very kind in you, I'm sure.''

He didn't answer, but instead walked over to the window and stood there, staring out at the rose garden and trying to collect his wits.

It was a blow—and a peculiarly, sharply painful one— to be forgotten. Irrationally, it struck at his pride; it hurt him personally, as if somehow he'd not meant enough to her for her memory of him to survive.

Thaddeus she remembered, and her home and her scaffolding and her hedgehog, even. But not Ransom.

But nor, he reminded himself, did she recognize Woodrow's name or the twins or Mount Falcon. In fact, it seemed apparent that the head injury had robbed her of a whole block of recollection, since some vague date before he had even entered her life . . .

He turned and looked back at her. He could not help himself—the advantages of the situation were too clear. A lifetime of reflex, of training in when to seize the initiative commandeered his higher impulses. Ransom was not his father's and grandfather's son for nothing. He recognized a golden opportunity when he saw one.

With sudden resolution, he pulled a chair up next to the bed and sat down, lifting her hand and clasping it gently between his.

"Merlin, I know how you must be feeling. It's confusing . . . it's even a little frightening, isn't it, to find yourself here in a strange place?"

Her fingers curled between his. She cast down her eyes. "Well . . . a little."

He stroked the back of her palm with his forefinger. "You had this accident, and you've forgotten some things, you see. Quite a lot of things. You realize that, don't you?"

She glanced toward Thaddeus under her lashes, as if to confirm that. The old man said nothing. After a moment, she nodded.

"You don't recognize me," he continued with a little wry twist to his words, "and that is rather . . . embarrassing. Would you look at me, Merlin? Look at me very hard, and make *sure* that you don't remember anything about who I am and why you came here."

He lifted her chin with the tip of his finger, gazing solemnly into the misty depths of her eyes. For an instant he lost himself, forgetting what he was doing in the aching urge to gather her up in his arms and kiss her.

She stared at him. She closed her eyes and opened them. The crease between her brows appeared, until she looked so distressed that Ransom broke the moment himself, squeezing her hand as he looked down.

"You don't remember," he said.

She bit her lip. "I'm trying. I'm not very good at faces."

He drew an aimless pattern on the back of her palm, and then slid his finger between hers, working the ring upright to view.

"I gave you this," he said huskily—and began the calculated tangle of truth and lies that he was sure would bring him what he wanted.

Chapter 19

"This ring?" Merlin asked, gazing down at the stone that held all the colors of a moon-drenched forest glade in its smoky depths. "*You* gave it to me?"

The man nodded. Merlin met his eyes, fascinated by the golden-green intensity there. Everything about him interested her, drawing her scattered attention into a single focus. He was a presence in the room, even when he was not speaking. He disturbed her: tall and mercilessly immaculate, as if not even a thick lock of his dark brown hair would dare to curl out of place. The slash of his brows intimidated her whether he frowned or not, but then sometimes he would smile—and the strong jaw and ruthless features became something else . . . something that sent hot agitation boiling through her already tattered composure.

"Thank you," she said, and felt color rise in her cheeks. "But did you really— I mean, no one ever . . ." She ducked her head in confusion. "Did you mean for me to keep it?"

He touched her cheek. "Yes. Of course I did. I mean for you to keep it forever."

Merlin frowned. "And did I give you something in return?" She glanced at the bed, and said suspiciously, "I didn't give you my hedgehog, did I?"

His mouth quirked. He shook his head.

"Not that you couldn't have it, if you wanted," she added quickly. "I mean, you've been so very kind and everything. It's just that . . . perhaps I could show you how to catch your own, if you really need one. Mine is very attached to me.''

''Yes, I can see how affectionate it is.''

Merlin peered at him, not sure of the gleam in his golden eyes.

''But you see''—he played with the ring on her finger—''there's no need for me to find my own hedgehog. We are engaged to marry, Merlin. You and your hedgehog are going to live here with me.''

''We are?'' she said stupidly.

''Yes.''

''Engaged! We are engaged?''

He lifted his eyes and looked directly into hers. ''Yes.''

Merlin drew a breath. ''Oh, my—I don't remember that!''

His mouth twisted a little. ''I know.''

''But . . . married! Do you mean you *want* to marry me?''

''Very much.''

''Whatever for?''

He left off playing with the ring on her finger and lifted her hand, tilting it back until his palm lay pressed against hers. He kept his face averted, looking down at their clasped hands. ''Because,'' he said in a strange, muffled voice, ''it has become painfully clear to me that I cannot live without you.''

''Oh,'' she said.

''Merlin,'' he said, looking up again, ''you would not change your mind, would you? You would not—cry off?''

''Oh, well—'' The sudden concentration in his gaze took her aback. ''Well . . . ah—''

He let go of her hand and stood up, turning away. ''I knew it,'' he said roughly. ''God . . . I knew it.''

''Knew what?'' Merlin cried, distressed by the abrupt violence in his tone.

He looked over his shoulder, his elegant figure stiffly erect. ''I cannot hold you to it, can I? I can't hold you to a promise you don't remember.''

''A promise—''

''You said you would marry me.''

Merlin bit her lip.

"But you don't remember." He flung out his hand. Merlin winced in preparation to see the spirit decanter go flying, but he checked himself an instant before he hit it. "You don't even remember *me*."

"Perhaps if I try harder . . ."

He turned back, his face harsh and handsome in the morning sun. "No. I release you. I am that much a gentleman, at least."

"Wait," Merlin exclaimed. "Wait, I—"

He shook his head. "You cannot marry a man who is a stranger to you." The set of his mouth turned bitter. "After all we've shared, and now—what do you know of me now? Only what you see—a face and a shape, the clothes I wear and the room where I sleep. How could you commit yourself for a lifetime on so little as that?"

"But I like your face," Merlin protested. "And your shape, too. And your clothes are very smart, although I don't think you could keep them so clean if you stayed around me very long."

"Merlin, you know I care nothing for that, if only—" He stopped. He spread his hand over his eyes as if they pained him. "But you don't know, do you? How can I tell you of my feelings? 'Tis farcical, to come as a stranger and say that I love you. To tell you that you loved me, too; that when I asked you to do me the honor"—his deep voice broke a little—"the very *great* honor of becoming my wife, you looked at me with joy in your eyes and said yes!"

"Oh." Merlin touched her lower lip. "I'm truly sorry to have forgotten that."

He made an odd sound and turned away, looking out the window. "I'm sorry for it, too."

"Perhaps if you gave me a hint," she suggested. "Where did this conversation take place?"

His broad shoulders straightened. Without turning, he cleared his throat. "Just there—" He lifted his hand and gestured out the open window. "Beneath the rose arbor. It was morning, a moment after the sun had touched the blossoms and turned the dew to perfume."

Thaddeus gave a derisive snort.

"I think it sounds very nice!" Merlin frowned at her elderly retainer.

The stranger turned, and she felt a little thrill of pleasure to observe his strong profile as his gaze locked with Thaddeus's for a long moment.

"I know," the duke said to Thaddeus in a low voice. "You've never championed my cause."

Thaddeus harrumphed. "Much ye care what I think."

Merlin looked uncertainly at her old friend. "You don't like Mr. Duke?"

The manservant busied himself with the tea tray. "He'll do. I seen worse rapscallions." He stacked the plates and added darkly, "But they was lurkin' behind a Punch 'n' Judy at the horse fair."

Merlin glanced at the duke, afraid he would not take kindly to the disparagement. But the tall man only looked at Thaddeus a moment more and then lifted his hand to cover a light cough as he turned away and stared out the window again.

She bit her lip, still frowning in question at Thaddeus.

He shrugged. "I tol' ye he'll do, Miss Merlin. A duke, an' all that." He dropped a spoon onto the tray with a clatter.

That was high praise and strong recommendation, coming from Thaddeus.

"Excuse me, Mr. Duke," she said. "But—um—could you tell me . . . had a date been set for—ah—"

"Today."

He didn't even turn around as he said it, but the word hung in the air between them.

"Oh," Merlin said.

"Of course, there's no question of it now."

"There isn't?"

He stretched out his arm, bracing against the window frame. In a harsh voice, he spoke downward to the cushioned windowsill. "You need time to recover. Time to know me. Perhaps I can—perhaps you might come to—" He straightened and twisted around. "I *will* win you again. I must. It's only that I've waited so long, been so afraid you were lost to me. To see you lying here, fearing for your very life . . . and then, when my prayers are answered"—he gave a bitter laugh—"to find I've lost all!"

Merlin touched her lip. "Yes, I can see how that would be vexing."

"Vexing!" His green-gold eyes narrowed. He took an abrupt step toward her. "You have indeed forgotten me, if you think that is all I feel."

She tucked in her chin as he neared, not quite certain how to interpret the decisive set of his jaw. He dropped to his knees by the bed and took her hand, pressing it to his mouth. "I'm not a patient man." His breath brushed her skin, his lips moving against the back of her palm. "I'm not. I've waited—ah, God, it seems so long! But somehow"—his fingers closed painfully on hers—"somehow I'll wait longer."

"Well, really, Mr. Duke . . . if you feel that strongly about it . . ."

He let go of her as suddenly as he'd taken her hand. "No! I must give you the chance to decide for yourself. It would be selfish—dishonorable—to do less. I could not face myself in the mirror."

"Surely it wouldn't be so bad as that."

He came to his feet. "I shall go away. You must have time; you must. I can't trust myself. I might—" He lifted his eyes, gazing at some unfocused point in the distance. "I might lose what little endurance I possess."

"Oh, dear—" Merlin touched her lower lip. "Go away? But where?"

He shaded his eyes with one broad hand. "I don't know. Italy, perhaps, or Brazil, but I must think. Let me think."

"How 'bout Cheltenham?" Thaddeus suggested. "I hear they likes a good hair-pullin' tragedy."

But the duke did not answer, engrossed in his own dark deliberations. At the words, his expression tightened queerly, and he raised his other hand, covering his face entirely with his palms. For a moment, his powerful torso seemed to shudder with distress.

"Now—see what you've done, Thaddeus! Please, Mr.—"

"The army," the duke said, dropping his hands. "I'll buy a captaincy."

"The *army?*" she squeaked. "But aren't we at war?"

"Yes, of course. That French fellow. 'Twould be a great relief for my suffering to run a saber through his black heart."

"But you could be hurt. Killed, even!"

Suddenly his fierce yellow-green gaze focused on her. "Would you care?"

"Well, I—uh—yes, I would! I haven't even gotten to know you yet." She looked down, worrying the ring on her finger, unable to hold in the face of his golden intensity. "That is—I mean, *again.*"

"Ah, Merlin," he said. "I do love you."

It was spoken so softly, with such a keen, gentle warmth, that she almost doubted her own ears. She looked up from under her lashes.

It seemed too incredible—this man, this room . . . and between the two, more physical grandeur than she'd seen in her life. If Thaddeus had not been there, she would have called it all a dream and drifted back to sleep.

But here was this duke—amazing, intimidating, magnificent creature that he was—looking at her like that, and saying that he loved her . . .

He broke the moment with a sudden move, turning toward the door. "I cannot stay. You see, already I press you too hard."

"No, wait," Merlin said.

His hand was on the knob. "I can't wait, Merlin dear. If you value your freedom to choose, you will not ask me."

"But—"

He pulled the door open. "No! No. Let us say no more. I cannot bear it. Goodbye, my love."

"Mr. Duke—"

"Wish me Godspeed." He was halfway out, pulling the door shut behind him.

"Wait!" Merlin struggled with the bedclothes. "Wait! Just a moment—oh, please, wait!"

Half an inch from closing, the door paused in its swing. It hung there a moment, <u>and</u> then silently reopened a few inches. "What is it?" he asked roughly.

"Please wait, Mr. Duke. I'll marry you."

The door opened another few inches. "You will?"

"Yes, I—today. I mean, if I've already made you a promise . . ."

He moved into the room and leaned back against the door, both hands behind him on the knob. "I released you from that promise."

"Well, I don't release myself."

He took a few steps toward her and stopped. "You're certain?"

"Yes."

"You must be sure." He moved closer and hesitated again. "Merlin, you must not feel that I'm forcing you."

"No. No, I'm sure that if I said I wished to be your wife, then I still wish it. Truly." She felt shy, and looked down at his shoes. "I can understand . . . why I said yes the first time."

"Merlin." Suddenly he was at the bedside, on his knees again, kissing the ring on her hand and speaking in that husky, warm murmur. "You've made me the happiest man alive."

She bit her lip, melting into rivers of wax inside.

He squeezed her hand. "Today! Truly? Oh, God— where are my wits?" He stood up. "What must I do? The minister, witnesses—we'll have the ceremony right here, of course. I won't have you press your health."

Merlin watched as the bemusement on his face gave way to something else. He let go of her hand.

"Thaddeus—" A new snap came into his voice, a tone of command that she hadn't heard before. "Ring for Collett, and send a message to the Duchess May. I shall see them both in the library immediately."

"Hmmpf," Thaddeus said, and shuffled toward the door.

"No, leave that tray," the duke ordered, escorting the old servant out. "Send a maid for it. I shall want you to verify your mark as witness on that special license, and . . ." His voice was lost as the door shut on the two of them, leaving Merlin alone. She gazed at the back of the door for a moment, and then looked down at the smoky diamond on her hand.

She closed her eyes, and hoped sincerely that this man who'd decided to be her husband would not always make her head ache so.

Ransom stopped outside. He allowed one corner of his mouth to curl a fraction as he lifted a brow at Thaddeus.

"Gi' me a rotten egg to pitch," the manservant grumbled. "Silliest damned moonin' about I never hope to see."

"It worked, did it not?" Ransom could not contain his grin.

"Only because she ain't got the common sense God gave to a peahen."

"Jealous?" Ransom cocked his head. "Never mind! You may give away the bride."

Thaddeus grunted. "'Bout bloody time."

Ransom just tucked his hands in his pockets and sauntered down the corridor, whistling a wedding march.

Merlin had never imagined getting married. At least, if she had, she didn't remember it. It was all quite bewildering. She sat in a chair waiting for the ceremony, dressed up in a pretty lemon-yellow gown and a lacy white shawl provided by a very nice, very petite lady who hugged her and kissed her cheek without saying much except that she knew Merlin would make her son happy. She also promised, three separate times—as if she weren't sure that Merlin believed it—that he would make Merlin happy, too.

Merlin concluded that this lady was the duke's mother.

He had a brother, too, who looked like one of the gods in Uncle Dorian's illustrated volume of Greek mythology. And a sister and nieces and nephews and friends, who all seemed to want to crowd into the magnificent bedchamber and smile and laugh and stare.

Merlin was glad that Thaddeus was there. And Ransom—that was his name, this man she was going to marry—she was glad he was there to stand beside her, too.

It was all over very quickly. Thaddeus helped her out of the chair at the proper time, and led her the short distance to where a clergyman and Ransom and his brother waited near one of the great velvet-hung windows. Just when her knees were shaking a little too much to stand up, Ransom took her arm, and somehow made her lean on him without seeming to. She could feel him through the fabric of his coat—solid warmth and easy strength. Then he turned, lifting the little scrap of veil someone had pinned in her hair, and held her by the shoulders and kissed her.

Not a long kiss. A brush of his lips on hers, a light pressure, but his fingers went tighter on her arms and his body seemed to grow taut beneath the formal clothes as he bent his head. He made her feel small and light, as if she might blow away in the faint breeze from the open window. But he was the anchor, his hands on her shoulders and his golden-green eyes that looked down into hers with a promise that her body seemed to long to answer.

She swallowed. He made her nervous. She felt positively giddy when he looked at her like that.

Afterward, she had to sign a paper, and then there was a great outbreak of conversation and laughter as the other people tossed things over them, satin slippers and rose petals, which seemed odd and silly to Merlin. But she could tell that it pleased her new husband, for he held her arm very tight and kissed all the ladies on the cheek and grinned the whole time. She thought he was wonderfully handsome, and he seemed to know exactly what to say to everyone while Merlin could only stand there and cling to him and nod as often as possible. She had her own share of kisses, and not all on the cheek—but none of them were like Ransom's.

After cakes and tea and much raising of glasses of champagne while predictions on future happiness were made, Ransom announced with calm authority that Merlin was exhausted and the reception was over. She opened her mouth to protest. She was a little tired, but all the laughter and company fascinated her. She was enjoying it, and besides, she wanted another of the delicious little cakes with a glass of champagne.

She looked up at him, where he stood beside her chair, and said, "I'm not exhausted at all. Can't they stay longer?"

He smiled down at her, not even answering. He continued to accept the final-sounding congratulations that everyone made before they left the room.

Even Thaddeus left, with a pat on Merlin's head and a gruff "High time you was made an honest woman," a comment which brought a quick scowl to Ransom's face. The frown lingered when they were alone.

"What did he mean by that?" she asked.

"Nothing." Ransom stood behind her, unpinning the veil. "He just likes to take a poke at me whenever the chance arises."

"Yes. Thaddeus is that way. But I think he must like you, or he would have told me not to marry you."

The veil came free, along with her coiled hair. He slid his fingers into it, caressing her nape with the back of his hand. "Merlin," he said softly. "Do you want to rest?"

"No," she said. Her breath came a little faster. "I'm tired of resting. Why did you make everyone leave?"

He gave a low sound of amusement. "Hmm. Pure selfishness."

"I wanted another cake."

He cupped her cheeks and tilted her chin upward, bending over to brush kisses along her forehead and down her nose. "I should put you to bed and let you rest. You don't know how much strength you've lost."

"I feel fine," she said—a small fib. She did feel weak, but the way he was moving his lips in a whisper of warmth across her temple, over her eyelashes, down to the curve of her throat was enough to make anyone feel like jelly. "Oh—" she mumbled. "Whatever are you doing?"

"Loving you, Wiz." He lifted her hair, his jaw smooth and warm against her cheek. "Just . . . loving you."

"Why?" She took a deep breath. "Because we're married?"

"Mmm . . . the other way 'round. 'Better to marry than to burn'—have you never heard that? And I've been burning, Wiz."

A funny, small whimper escaped her as he slid his hands downward and rested them under her breasts, enclosing her in his embrace. She tilted her head back against his shoulder. His arms tightened. He pressed his mouth to the base of her throat.

Yes, she thought, as sensation spiraled through her body from the point where his lips touched her skin. *Much better to marry.*

He drew his hands away and straightened. "I'll come back later. I want you to rest."

"Rest?" The word seemed to have no context, no relation to the pounding in her blood or the way her throat tingled as if he were still kissing her. "But I like what you were—" She looked up at him. "I don't want to rest."

"I'll send my mother's maid to help you change."

"But, Ransom—"

He opened the door. "Rest," he ordered. "Take a nap."

"A nap!"

"Merlin," he said huskily. "I'm going to come back tonight."

There was a promise in his look, a glimmer of flame in his golden eyes. Merlin wet her lips.

"Will you stay longer then?"

He smiled. "I believe," he said slowly, "that I could manage that."

Ransom walked down the corridor, heading for the saloon where he reckoned the guests at his hastily arranged wedding would have migrated to continue their celebration. He'd given instructions to Collett that Mount Falcon's legendary hospitality should not fail them. He had a notion he could stand a few glasses of champagne himself. Leaving Merlin, all soft and misty-eyed from his caresses, had taken almost as much as Ransom was worth. But she needed the time to relax and adjust. He could tell that; could see the way her face had grown more and more bewildered as the ceremony proceeded.

Besides, he'd be a laughingstock if he closeted himself all day and night in the bedchamber like some half-grown stag with his first doe.

Burning. He closed his eyes with a self-conscious grin. *You're smoking like a chimney. Get a grip on yourself.*

He ought to be thanking God she was alive and awake. And he did. Oh, he did. And then he thought of her full lips parted beneath his and his hands in her hair, and his blood ran hot as ever.

He met his valet emerging from the room where Ransom had been sleeping temporarily.

"Your Grace," the man said. "Congratulations, Your Grace. And we're all happy as tuppence that Miss—ah—Her Grace the new duchess has recovered. Shall I be moving your things back into your own dressing room?"

Ransom nodded thanks. "Yes. Miss—" he began, and stopped himself. He shared a grin with the valet. "My wife is resting now. I think we can put off major removals until tomorrow morning. Wait on me in my dressing room then."

"Your Grace. Oh, and there is something else—in all that's happened, I hadn't wished to bother you with trifles. That hat you asked about . . . it most probably belonged to Lord Shelby. Or possibly Major O'Shaughnessy—it so happens they both use the same haberdasher and wear the same size. But His Lordship's man said that one of his beavers had turned up missing lately. The major has no valet, so I couldn't say for certain there."

Ransom cocked his head. "Do you have the hat?"

"Yes, Your Grace. It's with your things."

"Bring it to me."

The valet bobbed and disappeared back into the bedroom. He emerged a moment later with the hat. Ransom took it, turning it over and examining it again.

Yes—Shelby's, in all likelihood, and so a false lead. His brother might have lost it in The Wilderness anytime in the past two months. But it was an intriguing circumstance that Quin wore the same size and make . . . and even more intriguing that Quin had been so prompt in beginning an immediate search of Mount Falcon's grounds after the kidnapping.

Ransom spun the hat on his finger. He headed again for the saloon, glad to have a little fishing to do, to take his mind off the amorous messages that his impatient blood kept pumping.

"Hullo," Merlin said to the slender boy who'd knocked shyly on the bedroom door. "Who are you?"

His mouth dropped open. "Ma-Ma-Miss Ma-Ma-Merlin! I'm Woodrow!"

She put her finger to her lip. "I'm sorry. Are you a friend of mine? Ransom says I've forgotten things. I suppose I've forgotten my friends, too. I'd even forgotten *him*."

"Forgotten ma-ma-my uncle?" Woodrow stared at her. "I ca-ca-can't imagine anyone da-da-da . . . doing . . . that."

Merlin shrugged apologetically.

"Well," Woodrow said, "it's a ga-ga-good thing I've ca-ca-come. You haven't forgotten the flying ma-ma-machine, have you?"

"Of course not. I'm going to go back to work on it immediately. The wings are almost ready to be tested."

His eyes became round and distressed. "Oh, ba-ba-but—have you forgotten that, too? The ca-ca-crash?"

"Crash?"

"Yes. Your accident. You da-da-don't remember it?"

She shook her head, frowning. "Do you mean— You can't mean I had an accident in the flying machine?" she exclaimed.

Woodrow looked at her, chewing his thumb. He started to speak and then hesitated. "Uncle Da-Da-Da-Damerell hasn't told you?"

"No, I— All he talked about was that we were to be married."

"That's why you've ba-ba-ba-been sick. You fell from a very ga-ga . . . great . . . height, and hit your head, and you've ba-ba . . . *been* sleeping ever since." He moved closer to the chair and took her hand. "It was horrid. Everyone was afraid you would never wake up!"

"I was flying? I was flying in my flying machine? But I don't even remember bringing it to the point of being tested!"

"Yes, you da-da-did! And it flew, Ma-Ma-Miss Ma-Ma-Merlin. It flew! You ba-ba-ba . . . *beat* Mr. Pa-Pa-Peminney!"

"But I don't remember Mr. Pem— whoever. You say I beat him?"

Woodrow nodded vigorously. "Yes! It was flying, and it da-da-didn't ca-ca . . . crash . . . ba-ba-because it wouldn't work! It was da-da-da . . . *deliberate!*"

"What?" Merlin cried.

"I sa-sa-saw it! There was a ba-ba-ba . . . break . . . in the na-na-number ta-ta-ta . . . *two* strut, and I *know* it had ba-ba-been weakened with a ca-ca-copper screw, ba-ba-because I pa-pa . . . put . . . the steel one in ma-ma-myself! I ta-ta-ta . . . *tried* ta-ta-to ta . . . *tell* Uncle Da-Da-Damerell, ba-ba-but he was so . . . oh, he was horribly upset about you, Ma-Ma-Miss Ma-Ma-Merlin. He wouldn't ta-ta-talk ta-ta-to ma-ma-me." Woodrow bit his lip. "I think . . . maybe . . . he even ca-ca-ca . . . *cried.* It was scary."

"But I don't remember! I don't remember any of this! You're saying that I flew, and I don't *remember!*"

"Oh, yes. You da-da-did! Right here at Ma-Ma-Mount Falcon."

"Here? I worked on my flying machine here?"

"In the west ba-ba-ba-ballroom."

Merlin stood up resolutely. "Take me to see it."

Woodrow's eyes widened, and then dropped. "Ba-ba-but . . . it isn't there anymore."

"Where is it?"

The boy looked at the floor. He clasped and unclasped his hands nervously.

"Take me to the west ballroom, please." Merlin walked to the door and opened it, waving Woodrow through. "I want to see it."

She saw it. And the sight of the huge, silent, empty room, the painted ceiling, and the trailing strands of hemp that cast long shadows in the afternoon light . . . Like a mist dissolving to reveal the sky, the fog on her memory began to lift.

Her flying machine; her beautiful white wind-dream made real . . .

"Where is it?" she whispered.

"Ma-Miss Ma-Merlin . . ." Woodrow's voice was painful, small, and grieving in the echoes. "He burned it."

Chapter 20

The Godolphin Saloon glittered with celebration, with hastily donned elegance—bejeweled ladies and high-collared men who succeeded admirably in their determination to make this wedding as worthwhile as any event that had been planned for half a year. Ransom walked in with the hat on his fist, playing with it a little, accepting more congratulations, allowing some slightly tipsy guest to prop the misshapen beaver on his head at a rakish angle. He left it there in what he modestly judged to be a masterful imitation of sporting good humor, and worked his way around the room toward Quin.

Somehow—oddly enough—he tilted his head and the hat fell off as he reached the little group where Quin stood talking to Mr. Peale. Quin caught the headpiece just as Blythe glided up to take Ransom's arm.

"Damerell," his sister said. "I hope you know you look ridiculous."

"Thank you, Blythe. But I've just gotten married, you see."

"I fear your new bride's personality is already rubbing off. Wherever did you get that disgusting soiled hat?"

"Do forgive me, Lady Blythe," Mr. Peale said in a pained voice. "I'm afraid I gave it to him."

"Mr. Peale, by the Powers!" Quin said. "I'm shocked, that I am."

The reverend blushed. "It was not meant as a—a common jest, of course. I merely found it. Several weeks ago, in fact. Just after His Grace's new bride was abducted.

295

Of course, she was not his bride at that time, she was Miss Lambourne, but—''

''The heavenly Father,'' Quin said. ''I do believe this is my hat.'' He popped it on his head and grinned.

''Perhaps it is, sir,'' Mr. Peale said with heavy dignity. ''I apologize if you feel I was remiss in not returning it directly to you, but I did not know to whom it belonged. I was going to make inquiries before I put it in the charity box, but His Grace wished to give it to the little girls to play with.''

''Is it indeed your hat, Major O'Shaughnessy?'' Ransom lifted his eyebrows.

Quin took the hat off and glanced inside it. ''Bekins and Sons, Haberdashers.'' He clutched his heart with a theatrical grimace of surprise. ''Faith, can there be another gentleman in the whole of the King's realm who knows just where to steal a fine hat for a song? Howsomever''—he handed the hat back to Ransom—''not havin' lost one to me knowledge, I daren't try to claim this beauty. Where was it found, now?''

''The Wilderness, did you say, Mr. Peale?'' Ransom set the hat back on his head at the jaunty angle. ''Several days after I located Miss Lambourne.''

Quin looked at Ransom, rather too quickly. Ransom smiled. There was an instant of some emotion in the officer's face—a flow of confusion in the green eyes, a trace of tightening between his brows. He dropped his gaze, but not before Ransom recognized the faint, faint signs of guilty discomfort.

He'd expected that. Even if it weren't Quin's hat, which seemed most likely, Peale's find showed the officer as a poor hand at the investigation Ransom had assigned him.

But Ransom merely nodded, and turned to speak to Blythe, preparing to use his sister to ease away. As he shifted to take her arm, she looked up. Her pale face had turned to chalky white; she looked at Quin, and at Mr. Peale, and then at Ransom with eyes gone huge with distress.

"Lady Blythe—" It was a chorus of male concern, with Quin and Peale and Ransom all reaching at once to support her. She clutched at Quin's arm.

"Oh, my," she said weakly. "I feel quite faint."

"Lean on me, darlin'," Quin said.

He caught her around the waist, but Blythe struggled upright, pushing him away. "No! No, Major, I—mustn't! Ransom—"

There was a frantic tone in her voice, a plea that Ransom answered in spite of his exasperation at this excess of prudish sensibility. "Never mind," he said with soothing gruffness, supporting her as she flung herself away from Quin. "Major O'Shaughnessy won't eat you, I'm sure, but Mr. Peale and I will—"

"No!" Her lips worked. She made an effort to straighten, but he could feel her trembling. "I'm quite all right now. I don't need any help from Mr. Peale. Just let me sit down, Ransom. I want to sit down."

He led her to a chair. The commotion had attracted his mother and some other women; thankfully, he left Blythe in the midst of ardent female care. He strolled over to Shelby, who stood sipping champagne near the door, beneath the huge portrait of the Arabian stallion that had given the saloon its name.

Ransom swept off the battered hat and placed it in his brother's hands. "Yours, I believe?"

Shelby slapped the hat on his head and took it off again, grinning. "No. Not in my style at all, I'm afraid."

"Isn't it? I understand Bekins and Sons make your hats for a song."

"Aye. Otherwise they wouldn't be making them at all. Who told you that?"

Ransom took a glass of champagne from a passing footman. "O'Shaughnessy," he said pleasantly. "The two of you share an excellent haberdashery, it would appear."

Shelby looked puzzled. He turned the hat and examined it. "Ah. Well. Perhaps Bekins is coming down in the world. Give it back to Quin, then, and advise him to take better care of his furnishings."

Ransom shrugged. "I think it's more likely yours, Shelby, though it's ready for charity now. You've lost one recently, haven't you?"

"No."

Ransom looked up. "No? Think again. Somewhere in The Wilderness?"

"Of course not. You think I can't tell when a hat's on my head? I didn't even misplace my midnight-blue beaver when that villian of a tinker set upon me. Found it in the bushes."

"You're certain this one isn't yours?"

"Yes, quite certain. How could it be? I haven't lost a hat."

Ransom frowned at his brother.

"What difference does it make?" Shelby asked. A trace of belligerence had crept into his voice.

"Some. Shelby, I'd like to know the truth."

His brother straightened. "You think I'm not telling you the truth?"

Ransom laid a hand on his arm. "Don't go off half-cocked, thank you. I only mean I'm not jesting. I'd like to know if this hat is yours."

"Well, it ain't. I said it wasn't. All the hats I can afford are safely stored in my dressing room, I assure you."

"Your valet keeps better count." Ransom was smiling slightly, expecting Shelby to look chagrined.

Instead, his brother looked incensed. "You interrogated my valet about this?"

"I had my man ask around about the hat. It's your size, your tailor—you've lost one. Fine. No more to it than that."

"Fine," Shelby hissed. "Fine. And where was it found? The Wilderness? You think I don't see what you're leading up to?"

For a moment Ransom looked at his brother, at the proud, angry twist to Shelby's mouth. "I wasn't leading up to anything," he said slowly.

"The devil you weren't." Shelby's soft voice held a sneer. "I know you, brother. I know you well. And the case is building, isn't it? I thought for a time that all this fraternal affection was real, but I might have guessed that as soon as you were on your feet, black-sheep Shelby would be right at the top of your list of suspects!'' He downed the last swallow of champagne in his glass and tossed it into the fireplace. It shattered across the grate. ''Felicitations!'' he said loudly, and then turned to stride out of the room.

Before he reached the entrance, the double doors swung inward, impacting the brass doorstops with a booming crash.

Merlin stood in the doorway. She was shaking, her gray eyes huge and wild, her despairing gaze on Ransom. In the silence that followed her entrance, she walked up to him, lifted her foot, and kicked his shin with her satin slipper.

''You *burned* it,'' she cried into the hush, a cry that drew out and smeared into a moan like a wounded animal's. ''Oooh . . . I hate you; I despise you; I *loathe* you. How could you . . . do . . . this? How could you . . . do . . . this . . . to . . . me?''

''Merlin,'' he said.

''I've remembered.'' She sobbed for breath, and began backing away toward the door. ''I've remembered. I never said I would marry you. It was all a trick; you tricked me and you *burned* it. You burned my notes—'' Her voice rose in hysteria. ''My flying machine and all my notes and everything that I could use to build it again.''

He walked toward her, the only thing that moved amidst the frozen company. Her reaction numbed him; the words and her frenzied expression, the undiluted rancor in her eyes sent pain so deep that he barely even recognized it except as a strange sort of detachment.

He had not wanted this so soon. He had not wanted it at all. If she had never remembered, he would have been glad. He would have thanked God for the chance to win her freely.

But he had not understood until this moment the breadth and depth of his mistake.

''Merlin,'' he said again, at a loss for anything else.

She took a step backward away from his touch, a gesture of aversion that lanced through the numbness, a shaft of bright torment in arctic silence.

"I'm leaving," she said, and her voice was a hiss that carried all over the room. "I'm going home. I won't stay here in this house with you an instant."

She turned away, and he caught her. She shrank from him, a frenzied twist to pull away. "I won't stay here," she cried. "Do you hear me? I hate you; I hate you; don't *touch* me!"

He let her go. He had to think to breathe; his chest seemed paralyzed in a frozen ache.

She spun away. "I'm going . . . home!" Her voice was breaking, quivering up and down in violent notes. "You've tricked me and . . . forced me . . . and plagued me long . . . enough!" Chestnut hair fell thick and tangled over the daffodil dress. When she looked at him, wild-eyed, he did not even think she saw him. She was lost in her anguish, in furious grief. He was only a contemptible thing that was the cause of it.

A murmur rose from the party, not quite covering the light sound of her slippers on the marble floors. Then she was gone; fled down Mount Falcon's miles of corridors, the froth of yellow dress a memory in the cold hall.

He turned to the guests. He supposed they thought he should be mortified; he saw the shock and fascination on their faces. But that was easy to deal with. Easy. Let Blythe and his mother do it: let the fabled Falconer diplomacy smooth and distract and cozen away the scandal.

He felt only this rising outrage, this fury at himself for playing with fate and allowing it to beat him.

While the company still stared, he raised his glass with a feral lift of his lips and then tossed it after Shelby's into the grate. "Felicitations," he said, a vicious mock of Shelby, the party, and himself. "I believe I shall need them."

She was trapped.

She had no clothes but the billowy wedding dress and satin slippers. She couldn't find her own. The wardrobe in her old bedchamber upstairs was empty, and she dared not ask the maid for fear the girl would summon Ransom. Merlin knew he had followed her out of the saloon, but Mount Falcon was an excellent place to slip down a side corridor and vanish. She'd ceased to hear the sound of his stride behind her when she'd reached the stairs and hurried up them.

She'd thought of going to Thaddeus, until she remembered that he'd been a part of the trick, too. He'd not warned her of Ransom's treachery; never told her what Ransom had done. Her memory returned in bits and flashes: the way Ransom had ridiculed her flying machine, the times he'd bullied her or deceived her or cajoled her into obedience. He was a tyrant, worse than the worst of Pharaohs and Huns and Oriental Despots she'd read about in her great-uncle's books.

And her flying machine . . .

It was gone. He had burned it.

Burned it. She closed her eyes, shuddering as if the flames seared her own skin.

The walled garden where she sat hunched on a marble bench was dimming in the late sun, the big pool and neat flowerbeds sunken and hidden from the windows of the house. The fountain spun—four arcs of water that whirled languidly from the mouth of a gilded fish, catching the orange and pink gleam of sunset at their zenith, then landing with a light ripple that made shadows dance with silver on the water.

She watched it miserably, grieving for shattered dreams.

The fountain poured. The rotating streams of water paused, dribbled for an instant, and reversed direction, circling the other way.

Merlin lifted her head. A trifling memory came back to her, of wishing she could investigate the mechanism that controlled the rotating flow. She lowered her chin again. Another thing forbidden, another path she was not to take. She hated it here, where every impulse had to bow to some decree she failed to understand.

Well, she was going to leave. There was only tonight to be endured. Tomorrow, as soon as she found her hedgehog and some real clothes, she would be gone, escaped from the confines of wedding gown and satin slippers.

She lifted her head again. And in a burst of defiance, she stood up and kicked off her slippers and stockings, and dropped her gauzy shawl, wading barefoot into the pool.

It sloped rapidly downward, deeper than she'd realized. By the time she reached the fountain, the warm water was up to her waist, and the dress floated out like a pale yellow lilypad around her. She grabbed a gilded fin, preparing to scramble up onto the slick curve of the fountain's base.

"Merlin."

The word came sharply above the soft splash of water. She jerked upright. Her feet slipped, and she landed backward with a splash in the deepest part of the pool. Surprise and the dress hampered her; by the time she came up, she was gasping for air. Something hauled at the back of her dress—she choked and staggered and found her feet on the smooth marble floor, and twisted around to see Ransom in his sopping shirtsleeves.

He gripped her shoulders and shook her. "In the name of God," he shouted, "what do you think you're doing?"

Merlin went limp and morose in his hold. She might have known that even the smallest rebellion would be unsuccessful.

"Nothing," she said sullenly. "It's no business of yours."

"The devil it—" He stopped short, and let go of her. White linen clung to him wetly, outlining the shape of his torso in the last light of evening. The starch had melted from his collar; his lace jabot drooped on his chest. He expelled a deep breath. "Merlin," he said, in a voice that shook amidst the slosh of water. "When I saw you there, with that dress floating out, I thought—" He drew his hand down his face, wiping water. "God, you gave me a fright."

"Why?" She turned away from him, pushing wet hair from her face. "Are you afraid I might ruin your fountain by trying to find out how it works?"

"Is that what you were doing?"

"No." She ducked as a spray of water passed. "I didn't get a chance."

"Tomorrow I'll have it turned off. You can take it apart and see everything you want."

"Tomorrow I won't be here."

"Merlin," he said, and there was quiet anguish in his voice.

She put her hand on the golden fin, feeling tears rise. The spray passed again, a gentle ripple and a mist on her cheek.

He touched her arm, below the sodden puff of sleeve. She barely heard him above the water's light gush as he said, "I'm sorry."

"You burned it."

"I'm sorry," he repeated. "Will you let me explain?"

She twisted, sloshing water, staring up at him through the mist that had begun to rise. "How could you explain? It's gone."

His face was a contrast of paleness and shadow. In the twilight, his deep brown hair and eyebrows looked black, dusted with fine droplets from the lazy arcs of water that passed rhythmically over their heads. He looked at her, a long, strained look, and closed his eyes. "No. I can't explain. Not so that you would understand."

Her lips trembled. Through a blur she saw his arm move, lifting a thin sheet of water as he touched her cheek. His fingers drifted down her throat, sliding on warm liquid.

"I love you," he said. "I wanted you to be happy."

"Happy." Her throat worked in a sob. "How could I be happy in this place? How could I be happy with you?"

"Oh, Merlin," he whispered.

"Why?" she cried. "I don't know why you . . . *keep* me . . . here." Her voice had gone squeaky and out of control. The words began to rush in gasps of fresh despair. "I don't know why you . . . took away . . .

everything I've worked for all my . . . life. I want to go home, I—hate you! Oh, I want to go . . . home!"

He caught her shoulders. "You can't go home. Not yet."

"I *can.* Why not? I can't stand it here!"

"You'll have to wait—for a while, at least." His voice had grown gruff. He gave her a little shake that set water gurgling at her waist. "You're still in danger. You can't go now."

Desolation welled up in her. She leaned back against his grip, her fingers sliding on his wet sleeves as she pushed at him for release. "I can't wait. I'll forget. I won't be able to remember everything."

"You can't leave."

"I'll forget," she wailed, struggling harder. "All my notes, all my drawings. You *burned* it all."

"Merlin—"

"*Let me go!* Let me go; let me go." She fought him, blinded by tears and water. "I hate you. You burned it. It's gone. It's gone . . . and I tried so . . . hard! I was . . . so . . . close . . ." Her voice disintegrated, tearing apart into huge, choking sobs.

He was stronger than she was; his arms came around her shaking shoulders and drew her close against him. He kept saying her name, over and over, rocking her and holding her, his embrace sure and gentle, offering solace that no one in her life had ever offered.

He pressed his cheek to her hair. Through the racking sobs he stroked her. He hugged her until she leaned on him, crying harder, crying suddenly for all the times she'd failed and there'd been no one there to hold her, no one there to whisper what he did: that it would be all right; that he was there, he was there; that he loved her.

She finally held herself away, her breath short and hiccoughing. "Now I can't . . ." She swallowed and then moaned, pressing her wet forehead to his chest. "Now I . . . can't even . . . hate you."

"Good," he murmured, and kissed her hair. "Good."

"But what will I do? What will I do? My flying machine . . ." A sound of grief came from deep in her throat. "Oh—what will I do without it?"

"Investigate fountains?" he offered. "Invent electric carriages?" He tilted her head back between his palms. The hard planes of his face were softened, hopeful. "Make love to me?"

She closed her eyes, leaking tears.

"You're my wife." His lips moved over her skin, tasting the mingle of fountain and salt, touching the tender skin beneath her lashes with his tongue. She could hear the fountain spin lazily around them. It splashed like gentle weeping into the pool.

"You tricked me."

"I was wrong. I was impatient. I was scared a little, Merlin. I was afraid you wouldn't remember—that you wouldn't have me."

"I don't remember. Not much. I remember"—she hesitated, ducked her head—"when you came. I remember that. I remember saying I couldn't marry you."

His hands cradled her chin. Warm water caressed her where his body moved against hers. "Do you remember when I said I loved you?"

"How can you say you love me?" She pulled away. "How can you say that when you burned my aviation machine?"

"Merlin, it had crashed. It was ruined."

"And all my notes. Everything." She looked up at him, trying to find the malice in his face that might explain that betrayal. "As if you wanted to be sure I can never build it again."

There was no trace of spite in his expression; there was only a kind of pain, and behind it, a stubborn answer to the question "Why?" He pressed his forehead to hers. "I want you safe. I want you alive. It won't fly, Merlin. It never would have."

"It did!" She jerked back away from him, coming up against the marble curve of the fountain. "Woodrow said that it did."

"It got off the ground. And it crashed. Don't you remember?"

She shook her head miserably. "No. And that's the worst of all—that I flew and I can't remember it! I remembered you, and coming here, but after that everything goes to bits and pieces, and I don't remember flying at all, or even how I did it."

"The thing fell apart in the air."

"Woodrow said it was deliberately weakened."

"Woodrow is twelve years old. Merlin, I'd thought I could let you do it—that you could build the thing and I'd hire someone else to test it. But having seen what happened . . ." He gripped her arms and frowned. "It's a death sentence, to put a man in a machine like that and tell him to fly."

"It's not. And how do I know *you* didn't change the steel screw to a copper one, if you hate the idea of flying so much?"

"Me!" He grew taut, crowding her back against the fountain. "Are you mad? Do you think I would risk—" His voice broke, seemed to fail him for a moment. His fingers closed hard on her shoulders. "God, do you suppose I give a damn whether the thing worked, except for your sake? Do you know what I felt when I saw you lying there under that wreck?" He leaned on her suddenly, taking her mouth in a bruising kiss that Merlin could not push away. "I want you," he said in harsh answer to her struggles. "I want you. I won't lose you again."

She grew still, panting, not nearly strong enough to break his hold and knowing it. He bent and pressed his mouth to her throat, his warm tongue mingling with the water that slipped from her hair. Her wrists were trapped, pinned by his hard fingers against the marble, sliding slowly downward on the smooth film of water until their hands dipped together into the pool.

"Do you remember this?" he said against her skin. "Do you remember what it's like to have me love you?"

Merlin let out a sharp breath, feeling his body come against her through the layers of water and clothes. He was warmer than the water. She shuddered with it, with the sudden contrast of evening air on her sodden dress and the liquid heat that flowed around her and pressed into her.

"Ah, Merlin . . ." He buried his face in the curve of her shoulder and throat. "Don't be frightened. Let me love you."

She made a helpless sound, wanting this and not wanting it. She remembered—oh, yes, it was easy to remember what his loving was. The night had come down, but his white shirt glowed against the dark garden, defining his shape the way the sound of falling water defined a circle that enclosed them.

The muslin gown drifted and flowed about her. As her resistance softened he let go of her hands and gathered it up, tugging free the ribbon beneath her breasts. The tight bodice came loose. He pushed the filmy sleeves off her shoulders and down under the water, sliding his hands over the linen chemise that still clung to her body, kissing her bared shoulder. An ardent sound came from low in his throat, a masculine note of excitement that sent response shivering through her.

She lifted her hands to his shoulders. But he pushed her back against the smooth stone, fumbling at each tiny bow that held the wet chemise closed across her breasts. The linen garment came free and followed the gown, leaving her skin to slide uncovered in the warm lap of water at her waist.

"Are you cold?" he asked in her ear, when she trembled under his hands, under the sensation of the polished marble at her back and his palms against her naked hips beneath the pool.

She shook her head, feeling dreamlike, there and somewhere else at once, as if her body was his while her mind had gone far away. He moved back suddenly and an instant later pulled his shirt over his head in a cascade of white cambric and shimmering droplets. He let it go. It floated, a light roughness at her waist. He came to her with water coursing down his face and between their lips as he kissed her.

Merlin covered his hands at her hips and slid her palms up the slick length of his arms. Near his shoulders she paused, encountering the rough width of damp linen pinned around his upper arm.

In the darkness it was a pale slash, catching the first dim glow of moonlight above the wall. Merlin touched it, frowning. Remembering.

The place and moment came back to her clearly—another dusk gone to darkness with him, and blood flowing free instead of water.

Her fingers slipped over his glistening skin, following the curve of muscle that swept upward in a fine arc of living flesh to his shoulder—perfect harmony of form and strength. As beautiful as the symmetry in a curving wing. As precious.

"Ransom," she whispered in the ripple of water. "I have to leave, but . . ." *I love you. I still love you.*

She did not say it. The words came from nowhere, out of memories too hazy to make sense.

Liquid murmured as he took her in his arms. "You won't leave. I won't let you."

She did not argue with him. There would be this night to keep when he wasn't there. This memory; this time with him when his intensity and his power did not try to crush her dreams, but flowed and blended with them the way the fountain poured into the waiting pool.

She closed her eyes as he caught her mouth hungrily, pressing her back against the stone. She wanted what he wanted. For now.

Ransom felt her yield, felt her body go soft and willing as she arched to fill the space between them. His own responded instantly. He was already on a violently ascending edge with the provocation of water and darkness and her sleek, warm, naked shape that had teased and withdrawn and teased again—all unknowing, all that unblinking innocence of hers that accepted his outrageous overtures as if it were the most conventional thing in nature to be undressed and ravished in a garden fountain.

It was why he loved her, he thought recklessly. Because he'd always wanted to take his wife in a fountain, and never before known it.

The moon cleared the wall behind him, pouring cool light over her face as she tilted it back under his caress. Her lips parted in naive pleasure. The tiny motion sent him soaring: the sharp edge of passion hit its limit like metal searing glass, diamond-hard, pouring sparks into his bloodstream and heat through his brain.

He groaned, regretting the formal silk breeches that kept him from touching every inch of her and too impatient to get rid of them. And then, moving against her, pulling her down with him as he went to his knees with his hand between them for a hasty instant to free himself, he found the smooth material was an added sensation—water and silk and her skin like no silk ever made by the hand of man.

He slid between her legs, with his knees braced where the fountain's base curved into the marble floor. Water, moonlight-silver, lapped high at his chest and covered the tips of her breasts. He held her on his thighs, put his forehead against the base of her throat, and pushed into her.

He thought he was going to explode.

He went still for a desperate moment to prevent it. His muscles trembled a little, straining to move against his will. He turned his head, tasting her throat, catching a drop of water and sweet salty skin with his lower lip, scooping the flavor into his mouth on his tongue. He could feel her pulse, strong and fast against the corner of his mouth.

She did not move. She gave him nothing, but waited on his advance, not having been taught the nuances of loving yet. He thanked God for it; his control was stretched to taut impossibility. But some devil of impatient pleasure took possession of his hands: he slid them upward and spread his palms under her arms. His thumb slipped over one nipple, rubbing a provocative circle around the soft swelling of her breast.

He got what he deserved. She tightened on him, nestling and arching in his lap. Ransom closed his eyes and tilted his head back, breathing hard. She moved again, and a low moan escaped him.

"Ransom," she said, a faint, pleading sound, and it was not a plea he could deny. He swallowed, made himself open his eyes. He moved his thumb across her breast again, slowly. His lips drew back in savage pleasure at the way her head sank backward and her body lifted, asking for more.

He forced himself to keep his eyes open, maintaining control by watching her. Like a sea-nymph she lifted her dripping arms and circled his shoulders, sending streams of water down his back and chest. He saw her smile, saw her throat tighten as he brushed her nipples again, rotating his thumbs around and around the tender, swelling warmth of her, setting a rhythm that she began to echo with her body.

It was hard not to move with her. *Watch her face; watch her face,* he commanded himself, holding back his own response with grim humor. Her fingers worked at the base of his neck, slid down his shoulders, pulling her into him. He ceased to breathe. His muscles corded, wanting to match the rising tempo.

The faint mists rose around them. She looked like a living sculpture, carved from the night and the moon. There were dreams in her face, in her half-closed eyes as she arched beneath his touch. Her belly slid against his in the water, demanding whatever he had to give.

He cupped her breast and bent, licking his tongue across the tip that peeked above the water's surface.

The sound of her pleasure sent bright torture through his loins. He was shaking now, fighting himself. He played and tugged and caressed her with his tongue while every move she made drove shivers of reaction from his thighs to a place deep and unbearable in his chest.

She panted, grasping at his back. He dropped his arm, crossing it under her to help her. Like a beautiful sleek fish she flexed and rocked against him, making little moans that blended with the ripple of the fountain and the tiny waves that lapped and quaked against his skin, spreading out in a web of silver across the pool.

Her moans quickened. She wrapped her legs around him, a move that came as near to killing him as sweet agony could come. He squeezed his eyes shut and buried his face in the tender, slick skin beneath her arm, every muscle in his body frozen while she shuddered against him.

He heard his name beneath her breath, a frantic, beseeching repetition. It drew out into a long note of wordless bliss. She clutched at him. And he came up suddenly off his knees, holding her against him by the firm curve of her buttocks, shoving her back against the unyielding surface of the fountain where she could not slide away from him, where he could pump his life into her in long, deep thrusts.

Pleasure exploded around him before the water sheeting off their bodies had cascaded back into the waiting pool. He heard himself: a luxurious groan of climax, a fierce tremor, and then he was breathing in harsh gusts in the aftermath, his weight slipping downward on the film of liquid that covered everything.

Before that lazy slide could drown them both, he lifted himself, pushing away from the slick marble surface.

"Oh, my," Merlin said. "Oh, my. That was wonderful."

He laughed. With an excess of splashing, he pulled her up and cradled her against his chest. "Wonderful." He rocked her back and forth, setting up new webs of ripples.

She relaxed, slipping out of his embrace like quicksilver and leaning back against the fountain with her eyes closed and her faced tilted up to the moonlight. "I'd like to stay here forever."

"Not likely." He moved next to her, leaning his elbow on the gilded fish. "I'm not spending my wedding night in a fountain."

She yawned. Ransom slid his arm around her shoulders and let her rest against him. They watched the languid streamers of water spin around them and fall in arcs of liquid light. Merlin snuggled closer and yawned again.

He kissed the curling tendrils of damp hair beneath his chin. "You're exhausted. Lord, I've pushed you hard today, and you're barely recovered." He squeezed her. "Come, I'll take you to bed."

She let him lead her up out of the pool, where she shivered in the night air. He found his waistcoat and ran it over her shoulders and legs, soaking up the worst of the water before he draped around her the coat he'd thrown to the pavement. Merlin sat on the edge of the pool and dangled her feet as he waded back in and retrieved her gown and his shirt.

She thought he looked like some pagan god, emerging from the pool with the white silk breeches molded to him and water glistening on his hair and chest. But he had to wring out the garments like an everyday washerwoman. Then he gathered shoes and stockings and made a damp bundle. "Here. Carry this, if you please."

Merlin stood up to take it. As soon as she did, he swept her up and carried her out of the garden with her bare feet dangling. He was breathing a little more heavily than normal by the time he climbed the terrace and then the single set of stairs that led to an open, floor-length window in the dark wing of the house that overlooked the gardens. He ducked through the open window and set her on her feet.

He kissed her forehead. "Wait here."

Merlin obeyed, too tired even to try to peer around the room and identify it. When he came back a few moments later, he had a pair of towels. She stood passively as he rubbed her hair and his own and stripped off the sodden breeches. In a shaft of moonlight she could see him, naked, all polished planes and muscle like a work of Grecian art. In hazy curiosity she reached out and smoothed her hand over his hip, brushing the part of him that was so different from herself. He stirred as she watched in fascination; his hand tightened on the nape of her neck.

"Mmm." He breathed lightly on her skin, pushing himself into her hand a little. "Merlin. Come to bed."

When she only stood there, swaying with weariness, he picked her up again. He carried her through one door, then laid her on a bed and sank down behind her. The bedclothes smelled of lilac. He took her in his arms and curled around her, his face in her shoulder, his legs drawn up under hers so that the warm evidence of his arousal pressed lightly at her back.

But he did not initiate any loving again. "Tomorrow," he whispered when she asked. "There's time enough. All my tomorrows belong to you." He stroked her skin and curled his arm beneath her breasts. "Just sleep with me tonight, sweet Wiz."

She tried, experimentally, to move away from him. His embrace tightened, holding her prisoner.

"Rest now," he ordered softly. "Stay here and sleep."

She stared into the dark and pondered that command. So simple, and so crushing in the knowledge that he could enforce it. That all the power in this world was his—he was stronger than she, and slyer, and more ruthless. Like a prince in a fairy tale, he would slay all the dragons and leave none for her. She would be safe. And dull, and pointless.

She swallowed, feeling his arm relax, his chest rise and fall in steady slumber against her spine. Then she sought his fingers, entwining them with hers.

One silent tear fell on her hand. Another followed. One for being free of him. And one for being lonely.

Chapter 21

She slipped away by kissing him. There was hardly light enough to see when he half-woke as she tried to work her way out of his arms. He hugged her to him, mumbling something about no ride that morning. "Better ideas," he murmured with a sleepy squint.

She leaned above him and whispered, "I have to get up. I'll be back in a moment."

He turned over and stretched with an indolent smile, sliding his hand around the nape of her neck and drawing her down for a slow, heady kiss. Merlin's resistance flagged. She pressed herself against the length of him, fascinated by the naked, smooth power of his sleep-warmed shape. But when he crossed his leg over hers and rolled toward her, she scrambled back, out of reach and off the bed.

He lay with his eyes barely open, his hand outstretched where she'd evaded it. "Don't be . . . ." He sighed and pulled her pillow toward him instead, shoving it up beneath his head. ". . . gone . . . ." His thick lashes drifted closed. "long . . ."

"No," she whispered. "I won't."

She stood by the bed. It was hard to leave him. Hard. Painful to deceive. She pressed her fist to her mouth and watched him as he rested in that drowsy, sweet contentment, believing her lie.

Knowing well that if he hadn't, it would never have been so easy.

In his dressing room she found clothes. They were Ransom's, true, a pair of tawny doeskin breeches laid neatly over the back of a chair, and a voluminous shirt on the horse by the fireplace. Merlin touched her lower lip as she looked at his midnight-blue coat, white waistcoat, and razors, all stiffly awaiting the duke's pleasure as if in silent attention.

She wrinkled her nose and grabbed the shirt, pulling it over her head. The breeches came almost to her ankles and were loose at the waist, but she remedied that by utilizing a conveniently long, starched length of snowy linen as a sash. Footwear was a bigger problem. She was obliged to choose between a pair of top boots which were far too large and some knee-high leather gaiters to fasten over the satin slippers she'd worn the day before.

She straightened from buttoning the gaiters and squinted through the early morning gloom at her figure in the mirror. With the chestnut tangle of her hair too wild to speedily tame to order, she looked absolutely indecent—like some gypsy boy about to make off with a stolen horse.

She bit her lip, and glanced around. Ransom's crimson silk dressing gown hung behind the wardrobe door. She shrugged into that and peered into the mirror again. Satisfied that the floor-length folds gave her a reasonable degree of countenence, she dragged the excess length behind her to the corridor door.

A soft scraping sound disturbed the silence behind her. She paused with her hand on the knob, looking back. On a table next to Ransom's shaving articles there was a bandbox, its lid shifting restlessly. As she watched, the paperboard cover lifted, and a beady, black nose thrust out, followed by two paws and a familiar small face.

"Sshh." Merlin poked the hedgehog back into the box and swung it up by the braided strap. Gathering the dressing gown over one arm to keep it from rustling, she let herself silently out the door.

When she reached the Great Hall, she found the huge double doors already open. The footman looked at her, looked away, and looked at her again with his eyes a little wider. Merlin nodded at him and hurried out the door. Shelby was pacing the steps, flicking his riding crop, and staring impatiently into the court.

He turned at the sound of her footsteps. For a moment he frowned at her, and then he exclaimed, "Good God, Merlin, where are you going rigged up like that? You look like a Cossack."

"I couldn't find my clothes." She started to hurry past him, but he caught her arm.

"Where are you going?"

"To ride."

He laughed, but the sound he made didn't seem very amused. "Is that so? In my brother's dressing gown and breeches?" He tilted his head and peered at her more closely. "And his cravat for a sash! Very fetching!"

She pulled the gown around her. "I told you. I couldn't find my clothes."

"And I suppose you're taking along an equally fashionable chapeau in that bandbox? To embellish your mount's equine beauty, perhaps?"

"No, I—"

A cheerful hail made them both turn. "Your Grace!" Mr. Peale came along the terrace from the direction of the chapel at a measured pace. "Good morning, Your Grace. I have just come from my early devotions, in which you were foremost in my prayers. May I offer you my most heartfelt felicitations and best wishes, which to my great regret I did not have the chance to proffer to you in person yesterday?"

Merlin looked at him blankly as he swept off his hat and bowed so low that he almost touched the step below her. The first rays of the sun over the eastern arch sent his long shadow rippling across the stone.

"He means you," Shelby said, with a light edge of sarcasm. "Duchess."

"Oh." Merlin bit her lip. She twisted the bandbox around her wrist and bobbed in a little curtsy, holding out the dressing gown.

Mr. Peale looked at her breech-clad legs and cleared his throat. He seemed to be at a loss for words for a moment. Then he said, "And where might you be off to so early on this fine morning, Your Grace?"

"Oh," Merlin said. "Nowhere in particular."

"I can't think how I come by the notion," Shelby said in ironic tones, "but I have the distinct impression that the duchess is leaving her husband."

She frowned at him.

"I beg your pardon, Lord Shelby." Mr. Peale gave him a repressive look. "I believe your attempt at levity must be found by any person of sensibility to be in exceedingly poor taste."

"Ah. Yes, I see that you must be quite an expert on levity, Mr. Peale. How unfortunate that I was serious." Shelby regarded Merlin and her bandbox with a speculative eye. "Indeed, I'd advise Her Grace that if she has the good sense to want to desert my brother, she'd do better to let me hire her a post-chaise at the village than go haring off across country in a dressing gown."

"Now see here!" Mr. Peale moved up a step. "You can't do that!"

"Can't I? Why ever not?"

"But she's married to the duke now," Peale blustered, as the sound of horseshoes rang in the early morning silence of the court. "She cannot leave without his permission."

Shelby swung his crop dismissively. "Don't be gothic, Mr. Peale. The lady's not a prisoner here."

"Oh, yes, I am." Merlin looked at the prancing bay stallion that a groom struggled to control as he led it toward the steps. "Can I borrow your horse?"

Shelby rolled his eyes. "No, you cannot. Are you daft?"

He started down the stairs. Merlin went after him, meaning to ask the groom to saddle the dappled pony on which she'd been taking her riding lessons as a poor second choice. She doubted it could run half as fast as Shelby's Centurion. Mr. Peale laid a hand on her arm.

"Your Grace! Your Grace, I beg your indulgence; I don't mean to detain you, but surely—Lord Shelby is not correct? You don't actually mean to—to leave Mount Falcon without your husband's permission?''

"Not dressed like that," Shelby advised, swinging up onto the restive bay. "At least find some decent shoes."

"No—no, I can't wait! Saddle my pony, please," she said to the groom. "As quickly as possible. I have to leave before Ransom wakes up. He won't let me go, Shelby."

"But Your Grace," Peale spluttered in scandalized accents. "Your Grace! Are you running away? I can't credit this!"

The bay shied and pirouetted, anxious to be moving. Shelby reined him in. "You can't go crying off alone, widgeon. I'll arrange something."

"But I have to hurry." Her voice rose a little. "I have to."

The stallion circled on his forehand. His black tail swirled across flanks that gleamed in the red rays of the sun. He dropped his haunches and bounced off his forefeet a few inches—a strong hint to his rider about what he thought of the delay. "I can't talk now," Shelby said in exasperation. "Go pack some reasonable clothes, and don't go farther than the main gate, Merlin. I'll meet you there."

"I find this utterly appalling," Mr. Peale exclaimed. "Lord Shelby—the bonds of holy matrimony—you must not . . . You cannot intend to betray your brother in this way!"

"Why not, Mr. Peale?" Shelby asked with a mocking curl of his lips. The stallion started to rear in earnest. Shelby leaned forward. The horse dropped, shied, and bucked, and then stood with neck arched and nostrils trembling under his rider's command. "My brother's already got half a mind to think I sold Merlin to that damned tinker. What's one more crime"—he turned the horse—"out of so wonderfully many to my credit?"

The bay's hooves sent crushed gravel flying as Shelby let him go. Merlin didn't wait to see them disappear through the arched gateway; she hurried toward the stable after the groom.

Mr. Peale strode alongside. "Your Grace, this is most ill-advised. Think a moment. The intimation of the divine will was communicated to the first woman immediately after the Fall. The New Testament says: 'Let the wife see that she reverence her husband.' " He spread his hands as he walked, supplicating. "And: 'Wives, submit yourselves unto your own husbands as unto the Lord; for the husband is the head of the wife, even as Christ is the head of the church; therefore as the church is subject unto Christ, so let the wives be to their own husbands in everything.' "

"Poo," Merlin said.

"Your Grace, you go against both God and Nature in this rebelliousness. Think on what I myself have said on the subject of female education. 'Submission and obedience are the lessons of her life, and peace and happiness are her reward!' You cannot reasonably doubt that under the divine law, faithful and willing compliance is a branch of your connubial duty. And while the obligation is unimpeachable, Your Grace, let not the ends for which it is imposed be misconceived. Man has been furnished by the Creator with powers of investigation and of foresight in a somewhat larger measure than your sex."

She stopped and turned on him. "Yes, you would think so, wouldn't you? I suppose Ransom told you that."

"Why, no, Your Grace. It is a universal truth."

"Poo." She started walking again.

"Your Grace," he called after her. "I must warn you, I feel it is my duty to report this to your husband as soon as may be."

Merlin cast a glance over her shoulder. He was already walking back toward the house, his coattails flying out behind him. She pulled the cloak around her and began to run. There would be no time to wait for Shelby if Mr. Peale went in and woke Ransom now. She had to get away instantly.

In the stable the grooms were just rubbing down the gray pony. Merlin hovered around, urging them to speed. By the time she mounted, clutching the bandbox in one arm and tucking the crimson dressing gown around the sidesaddle, the sun was well above the horizon. Ransom was probably already awake.

She kicked the placid pony and sent it cantering down the drive. The broad meadows and woods of Mount Falcon's park glistened with dew, and ground fog still hung in the hollows. Up ahead, just as the triumphal arch of the main gate came into view, she saw the sun reflect on some pinpoint of a polished surface.

The reflection came again, and then as she followed the freshly raked drive down into a small valley and up around a sweeping turn, the famous vista on her other side presented the house itself, set like a crown on a bed of velvet green. From somewhere near the house came another pinpointed sun reflection. A flash: once, twice, and then a third time—that almost might, to a vivid imagination, have seemed to answer the one from the gatehouse.

She hiked the sliding bandbox closer up under her arm and slowed the dappled pony to a trot. As she approached the arch, the keeper emerged, standing beneath the painted and gilded ducal crest wrought in the center of the black iron gates. He turned a broken-toothed smile on her, doffing an old-fashioned tricorne as she came to a halt. He wasn't wearing the wine-red livery of Mount Falcon. Merlin supposed it was too early in the morning for that kind of faradiddle all the way out at the gate.

"Excuse me," she said. "Could you tell me which way to the village?"

"Aye, miss. But that pony's workin' on a loose shoe. Best get down a moment and let me have a look at 'er."

She clutched the bandbox and scrambled down, clinging to the saddle of the patient pony. But before she could even turn 'round again to face the gatekeeper, a hard hand and a handkerchief reeking a familiar, nauseating odor clamped over her mouth and nose.

Merlin didn't even bother to struggle.

Oh, drat it all, she thought, holding tight to the bandbox as her knees went to liquid and the darkness closed in. *Not again.*

* * *

"Well, she never showed up," Shelby said. "As I've told you five hundred times in the past two days." Candlelight glinted in his bright hair as he lounged back and tossed off a fourth glass of port in one swallow. He looked at Ransom with insolent blue eyes. "Still aching to find a flaw in my story?"

"A clue, maybe." Ransom ignored his brother's flushed sullenness. He was drawing aimless circles on the side of his glass, past angry desperation and sinking toward black furious despair. One night and two days and no lead, and he felt like howling, like standing up and laying waste to his glass and the decanter and all the furniture he could reach.

On the fireplace mantel a clock struck, and another across the room echoed it—nine deep-toned peals in tandem. He put his elbows on the tea table that graced the center of the Godolphin Saloon, resting his forehead in his hands. "A hint. One God damned place to start."

"Yes, our esteemed friend the major here has been a bit backward in his investigations, hasn't he?"

"By the Powers," Quin exclaimed. "Just what do you mean by that, sur?"

Shelby gave him a malicious, sidelong glance. "Take it any way you please. *Sir.*"

"Shelby." Blythe stood up. She bit her lip and walked in small, agitated steps across the floor. As she came within a few feet of where Quin stood by the bookcase, Mr. Peale stood up in ponderous formality, bowing as she passed. She hesitated, and turned back, putting her hand to her temple. "Shelby, I wish you would not start a quarrel. It gives me the headache."

"My profound apologies!" Shelby said unrepentantly.

Quin took a deep breath. There was a light flush above his collar. "You might be givin' your sister some support at a difficult time, Your Lordship—if I could be bold enough to suggest it."

"Oh, of course. If you're bold enough to hang about this house at all, you might as well."

Blythe pursed her lips. "Please—"

"Please what, Blythe?" Shelby flung himself out of his chair. "Please sit here quietly and watch Ransom go to pieces waiting for someone to find his wife's body at the bottom of a well?"

"*Shelby.*" Duchess May's voice was soft steel. "That's enough of that."

"Is it?" Shelby turned on her. "What *are* we waiting for? Search parties organized by this—this—" He waved his hand toward Quin in disgust, and then looked at Ransom. "Why O'Shaughnessy, damn it? Some half-pay major—for all we know of it, he's been cashiered for graft! Why him? I've offered. I know the country; I know the men. *He can't find her*, Ransom. For God's sake, let me try."

"It doesn't need your help," Ransom said. "I've organized the search—Quin's only carried out my orders."

"Aye." There was bitterness in Shelby's voice. "No orders for me, of course."

Ransom looked at his volatile brother. Shelby was primed to go off like a barrel of gunpowder at the least hint of accusation. "And there won't be," he said sharply. "There's something odd in this, Shelby. I don't want any of the family to venture outside the park." He lifted his glance briefly to Shelby's ex-wife where she sat a little distance away with Woodrow, who had adamantly refused to go to bed. "That includes you, Jacqueline."

She inclined her head.

Ransom looked back at Shelby. "And most certainly you."

Shelby opened his mouth to retort, and then closed it. He frowned at Ransom. But the resentful set of his mouth softened a little. "I can take care of myself," he said.

"This is my failing," Mr. Peale mourned. "If only God had seen fit to enable me to find the proper words to convince Her Grace of her Christian duty to obey her husband—"

"One might wish that while He was at it, He'd seen fit to give you a particle of sense," Shelby snapped. "I don't doubt it was your sermonizing that drove her off before I could arrange something suitable to placate her!"

He jerked his head in contempt. "Any cocklehead could have seen that she was in no mood to obey anything Ransom had to say after she found out he'd burned her flying machine."

Ransom stared at the decanter of port in front of him. "This cocklehead didn't," he said brutally.

Shelby picked up the decanter and poured two drinks, shoving one across the table toward Ransom. "So. Give a dog an ill name, and hang him out of the way at once!" He lifted his glass. "Join the ranks of Falconers who can't seem to hold on to their wives."

"Do go to bed, Shelby," Blythe said. "You make everything worse."

He took a swallow of port and sat down at the table, not even bothering to look at Blythe.

"Perhaps," Mr. Peale said, "we should engage in a period of prayer and meditation to calm our souls."

Unenthusiastic silence greeted this suggestion. Ransom barely even heard it. Instead he just sat, brooding in his fear and outrage.

Finally, the dowager duchess said, "That may be an excellent idea, Mr. Peale. Will you lead us in a prayer?"

"I would be honored, Your Grace. Most honored." Mr. Peale cleared his throat. "And if Major O'Shaughnessy would be so kind as to turn to his left and take down a book from the bookcase for me—I believe I know of a text appropriate to this situation. The work of the Reverend Mr. Caldicott . . . on the third shelf, Major, that thickest tome with the gold spine. No, no—not that one, I'm afraid! To the right—oh!"

Mr. Peale stood up as the volume Quin had touched slumped over and came crashing down onto the floor, bringing four more along with it. A slip of paper went sailing and landed at Ransom's feet.

He picked it up. In the candlelight he glanced at it briefly, started to hand it to Quin, and then held it back. He frowned down at the set of neat letters and numerals.

5,000£ in gold and 55,000£ in numbered bank notes received of Mr. Alfred Rule and accrued to the

*balance of Lord Shelby Falconer this twenty-fifth day
of July in the year of Our Lord eighteen hundred and
five. Your humble servant, Richard Corliss, clerk to
the Bank of England.*

Ransom stopped breathing. It froze him. He sat there
holding the slip and felt his body grow hot and then cold.

Five thousand in gold. Fifty-five in notes. A date one
week old and a betrayal that struck deeper than bright
steel through his heart.

For the first time in his adult memory, he had no in-
kling of what to do. He just felt blank. Helpless. He lifted
his eyes and looked at his brother—a long, stupid, baffled
look, and then back down at the receipt.

"What is it?" Blythe asked.

Ransom laid the paper on the table. Of a sudden, he
did not want to touch it. He stood up. He had to think;
he had to get away and think, but Shelby was already
leaning across the table to reach for the receipt. With an
ugly fascination, Ransom watched his brother lift the slip
and glance down to read it.

For an instant nothing happened. Then Shelby's face
changed, and Ransom could not tell if it was real or a lie
when his brother whispered hoarsely, "My God . . . oh,
my God. What is this?"

He looked up at Ransom. What emotion showed in his
own eyes, Ransom did not know, but the blood left his
brother's face. Shelby's throat worked, as if there were
words there that would not come out. He crushed the receipt in his hand and started to stand. Ransom didn't wait.
He found himself an abrupt coward, unable to face this,
unready for a confrontation. He shoved his chair back and
strode out the door, yanking it closed behind him.

In the dim corridor, a footman standing in a pool of
candlelight came to attention. Ransom hesitated. He had
an order to give, but he was afraid that his tongue would
not obey him. The stammer hung at the back of his
throat. He closed his eyes, gathering himself, trying to
collect the pieces of shattered illusion.

"Wake Mr. Collett," he said finally. "Tell him that he is to place a"—here Ransom had to pause, to force his tongue around a word that nauseated him—"body-guard . . . with Lord Shelby. At all hours. My"—Ransom had to wait again, for the physical mastery of his tongue to speak—"brother," he managed eventually, "is not to leave the house."

The footman bowed, impassive. "Your Grace," he said, and turned away.

Ransom walked a few steps down the corridor. Beyond the ring of candlelight, he lost momentum. The shadows beside a marble column made a refuge. Like some mongrel dog he hid in them, leaning his cheek against the stone to suffer a wound that was only just beginning to lose its numbness and turn to agony.

The saloon door slammed. Shelby's boot heels set up an echo in the hall. He passed Ransom, saw him, and stopped.

"It's not true," Shelby said.

Ransom wanted to believe that. He wanted it so badly that he did not trust himself to speak, or move, or think straight. He simply looked at Shelby.

"I had your bank draft delivered to Rule." His brother stood stiffly, hands locked behind his back. The faint candlelight picked out his features in perfect profile and turned his hair to sculpted gold. "I got my notes back. I gave them to you. I did what I said I would. This— *thing*—you saw—" He held up the crumpled receipt. "I don't know what it is, or whence it came. I've taken no money from Rule since you told me what he was. Before God, Ransom."

"Yes," Ransom said softly. "It would be necessary for you to claim so, wouldn't it?"

Shelby's mouth took on a grim curve. "*Claim* so?"

"Either way. Traitor or dupe . . . you have to protest your innocence."

The grim curve became murderous. "You don't believe me."

"Shelby." Ransom let out a slow breath. "I cannot afford to. Not anymore."

"Because of *this?*" Shelby cried viciously. He flung the paper to the floor and stepped forward. "I ought to kill you. I don't take the lie from man or mortal."

Ransom straightened. He was an inch taller than Shelby, and he used it. In a low, snarling voice he said, "You'll take from me what I hand out, my friend. There's enough suspicion hung around your neck now to drown an ox. Try to press me, and I'll forget family honor and do my task like any other of the King's magistrates—let the evidence swallow you whole."

"Family honor!" Shelby hissed. "Since what century have we concerned ourselves with that?"

Ransom stared into his brother's furious blue eyes. "You tell me. You tell me, Shelby."

His brother's gaze faltered; rose again. "Do you think I'm in Bonaparte's pay, then? Do you think for sixty thousand pounds I sold Merlin to that damned Corsican pirate?"

"He da-da-da . . . . *didn't!*" Light poured into the corridor from the saloon's open door. Woodrow stood in the portal, his small figure throwing a long shadow across the floor. "Ma-ma-ma . . . my pa-pa-papa wouldn't da-da-da . . . . *do that!*"

"Master Woodrow." Peale appeared in the doorway behind the boy, sounding flustered. "This won't be any of your concern, my dear child. Forgive my presumption, Your Grace—but shall I ask the boy's mother to take him to his chamber?"

"Unnecessary." Jaqueline glided into the corridor, taking Woodrow's hand. Instead of turning away toward the stairs, she drew him with her to Shelby's side. "I wish to hear, and Woodrow, too, these accusations against his father."

Ransom glanced down the hall, where the whole party was crowding now into the cool marble corridor. He swore beneath his breath.

"It's none of your affair, ma'am!" Shelby said, equally furious.

Jaqueline lifted her head, her magnificent violet eyes calm. "It is."

"Why?" He moved away from her a step and swept a bow to the others. "Anxious to see me hanged by the neck? State your case, brother—we've judge and jury here to try me!"

"Shelby," Ransom said in a warning tone.

"Nay—let's go at it! I'll begin myself. The suit is watertight, Your Grace; the evidence is heavy." Shelby flung out his arm recklessly. "You said so not a moment past! There's knowledge first—there's knowing what a muddlehead like Merlin is worth and why you brought her here. There's—"

Ransom caught Shelby's arm. "Don't do this."

Shelby jerked away, his fine nostrils flaring with temper. "No, let them hear! They deserve to know what a viper you've held to your bosom. Listen now—the tinker's camp—who took her there? I arranged it. I dangled the bait of a pinion gear, and she fell right into that little trap, didn't she?" His blue eyes glittered. "And I drugged myself, of course! To turn away suspicion. The temple was my triumph, though. Who but you and Blythe and I knew of the temple room till now?"

"No! Papa—" Woodrow tried to reach for his sleeve, but Shelby swung away.

"We took an oath on that, we three. Would I hold to a childhood oath? Look at the progress of my sorry life, ladies and gentleman," he sneered. "Look at the fact that I sank to the tune of sixty thousand under a gentleman of French connections and make your own conclusions. Oh, yes, and that amazing, incriminating hat! It's mine, you say? Well, how shall I defend against a blow like that? I haven't lost one, nay—but it must be mine. Why, the case must be rested on that point alone!"

"So rest it," Ransom said darkly.

Shelby turned a scornful look upon him. "Embarrassed now? You only care to assert your accusations in private?"

"I only care to recover my wife. And see that any bastard who put her in danger is drawn and quartered. If you're responsible, then count your days, brother. They have a limited number."

"But he's not!" Woodrow cried. "It wasn't my papa. *Everyone* knew about Miss Merlin's pinion gear and how she wanted it. And he isn't the only one who knew about the temple, either! I saw Aunt Blythe there, and she was showing Major O'Shaughnessy—"

"Woodrow!" Blythe hurried forward. "You little beast, you swore to me—"

"I'm not carrying tales! It's important, don't you see? He thinks my papa tricked Miss Merlin and put her in the temple, and he *didn't.*"

"Oh, I feel faint." Blythe put her hands to her eyes and moaned. "Shelby!"

He looked toward her keenly, making no move to support her as she swayed. "What's this? New evidence?"

"Mamá!" Blythe crumpled to her knees. "Oh, I'm ill. Help me!"

It was Quin who knelt quickly beside her, cradling her head against his shoulder. "Darlin'," he soothed. "It's all right; it's all right; don't be frightened, my love."

Blythe whimpered and clung to him, pressing her cheek to his chest.

"Now, see here, Major!" Mr. Peale exclaimed in a scandalized voice.

Blythe stiffened. "No!" She struggled to sit up. "Get away from me—don't touch me! Oh, God, I can't bear—"

"Be still," Ransom snapped. He stared coldly at Quin. "O'Shaughnessy," he said, "I'll have the truth from you, I think."

Blythe moaned and buried her face in her hands. The officer tightened his hold on her quivering shoulders.

"Your Grace," he said. "May I—in private—" He set his jaw. A deep flush was rising in his face. "Your sister, sir, for her sake—"

Ransom took a step forward. "I am out of patience, Major. Here and now. Did she show you the temple room?"

"Your Grace," Quin said in a rush, "I wish to marry Lady Blythe!"

Dead silence greeted his announcement. Then Shelby began to laugh.

Quin glared up at him. His face went from red to white, but he only gathered Blythe's hands and held them to his lips. "Don't weep, love. Don't."

"How touching." Shelby crossed his arms and leaned back against the marble pillar. "It very nearly makes me ill."

Quin kept his head bent, but his broad shoulders went still and tense.

"When did she show it to you, Major?" Ransom asked.

Still Quin did not look up. He pulled out his handkerchief and bent over Blythe, gently applying it to her cheeks. She grasped at his hands, shaking her head violently.

"Sshh, darlin'," he murmured. "It will be all right." He looked up finally and met Ransom's eyes. "I first went there with her not long after I arrived, sir."

Blythe began to rock and whimper. Quin held her close.

"I suppose I needn't inquire as to why," Ransom said.

Quin took a deep breath. "Your Grace. I love her."

"Yes, I think you'd damned well better. Any other reason for your actions chills me."

Blythe buried her face in the handkerchief. "I'm sorry. I'm sorry. Oh, I want to die!"

"Lady Blythe," Mr. Peale said in a stricken voice. "Lady Blythe. Has this criminal used you ill? Has he ruined your good name, and for no more reason than a villainous plan to abduct Miss Lambourne?"

Quin jerked around. "You slimy little—I'll horsewhip you for that!"

"Your paltry threats do not frighten me, sir!" Peale cried. "I'm a man of God, but choose your weapon—I'll go out with you to avenge this calumny! She is far above you, and yet you've dragged her down into the muck of your base de—"

"Good God, Peale," Ransom interrupted. "Take your-self off. I can't stomach a rejected suitor's hysterics right now."

Mr. Peale gave Quin a trembling glare. "Your Grace," he said without looking at Ransom. He turned around, and with a jerky stride, disappeared into the dark.

The Duchess May came forward. She gave Quin a look that Ransom found unreadable. "Please help my daughter to her feet, Major O'Shaughnessy. I believe she had best retire now."

"Oh, Mamá," Blythe said, muffled in the handker-chief. But she leaned on Quin as she rose, and let him hold her for an instant in a tighter grip before she turned into her mother's arms.

"So affecting," Shelby said when Blythe and the dow-ager duchess were gone. Quin stared at a point near Ran-som's feet, not answering.

"I would like to hear all of this story," Ransom said to him. "From the beginning."

Quin's lips tightened. He glanced toward Woodrow and Jaqueline.

Ransom nodded in mocking answer to the unspoken question. "Yes, Woodrow will stay. I need one word at least that I can depend upon."

The boy looked up at him, eyes wide. He stood a little straighter.

"Major," Ransom prompted with a nod of command.

"There's little to tell, sir. Her Ladyship is blameless."

Ransom's mouth flattened. "So blameless that you'd hang for it? I have some choice, you know. I can believe you forced yourself on my blameless sister and then blackmailed her into telling you the key to that room, or I can believe she was not so innocent, but a willing party in a flirtation that went a bit far."

"It's not—" Quin scowled. "I meant that— Damna-tion, what do you want me to say? I flirted with her, aye! It was a challenge at the start. And then, when she came to me—when I learned to see—" He paced away, stopped, and looked at Ransom suddenly. "You don't know her! No one here knows her, or looks past the damned Falconer fortress she's built around herself. She's lived in your shadow until she's almost lost her own will. That puffball Peale—that pompous little bag of air—why do you suppose she suffers him, but that he has your sanction? She would have married him a half dozen times over if I'd not begged her to think. If I'd not—'' He turned his face away, rubbing his mouth.

"Damaged the goods?" Shelby suggested dryly.

Quin swung back. For an instant, there was murder in the air. Ransom moved a step, putting himself between them. "If you were meeting my sister at the temple, why didn't you find Miss Lambourne when she was held there?"

"We didn't go then. We hadn't gone. Not for weeks. Apparently Mr. Peale told her he had been walking in the vicinity. She grew quite . . . panicked . . . over the possibility that you would find out. You saw her—that day you brought the hat to me and she thought that it might have been mine! She almost swooned." He shoved his hands in his pockets. "She was terrified. How could I have told you that I knew of the temple without explaining how and why? Without doing what she fears most in the world—lessening her in your eyes?" He set his jaw. His scattering of freckles stood out against the white lines around his mouth. "It's been a month—a full month since she's allowed me to . . . meet her—in private."

"Do you believe this?" Shelby asked scathingly. "Let me tell you a different version. This fellow made love to our sister until he seduced her. He found out about the temple from her and planted that tinker with his damned pinion gear at the gate where I come and go. When Merlin and I fell right into the trap, he made his move, and put her where no one would think to look."

Ransom grimaced. "Shelby, what the *devil* is this damned pinion gear you keep raving about?"

"Miss Merlin's!" Woodrow said. "She needed one very badly for her wing control. We all knew it."

Ransom narrowed his eyes. "All?"

"Oh, yes. Quin and Papa and Aunt Blythe and Mr. Peale and Mamá and I. Everyone who was helping with the flying machine."

"I see." Ransom frowned. He looked at Shelby. "It was a bluff. It wasn't ribbons she wanted from the tinker, then."

His brother shifted his feet and nodded. "I should have known, of course. I thought it an odd coincidence, that the shabby fellow carried pinion gears with his pots and pans. But that's not the point! The thing's being nailed on me, Ransom; I've been made to look as black as pitch. And now—I ask you—who pulled down that book with this supposedly in it? He kicked at the paper on the floor. "Who made sure it would be found? I am not stupid, brother. If I had something like this to hide, for God's sake, would I put it in a book in plain sight in the saloon?"

"I don't know," Ransom said slowly. "I don't trust myself to know."

Shelby made a sound of furious disgust and turned away. Other footsteps reverberated in the corridor. Mr. Collett, looking disheveled, came hurrying toward them with two footmen behind him.

"Your Grace!" He bobbed into a hasty bow. "I've men to stand bodyguard, as you asked. Something untoward has happened, I fear?"

Shelby twisted back on his heel. He stared at the footmen.

"A bodyguard," he said softly. "Oh, Ransom . . . Ransom . . . do you think I'll forgive you for this?"

Ransom kept his gaze hard and level. He did not, could not—would not believe that Shelby could betray him. And for that alone, for that one immovable conviction, he had to let his order stand. Because blind love made a miserable substitute for reason.

He turned away to Mr. Collett. "Put a guard on Major O'Shaughnessy also. By my authority as magistrate they are both under arrest. Neither he nor Lord Shelby leave the house at any time."

"But you can't!" Woodrow's high-pitched cry rang in the hall.

Mr. Collett bowed his head. With an uncomfortable cough, he began to issue low-voiced instructions to the footmen.

"Uncle, you don't think Papa kidnapped Miss Merlin?" Woodrow gave Ransom's coat a frantic tug. "You don't! He wouldn't do that; you know he wouldn't!"

Ransom put his hand to his eyes. "Woodrow—"

"No, listen to me! I'll find Miss Merlin! I'll find out who did it. It wasn't my papa. I know it wasn't!"

Like a coward Ransom chose retreat, with no way to answer or explain, no buffer against the scared disbelief in his nephew's eyes. As he started to move away, Jaqueline stepped out of the shadows where she'd stood, half-forgotten. She placed a hand on Woodrow's arm and hushed him.

Ransom came face to face with her, and halted.

"I understand you." She looked into his eyes. The faint flicker of candlelight turned her violet gaze to deep velvet. "You are a duke and a magistrate, and cannot be a man. But . . ." Holding her chin like an Amazon queen, she reached out and lightly touched his chest. "There is the law"—she lifted the hand that had touched him to her lips—"and there is the heart. So. Woodrow and I, we do you the service, Duke. We take your heart with us . . . to keep it safe where you wish it to be."

She reached down and grasped Woodrow's hand. He clung to her, giving Ransom one last trembling look. But when Jaqueline slid her arm through Shelby's in spite of his baffled frown, Woodrow instantly grabbed his father's other hand.

"Now. Come," Jaqueline said. "Perhaps we can persuade our bodyguard to play spillikens with us until it is time to go to bed."

Ransom watched them down the hall, the footman making a hesitant foursome as Jaqueline engaged him in bright banter as if he were a newfound guest. Shelby said nothing. But he held Woodrow's hand and he kept Jaqueline's arm, and the rigid set of his spine and jaw had gone to something less than killing fury.

Brava, mi prima, Ransom thought. *Bravissima one more time.* He closed his eyes. *Thank God you never miss a cue.*

Chapter 22

"They *are* the French," Merlin hissed. "Don't you know anything?"

"Now, see here, young lady!" Mr. Pemminey's chubby mouth pursed. "I think I would know it if my sponsors were French. Why, they speak the King's English better than I."

Merlin dropped her head back against the creaking wooden settle. She put her hands over her eyes, blocking out the cluttered, book-lined interior of Mr. Pemminey's tower room. "Of course they speak good English." She glared at him through her fingers. "It's a secret, don't you see?"

Wispy gray sideburns flew as he shook his head. "No, ma'am, I do not. They are high-minded, farsighted men, who have seen the value of my labors when others have laughed. Why, their generosity alone—"

"Yes, yes, I know it's very hard when people laugh, but you can't just go off and sell your work to the enemy!"

"The enemy!" Mr. Pemminey's round face turned as red as Ransom's crimson dressing gown. "I say, Miss—uh—what did you tell me your name was?"

"Merlin Lambourne," she said, and brushed a cobweb off of the cravat around her waist. "Well, I suppose it's Merlin Duke now. Or Damerell. Or perhaps Falconer. I'm a duchess, you know."

He gave her a skeptical look. Merlin glanced down at herself with a trace of chagrin. After her sojourn in the castle's dungeon before they'd brought her here, she was somewhat grubbier than usual. She rubbed at the cobweb again.

"A duchess," he said. "I suppose I'd as soon believe that as believe in this story about the French."

"Believe what you like!" Merlin stood up. "But why do you think I'm here? I was kidnapped. And we must think of a way to tell Ransom where I am, so that he can rescue me."

Mr. Pemminey huffed. "Nonsense. Rescue you from what? Who is this Ransom, then—I suppose he'll be coming along now disturbing my schedule just like you, young lady!"

Merlin stared at him in exasperation. "You don't know anything, do you? Ransom is the duke, of course."

Mr. Pemminey pinched his lips together, apparently in thought. His cheeks turned pink. Then he sucked in his breath. "You don't mean Damerell of Mount Falcon? Highly unlikely *he'll* dare to show his face here. He made it quite plain to me some months ago what he thought of my aviation project when I went to him desiring funds. No—he won't be welcome in my castle, miss. I should slam the door in his face!"

"Well, that wouldn't do any good," Merlin said. "He would simply knock it down. He's very clever at things like that."

"He sounds like a barbarian."

Merlin's lips parted in astonishment. "Ransom? Oh, my heavens, no. He's the most civilized person on earth. In the universe, most probably."

"Indeed. He was quite rude to me. And you say you know him, do you?" Mr. Pemminey's bright little eyes became even smaller, narrowing in suspicion. "How do I know you haven't been sent to spy upon me?"

"Spy upon you!" Merlin puffed up in affront. "I wouldn't do that."

Mr. Pemminey gave her a sidelong glance, and began surreptitiously shuffling the papers on the table away from her. Merlin looked down, catching sight of a diagram and a set of equations on the top sheet. Her lips parted. She bent over and grabbed at the pile.

"No, no!" Mr. Pemminey kept tight hold, and the vellum parted with a rip.

Merlin stared down at the torn sheet in her hand. "This is *my* diagram!" she exclaimed. "You've been spying on *me!*"

"I have not."

"But this is mine." She shouldered the protesting Mr. Pemminey aside and began leafing quickly through the papers. "These are my notes! There's my wing tip, and the equations on air weight and lift." She held them up in exultation. "They're safe! Do you have them all? Oh, they're safe! I thought they'd been burned. How did you get them?"

"Well, I—" Mr. Pemminey's mouth worked. "They're yours, you say? Are you quite sure?"

Merlin bent over a diagram. "Yes. You see—this is the way I've numbered the struts. Starting here at the apex and moving outward. And this crank and pinion here, that's to change the angle on the wing for landing. And the wheels are for—"

"All of this—" He spread a pudgy hand to indicate the pile of paper. "This is *your* work?"

"Yes." She nodded. "My flying machine."

"Well." Mr. Pemminey looked at her with a new expression. "I must say, I am impressed. These notes have been of great help to me."

"But where did you get them? I thought they had burned."

"Oh, no. I've been receiving these excellent communiques for some months now. Most useful. Most beneficial. I can't agree with your emphasis on catgut at the expense of metal, but your notions on wing contours are absolute genius, if I may say so. I've applied them rigorously. I do appreciate your generosity in sending the notes along."

"But I never sent them." She peered down at the paper. "This isn't my handwriting at all."

"Did you not send them? Oh, but a young man has brought them for you. A very nice, pleasant young man. I don't recall his name, but you will, no doubt."

"Not Woodrow!"

"Eh?" Mr. Pemminey stroked his chin. "No—that's the boy: Woodrow. He mentioned you, too, now that I recall. I've let him watch me now and then. Most clever lad."

"He didn't bring my notes?"

Mr. Pemminey was staring down at the diagram in her hand. "No, no—it was the other one brought them. The young man. I say, do you suppose that this stay attaching to the number six strut could be lengthened and replaced with steel?"

Merlin looked where he was pointing. "Steel! I thought you were using aluminium. But short stages of catgut are the thing. As I've told Woodrow over and over, the strength must be in the skin over the bamboo framework."

"I've been using steel wire. I had to abandon the aluminium when I found out it stretch—"

A pounding on the oaken door interrupted him. Merlin stiffened. "The French!" she whispered.

"Rubbish," Mr. Pemminey said. "It will just be Thomkins with my lunch. Good fellow, that Thomkins. I never have to go anywhere anymore; he serves me so well I just stay in this room and work. Only time I have to leave is when I go up onto the battlements to tinker with The Matilda herself. I named the gliding machine that, you see. The Matilda. After a girl I knew once." He rubbed shyly at his thinning hair. "But you wouldn't be interested in that, no, no. Would you take luncheon with me?"

Merlin had no chance to answer the question. The door opened, and a man of intimidating size and shape stuck his head in. His sword clanked against the iron bolt on the outside of the door. "That lad is here to see you, Mr. Pemminey."

"Ah, of course. Woodrow!" Mr. Pemminey rubbed his hands. "Ask him up. We can all have lunch."

"Nay—you ain't to see him today, I'm told. They want you to write him a note and say you're occupied."

"Oh, but I'm not. Tell him that Miss—uh—"

Merlin stepped hard on Mr. Pemminey's toe.

"Ow! My dear, do have a care, if you please!" He turned toward her. Hidden from the guard behind his wispy halo of hair, Merlin mouthed, *The French* in silent urgency.

"What's that?" he asked. "Dear me, are you choking?"

Merlin rolled her eyes and abandoned the attempt. She bit her lip, staring at the guard as Mr. Pemminey said again that he wasn't at all too busy to receive Woodrow for lunch.

"Yes, you are," the burly man said placidly. "Write us the note, now—there's a good fellow."

Mr. Pemminey rubbed his palms together, looking flustered. "Well, yes—I suppose perhaps I am. The Matilda is quite ready for her first flight, and I've much to do to prepare myself for it."

He shuffled among the papers, searching out a pen and inkwell. Merlin chewed her knuckle. She had to get a message out; she had to *do* something. Woodrow was outside. That note was going to go to him . . .

And suddenly it was as if Ransom himself stood behind her, issuing orders and taking control of things as he always did.

She must not let Woodrow know she was here.

She could almost hear that command as if Ransom had snapped it. The boy was in danger—clearly he'd been allowed to come and go here only because he knew nothing of Mr. Pemminey's "sponsors." No one took him seriously. But Merlin was learning the ways of kidnappers and Frenchmen. If they discovered that Woodrow had seen or heard of Merlin—then, of course, they could not let him go back to Mount Falcon.

She looked at the heavy-set guard standing over Mr. Pemminey, and wondered if he could read.

No, Ransom's incisive, imaginary voice warned her. *Too risky.*

"We," the guard had said. Even if this one were illiterate, he wasn't alone in defending Mr. Pemminey's castle.

She watched Mr. Pemminey fuss with the inkwell, blotching the table with black and deciding that he needed to cut a new quill. She put her palm to her cheek. The guard looked up at the sudden move, his hand twitching toward his sword. Wetting her lips, Merlin gave him a wan smile. He grinned back at her.

"Mr. Pemminey," she said, "have you ever tried a hedgehog quill?"

He cast her an impatient glance. "A hedgehog quill! You don't mean to write with?"

"Oh, yes." She turned to the wooden settle, where her kidnappers had kindly placed her bandbox, and swung it up by the braided strap. "Look!"

She dumped the hedgehog out onto the table. It rolled a few inches and began to uncurl.

"You see," she said with an excess of enthusiasm, "the spines are quite sharp. Just the thing for making a very fine line."

"Nay, don't muddle him about while he's trying to think, miss," the guard said.

Mr. Pemminey nodded. "Really, my dear. You have the most peculiar notions." He bent over the hedgehog. "Why, the quills aren't more than an inch long! How in heaven could one hold on to the thing?"

"It's quite simple." Merlin reached for the hedgehog and caught its hind legs, pulling it toward her and knocking over the inkwell in the process. "Oh! Oh, I'm so sorry! Here, quickly—" She plopped the hedgehog paws-down in the puddle of ink, as if to sop it up.

"Now see what you've done," Mr. Pemminey exclaimed. "And there it goes, making footprints right across my note paper!"

"Forgive me!" She used the tail end of Ransom's cravat to wipe up the excess ink from the table.

The guard waved dismissively as Mr. Pemminey began to rummage for another piece of paper. "Never mind that.

You ain't writin' to the prince. I need to get back down to the gate with it.''

Merlin dabbed at the hedgehog, pretending to clean off the ink, while she tried to see if a clear paw print showed through Mr. Pemminey's letters. But the animal had had enough of espionage. It rolled up tightly and would not uncurl.

Mr. Pemminey dashed off his signature and sanded the paper. "There you are. And bring us a bite of lunch, if you please."

The guard made a casual salute with the note. "Soon's I deliver this." He grinned again at Merlin, and gave her a suggestive wink. She bit her lip and let her mouth curl upward just a little, peeking at the man under her eyelashes.

The door closed behind him. Merlin heard the bolt slide into place.

"There," Mr. Pemminey said. "You see?"

"See what?"

"Why, the fellow's going to bring us lunch! How could he be French? And an excellent lunch it will be, I'll wager. Lobster and boiled artichokes with some melted butter to go along."

"But he's locked us in," Merlin said.

"Nonsense. Why ever would he do that?"

"Because." She held back an urge to pick up the ink-pot and dash it on him. "They're *the French.*"

Mr. Pemminey trotted to the door. "Locked us in," he muttered. "What a pack of—" The door shifted and clunked under his tug. He pulled at it again. "Good God," he said.

Merlin looked at him smugly and clasped her hands behind her back.

"But—" Mr. Pemminey ran plump fingers through his mist of gray hair.

"We're prisoners."

"Oh, come now. I'm sure . . ." He wet his lips, looking at her dubiously. "It must be an oversight."

"Hah." She walked to the narrow window and pushed the leaded casement wider, leaning out. Below, it was an unimpeded drop from the tower to the smooth hazy silver of the Channel. "Look at this. We've been kidnapped, I tell you."

"*I* haven't been kidnapped, young lady. I live here in perfect freedom."

"When your servants wear swords, and won't let you out of the room!" She gave a scathing snort. "Don't you know *anything?*"

Mr. Pemminey tapped nervously on the tabletop. "Well. I suppose the domestics have become a trifle high-handed." He watched her peering out the window. "You aren't expecting that I should do anything about it, are you?"

She looked back at him. "Whatever could you do?"

"Oh—" He cleared his throat. "Fight our way out. Swords and pistols. Things like that. I'm not as young as I used to be, you know."

Merlin rolled her eyes. "Of course not. You'd be killed."

"Yes, yes, I did think that might be a consideration."

"You won't have to do anything." She peered out the window again. "I've been looking the situation over. The front gate is quite ineligible, of course. But that path on the side of the cliff—" She pointed outside along the coastline, where the vertical face of white chalk plunged down to the water below. "Do you see? It goes right 'round the edge at the gatehouse wall and out onto this peninsula. It isn't very wide . . . and there's that one ravine to cross, of course. But I'm sure that's a leap of only a few feet." She turned around and smiled at Mr. Pemminey. "So there," she said comfortably as she rolled the hedgehog off the table and back into the band-box. "We might as well have lunch. It will be a little while before Ransom can come to rescue us."

This is stupid, Ransom thought.

He stood beside his horse in the dubious cover of wind-dwarfed brush, looking up at the crumbling walls and towers of Pemminey Castle.

Behind him, the South Downs rolled away in gradually descending billows of olive-green. Before him, the smooth, grassy hill rose up and up, crowned by the half-ruined castle walls standing cinder-gray against the hazy sky.

As far as Ransom was concerned, attacking fortified positions single-handedly was something best left to fairy tales and the rather ill-advised knights who inhabited them.

Very, very stupid.

Almost as moronic as believing that a smudge between a "b" and a "u" on a sweat-grimed note matched a smudge on the leather blotter on his desk at Mount Falcon. And that both ink stains represented the literary ramblings of a particularly well-traveled hedgehog.

Listening to twelve-year-old boys: that was his mistake. Letting a pair of earnest, tear-filled eyes look up at him in spite of a murderous scold and the sentence of a week's confinement to the nursery, and allowing a bravely stammer-free voice to say, "Begging your pardon, sir; just a moment of your time, sir. Would you look at this before I go? I think I might have found Miss Merlin, sir."

The Machiavellian young cub. He'd probably timed it for maximum effect. But if Woodrow thought anything was going to soften his punishment for disobeying Ransom's direct order not to leave the estate, he could think again. Hedgehog footprints be damned.

It was no doubt smugglers who'd taken over Pemminey Castle, as Ransom had been at pains to explain to Woodrow. Since Bonaparte had turned his attention to more promising shores, the Gentlemen of the Sussex coast had expanded their illegal activities tenfold. It would come as no surprise to anyone if the impoverished Pemminey had decided to finance his eccentricities by hiring out his strategically located castle to run a few contraband kegs.

So Ransom had a choice. He could march up to the gatehouse, which effectively cut off the castle itself on its little peninsula, and begin negotiations for a new supply of brandy, or he could skulk about like some revenue officer and try to find a covert way in. The first, he felt, would get him laughed at. The second was like to get him shot.

Then there was the third possibility, of course: the remote chance that Merlin and her abductors *were* here—a secret in plain sight.

It had a certain consistency, that notion. Like imprisoning her the first time in Ransom's own park. If it were so, he could begin to get a feel for the mind behind these schemes: the sharp eye for character and how a person would respond to pressure, the detailed knowledge of events at Mount Falcon, and the clear familiarity with the countryside around.

If it were so.

All he had to go on was a smudge on a piece of smudgy paper. And hope . . . which he didn't trust for a moment.

He'd sat at his desk half the night, thinking. Early this morning, he'd abandoned thinking and proceeded ahead to foolishness. He'd saddled his horse and ridden out to Pemminey Castle alone.

He dug in his saddlebag and took out a spyglass, steadying his arms on his hunter's back. The castle looked like a hundred others, stone walls kept in repair in a few places, falling down in most. The curtain wall, with its gatehouse pinched between two ponderous towers, curved around and out of sight at the crest of the hill. Somewhere beyond was the limestone cliff of Beachy Head, highest on a coastline of dauntingly high cliffs.

Perched at the edge, Pemminey Castle was doomed. The sea ate away at the shore. A fortress that must have stood on a solid promontory centuries before now balanced on a crumbling peninsula, with half the ramparts already fallen away.

At least, so Ransom had been told. He had never in his life entertained the least desire to see this phenomenon for himself.

He closed his eyes at the very thought.

Stupid, stupid, stupid, stupid.

He opened them again and focused on the gatehouse. There were figures there. He counted four men, and possibly more, slouched against what was left of the crenellations in a casual, confident watch. If they were smugglers, it was a major operation and an unusually delicate one, to require any more safeguard than a good hiding place and some well-greased palms.

Beyond the curtain wall, there seemed to be an interval of empty space—a courtyard, most probably, hidden behind the stone fortifications. Much farther back, the castle walls mounted into view again, and rose to a culmination in the highest tower of all. Through his eyeglass, Ransom followed the wall of wind-scoured stone upward, from window to narrow window, until he reached the topmost one.

"Damnation," he muttered.

The window flew a pennant of crimson. Hidden from the gatehouse by the curve of the tower, the splash of color waved and fluttered. As an odd gust of wind flattened it against the wall, he made out the sleeves and voluminous outline of his truant dressing gown.

He closed the eyeglass, crossed his arms, and buried his face in the leather curve of his saddle.

It took a few moments to compose himself. The elation at finding Merlin here was dampened considerably by the circumstances. He discarded any ideas of calling out the garrison at Eastbourne to storm the place. It was highly unlikely Merlin would be allowed to survive a direct attack.

He squinted again at the castle. He knew nothing of its layout, despite having lived in the neighborhood his entire life. Castles on cliff edges were not prominent on Ransom's list of places to spend time. Poor Pemminey, last of his noble Norman line, was clearly a lunatic. No sane man would choose to live in that sea-girded ruin while there was a leaking hovel to be found anywhere.

Ransom thought of returning to Mount Falcon for help; of waiting until night for a secret attack. He abandoned both ideas. Time crowded at him. It seemed likely they meant to take her to France in the dark of the moon like any other sensible smugglers of humanity or brandy. And with the help of an overcast sky, it would be dark enough tonight.

He looped the horse's reins in a bush and took off his hat. He was armed, at least—with a rapier and two pistols. When he left his mount, he moved away from the castle, staying amidst the gnarled bushes to angle around the hillside. When he'd gone far enough to be hidden from the gatehouse entirely, Ransom began to work his way higher, toward the castle itself.

The blind crest of the hill still hid the peninsula. Amidst the increasing roar of the wind in the bushes above him, he could see only the tower and its telltale crimson pennant floating over the curtain wall. The path was leading him straight toward the place where the wall took an abrupt turn and disappeared from view at the crown of the hill.

When he straightened from the cover of the scrub, hard wind caught his hair. In front of him the bushes came to an abrupt end, giving way to the grassy summit a few yards ahead. Beyond the crest, he could see nothing but sky, bluish-gray in the haze.

The castle wall was deserted, the protective crenellations long since crumbled away. Ransom judged that any threat along the top of it would have been visible. He looked up, eyeing the place where it made a corner and vanished over the crown of the hill. If he could reach that spot . . .

He put his hand on his sword and ducked, keeping low to cross the short space of open ground. Wind buffeted him the instant he left the cover of the bushes. He headed up, across the slant of the incline, looking back toward the gatehouse towers. No alarm came. He had nearly reached the crest and the safety of the wall when he glanced to his other side.

His stomach turned. He lurched to a sudden, frozen halt.

Beside him, there was nothing. No hill curving down from the summit, no wall, no bushes, no grass . . .

nothing but wind, in ferocious force, and the blinding white face of a perpendicular drop.

His wits deserted him. His body arched back in a wild hiss of recoil. Hummocks of wind-ripped grass clung where the castle masonry had long ago torn away, stone evaporating into space at a ragged edge. Below it, the chalk cliff plummeted toward nothing.

He crushed his fist over his mouth and took one step backward. Then terror and vertigo made him wrench around in a crazed dread that the ground had opened up behind him, too. The wind seemed to grab, pushing and pulling in willful violence. He flung himself toward the nearest solid thing, the wall, and pressed back against it as if he could drive his fingers and skull and spine right into the stone.

He braced there, his heart and the wind a mad battery of sound. The rapier angled awkwardly, its sheath stabbing his thigh, but he could not bring himself to move enough to ease it. His body twitched, wanting to curl, wanting to roll up in frantic self-protection.

He let his knees collapse, a quick, hard drop to the solid ground, with his heels braced in the dirt and his back shoved as vigorously against the stone as his muscles could manage.

He closed his eyes. Sickness rolled in his chest and stomach. He tilted his head back against the stone, taking air in great gulps that gradually slowed as his mind began to agree with his senses and assure him that he was on firm earth.

When his breathing had come back to something more or less like normality, he ventured a brief look. From his position at the base of the wall, the cliff was invisible again. On one side of him, the hill sloped up from below, unfaltering in its even incline. On the other, grass tossed and rippled at the summit, creating the comforting illusion that the land went on beyond.

A harsh cry made him jump. A seagull sprang into view, exploding up from the deceptive crest as if it had been shot from some hidden cannon. It hovered at eye level, wings kinked, and then tilted and fell away, disappearing with a swoop that sent queasiness rippling through his body.

Perhaps he should call out the garrison and let them storm the place after all.

Perhaps he should walk up and knock on the front door.

Perhaps he should go home.

Forget the whole thing.

He put his hand over his eyes. It still shook a little. He clenched it into a fist to stop it, curling the other around the handgrip of his sword.

He took a deep, slow breath.

All right.

Keeping his back firmly to the wall, he twisted until he'd worked off his coat. He settled the rapier across his lap and slid a few inches in the direction of the edge. He craned a little. Beyond the whipping grass, he could just see the hazy horizon, where the blue-gray of the sky shaded to the deeper bluish-silver of the sea.

He took another breath.

He moved as far as the corner of the wall. Keeping his hands firmly in contact with the ground, he peered around the angle.

Vertigo flooded him.

He clutched at a root, blinking rapidly. A yard past the corner, the wall ended, hanging by some insane concatenation of stone and mortar a full foot beyond the cliff itself. The undercut face fell away, a blaze of white rock beneath the dark olive vegetation and the stones and towers that sprawled in magnificent ruin across what was left of the jutting peninsula. Down and down and down, the cliff wall finally met the shore at a beach of silver and ebony shingle, in a sheer drop that made his eyes water and his stomach heave.

There was a particular pebble far below on the beach: oddly shaped, yellow and green against the more natural black ones. With wind tearing at his hair, he squinted down at it.

It looked like a pebble. It was a fishing boat. He swallowed and moaned softly, clinging to the root.

Merlin's crimson banner flew free and slapped back against the stone. She expected him. She needed him. Her life depended on him.

He felt like being sick.

The seagull soared up from below again, startling him with a raucous cry. It looped on the wind and pitched downward, drawing his gaze with it. His fingernails dug into the bark.

He closed his eyes and wrenched them open, breaking the fatal fascination of the bird's lift and plummet. On the opposite cliff, a faint line of vegetation descended gradually across the chalk face, disappeared from his view, and then reappeared, emerging as a narrow track just beneath the overhanging end of the stone wall where he sat.

Ransom stared at the footpath miserably. It was only what he deserved, he thought. God had been going easy with him, lulling him, leading him inexorably to this point where he would have to pay for all the sins he'd committed in a wickedly sinful life. He could hear the celestial snicker now.

Carefully, Ransom transferred one hand from the root to his sword. Then he sat for a moment. He gathered himself, mind and body, and carefully inched his heel toward the bare spot between two tufts of grass, where the path emerged onto the hill.

He kept his eyes resolutely on the ground. By the time he had his boot over the brink far enough to feel the ledge beneath, the root to which he clung was slippery with his sweat.

He leaned into the wind, trying without loosening his hold to see around the corner. The path dropped down to clear the curtain wall, and then rose again, curving out of sight. What he could see of it looked to be about half an inch wide. But it was a path: right beneath his feet were the indentations of sheep or goat prints, cut into the soft chalk.

Transferring his slick grip to a solid hummock of grass, he said a brief prayer and stood up. Wind buffeted him. His sword—on the inside—caught, held, and broke free with a little jerk that sent him forward in a stumble. The grass tore beneath his clutching grasp. He scrambled and swayed wildly, twisting, coming up with both hands braced above him on the rough overhang of the wall and his heart clamoring for mercy.

He leaned his cheek on his sleeve and thought of abandoning the rapier. Not rationally, but rather with the intention of tearing off the awkward sword belt and the two pistols and tossing the whole rig into the sea below.

The only thing that prevented him was the notion that this insane clinging to terrifying cliffs would be wasted if he did so. He'd not be likely to save Merlin from her captors bare-handed.

He kept his eyes rigidly ahead on each inch of path as it appeared in front of him. The gull kept swooping in and out of his vision, tormenting him with mocking cries. The wind blew, pounding at him, plastering him against the cliff until an instant's abeyance in the gale made it seem that he was swaying suddenly outward. He scrabbled at the rock. The wind resumed. He put one foot ahead of the other in his painful shuffle, never lifting his eyes from his boots.

He came to where the cliff face retreated into the deep bite. The path narrowed. The cliff itself had an undercut slant, the top hanging farther out than the path. He inched himself around until he faced the stone, and leaned sideways to look ahead.

Wind hit him, howling in the opposite direction. It billowed out his shirt, eddied, changed to push him from behind and changed again. He snatched back from the corner and pressed his forehead to the chalky wall, his fingers working in a futile search for security.

He stood there, eyes screwed shut, the rock jagged against his face, and counted to ten. Then he counted to twenty. He considered the merits of counting to forty-five million. He wondered if anyone would find his skeleton, hung there a hundred years from now.

He could still go back. He could inch his way up the path, under the wall and onto safe ground. He could slink through the bushes and mount his horse and go home.

The chalk beneath his spread fingers crumbled a little. He moved his hand, and then his foot, and began shifting by degrees into the wild play of wind around the corner.

He learned, in those moments, what limestone looked like at eyeball range. It scraped his cheek and his chest and his thighs as he slid forward. The wind tugged at him, pushed: one way, the other, and all the time behind him was the fall, that unthinkable drop into empty space.

When the curved face seemed to flatten and the wind eased, he ventured a look forward. He was around the corner, into the bite. The path widened a little. Looking up at him from a few yards ahead was a startled, black-faced sheep with a stalk of dry grass protruding from its mouth.

Ransom closed his eyes. *Oh, thank you, God. Thank you very much.*

He rested a moment. He eyed the sheep. "Back off," he muttered. "Or I'll kick you off."

The sheep gave a few quick chews on the stalk of grass.

Ransom pressed his cheek to the cliff. "I swear I will," he shouted.

The beast suddenly seemed to take his meaning. It rolled its eyes, bunched itself, and made a neat reversal. An unkempt, woolly rump bounced up the path. He watched it until the animal came to a stop at the apex of the ravine, looking back at him.

"All right," he said, looking down at his boot again. "We'll discuss it when I get there."

He crept along, and was almost upon the sheep again before he looked up and found it was still ahead.

"Hup!" he barked.

The sheep tripped forward and sprang into a leap, landed, and hurried on up the path. Ransom paid it no attention as it disappeared above. He was staring at the crevice the animal had jumped.

He swallowed. He wet his lips.

It was a shadow in the white glare, with no other way around. Ransom began to breathe faster. He inched forward to the edge, and allowed himself a glance downward.

Stupid. Oh, stupid, stupid, stupid, stupid.

He twisted back and pressed his face against the stone. *Oh, Merlin,* he thought. *I can't.*

He stood with his shoulder jammed against the cliff, the sword banging awkwardly between his thigh and the rock, and looked again at the plunge before him. The cliff and the sky and the sea below began to make a slow, tilting spin around his head. With every breath, he heard himself make a hollow, desperate, huffing noise, like a horse driven past endurance.

He set his jaw, gripped the sword, and jumped.

Chapter 23

"Yes, of course, The Matilda will fly," Merlin said. "You built her from my plans, didn't you?"

The little man rocked up on his tiptoes. "Now, see here! Not entirely! I did draw heavily on your plans, yes, but it's quite another matter, building a machine that will carry two persons."

"Why, Mr. Pemmican—"

"Pemminey."

"Mr. Pemminey, it is the same design, right down to the last strut! Only larger, and with steel cable." She bent over the paper on which she'd been scribbling. "I wish I'd thought to use wire from a pianoforte. There were several at Mount Falcon that would have done quite well." She flourished her pen. "In any event, I think these equations you've done to enlarge the scale are perfectly valid. But wheels for landing . . . really, are you quite sure?"

The sound of someone pounding up the stairs interrupted her, but Mr. Pemminey ignored the noise, plunging into a defense of his wheels. "I suppose you will say that they will not take the stress, but I assure you that I have calculated spoke and diametric ratios down to the fraction."

The oaken door shook under a heavy blow. The bolt crashed back, and the barrier swung open.

"Merlin!" Ransom shoved into the room, kicking the door aside. He was all in white: shirtsleeves and waistcoat and pale breeches. Even his face and his boots were marked with chalky dust.

"Hullo!" She stood up. "Here you are."

He looked quite wickedly frightening, with a drawn sword in his hand and pistols at his waist. His dark brown hair was windblown, powdered with white. He strode toward her. "Are you all right?"

"Oh, yes, of course; I'm quite well. Did you get my hedgehog footprint?"

The hand he placed on the curve of her throat was trembling. He jerked her toward him, his grip pressing painfully into the back of her neck. He kissed her harder than he'd ever kissed her before. She whimpered under the brutal pressure.

He let her go.

"Are *you* all right?" She frowned at him, touching her bruised lips. His movements were odd and temperamental. Beneath the white smudges, he looked as pale as he had after he'd been shot.

"Oh, God," he said, wiping at a streak of sweat with his sleeve. "Don't ask."

"Good day, Your Grace," Mr. Pemminey said politely, and then added with a trace of reproach, "We thought you would arrive yesterday."

Ransom looked at him.

"Never mind that," Merlin said hastily, unnerved by the expression on Ransom's face. "Can we go now?"

"Instantly." He hefted the sword in a graceful sweep. "Stay behind me."

"You're going to rescue Mr. Pemminey, too. Is that all right? He really didn't know his new servants were the French."

Ransom was already at the door. "Look sharp, then," he ordered without turning around. "I'm not coming back for anybody who isn't on my heels. I say stop, you stop. I say go, and you go. No questions."

He was gone down the spiral staircase almost before Merlin had a chance to grab her bandbox. She heard Mr. Pemminey come panting behind her.

She reached the bottom just as Ransom hissed, "Stay back!"

Merlin stopped, but Mr. Pemminey ran into her from behind and pushed her out into the octagonal room at the base of the tower. She sucked in her breath. The large guard was silhouetted in the doorway with a sword sliding noisily out of his sheath.

Ransom stood still, balanced over his toes, his weapon at the ready. He snarled something that sounded vaguely to Merlin like "Ah, guard," which seemed an unnecessarily obvious remark. The point of his blade circled. The other man lifted his longer, heavier weapon. Just as he lunged, Ransom moved, lightly and fast. Metal clashed, and the guard's sword went flying.

Merlin blinked in astonishment. She wanted to ask how Ransom had done that, but he was already closing in on the guard with an intent that looked murderous.

At the last moment, he swung his sword point aside and brought his knee up to drive it into the man's abdomen.

"I ought to turn you on a spit, traitor." He pressed the point of the weapon on the back of the prostrate man's neck. "Who do you work for?"

The guard was holding his stomach, heaving for breath. "No—" he gasped. "What d'ye . . . mean . . ." The sword point drew blood. The guard jerked. "Not a traitor!" he yelped.

"Who?" Ransom demanded.

"English. English." The man took a deep breath. "Call him . . . Mr. . . . Bell. I'm not a traitor!"

"Just a common bandit," Ransom sneered. He looked up at Merlin. "Go. Outside; turn left. Wait for me behind the rocks."

"Oh, yes," Mr. Pemminey said. "Are we taking the shortcut into town?"

Ransom glanced at him distractedly. "What?"

"Along the cliff. You came that way, I presume? A most scenic stroll when the weather is so mild, don't you agree?"

Ransom looked at Mr. Pemminey as if he had lost his mind. "I told you to go. You—Pemminey—take that sword. Carry it if you can. Throw it over the edge if you can't."

"Oh, no, no, no!" Mr. Pemminey scurried across to lift the guard's weapon. "That won't be necessary. It's not at all heavy. I used to carry twice this much on my way back from market day."

Holding the rapier in killing threat, Ransom watched his two charges hurry obediently out the door. He looked down at the kneeling guard.

"Forgive my poor manners," he said, and swung the sword in a hard reverse, using the handle to deliver his blow. The man slumped. Ransom moved away fast, sorry there was no way to tie him. He wouldn't be unconscious long.

Merlin and Mr. Pemminey were waiting as Ransom had ordered, where the head of the footpath was hidden by a pile of stone rubble.

"You first," he ordered Merlin. "Go slowly; face the cliff. Don't be afraid, and don't look down. I'll be right behind." He watched her skirt nimbly around the rocks in his ink-stained, stolen breeches. "And for the love of God, be careful!"

She disappeared. He had a sudden, wrenching fear that he would never see her again. That cliff . . . oh, God, that cliff . . .

He shoved the thought away and turned to Pemminey. "You next. No, get rid of that damned sword—Christ, do you know where you're going, man? You'll never make it with that!"

"Oh, I know the way perfectly well, I assure you. Since I was a babe in arms." Mr. Pemminey turned, lifting the sword like a walking stick, and strolled after Merlin.

Ransom looked back toward the tower, and then the gatehouse. There was no sign yet of alarm. They were damnably lazy and sure of themselves, these fellows. It made him uneasy. He sheathed his sword and moved between the rocks.

Wind shoved at him. The cliffs came into view, white rock and dizzying fall. He put out his hand, grabbing at a stone face. The path descended in front of him, with Mr. Pemminey a short distance ahead, moving slowly and comfortably along it. Merlin was far away already, at the apex of the ravine. She wasn't following Ransom's orders at all. She moved quickly, casually, carrying her bandbox under one arm and not even touching the cliff with the other.

The seagull swept up from below, hovering beside her an instant. She stopped, leaning out, and held up her hand as if to offer a perch. The bird fell away, swooping outward, soaring below Ransom to become a speck against the towering white cascade of the cliff.

Without hesitation, Merlin turned back to the path. She took a little running step and cleared the crevice.

Ransom looked down at his feet. He ordered one to move.

It did not. Only his fingers shifted, clutching harder at the rock.

He coughed to clear his throat. His heart was beating so hard that he could not hear the wind. He put up his free hand, as if to shelter his face from the glare, but the blinder was so comforting that he held it there, turning his face aside.

He tried to let go of the rock. He stood there, not quite shaking, looking at the back of his hand.

A diversion, he thought suddenly.

That was what he ought to be doing. He ought to be creating a diversion. It wouldn't do to have the guards discover Merlin and Pemminey exposed on the cliff.

A feeling of vast relief jolted through him.

"Pemminey!" He put both hands on the stone, leaning hard against it. Careful not to look outward, he called after the old eccentric again.

Pemminey was only a few yards down the path. Ransom waited, braced against the stone, until the other man had worked his way back.

"Here—" Ransom wrenched at his right hand, pulling off his gold signet. "My horse is hidden down the hill.

Leave my wife in East Dean. Take this to Colonel Torrance at the Eastbourne encampment. Tell him to get back here with a detachment on the double.''

"Your wife?'' Mr. Pemminey tucked the sword handle under his arm and examined the ring. "Oh, you mean Miss Lambourne, I expect. She did say she was a duchess. But pardon me—I thought you were coming with us?''

"No. I mean to hold them off until you get away.''

Pemminey blinked, looking around nervously. "Hold who off?''

"The guards.'' Ransom backed up a step.

"Oh dear. Have they seen us? I thought we'd quite slipped away.''

"Go on. I'll take care of it.''

"But they have weapons. Guns. Shouldn't you just come along with us?''

"No,'' Ransom said.

"And aren't there rather a lot of them? Ten or twelve, I believe. And only one of you. Really, Duke, I think you might consider coming now.''

"Go!'' Ransom exclaimed harshly. "Get away from here.''

Mr. Pemminey patted his throat. "Pray don't shout at me.'' He slipped the ring into his pocket. "I'll do as you say, but I really think—''

Ransom left him thinking. He gripped his sword and turned back toward the tower, his boots scraping as he vaulted the jumble of rocks. He moved quickly to the shadow of the tower's wall and leaned there, looking back. Mr. Pemminey had disappeared. From here, Ransom could not see the cliff face.

He waited, watching around the curve of the tower. Eventually, long after Mr. Pemminey had gone, the battered guard stumbled out from the tower room, rubbing the side of his head.

Ransom made his move.

"Hold!'' he ordered, stepping out from the wall and aiming a pistol at the guard's middle. As the man whirled, Ransom shifted quickly, putting himself between the guard and the door. He backed inside and aimed a shot at the man's feet. As dust and a shout erupted, Ransom kicked the door shut and lunged to bar it.

He heaved the wooden plank into place. In the dim light from a high window he strode in a circuit of the octagonal room, looking for other entrances. There was one door, a continuation of the spiral stair downward. He peered down into the dark, decided it most probably went nowhere, and barred it, too. He busied himself reloading his pistol.

More shouts came from outside. A gunshot thudded into the solid oaken door.

Ransom grinned. "Fire away," he muttered, packing powder into the gun barrel.

Another shot hit the window, shattering leaded glass. It tinkled harmlessly to the floor.

He congratulated himself on an excellent diversion, picturing Merlin and Mr. Pemminey riding safely away while her abductors drove themselves to a frenzy trying to attack him in an unassailable position. He'd tease them; keep them busy until the infantry arrived. Perhaps if he was lucky, this Mr. Bell himself might be in the captured crew.

But Merlin was safe, if she'd made it around the cliff. That was what mattered.

Yes, a most excellent diversion.

He hefted the pistol and moved toward the stair. Just as his boot mounted the first step, there was a rattle, and a faint female voice.

"Ransom?" it asked hopefully. "Are you in there?"

He kicked back off the stair, whirling. The wooden rattle came again from the barred cellar door. Ransom flung it open.

Merlin looked up at him from the dark. "Aren't you coming?"

"Are you mad?" he shouted. "What are you doing here?"

"They're shooting. I couldn't come in the other door. Mr. Pemminey told me about this one—there's an old side passage that comes out among the rocks at the edge, you see.''

He grabbed her arm and jerked her up inside, slamming the door behind her. ''Good God, you crazy—'' He stopped, finding words sufficient to the occasion beyond his grasp. ''The devil take it,'' he grated finally. ''Did Pemminey get out?''

''Yes, I left him outside the wall. He said you gave him instructions. I hope he can manage to mount your horse. He says he isn't very knowledgeable about horses.''

Ransom looked toward the main door. The gunshots were silent for the moment. He suspected the men outside were looking for something to make a battering ram. ''Pray God he can mount. You'll have to stay with me now.''

''Oh, no. We can go right along the way I came. No one saw me. I don't believe these mutton-headed French even know about it. It's quite hidden by the cliff edge.''

Ransom looked at her. Her hair was pinned in a sagging bun, with windblown wisps curling around her face. In her breeches and baggy shirt, she appeared small and adorably kissable. There was already combat-induced excitement singing in his brain, and passion rode just below the turbulence. He released her and stepped back. ''You go.''

She put a hand on the door. When he did not move, she slanted a glance toward him. ''Are you coming?''

''No. I'll keep them busy.''

Her lips parted. ''But they're shooting.''

''I'll be safe enough in here. Go on. Quickly.''

She frowned. Her mouth took on a stubborn set. ''I can't go without you. You're rescuing me.''

''Yes,'' he snapped, ''and I'd be making a damned lot better job of it if you'd see your way clear to do a thing I tell you.''

She drew herself up. ''I'm staying with you.''

''Hell,'' he said. ''Hell and damnation.''

''Just a moment ago you said I should have to stay with you.''

Shouts and scuffles floated through the window. Something heavy slammed into the door.

"Fine." Ransom grabbed Merlin's elbow and shoved her toward the stairs. "Up!" He put his hands on her rump, distracted momentarily by a flash of appreciation for the fit of his pants, and then gave her a push.

Merlin yelped, banging her shins on the next higher step, and scrambled on without further instructions. At the top of the stairs she stumbled into Mr. Pemminey's tower room, panting hard. Ransom came pounding up behind her. He did not stop to catch his breath, but grabbed the trestle table and dragged it toward the door, ignoring the way papers went flying.

Before Merlin could scrabble up the piles of notes and books, he overturned the whole table, throwing everything in a shower to the floor. With a hollow scrape and a crash, he sent the heavy trestle tumbling down the spiral stairs, where it wedged in the first turn. Two benches, the wooden settle, and a chair went after it.

An explosion of splintering wood echoed up the stairs as the door below gave way, and then came the sound of many boots. Ransom pulled out his pistol and stood at the top of the stairs, looking down. Merlin twisted her hands together. She jumped at the crash of gunfire from below, and saw Ransom's mouth jerk a little, but nothing made it past his barrier.

He leaned his shoulder against the open door at the top of the stairs, keeping watch.

Merlin went to a window, pushing open the leaded glass.

"Careful," Ransom said. "Stay back a bit. Can you see anything?"

She squinted, craning back and forth to get a view from the narrow casement. "There's someone riding in the front gate."

"Uniforms?"

"No. He isn't wearing a uniform, I don't think. Just a dark coat." She tilted her head. "He's getting off now. He's walking out here . . . The French are running up to talk to him."

"Hah. Perhaps we've lured the mastermind for this little project. The mysterious Mr. Bell, no doubt."

"No," Merlin said. "He looks more like Mr. Peale to me."

"What?" he exclaimed.

She lifted her knee into the embrasure, moving closer to the window. "Yes—I believe that's who it is. Has he come to rescue me, too, do you suppose?"

"That meddling little ass—" Ransom bit off his words with a sudden sharp hiss. "*Peale.* Good God." He strode over to the window and thrust Merlin aside. "Oh, my God. *Peale.*"

"I must say, that's rather brave of him, to ride right in among them," Merlin said. She stood on tiptoe to look over Ransom's shoulder. "But he seems to be getting along with everyone quite well."

"Too damned well by far," Ransom exclaimed. "I'll see him hang for this."

"Oh, but I'm sure he doesn't mean to upset you. You know how hard he tries to please."

"Aye," Ransom said through his teeth. "It makes sense now, doesn't it?" He leaned forward and shouted, "*Peale.*"

The man far below looked up. "Your Grace!" he called, with a sweeping bow. "How convenient to find you here. I wished to speak with you."

Ransom made a growling noise in his throat. He did not answer.

"Come down, Your Grace," Mr. Peale called. "Let us have a drink and be civilized."

Ransom narrowed his eyes. Merlin could see the pulse beating furiously in his throat. "Nay," he shouted, "I can smell the carrion from here. It puts me off my appetite."

Mr. Peale's thin figure stiffened. "Come down," he repeated.

"Why?"

"As well now as later." He moved his hand, and one of the men grouped around him took a shot at the window. The blast echoed among the ruins. "As well alive as dead."

Ransom pulled back. He scowled at Merlin and then at the door with a thoughtful, calculating look.

"Ransom," she whispered, "is Mr. Peale one of them?"

"I venture to say he's the leader of 'em. Blind fool that I've been, to miss it all along. He worked with you often, didn't he? He must have—"

Merlin gasped. "And he copied all my notes. He brought them here for Mr. Pemminey to use."

"Damn! Do you mean Pemminey's already built a speaking box?"

She waved her hand. "No, of course not. Not those notes. That was to be a secret, wasn't it? No, listen, Ransom—" She grabbed his arm. "Mr. Pemminey's built a flying machine. From my plans!"

He gave her a startled look and then a stare. After a moment, a slow grin spread across his face. He threw back his head and let out a howl of laughter. "A . . . flying machine!" he exclaimed. "Do you mean they thought . . . everything's been for a . . ." He put his hands over his face and went into another shout of amusement. "The abductions—all your notes he copied— were for . . ." Ransom kept trying to speak and spluttering off into more guffaws. When finally he caught his breath, he said weakly, "Ah, God—what poetic justice!"

"What's wrong with you?" Merlin demanded. "This is serious."

"Where are they? These notes. All this?" He swept his arm toward the mess on the floor.

"Yes. I kept telling you, if you'd just have let me move them before you overturned the table."

"And he's actually built the thing?"

"Yes. It's upstairs on the parapet."

He leaned back to the window. "Peale!" he shouted. "Let's make a bargain."

The little huddle of men in the courtyard below broke up. Several of them ran off in various directions. Mr. Peale looked up. "What kind of a bargain?"

Merlin didn't think he sounded very interested.

"Let us go"—a trace of mockery hung in Ransom's voice—"and I'll tell you what Merlin was really working on."

"Something else beyond the aviation machine?" Peale answered Ransom's irony with a laugh of his own. "Ah, but all the more reason why I'm afraid I can't let her and Pemminey go, Your Grace. They're too valuable to waste, and a danger, left in your too-capable hands. Who can tell what other technological wonders your wife might dream up in that marvelous head of hers for you to put to use?"

Merlin clutched Ransom's arm, her eyes widening. "What does he mean by that—that he can't let us go?"

He glanced at her and patted her hand. "Nothing to worry over. He must think Pemminey's still here. That's good. If he made it to Eastbourne, God willing, we'll have the infantry here while Peale's standing around talking."

"Oh. I hope he didn't fall off your horse."

Ransom turned back to the window. "I hope so, too. I think Peale may have an idea something's in the works."

"Well, we can always use the flying machine, if he won't let us out any other way."

He patted her hand again absently. "It won't come to that."

"All of you," Peale called. "All of you come down. And no one will be hurt."

Ransom lifted his pistol and fired it out the window. "That's what I think of that idea," he muttered.

The men below ducked and scattered. One clutched at his shoulder and sank down behind a rock. The rest of them moved out of range.

"Damerell," Mr. Peale shouted in a rougher voice than before, "if you have a care for your wife, send her out."

Ransom's lip curled. He lifted the other pistol and fired it.

Merlin chewed her finger. She'd come to dislike the sound of gunfire excessively. While Ransom was reloading, she peered out the window herself.

The jumbled courtyard seemed much emptier of men than it had before. While she watched, a guard emerged from the gatehouse. He dodged around the piles of stone and ran up to Mr. Peale. For a moment the reverend stood listening while his aide gestured wildly, pointing east.

"Ah," Ransom said, looking up. "They'll have spotted our reinforcements arriving."

Mr. Peale turned his face back up to their window. "Last chance, Damerell! I want all of you."

Ransom said something about Mr. Peale and his mother that Merlin didn't understand. But it sounded quite impolite.

Peale bowed. He shouted, "We've been storing munitions here, Your Grace. There's seven tons of black powder in the foundations of this place."

"Oh, dear," Merlin said. "I forgot about that."

Ransom slanted a look toward her. "You're joking."

"Will they blow us up, do you think?"

His eyes widened. "You're joking. He's got seven tons of powder in the cellar?"

"I didn't count the kegs," she said apologetically. "There's a lot."

Ransom turned abruptly to the window. "Peale," he shouted, "I'm sending Merlin out."

"Wait," Merlin exclaimed. "Are you coming, too?"

All the humor had left his face. Beneath the streak of chalk on his cheekbone, his mouth was grim. He touched her throat. "No. I can't, love. You do what he says—I don't think he'll hurt you."

"You aren't going to stay here?" she cried. "And let them blow you up?"

He shook his head. "Maybe that won't happen. Come on, I'll move as much of that barrier as I can, and you slide through. They'll be helping from below."

"But Ransom—" Her voice rose frantically. "Why won't you come?"

He took both her arms and kissed her, then pushed her away. "You're a little fish. Unfortunately, I'm a rather large one. I know too much, Merlin."

"Too much about what?"

"Everything. The war. You just do exactly as Peale says, and get down flat if anyone starts shooting. Please." He gripped her arm. "Please don't make this hard."

"But . . . the gunpowder . . . Ransom!"

He gave her a bitter smile. "I'm counting on it being damp. Belonging to the French, and all."

"It's not damp!" She was resisting him every step. "I won't go without you. We'll use the flying machine!"

"Suicide is not the answer."

She set her feet at the top of the stairs. "Then why are you staying?"

"Merlin—"

"I won't go!" she cried. "I won't go without you!"

He let go of her, and dropped down into the staircase. He pulled one of the chairs free and tossed it back up into the room. "She's coming," he yelled, and someone answered something, a muffled agreement from below.

"I'm not." Merlin sat down in the middle of the floor. Another chair clattered up from the stairwell and fell over. Ransom was working on the settle when the voice from the lower stairs spoke again.

"Too late, the man says. We ain't got time."

Ransom flung himself up the stairs and into the window embrasure. "*Peale,*" he bellowed. "I'm sending her out. Do you hear me?"

"Your Grace," Mr. Peale's thin voice answered, "I'm afraid I have no more time for sentimentality. You may blame yourself—'twas you who called out these troops, was it not? It does put me in a difficult position."

"Take her! Let her out!"

"Nay. You have thirteen minutes, I'd estimate, Your Grace. They won't be in time for you, I fear."

"*Wait!*" It was a howl. Ransom shoved backward. "That bastard. That bastard." He started down the stairs to the barrier. Someone yelled from below, and there was a new smell in the air—a trace of smoke. From the spiral staircase came a curl of gray that increased to a billow. She could hear Ransom's grunts turn to coughs as he tugged at the settle.

"Come up," she cried. "They've set a fire. We can't get out that way!"

There was no answer but coughs and scraping wood. Merlin held her breath and dove down the stairs. She groped with her eyes closed and found Ransom's convulsing shoulders. He resisted her for a moment, and then gave way to her pull on his arm, stumbling after her back up the stairs. She threw the door shut and barred it. Smoke swirled at the ceiling and dissipated, while more crept in the crevices around the door.

Ransom choked and wiped his eyes, his breath rasping. "Rid of us—" he said hoarsely. "Wants to be sure."

"We'll use the flying machine," Merlin said.

His face was a patchwork of black and white now. "Don't be ridiculous." He began a quick circuit of the room, pulling back the musty tapestries, sweeping books from bookcases. "No more doors," he said. "Just the stairway up."

"Yes. The flying machine is up there."

"Merlin—"

"It will fly! You saw mine fly, and this one will, too!"

He went to the window. "Maybe the powder won't blow."

A crescendo of sound throbbed through the tower, rattling glass and reverberating in Merlin's bones. Ransom grabbed the casement. "Jesus Christ," he said.

Merlin ran up behind him. Through the curtain of dust, she could see the empty courtyard—or rather, two-thirds of the empty courtyard. The other third was gone . . . transformed into vacant space. A white scar marked the site where a huge chunk of the peninsula itself had fallen into the sea.

Ransom coughed weakly. "Blew up the wrong spot. Stupid—"

Another detonation rocked through the air. Merlin saw it this time; she felt the blast of wind and closed her eyes against the arching cascade of rock and dust. Stone missiles crashed against the tower and fell back in clatters of splintering sound.

Another stark slash cut into the peninsula, carving out a gap closer to their tower than before.

"It must be fused along that corridor in the cellars," Merlin said. "There were four rooms full of kegs."

"Four." He took a deep breath. "How close is the nearest?"

"Underneath us."

Ransom cleared his throat. "Perhaps we'll try the flying machine."

"Good." Merlin clapped her hands. "Come on."

She raced ahead of him up the stairs and out onto the flat-topped parapet. The Matilda was protected from the strong coastal winds by a sturdy shed, but in her time with Mr. Pemminey, he'd shown Merlin how to ready the machine for flight. She began tearing down the wooden cover, with Ransom helping to toss the boards aside.

The machine sat perched at the top of the tower, overlooking a ruined gap in the crenellated wall. Merlin unfolded the wings by degrees, locking the joints that were exact replicas of her own into place.

Ransom hovered near the center of the parapet. "Hurry up," he said.

"Oh, yes." She checked a strut. "I'm hurrying." She looked up at Mr. Pemminey's wind vane, and saw that the steady onshore breeze was adequately oriented—she wouldn't have to use his gearing mechanism to direct the take-off tracks to another angle. She leaned over the broken section of wall, looking down to check the lubrication on the tracks themselves.

The steel furrows hung suspended over the water, polished and measured to a fine, smooth fit against the metal wheels that would move in a greased swoop down the sheer drop. The triple tracks descended the full height of the tower, curving up at the end.

It was a close replica of the tracks she'd used with her skis at Mount Falcon, except Mr. Pemminey and his tower had gravity and height instead of horsepower to provide the initial momentum. It meant his machine could be heavier—had to be heavier—to stay on the tracks and gather speed and lift, and then meet the wind rushing up off the cliff face with forward velocity enough to soar.

Merlin made a little hop of excitement. "It's ready. How much do you weigh?"

Ransom licked his lips. "Oh, God, does it make a difference?"

"There's a range. I'm eight and a half stone."

"Fourteen," Ransom said. "Maybe a little more."

"How much more?"

"I don't know." His voice cracked a little. "Three pounds more," he said quickly.

"That's all right, then."

She was about to give him instructions when Ransom yelled, "Get down!" A sheet of sound smashed into her ears, and rock dust cascaded in stinging pinpricks on her cheeks and ears. She coughed and sprang up, checking frantically over the taut canvas wing surface for any damage. It appeared whole.

"God damn," Ransom hissed. "We're on an island now."

"What?" Merlin asked, distracted.

"Is it ready? Hurry, for heaven's sake."

"Here, get in. You put your feet here, on this bar, and lie on your stomach. Rest your chest in this netting. It's rather like a cradle, you see. Then buckle the straps."

He moved over toward her. Merlin motioned, pointing out where to put his feet. He put his hand on a wing strut and stopped, looking down past the ruined wall at the slope of the metal tracks.

Even beneath the smudges, she saw his face turn white.

He jerked his hand off the strut and backed up. "I can't," he said.

Merlin blinked at him. "Why not?"

"I just can't." He was breathing harder. He shook his head. "You go on."

"And leave you here?"

He swallowed and shook his head again.

"But I can't leave you here! Hurry, you have to get on. I'll do the straps for you."

"No."

"Don't you think it will fly?" she cried. "It *will* fly! You'll be blown up if you stay here! Get on!"

His mouth curved in something not at all like a smile. "I'd rather be blown up."

"Are you mad? We'll die here!"

"You go." He turned his head a little away from the view. "I can't, Merlin. I cannot."

She marched up to him, and took his cheeks between her hands. "Are you afraid it won't work?" she yelled in his face.

He made no answer. He was absolutely rigid. Beneath her fingers, she could feel a very faint quiver.

"Now, you listen to me, Mr. Duke," she shouted. "I designed this machine, and I went over every inch of it with Mr. Pemminey yesterday. *It . . . will . . . fly!* Do you hear me?"

"Yes! Yes, damn it, fly the thing out of here." He tore her hands away. He pushed her toward the machine. "You can do it."

Merlin stared at him. She watched the way he glanced again toward the break in the wall and the tracks almost furtively, saw how his jaw grew taut and his hands clenched.

He jerked his eyes back to the solid floor at his feet. "Go on," he yelled.

Merlin put her finger to her lip. She had never seen Ransom terrified before, had never even imagined it was possible. But he was beyond reason now. He admitted her machine would fly, he knew the tower was going to blow up, and yet he stood there, telling her to go by herself and leave him.

She turned around, looking over her shoulder down the steep swoop of the tracks, at the sheer drop from the cliff and the sea below. She looked back at Ransom. In a moment of blinding revelation, she knew exactly what vile, manipulative, bullying thing he would do, if he were in her place.

"Ransom," she said sharply.

He slanted a look toward her, one that did not rise past her waist.

"Do you love me?" she demanded.

"Merlin." Her name was a painful rasp in his throat. He looked down at his feet, gripping his sword handle until his knuckles turned white.

"If you do," she said coldly, "you'd better get on that machine . . . because it won't fly with a smaller load than twenty stone. It will come off the track too soon, before there's enough velocity—it will just blow sideways and fall."

"Oh, God," he said with a groan.

"You have to rescue me," she added. "I need you."

He lifted his eyes to hers. For a moment she thought he would realize her ploy, that he was still cleverer and stronger than she—strong enough to see the obvious thing: that there was a container filled with rocks right beside the machine, ready to be fitted into place so the apparatus could be flown by one person alone.

He looked past her, at the machine and the top of the tracks. His jaw worked. With a sudden shudder, he moved, stepping close to the machine and shoving his boot onto the bar as she'd shown him.

Merlin threw herself into the other webbed cradle, working at the straps. Ransom finished buckling and twisted his head. "Damn you, Wiz," he said. "I'll see you in Hell if I die like this."

"Pull!" she ordered, and looked toward him.

He wrenched one eye open. "What?"

"That lever there. I can't reach it. Pull it, and we'll go."

He lifted his head. She heard him moan as he looked down at the track, but he put his hand around the lever.

"Go!" she hissed.

"Merlin—"

Gunpowder detonated. Ransom's body jerked. In a shriek of metallic friction and thunder, the flying machine dropped. Merlin's insides made a wild, exultant swoop. The machine hit the curve with every wire taut to contain the energy of their take-off. With a powerful flex of canvas and steel, it burst into the open air.

Chapter 24

They were flying.

Ransom had his eyes closed. The reason he knew they were flying was because he wasn't dead yet. He could hear the wind and feel the netting under his belly and taste the coppery tinge of terror in his mouth.

"Look," Merlin cried over the sound of wind thrumming through the wires. "There are the troops."

Ransom didn't open his eyes. The flying machine rocked upward on a gust, leaving his stomach in his mouth.

"And look . . . Oh, no—" She sent the machine into a tilt. Ransom gritted his teeth. "Is that Mr. Peale? He's going to get away."

Ransom felt his body grow heavy on one side, pressing into the netting. His sword handle dug into his ribs. He would have scrabbled for purchase, but his fingers were beyond his control. He opened his eyes and saw the wild angle of the earth beneath them. It was such an insane sight, that dizzy mass of green tilted up against the blue, that he decided to stop worrying. He was doomed. He thought he might as well make the most of the time he had left.

He squinted against the wind. "Where?"

The machine tilted the other way, and he realized the band of twisted white ribbon that seemed to rotate in front of him was the coastline, chalk cliffs rising and falling in a line down the shore. He managed to sort out land from sea in his mind.

"In front of us," Merlin called over the wind. "I'll go closer."

The white ribbon grew larger with alarming rapidity. The cliff loomed up, still blowing a haze of pale dust from the last explosion. The peninsula was gone entirely, leaving a blazing scar in the light-colored cliff and a salt-and-pepper wreckage below. Then suddenly they were past the cliff and over the gray-green downs. Ransom stared and squinted at a splash of red in the landscape. He finally realized it was soldiers. The size of them made him feel ill.

The flying machine was over and past the troops before he had time to think about it.

"There," Merlin cried. "See, by that square of rusty color. That must be a plowed field. Do you recognize him?"

Ransom grunted. The dark speck in the distance with a small puff of white behind might conceivably be a horseman. The pale string that looped over hills and dales was obviously a road. "Never mind," he shouted. "Put this thing on the ground."

"I have to decide where!"

"Decide!"

"More troops," she cried. "From the other way. Oh, but they won't catch Mr. Peale, I'm afraid. Not unless they cut off through the fields to go after him."

"Merlin," he groaned. "For the love of God, get us down!"

"There," she said, sending the machine into another sickening tilt. "We'll land there. I'll go over it once and make sure there aren't any bushes."

The machine took a sudden dip. Ransom squeezed his eyes closed. Merlin kept up a running commentary on what she was doing. He opened his eyes once in the middle of it and found the ground very close, streaming past in a flood of mottled greens and grays. Suddenly the cliff edge flashed by and water was beneath them. The machine took a leap and a long, long tilt in the air, circling. When Merlin started yelling about how she'd never landed before and how difficult it might be on Mr. Pemminey's wheels, Ransom said his last prayers and quit listening. He buried his face in his sleeve.

The first impact jolted his arm free. His chin cracked on the strut in front of him. They bounced into the air again, with wind and ground in a confusion around him, then hit once more, skidding up the hillside in a series of rebounds and rattling slides. The machine came to a stop with its front angled into the hill. Ransom's feet were higher than his head.

He put his face in his arms. "God Almighty," he muttered. "I will never sin again."

By the time Merlin struggled out of the straps, Ransom was already free. He grabbed her waist and helped her stand.

"See," she said. "It worked! Did you like it?"

He pushed her away—not roughly, but not very gently, either. "Oh, excessively." He stepped away, making a great show of dusting off his pants. In a muffled, vicious voice, he added, "All that tilting was marvelous, but I thought the landing was by far the best part."

He straightened up, looking beyond her. Merlin turned. From one side, the scarlet-coated troops from Eastbourne marched toward them, and from the other came a small cavalcade of horses, with militia in dark-blue uniforms farther behind. Ransom walked away from her, down the hill to meet them.

Merlin looked at the flying machine. The canvas surface was fluttering dangerously in the breeze, trying to lift. "Ransom!" she shouted.

He turned.

"I need help—to hold it down!"

He looked at her a moment, nodded, and went on. He met the mounted officer who cantered up, and they stood talking. After a moment, the officer gestured, and four men came running toward Merlin. She stationed them at the corners of the wings, and ran down the hill after Ransom.

She reached him just in time to recognize Shelby in the lead of the group of approaching riders. Ransom was talking to the officer in his usual fashion—making suggestions which sounded like orders. The officer seemed happy to act on them, but Merlin paid little attention to the commands and regroupings of the military. She was busy being enveloped in hugs from Shelby and Jaqueline and Quin and Woodrow and even Blythe, who had come rattling up with Woodrow in a phaeton a little distance behind the others. The militia arrived, mixing with the other troops, and everything was a blur of shouts and color and nervous horses.

"Miss Lambourne," someone cried, and Merlin looked around to see Mr. Pemminey half-sliding, half-falling off of Ransom's gray gelding. He handed the reins to a soldier and trotted up to Merlin.

"Your bandbox." He shoved it into her hands and turned to gaze ecstatically toward the flying machine. "Tell me, tell me! How did it perform?"

"Perfectly," Merlin said. "I'm awfully sorry about your castle."

Mr. Pemminey waved his arms. "Never mind that. Did the wheels work for landing? Did the steering gears function?"

"Of course," Merlin said. "The steering was excellent. I think the landing could use some refinement. There's no brake, you know." She eased the lid off the bandbox and peeked inside. Her hedgehog blinked in the sudden light and rolled up. She put the bandbox in the phaeton, with Mr. Pemminey and Woodrow dogging her steps and asking questions with every breath. Finally they grew impatient, and ran off up the hill to look at the machine.

The militia and troops had thinned, sent off in pursuit of Mr. Peale and his minions. Merlin saw Ransom rest his hand on his sword and look around. A silence fell in the remaining group when he walked up to his brother.

Shelby straightened his shoulders, looking belligerent and uneasy and eager all at once. Ransom's white shirt and waistcoat stood out against his brother's dark green frock, making them a striking pair as they stood at the center of attention.

"I ask your pardon," Ransom said. "I've wronged you, Shelby. I'm sorry for it."

Shelby looked at the ground, and back up at Ransom. Before he could speak, Jaqueline took his hand.

"The duke is not alone," she said in a clear, carrying voice. "I, too, ask your pardon. For all the times I should have stood with my husband, and not against him."

"Your husband?" Shelby's words held a faint bitterness.

"In my heart," Jaqueline said. "Always."

Shelby turned her hand over in his, looking down. "Do you mean that?"

Jaqueline's proud figure seemed to wilt a little. Merlin thought she looked smaller suddenly, like a marble statue of a goddess relaxing into something softer, more human and vulnerable. She looked up at Shelby and nodded without speaking. He took her in his arms.

Merlin tilted her head in curious interest, wondering if Shelby would kiss Jaqueline the way Ransom kissed her. But Shelby seemed to change his mind at the last moment. He lifted his face with a self-conscious cough, and loosened his hold a little.

He looked at Ransom. "You know it was Peale, then?"

"Yes."

"Jaqueline worked it out," Shelby said.

Quin stepped forward. "Aye, and your clever sister." He bent over Blythe's hand with a kiss. "The charmin' ladies."

She turned pink when everyone looked at her. "I knew it wasn't Qui—" She paused, and the pink turned to scarlet. "Major O'Shaughnessy. I knew it wasn't."

"And my Shelby is no traitor." Jaqueline straightened again and moved her hand in a theatrical sweep. Then she slanted a look up at him and added, "Although he is no saint."

"I'll reform," Shelby said.

"No, you will not." Jaqueline patted his shirtfront. "I have no hopes of that."

"I mean it," Shelby said. "'Twas no more than I deserved, to live my life so that I fit so easily into the mold Peale cast for me." He looked toward Ransom. "It would have ruined you, wouldn't it? To have me hanged for a traitor. That was what he intended."

Ransom said slowly, "It would have ruined me."

"'Tis I who beg pardon, then." Shelby held out his hand.

Ransom took it. For an instant the grip held, and then broke.

Ransom turned to Quin. "I owe you an apology also. I only say in my defense that I was looking for a suspect besides my brother."

Quin grinned and looked down Ransom's offered hand. "By St. Patrick," Quin said. "Give me your sister's, and I'll be satisfied."

"Oh, we'll discuss that, I assure you." Ransom narrowed his eyes. "In private."

"Don't blame him," Blythe cried. "I've been wicked and . . . and *wanton* . . . and Mr. Peale would never have known of the temple, but that he must have seen me showing Major O'Shaughnessy. Ransom, don't blame him, please; it's my fault! I've violated every moral—"

"In private, Blythe," Ransom said.

She stood with her lips trembling. "I shall run away with him if you won't give us your countenence."

"I'm quite certain it won't come to that." He began to unbuckle his sword. "I have a wedding trip in mind for you. Afghanistan. On your way to take up a promising post in India."

"India." Blythe gasped.

Ransom tossed the sheathed sword into the phaeton. "In private, Blythe. Not now."

"Miss Merlin!"

Merlin turned. Woodrow had run back from the flying machine. He was panting, tugging on her elbow, his eyes bright with excitement.

"Miss Merlin, the castle blew up! Did you see it? Were you in there? Are you all right?"

"Oh, yes," she said. "I'm quite all right. Ransom rescued me."

Ransom looked up from unloading one of the pistols. His mouth curved into a mocking line. "Oh, did I rescue you?" he asked coolly. "You'll have to tell me about it someday."

"Look!" Woodrow gasped.

Up the hill, an odd gust of wind had torn the flying machine away from one of the four soldiers. The apparatus was lifting, one wing rising high in the air. Unattended, the horses began to dance anxiously at the peculiar sight. While Merlin watched, everyone else started to run. The canvas expanse shuddered as it caught the wind under its full surface. In a majestic tumble the machine wheeled over.

Horses bolted everywhere. Ransom grabbed at the harness of the black mare in the phaeton's traces. Up on the hill, someone managed to grapple a wing tip, but the wind had sway now. It snatched the machine and sent it in another graceful somersault toward the cliff. Frantic figures pursued it, clawing and clinging to any purchase. In devilish cooperation, the wind and the spread of canvas worked together to defeat recovery.

In a succession of flips and kite-wheels, the flying machine evaded every attempt to restrain it. Struts began to break, but the spread of cloth was still enough to catch and hold the vigorous wind. At the summit of the hill, where the cliff dropped down to the sea, the machine seemed to pause and hover tauntingly, one wing raised like a drunken salute.

For a moment the white surface was silhouetted against the sky. Then it fell, vanishing behind the summit. A row of human figures lined the edge, staring downward where the machine had gone.

"Aren't you going to help?"

Merlin turned to see Ransom leaning against the phaeton's traces, his shirt-sleeved figure white against the mare's shiny black hide. The horse had calmed again once the flying machine had vanished. He let go of her bridle and crossed his arms.

"I don't think there's much to be done," Merlin said. "Poor Mr. Pemminey! First his castle, and now this."

Ransom looked at her in a strange, intent sort of way. Merlin touched her lip, remembered not to chew her finger, and clasped her hands behind her back. It was never very comfortable, being subjected to the Falconer stare. "What have I done?" she asked defensively.

"Get in," he said, straightening suddenly and motioning at the phaeton. "I want to talk to you."

Merlin wet her lips. At a second dose of the Falconer stare, she wiped her hands on her pants and obeyed. Ransom gave her a hand up into the high perch. He walked around the other side and swung himself into the seat. The carriage rocked forward.

"Are we going home?" Merlin demanded. "What about everyone else?"

"The lovebirds can ride double," he said sourly.

She clung to the seat as the phaeton jolted on the country track. For the first time since Ransom had arrived, she recalled she wasn't wearing a skirt. She pressed her knees together in embarrassment and hunched over, trying to hold on and cover her legs at the same time.

"Never mind that," Ransom said. "You aren't in imminent danger of ravishment by me, you know."

"I'm not?"

"No."

"Oh," she said. And then added hopefully, "Perhaps I will be later on."

The phaeton had followed the limestone track down into a little hollow. Ransom reined to a halt. "Merlin," he said, turning toward her, "I want to say something to you. Something important. What's happened today has been a monstrous revelation to me."

She nodded and smiled. "Yes," she said. "Flying will do that."

He took a deep breath and looked ahead. "It certainly will." He set his jaw. "Merlin . . . I'm afraid I've forced you into a very unfortunate mistake. I—" He frowned. He rubbed the reins between his fingers. "I've come to see today that I would never make a satisfactory husband for you.''

Her eyes widened. ''You wouldn't?''

''No. You've been right all along. We shouldn't have married.''

''Oh.''

''I've tried to stifle you, Merlin. And you should not be stifled. Nor hedged about with rules and restrictions. You should always be free to go wherever your mind can take you. As high and as far . . .'' His mouth tightened. He shook his head.

Merlin frowned down at her lap. Wind rustled the long grass around them and lifted the strands of the mare's silky tail.

''I've never done you justice, Wiz,'' he said. ''Not for one moment. It makes me ashamed.''

She fitted her fingers together, rocking back and forth a little. ''I don't mind.''

''It flew. You said it would. It was your design—I don't believe for an instant that Pemminey had the wit to devise it.'' He stared off at the horizon. ''I found out some unpleasant things about myself today. I'm an overbearing idiot. I've a dread of heights. I knew that, of course, but I never knew I could let it interfere with my judgment. Not so very far.''

Merlin looked up. ''You're afraid of heights?''

''You didn't notice?'' he asked dryly.

She blinked at him. ''Oh,'' she said slowly. ''I see! And you were going to get on the flying machine, weren't you? Until you looked over the edge. I expect it was seeing those tracks. And the cliff. Yes, I can imagine that would be very daunting.''

He cleared his throat. ''I'd prefer not to discuss it.''

''I'm afraid of snakes,'' she confided. ''I understand.''

''Do you?'' His fingers tightened on the reins. Chalk and soot mingled in smudges on his strong hands. ''I was going to stay there, Wiz. I was so . . . beyond reason . . . that I was going to stay there on top of a powder keg and be blown to Kingdom Come rather than face that fear.''

"But you didn't."

He scowled and shrugged.

"And there was the cliff," she said. "You stole in on that path around the cliff, didn't you? Why, that must have been just as difficult—right there on the edge, with the cliff down below you, and the wind blowing so hard— as if it would knock you off on purpose. And having to look down at the rocks, and see the birds flying down there—I should think that would be very distressing for someone with a dread of heights. And then there was that steep ravine that one had to jump, with nothing to hold on to—"

He coughed uneasily. "Must you be so descriptive?"

"I think you were very brave." Merlin looked up at him, at his harshly marked face turned partially toward her. "I think you're the bravest person in the world."

"Well," he said. "I certainly have you fooled, don't I?"

She leaned on his shoulder, tucking her arm through his elbow. "I'm not so stupid."

"I am." He disengaged her gently and moved away. "It's taken me until today to see it. I've run roughshod over everyone I care for. I've thought I knew what was best, and I've used every advantage and prerogative and chance I could find to bend you to my will. To make you give up your flying machine. And look what my will has been based upon. On fear, not on wisdom. A child's bugaboo instead of principle."

Merlin sat up straight, faintly piqued that he would not respond to her overture. "What difference does that make?"

"What difference! All the difference. Don't underestimate me, Merlin. I'm damned good at what I do. And what I do is manipulate and pull strings and play politics until I get what I want. I've been brought up to it. I've been told all my life that I'm the one who makes the decisions. I've tried my best to make the right ones, but now . . . I don't know . . ." He ran a hand through his dusty hair. "I just don't know anymore."

She pursed her lips, looking at him sideways. "I'm sure no one can expect to be right all the time."

"If I can't expect to be right, then I'd better not be managing things." He squinted at the horizon. "Shelby said something to me, almost the first day that you came. He said I would make you miserable. And I would. That I'd run your life to suit my convenience. I don't want to do that, Merlin. You deserve more than that . . . so much more."

"Wings," Merlin said softly.

He looked toward her, an arrested look that softened into a brief nod. "Yes," he answered. "Not a cage of my building." He frowned, his golden-green eyes darkening. "I want to say that I would change, but I'd be lying. To myself and to you. I'm too old to change what I've been brought up to."

"I don't want you to change."

"No. You're wiser than I." His mouth curved downward, the scowl deepened by a smear of black at the edge of his lips. "You had the right of it when you ran away from me."

Merlin sat still, gazing at her hands. "I wish I hadn't," she whispered.

If he heard her, he took no notice. "I'm sorry, Merlin. I was a selfish, love-blind fool to think I could force you to live under my control."

She felt a knot gathering in her chest and a growing dread of what he would say next.

"You didn't force me, exactly," she murmured.

"No. Nothing so crude." He flicked his hand. "We have a little more finesse than that, we Falconers. I only took advantage of you when you were weak and confused, and tricked you into it." The bitterness in his voice hardened into determination. "But that can be remedied, Merlin. I want you to know that. The marriage can be annulled. You weren't in your right mind when you agreed to it. You were coerced. Your legal guardian knew nothing of it. I'll have the best solicitors in the land put to work. The marriage can be dissolved, never fear."

The knot in her chest grew to a lump. She tried to swallow it and did not succeed.

She gripped her hands together. "You mean, I would go home and everything would be just as it was?"

"Yes." He turned toward her and took her hands in his. "Just as it was. Or any way that you want it to be. I'll see to that. Whatever you need, Merlin; whatever you wish for—you can write to me, and I'll see that you have it." He looked down at her hands with a painful smile. "Even a Vaucanson pinion gear."

"I don't know . . ." she said timidly. "What if I thought that I would like to stay married?"

"That's all right," he said without hesitation. "That would be far easier than an annullment. But you wouldn't be free to marry elsewhere in that case, you know."

"Elsewhere."

"If you met someone else. That might happen, Wiz." He touched her cheek. "You won't wish to live alone there forever."

She kept her face lowered, blinking at the blurriness in her eyes. "But if I was kidnapped," she said, "who would rescue me?"

He caught her chin. "Merlin, Merlin—don't you understand what I'm saying? You have this talent, this marvelous genius—and I'd be forever in your way, trying to turn you toward my goals, the way I did on the speaking box. Keeping you from your own dreams when yours might be the greater." He cradled her face, moving his thumbs across her cheekbones. "If you were a different person, it wouldn't matter. But with you . . . I feel like a fox trying to mother a newborn chick. Sooner or later, my discipline would break. I'd swallow you in one gulp."

"I'm not a newborn chick."

His thumbs traced her lips. "You seem like one to me. You feel like one."

Merlin looked up at him through her eyelashes. His face was very close, the stern set of his mouth softening. He lowered his head and brushed her lips, then tilted her chin up and deepened the kiss, sharing the taste of chalky dust and his warm skin, the familiar shape and scent of him.

"My discipline's breaking already," he murmured against her mouth.

"Oh, Ransom," Merlin said, sliding her hands around his waist. Her voice had gone vague and dreamy as he pressed light kisses at the curve of her throat. "I don't think I . . . want to . . . go home anymore."

Abruptly, he pulled away from her. Merlin opened her eyes, an objection and a plea on her lips, but before she could voice them he retrieved the lines and slapped the mare on the rump. The phaeton bounced into motion. Merlin grabbed the seat for balance.

"Do you see?" he said, over the creak of the wheels. "You're too damned easy, Merlin."

"What does that mean?" she demanded.

"It means I can make you do just about anything I wish by dangling the right carrot. I don't want that kind of power over you. It isn't good for you, and it isn't good for me."

"Make me do anything!" She glared at him. "And what is it you wish me to do? Take Thaddeus and Theo home and forget all about you?"

"Yes."

"I won't." Merlin crossed her arms. The phaeton jolted over a rock, and she had to hastily uncross them again. "Do you know what I think you're doing?" she yelled. "You're just being a bully again. First you bully me into marrying you, and now you're trying to bully me back out again."

He looked at her and then at the road. "I'm not bullying you, for God's sake. I'm trying to do what's best for you!"

"I call it bullying."

"I thought you wanted to go home. You packed up your bloody bandbox and left me."

"I changed my mind."

He gave her another glare that lasted until the carriage bounced over a rut. "You mean you've decided to become obstinate."

"So—" She shrugged. "Just dangle a carrot! Or kidnap me and put me where you want me."

He jerked his head. "Yes. And see how long you'd stay there. You and that damned peripatetic hedgehog."

"*That's* what I'll do!" She sniffed. "Now that I've learned how to get on in the world, I think I'll go and see more of it."

The carriage slowed. "Is that right?" He gave her a narrow look. "How much more of it?"

"Where is Afghanistan?"

The black mare bounced to a halt.

"Can I hire a post-chaise?" Merlin asked haughtily.

He dropped the reins and gave her the Falconer stare. Merlin lifted her chin. "Shelby will tell me."

She could see Ransom's jaw clench. He turned away from her and transferred the Falconer stare to the mare's rump. For a long time, there was no sound but wind and the jingle and creak of the mare's harness when she moved.

Merlin bit her lip. "Ransom," she said in a small, hopeful voice, "if I got to Afghanistan, do you think you might come and rescue me?"

He turned his face a little away from her. "You have a few carrots of your own to dangle, don't you?"

She flipped the trailing end of his cravat back and forth across her knee. "Would you come?"

"You left me," he said gruffly. "You ran away."

"I suppose it must be very hot there. Do they have tigers in Afghanistan?"

"I won't change," he said.

Merlin frowned at the gray-green horizon of the downs. "I would need to be rescued from tigers, I should think."

"I'm too old to change."

"And snakes!" She stiffened and looked at him with wide eyes. "Do they have snakes?"

"God knows."

"You'd rescue me from snakes, wouldn't you?"

He slanted a look toward her. "I might. What would I get out of the bargain?"

Merlin touched her lower lip, thinking.

"Obedience?" he suggested. "Deference? Respect for my opinions?"

"All that?" she exclaimed. "It's only snakes."

"Yes," he said sweetly, "but I'll have to go all the way to Afghanistan to fight them off. And one doesn't get there in a post-chaise, my dear."

She cocked her head curiously. "How does one get there?"

"I don't think I'll tell you," he said as he pulled her into his arms. He buried his face in the curve of her throat and began to kiss the tender skin beneath her ear. His hands shaped the outline of her body from her breech-clad hips to the base of her breasts.

Merlin tilted her head back, taking a deep, luxurious breath. "Why won't you tell me?"

He held her chin up with his thumbs and kissed her parted lips. "Because," he muttered between warm caresses, "I damned well don't have the time to go."

A harvest moon hung full and heavy over the garden, sending cool light to turn the gilded furnishings to silver. Merlin stood at the window of the darkened bedchamber. She crossed her arms, draped in Ransom's borrowed dressing gown because she'd managed to mislay her own so badly that even the maid couldn't find it.

She heard him move behind her and turned.

"Aren't you cold?" she asked, eyeing his unclad figure in the moonlight. "It's November, you know."

He put his arms around her and pressed against her back. "Do I feel cold, Wiz?"

She leaned against him. "Not in some places."

"Mmm." He brushed aside her loosened hair and kissed her neck. "What are you doing staring out the window, Mrs. Duke?"

"Thinking."

He groaned. "About what?"

"Things." She twisted a little, looking up at him. "What happened to our speaking box?"

"Ah." He rocked her gently. "I'm afraid it's been swallowed up in the Admiralty's confidential files."

"Was it never put to use?" she asked in disappointment.

"It's the Admiralty's secret. It may be we'll never know."

"I'll wager you know," she said wisely.

He raised his eyebrows. "Do you care so much what happened to it?"

"Well . . . I hoped that it would do some good. You said it would."

He kissed her nose. Then he ran his forefinger down it and gave her a subtle smile. "Nelson won at Trafalgar, did he not?"

Merlin tilted her head. Her lips curved upward in an answering smile. "Ah. I probably saved thousands of lives," she said. "I'm good at that." She settled back against him and watched the moonlight. "I'm rather glad that you arranged for Mr. Peale to get away. I shouldn't have liked for him to be hanged."

"Merlin," Ransom said patiently, "I wish you will not say that I arranged for him to 'get away.' Not in public, at any rate."

"I won't," Merlin promised.

His low chuckle vibrated against her back. "The incident did have a nice Falconer twist, I must say. Full confession of activities and a list of members in his spying ring in return for dropping charges of treason. How was I to know there was a Navy press gang prowling just outside the door as he left?"

"Hmmpf," she said. "You always know."

"Oh, always. I'm infallible." Ransom nibbled at the curve of her ear and then said softly, "I do have one question, though, Wiz."

"What?"

His arms tensed a little around her shoulders. He laid his cheek on her hair. "Merlin, when are you going to start working to rebuild your flying machine?"

"My flying machine?" She half-turned in his arms. "Oh, I wasn't going to rebuild it."

He held her away from him and peered into her face. "You weren't?" There was the faintest trace of hope in his voice.

She shrugged. "I'm finished with that. I said I would build a machine that would fly, and I did. I flew. I've forgotten that first time—I never can seem to remember anything about that day at all—but you and I flew in a machine that I designed."

"And that's it?" He sounded stunned. "That's all you wanted?"

She nodded.

"You're sure?"

She nodded again.

"Thank God." Air came out of him in a whoosh. He drew her close and hugged her. "Oh, Merlin, thank God for that. I was going to try not to interfere; I swear I was, but I've been dreading it worse than death by slow degrees."

She smiled. She could just see his eyes in the moon-shadow, pale gold in the metallic light. She stood on tip-toe and met his kiss, felt his arms grow taut around her. For a long, long moment all she thought of was Ransom, of his body and his arms and his kiss—all pressed hard against her—and the assurance of pleasures to come that those things promised.

When he let her go, she turned around in his arms to look back out the window at the sky. She tucked his hands up between her own and intertwined their fingers. She liked the feel of him at her back, solid and warm, so much larger than herself. He tightened his hold, exerting a steady pull on her to draw her toward the bed.

She patted his hand. "No, you have nothing at all to worry about. I'm quite done with the flying machine. I have something else in mind."

He squeezed her. In a husky murmur, he said, "So do I, Wiz."

She relaxed in the velvet strength of his hold, allowing herself to be pulled along backward on her heels. "Yes," she announced complacently as she was towed across the floor. "*Now* I'm going to start building a rocket to reach the moon!"

Author's Note

The battle of Trafalgar predates by a century both Reginald Fessendon's radio broadcast from Brant Rock, Massachusetts, on Christmas Eve, 1906, and the Wright Brothers' controlled flights in Glider Number Three at Kitty Hawk. In light of these facts, Merlin's achievements may seem unrealistic. But in 1805, the elements of radio communication and heavier-than-air-craft flight existed. An electric current made magnetic fields. The wind provided lift for birds' wings according to the laws of aerodynamics. Countless amateur and professional scientists dreamed dreams and flew models and sent currents through the wires.

The names we remember today—Wright, Marconi, Morse, Cooke, and Wheatstone—are legend. They had genius, and more than that: the luck to have it at the right time. In the shadows behind them stand all those who tried and failed . . . or tried and might have succeeded, only to be ignored by a complacent world.

In 1816, eleven years before Cooke, Wheatstone, and Morse entered their claims of inventing the electric telegraph, a young aristocrat named Francis Ronalds sent a memorandum to the Lords of the Admiralty. He offered them his plans for the first practical, effective electric telegraph, which he had erected in his garden. After being denied an interview with Lord Melville, Ronalds received a letter from the Secretary of the Admiralty, which stated: ". . . telegraphs of any kind are now wholly unnecessary, and no other than the one now in use will be adopted.''

I like to think the Lords had their reasons . . . concealed deep in the Admiralty's secret files.

Ad astra per aspera.

L.K.

LAURA KINSALE

LAURA KINSALE began her working life as a petroleum geologist—a career which consisted of waking up at three a.m. on random Saturdays and driving hundreds of miles across west Texas to visit drilling rigs, wear a hard hat, and attempt to boss around oil-covered males considerably larger than herself. This, she decided, was pushing her luck. After six years with Sun Company, she packed up her dog Sage and her husband David, whose greatest sorrow is that he Never Gets To Go Fishing, and moved into her great-grandmother's restored 1890s' farmhouse near Dallas to write. David still Never Gets To Go Fishing, but Laura finds her book deadlines a great excuse to get him to go to the grocery store. She has since acquired a horse named Firedrake, was accidentally elected a regional representative for Romance Writers of America (no one else ran), and is planning to get some exercise and go on a diet tomorrow.

The Sizzling *Night* Trilogy by
New York Times Bestselling Author

NIGHT STORM
75623-4/$4.95 US/$5.95 Can

Fiery, free-spirited Eugenia Paxton put her heart to the sea in the hands of a captain she dared not trust. But once on the tempestuous waters, the aristocratic rogue Alec Carrick inflamed her with desires she'd never known before.

NIGHT SHADOW
75621-8/$4.95 US/$5.95 Can

The brutal murder of her benefactor left Lily Tremaine penniless and responsible for the care of his three children. In desperation, she appealed to his cousin, Knight Winthrop—and found herself irresistibly drawn to the witty, impossibly handsome confirmed bachelor.

NIGHT FIRE
75620-X/$4.95 US/$5.95 Can

Trapped in a loveless marriage, Arielle Leslie knew a life of shame and degradation. Even after the death of her brutal husband, she was unable to free herself from the shackles of humiliation. Only Burke Drummond's blazing love could save her... if she let it.